THE DAFFODILS OF NEWENT

The Second Instalment in the story of the Rising Family

THE DAFFODILS
OF NEWENT

Susan Sallis

This first hardcover edition published in Great Britain 2000 by
SEVERN HOUSE PUBLISHERS LTD of
9–15 High Street, Sutton, Surrey SM1 1DF.
Previously published in paperback format only
in Great Britain 1985 by Transworld Publishers Ltd.
This title first published in the USA 2000 by
SEVERN HOUSE PUBLISHERS INC., of
595 Madison Avenue, New York, NY 10022.

British Library Cataloguing in Publication Data

Sallis, Susan
  The daffodils of Newent
  1.   Great Britain – Social life and customs – 1918-1945 –
        Fiction
  2.   Domestic fiction
  I.   Title
        823.9'14 [F]

ISBN 0-7278-5507-7

Chapter One

It was June the twenty-first, the longest day of 1919, and April Rising's wedding day. She woke at five o'clock and lay still in the bed she was sharing with her visiting sister May, watching the morning light around the edge of the blind in their attic bedroom, her body burning with fever one moment, shivering with panic the next. Eight months before on Armistice night, when she had still been sixteen, David Daker admitted his love for her in a kiss which had at last accepted that she was no longer a little girl. Now, only just seventeen, she had penetrated his post-war withdrawn soul, and together they had overcome the considerable family opposition to their marriage. She had no idea how it had been done, but here she was seven hours away from a proper white wedding with her two sisters as attendants.

She sat up very carefully so as not to disturb May who was, after all, seven months pregnant. Naturally May, innately indolent, merely puffed a little sigh and slid a hand over her abdomen. She was as beautiful as ever, her blonde baby-fine hair curled in wisps over her shoulders like the illustrations of Rapunzel in the book of fairy tales belonging to Mother. April smiled affectionately, hoping that she would have children, and as gracefully as May seemed to be having this one.

April's other sister, March, asleep next door with her baby son, had looked so thin and haggard when she had come home at Christmas.

April pushed her feet into the felt slippers Mother had made so long ago, and crept quietly out of the bedroom and down the stairs to her father's work-room where the dresses hung limply from their padded hangers. Her own, cream satin cut on the cross in panels that swathed themselves to her, was March's creation, inspired by sketches and descriptive letters from May. The two attendants' gowns were entirely May's idea, and had been copied down to the tiny roll hems from some Grecian dresses she had seen in Weymouth during the war. They were sleeveless and straight up and down like silken sacks. Will Rising, the girl's father, had refused to make them: 'I'm a tailor, not a French blouse maker,' he had protested. So May had come down three weeks ago and she and March had cut and stitched and talked as they never had before. May, engrossed in her own pregnancy, was flatteringly deferential to March, who had already 'gone through it'.

April let her fingers brush lightly against the fine materials and linger on her mother's grey chiffon, then she moved to the window. Through the frosted glass, inlaid with her father's name and trade, the sun was already warm. She put her fingers to the W. of 'W. Rising' and traced it carefully. She had not been close to her father since he had condemned David Daker two years ago, but before then she had been his favourite daughter. She thought that now he had forgiven David everything would be all right again.

6

She touched her fingers to her lips and smiled. Of course it would be all right.

She slid the catch of the sash window and lifted the bottom half with infinite care. There was a slight rattle from the weighted pulleys but no squeaks; Mother always soaped the cords. April put out her head and turned it to the left to stare up the street – Chichester Street – to the portly window of the Lamb and Flag leering across the road to Mr Goodrich's dairy. Behind that lay the playground of Chichester Street Elementary School where April Rising and Gladys Luker had sat on the coke pile and exchanged secrets. Beyond that still lay the silent streets of Gloucester: North, East, South and West converging at the Cross, supine in the early sunshine, waiting for whoever would tread them that day, be it Roman, Cromwellian, or the three Rising girls on their way to a wedding. April smiled at the thought, always conscious of her place in the long queue of Gloucestrians.

She straightened her neck painfully and looked at the house opposite, hoping one of the Luker family might be up and about and would pull aside their tattered curtains and wave to her on her wedding morning. But even energetic Fred was using the wedding as an excuse to lie in, and Gladys, exhausted after a week at the pickle factory, would not wake for another four hours at least. As for young Henry, he wasn't interested in weddings. And Sibbie was no longer welcome in her old home. Sibbie Luker was now the scarlet woman of Gloucester and owned her own house and did not care tuppence that her father barred his door to her.

So April turned her head to the right and stared towards the top of the road where Chichester House lay behind its high brick wall. Chichester House . . . where she had spent ten of her seventeen years . . . She smiled and pulled back from the window. She knew now what she wanted to do with her sudden gift of time and solitude. She wanted to walk in the garden of Chichester House again and remember her two dead brothers, Albert and Teddy.

She slid into the hall and reached into the darkness under the stairs for her old Melton coat. Upstairs someone used a chamber-pot and she froze, thinking it was Will and he would come down to investigate her own furtive movements. There was a creak of bed springs and silence. Huddling her coat over her cambric nightdress she turned the hefty key in the front door and eased it open. Morning smells of lilac and baking bread and vinegar from the pickle factory rushed into the house. She inhaled them blissfully and set off across the road for her old home.

It had not been Will Rising using the chamber-pot. He was awake before his youngest daughter, but not in the same house. Fretfully at four in the morning he turned in bed, hunching a shoulder towards his companion, and snapped, 'I'm not discussing it any more, woman! It's too late now. She's getting married tomorrow . . . Christamighty, this *morning* . . . d'you realize it's four-a-bloody clock? I'll have to go Sib, they'll be about early this morning and April's sure to bring me a cup of tea in bed as it's the last time—'

Sibyl Luker looked at the back of the ginger head

with unusual exasperation. 'That's what I'm trying to tell you, Will, but you won't listen. It needn't *be* the last time. It *mustn't* be the last time! You know what David Daker is like as well as I do – ' she caught her breath, unable to resist the provocative remark even during such a serious conversation, ' – well, perhaps not quite as well as I do—'

Will growled in his throat warningly, 'Sibbie!'

'Well . . .' Sibbie changed tactics and snuggled up to the unresponsive back. 'Will, darling Will. You always listen to your Sibbie. Why are you turning a deaf ear now? April is only seventeen, my darling. Seven*teen*!'

'I know how old my daughter is, thank you, Sibbie.'

'And you know what David is,' she said, swiftly abandoning her cajoling in sudden pique at his closing ranks on her. She – Sibbie Luker – who had always shared everything the Risings had. She moved away from him, hoisted herself up in the bed and folded her arms over her naked breasts. 'You yourself called him a pervert, Will. Do I have to remind you of that!'

Tiredness and anxiety made him snap back. 'Yet you let him do . . . whatever he did! Is it – is it perhaps that you can't stand the thought of any of your lovers going to someone else?'

Tears started in her eyes. 'Will. How could you say that? I've never taken – I've always shared. I could have made you leave your Saint Florence and come to me—'

'Don't be too sure of that, my girl!'

'But I didn't try! I didn't want that! I wanted you to

be happy, Will – that's all I've ever wanted! For you to be happy!'

She was crying in earnest and he turned and gathered her to him. Tears and laughter were always near the surface for Will Rising, they were as natural to him as bubbles to a spring. When they were suppressed, that was when he turned sour. Now he wept and let himself be comforted and then he laughed as she wriggled under him like a kitten and kissed his face with her tongue.

'Sibbie . . .' he crooned. 'Little Sibbie Luker. Kept woman. Kept for Will Rising. All these years . . . kept woman. For Will Rising.'

She waited until after, when he was spent and exhausted. Then she whispered against his mouth, 'Why, Will? Tell me why you've allowed this marriage? And don't give me any cock and bull about it being for old man Daker's sake. You wouldn't let David marry May. And April is your favourite.'

Will groaned, seeing the clock standing at five to five and knowing he must get up and leave for home. There seemed nothing for it but to tell the truth.

'David knows about us. He saw us that night. Armistice night. He told me that if I didn't agree to him marrying April, he'd tell her about you and me.'

She was very still, gazing into his face two inches away, knowing that with his near sight he couldn't focus hers.

'That's blackmail,' she said softly, with a kind of admiration.

'I don't know what it's called. But that's what he said.' He raised his head and drew it back so that he could see her. His beard trembled slightly and his resemblance to the Old King was striking. 'What could I do, Sib?' he pleaded. 'What could I *do*?'

'Nothing. But I wish you'd told me sooner. I could have done something.'

'What?'

'Warned her. Told her about David and me.'

'She knows, Sib. She guessed. It didn't make any difference. You don't understand April. When she loves, she loves. Not even death . . . she's still so close to Teddy.'

Sibbie said stonily, 'I should have told her exactly what he used to do to me. Not even you know that, Will Rising.'

'Oh God . . . Sib . . .'

'God's not going to help you over this. I could have done.'

He massaged her abdomen helplessly. And she lay still and thought about David Daker who wanted one of the Risings so much he was willing to blackmail for her.

Will said, 'Sib, I have to go. Really. Now.'

'Then go.' She gathered the neat square head to her shoulder. 'And Will . . . dear Will . . . I hope it goes well today. I wish I could be with you, I'm half Rising myself. But I'll think of you all the time, darling.' She put him from her and slid out of bed, standing proud and naked for an instant in the pale five o'clock light. 'I think I'll go out too. I shan't sleep any more. I'll walk along the canal bank and think of last night. And tonight.'

'Oh Sib . . .' He grinned as he dragged on his short

summer pants. After all it wasn't the end of the world. Naturally David would treat April quite differently from the way he'd treat Sibbie Luker, and there was a good chance the marriage would work out. If it did not, she could come home again as March had come home. Home to her father who would look after her without recriminations; even with understanding.

And meanwhile he had Sibbie. And because of having Sibbie he somehow had Florence again. His own quiet, gentle nun. His to protect and cherish as nuns should be. No more anger because of her purity, no more . . . degradation. With Sibbie love wasn't carnal and wicked. It was fun.

He strode along the canal bank into Bristol Road. Musing philosophically along these lines, he worried no more about April.

The blackcurrants were as big as the gooseberries and had a bluish tinge to them like black opals. The gooseberries themselves were all ruby red and sweet. April picked them and savoured them slowly as she wandered past the fruit enclosure to the group of gnarled apple trees, standing in the long grass like petrified dancers. How Albert had loved this garden. The long hours of solitude he had spent in it, thinking maybe of Harry Hughes, maybe of his beloved March. He had only to lift his neat golden head to see the cathedral spires where he had sung as a choirboy, and to sniff the air blowing up Westgate Street from Newent and Kempley and the countryside of his roots. April bent and picked up two tiny hard green apples fallen from the trees. She felt she knew Albert far better in death than she had done in life; he was easier to love as the ten years between them grew less. But of course he belonged to March. Just as Teddy had belonged to her.

She hurried down the path to the gate which led into Mews Lane. Teddy too had loved the garden, but as a rampager not a nurturer. Teddy would have gathered the hard little windfalls as ammunition for his catapult. They would have played David and Goliath. She would have stood on the wall and been Goliath and he would have made her fall off and crash into the pile of grass cuttings beneath – several times. Dear Teddy, instigator of so many games and so much trouble and so very much love; forever a child of six years old. Peter Pan. She hung on to the gate and looked all around the garden. In the eighteen months since the Risings had left Chichester House there had been three itinerant tenants, none of whom had done anything outside. The place was empty again and had a derelict air which fitted well with the war-deprived street and the gently decaying area around it. To April it looked like a shrine.

She turned to go into the stable and froze where she was. Walking down the cobbled lane, picking her way daintily on low-heeled satin shoes, was Sibbie Luker.

For two pins, April the courageous, April who had her beautiful red-gold hair cut off for the war effort and worked in the poisonous powders of the munitions factory, would have run. She was wearing her felt slippers, her old school coat over her nightie; her short curls were not yet washed and brushed and she was in a private world of her own. But Sibbie had seen and recognized her and was smiling without embarrassment as if the last two years hadn't happened. Everyone knew about Sibbie Luker: she had stolen May's childhood sweetheart from her, she had taken March's treasured job as secretary to Alderman Williams, she had bargained with her . . . yes, with her *body* . . . until he bought her the small wooden bungalow alongside the canal. And everyone also knew what went on there night after night. Even Harry Hughes, poor dead Harry who had been Albert's best friend, even he had been one of her . . . men. April felt her cheeks flame at the thought. But she couldn't run.

Sibbie said, 'Well, look who's here! Isn't that lucky – I was just going to sneak in and see Ma while Pa's still sleeping and can't throw me out – ' she laughed merrily at that, ' – and I was hoping Ma would give you a message. And here you are!'

April found she was the one who had to make excuses.

'I couldn't sleep—'

'Shouldn't think so!'

' – And I wanted to see the – the garden – just once more.'

'Oh April! You haven't changed, have you? I remember you standing in that kitchen over there – ' she jerked her head towards the back door, ' – and talking out loud. And when I asked who you were talking to, you told me. God.'

April recalled the Sibbie of then, her golden head a shade darker than May's, lighter than March's. She had always been in the house, part of the family, whispering to May, 'We always shares everything May, dun't we May? Dun't we?'

April swallowed sudden tears and said unthinkingly, 'May still misses you, Sibbie.'

Sibbie smiled, pleased. 'Course she does. She'll never have another friend like me. And I won't have one like her. Underneath we're still the same.'

There was a pause, uncomfortable for April, considering for Sibbie. Then the older girl said, 'You see, April, May knew. Long before I showed her, she knew there was something wrong with David Daker.'

April opened the gate and moved swiftly up the garden path again. 'I don't want to hear,' she said. 'Goodbye Sibbie.'

But Sibbie, unencumbered by slippers and long nightie, got ahead of her without difficulty.

'You must hear, April. I've always thought the world of you. And I know something about David that you don't.'

April tried to pass her left, then right. Sibbie grabbed her coat and stopped her. April clapped her hands over her ears.

'I know!' she said, her eyes wide and very dark blue staring furiously at Sibbie. 'I know you and he had – had an *affaire*—' She pronounced the word in the French way and Sibbie burst out laughing.

'Is that what it was?' She sobered and shook April gently. 'Oh April . . . don't make anything of *that*! That doesn't matter. If he was all right that would be a good guarantee for you.' She tried to put her free arm around the Melton shoulders, but April backed away. 'Listen April. Do you want children? Babies?' She shook her again, impatiently. 'Oh for God's sake don't look like that! You're as bad as your mother! Do you want kids or don't you?' April did not answer. She had backed right up to the gate now and was stuck there. She was taller than Sibbie and stronger too, but she could not bring herself to wrench away physically from the confining hand.

Sibbie sighed. 'Well, it doesn't matter. I'm just telling you, my girl, that if you marry him you won't have any. Do you understand that?'

'Go away Sibbie!' April gasped. 'Please go away and leave me in peace!'

Sibbie stepped back and dusted her gloved hands fastidiously.

'Righty-ho duckie. If that's what you desire. ' She put on a mincing, affected voice to hide her hurt. 'Don't say I didn't warn you though, will you? It's that shrapnel in his poor little groin, don't you know. Oh he'll give you a marvellous time – don't worry about that. But there won't be any results.' She tinkled a laugh, stopped dusting her hands and smoothed her fitted powder-blue coat instead. 'Maybe that will suit you. I don't know.' She looked critically at April. 'If I were you dearie, I'd get May to Marcel your hair and put a dab of rouge on your face. You Risings never knew how to make the best of yourselves.' She sighed dramatically and stepped around April and into Mews Lane. 'Toodle pip!' she concluded. And was gone.

May's actor husband, Monty, arrived at midday. No-one had found time to meet him from the Paddington train, so he burst in on them unannounced and in his rôle as one-of-the-family immediately slotted into place.

'Mamma—' He embraced Florence with a sort of passionate reverence. 'Will!' He shook Will's hand in both of his. 'My beautiful sisters!' He couldn't get near them for curling tongs and safety pins. May extended her neck to present her face and he kissed it without embarrassment. 'Darling May. I can see you're in the thick of it. I want to hear everything. May I change behind this screen-thing while you talk?'

In the event he did most of the talking. Will loved it; another man, a son practically, in the house again. He sent Daisy to the Jug and Bottle for beer and did not avoid Florrie's disapproving look.

'Special occasion, my love. Special occasion.'

She looked beautiful in the chiffon May had made for her; like a blue-grey cloud. He cupped her thin face in his needle-pocked hands and kissed her and she laughed forgivingly and fetched glasses.

'Want some help, son?' He passed a glass around the screen and caught a glimpse of Monty's sinewy legs. Some sort of dancer wasn't he? A bit of every-thing: actor, singer, dancer. And his legs weren't that much better than Will's own short, hairy pair.

'Thanks Dad.' Monty took the glass, grinned, flapped his shirt tail at Will. He knew his father-in-law loved the familiarity. Florence was so . . . formal. They all worshipped her of course, but sometimes Monty wondered just what went on in that marriage. Five children and she still looked like a nun.

Will said, 'How long can you stay, Monty? Time for a spot of shooting on Robinswood? D'you remember the last time I took you up there? First time too wasn't it? You bagged a handy rabbit.' Will had a rabbit shoot on one of Gloucester's two small hills. He never used it now, but he liked to talk about it.

'No R in the month, Dad. Besides I have to get back for tonight's performance. We closed last night at ten-thirty, open again at seven tonight.'

May removed the last pin that had held April's swirling skirt in place and put it on the kitchen table with the others from her mouth. She stretched luxuriously and put her hands beneath her abdomen. The Grecian dress revealed her size for the first time.

'Well . . . we're ready now . . . and in good time.' She went behind the screen. 'D'you want any help now darling?' In the spurious privacy she wound her arms around Monty's neck and kissed him with relish. He snapped his braces over his shoulders and put his arms round her enormous waist. They began to giggle.

March spat out her pins and looked irritated. 'Will you stop it, you two!' She pulled at her own straight tunic, dissatisfied. 'I wonder if these sleeveless dresses were such a good idea, May. I've never noticed before how arms go in before they go out.'

May emerged, deliciously flushed. 'They're all the thing in London, March. And arms are made that way. April don't *touch* your hair, it's perfect! No, not even to put on the veil, I'll do that. I'm the hairdresser of the family.'

Monty folded the screen against the door and they stood around April in an admiring circle. The screen crashed inwards as Gran opened the door. There was pandemonium, then Gran, Aunty Sylv, Daisy and

Hettie Luker crowded in. Hettie liked the way the panels of the dress were on the 'bee-ass'. She said, 'They sort of outline the – the – chest.' She glanced nervously at Florence.

May said matter-of-factly, 'Yes, April's got a nicer bust than March or me. Although mine is all right at the moment.' She laughed unaffectedly and Florence wondered wryly how darling May could say such things with such perfect innocence.

'Well.' March was not enjoying it. She never liked crowds and she was worried about letting Hettie take over Albert-Frederick. 'I suppose we'd better go.' She kissed April's cheek awkwardly. 'Dear April. I hope you'll be happy. If anyone can be, it will be you.'

Her words were significant to everyone there, and April reddened slightly as she returned the kiss. She decided on frankness and looked at her father as she spoke.

'Listen . . . everyone. Just believe me. I know David better than anyone. Better than he knows himself. Please trust me.'

The short speech lifted some of Will's hurt. Of course she was wrong; she had no idea what sort of man David Daker really was. He himself would never have guessed that the dark, suave chap with the constant half-smile was anything more than a reserved young man – a bit like Albert – who would come out of himself in time. The war hadn't helped of course, but he'd been one of the lucky ones really, invalided out before the casualty list could get him. He should have come back to his father's small drapery in the Barton and started the tailoring side up again – with

Will's benevolent help – and everything would have been as it was before. Maybe he would have married May, maybe not. Probably not. But before any decision could be made, Will had discovered David's true nature. He had discovered him and Sibbie in that tiny cutting-room of his behind the shop; with Sibbie spread out on the cutting table like a paper pattern.

Will felt his mouth go dry at the recollection and he glanced at the clock on the mantelpiece. Another ten or eleven hours and he'd be with Sibbie again. Meanwhile he'd put on a good face today, knowing that he was right and that April would soon be home again, weeping and hurt and needing him as she had when she'd fallen as a child. And her public statement – so like April – absolved him of present responsibility somehow.

They walked round to ancient Saint John's. May and Monty had been married at the fashionable Saint Catherine's at the top of Wotton Pitch, but April was a Sunday School teacher at Saint John's and loved the sooty, grimy old workaday church. The Lukers came out in force to wish her well and to admire their own two representatives at the wedding, Fred in his civilian suit and Gladys in a gaudy copy of the new sleeveless creations. Gran Goodrich popped out of the shop, dragging her son behind her, and the patrons crowded out of the Lamb and Flag to raise a cheer for Will Rising who'd had it rough in the past. April held her father's arm so hard it hurt, and Will, thinking nerves were overtaking her, patted her hand with his free one and said, 'There, there, little April. You're not far from home, you know. And the door will always be open.' And April smiled wryly, relieved that her father did not after all need comfort from her.

And then her sisters were fussing over her again in the porch and the dark cave of Saint John's nave was before her, the sooty windows casting purple and orange lights over the scant congregation. She remembered the Armistice Day service with a clutch of her heart; then someone next to the splash of vicar-white by the altar turned and looked at her. David Daker's face, giving nothing away to the world, opened for her with a kind of terror. He couldn't believe it either. He couldn't believe that happiness could still exist after so much death and stench and degradation. She had to convince him that it could and did.

She and Will paused, waiting for the first organ notes; everyone looked round and smiled at her beauty and her dress and her short orange-gold curls and her ridiculous, unfeminine height which dwarfed her strong, square father. And while their eyes were still on her, she stretched out the hand holding the tiny nosegay of primroses, and curved the slender arm towards David as if inviting him to her. There was a small gasp throughout the church; Florence put her ready handkerchief to her mouth to hide its tremor, and Gran clutched at Aunty Sylv feeling, suddenly, that she was an old woman. And then, while April followed that curving arm with her whole body, the organ notes reverberated, and David turned fully towards her, acknowledging her gesture, and held out both his hands and waited like that while she paced slowly towards him. Then he gathered her to him.

Daisy said afterwards it was the most romantic thing she'd ever seen; even more romantic than the meeting between May and Monty.

The Breakfast was at the Cadena; Will had found the money from somewhere to 'do' for May and April. It was a fairly quiet affair, just the family and a few very old friends: Gladys and Fred Luker, Bridget Williams and Tollie Hall. David's best man was someone no-one had seen before, a man met at the hospital where David had been 'patched up' as he put it. His undisguisedly foreign name was Emmanuel Stein. He and Mrs Daker sat together, looking very Jewish in this Aryan gathering. Even Florence's darkness could not compare with their olive-skinned difference. April sat by the strange lamenting woman who was now her mother-in-law and smiled at her tentatively.

'You don't mind too much, Mrs Daker?'

'Mind? Why should I mind?' asked Mrs Daker lugubriously. 'He has to marry some time and if it must be a Rising then you—'

She might have been going to say that April was the best of a bad bunch, but David, hovering protectively, swooped in. 'April, take Manny onto the verandah. Show him the view. I'll say goodbye to Mother, then we must leave.' They were spending a week in Scarborough.

Manny Stein stood up immediately. 'Gloucester is a very interesting and ancient city,' he pronounced dutifully. 'And I shall be obliged indeed if Miss . . . Mrs Daker will describe it to me.'

*   *   *

March said, 'Don't be ridiculous Fred. Of course I can't come away for a week to the Forest. What would happen to Albert-Frederick?'

'Your mother would be delighted to look after him. Anyway May won't go back to London for a bit.' Fred Luker folded a slice of ham in four, speared it on his fork and put it in his mouth. He spoke through it. 'You've got the perfect excuse, Marcie. You've been doing all these letters for me and I am going down to see the coal-miners themselves, so you could come with me to take notes. Nobody would think anything of it.'

March said tightly, 'Kindly do not speak with your mouth full.'

'And kindly don't call me ridiculous. And kindly come with me next week to the Forest of Dean.'

March breathed quickly. 'Why should I?'

He turned and looked at her, chewing slowly and rhythmically. On her other side Aunty Vi Rising cut her ham into postage-stamp squares and spread each one with mustard. 'Because you're the mother of my son,' Fred said quietly, but not quietly enough for March. 'And because in the eyes of God we are man and wife, and because we haven't been together since I rescued you from Edwin Tomms last January. And because I thought you would want to.'

March held her knife and fork so hard it shook slightly. She studied her plate.

'Rescued me? Is that how you saw it? Smashed my life to pieces – that's how it seemed to me.'

Aunty Vi said, 'What's smashed, dear? I din't 'ear nothin'. What was it?'

Fred smiled. 'You want a row, don't you, March? I wouldn't mind one either. Come down to the Forest with me and—'

March put down her cutlery with a clatter and turned her back on Aunty Vi. 'I don't want to. That's the other thing. I don't *want* to.'

'We all 'as to do a lot of things we dun't want to,' Aunty Vi mourned. 'D'you think I want to stay on at that dead 'ole with the boys? But 'oo else would 'ave 'em? They couldn't come yer. They'd be in trouble afore you could turn round. Poachin's bad enough, but yer, 'twould be out-and-out thievin'.'

Fred kept smiling. 'I don't believe you, Marcie. Remember that night at the George after we'd left Edwin? D'you remember that? You wanted to be with me then, didn't you?'

March did not flinch but the anger seemed to go out of her. She kept her tea-brown eyes on Fred's blue ones and spoke softly and reasonably. 'Maybe I did. But now . . . I've had enough of men, Fred. You don't know what it was like with Edwin. Pestering. It was disgusting. Now things are good. I want to be with Mother and Dad. Quietly.'

His smile died. 'You've had six months with them, Marcie.'

'I want it to go on. Six years. Sixteen.'

Aunty Vi's eyes watered with too much mustard. 'I'll be dead in sixteen years,' she said painfully.

March dabbed at her mouth with her napkin; her arms, naked in the fashionable tunic, were still thin but beautifully shaped. She said with a new assurance, 'This is how I want my life now, Fred.'

He smiled again and leaned towards her, taking her napkin from her hand and pressing the knuckles between his thumb and forefinger.

'If you don't come with me, Marcie, you'll be sorry,' he said pleasantly.

March stayed very still. Vi began to cough.

'Let me get you some water, Miss Rising,' Fred said and stood up. March looked at her hand and saw the dark bruise already spreading.

Monty said, 'May – sweetheart – I'll have to leave. Really.'

'I can't bear it,' May said with every appearance of bearing it very well. 'I simply can't bear it. You haven't felt Victor kick once. Put your hand on him – he must know that his daddy is here.'

He touched the front of her tunic dress lightly and she immediately covered his hand with her own and pushed it over the curve. Gran saw it and tut-tutted audibly.

'You are brazen, May Gould,' Monty laughed, putting his mouth to her exquisite neck. 'You tricked me into having this baby and now you want to show everyone—'

'Baby, darling, honey,' she crooned at him. 'How could a *woman* trick a *man* into having a baby. Silly billy.' She kissed his ear lightly and whispered, 'And hasn't it been wonderful since?'

He lifted his head, pretending to be outraged. 'You really *are* brazen May! I don't know what you mean!' He couldn't hold the pose and spluttered with laughter as he looked into the clarity of her eyes. They fed each

25

other scraps of meat on the end of a fork. Gran muttered to Aunty Sylv, 'If that's how they go on in London . . .' and Aunty Sylv muttered back, 'They're happy, those two. That's what matters.'

Monty said, 'I wish you wouldn't keep calling him Victor. Suppose it's a girl?'

'It has to be a boy. For Mother.'

'It's *our* baby, May!'

'Of course. Why do you think he's called Victor?' May looked at him and the laughter was between them again. 'It was victory night that night in more ways than one!'

Monty said, 'I really have to go, May!'

'You don't mind me staying on a few days? They'll miss April more than they realize.'

'I mind like hell. But I'll put up with it somehow.' He kissed her again. 'No, you're not to come with me to the station. Fred Luker said he'd take me round in his car, and I don't want any sad station farewells.'

May, who had no intention of leaving the Cadena until after April did, smiled beatifically. 'Monty, you're wonderful. I love you. I love you, baby-darling. Sweetheart. Mother's baby.'

Gran said, aghast, 'Look at them now! It's indecent.'

'They're all right,' replied Aunty Sylv.

April said, 'The Cloisters have a very beautiful fan vaulted ceiling . . . Did you know David before the hospital, Mr Stein?'

'No, Miss . . . Mrs Daker. And only two weeks in

the hospital. We were the only two Jewish patients, you see.'

'I see.' David had never made friends easily; perhaps his army friends had been killed. That he should be forced to choose this stranger to stand by him at his wedding was evidence of his . . . alone-ness. She swallowed on the pain of it. He would never be alone again.

'To the right you can see where Bishop Hooper was burned,' she said huskily.

'Hooper?'

'Reformation. One of our – Anglican – martyrs.' April straightened and took a deep breath. It was hot beneath the glass of the verandah and the potted palms smelled of mushrooms. 'He was burned at the stake. He burned and burned but would not die.' She turned away. 'He did eventually, of course.'

'David tells me you are a teacher, Mrs Daker.'

'A pupil teacher. That is all.'

'You should go to college and become trained.'

'Married women teachers are not allowed in Gloucester,' she said shortly.

'Ah. I see. So you help David with the small shop, yes?'

Why did he make it sound second-rate? 'Yes. Oh most certainly. Yes.' She smiled, trying to show him that nothing could be more wonderful than helping David with the small shop. He blinked, dazzled. David Daker had told him of the Rising girls, their two dead brothers, their ill-assorted parents. He had been disappointed: the father was stocky, bulldog, a typical British type; the mother, far from being beautiful, was thin and bent though she still had a certain elegance. The brothers – how could he know? But the girls themselves were merely fair and pretty and under-nourished. Until now. Suddenly he saw this one, as . . . quite extraordinary.

David said, 'Christ. When will this be over?'

'Soon, my darling. I'll get out of this ridiculous dress and we'll catch Fred as soon as he gets back from taking Monty to the station.'

'And everyone will come with us and throw rice. And that dress is not ridiculous. It is virginal and very pro-vocative. It is moulded rather than sewn. I shall get the pattern from May and make all your dresses from it.'

'We can catch an earlier train and change at Cheltenham. Let's do that, David.'

'I love you, Primrose Sweet. I love you. I love you. I love you.'

'David, stop it. You don't have to . . . it's *happening*. Just believe that and everything will be wonderful.'

'What's the matter? Something has happened. What is it?'

She almost told him about Sibbie. Maybe she would. Later. When they were at Scarborough. Tonight.

'Nothing. Everything is perfect. I love you. Oh, David, I do love you so much. Ever since that first time. When I was five—' She recalled him waiting for her on the landing outside the bathroom door at Chichester House. Full of menace and glorious attraction. Devil Daker she had called him. She shook.

He whispered, 'I feel like Mr Rochester marrying Jane Eyre when he's got a mad wife locked in an upstairs room.'

She knew exactly what he meant but she still whispered back, 'You haven't got a wife – anywhere. Have you?'

'No. But there's something mad somewhere.'

She looked into his dark, secret face and her heart accelerated.

'That's what makes it . . . like it is,' she said in a low voice. He encircled her wrist with thumb and forefinger and felt her pulse race. He squeezed, his eyes on her face. She smiled at him. He, too, blinked.

Fred did not wait at the Great Western Railway station and Monty walked the length of the Up platform, counting the Mazawattee tea signs just as his sister-in-law had before him, and hating the hiatus between one life and another. May's deliberate provocation had made him tingle, and he cursed himself for not demanding her immediate return to their shabby London digs. He ran through his two numbers for tonight's show: 'I love you dearly, dearly and I hope that you love me,' May's favourite; and 'Come into the garden Maud,' which he would sing with Maud Davenport. May pretended to be jealous of Maud, but knew there was no need to be. Darling May. Beautiful, wonderful May, who could enter into any rôle he chose to play. He paced past a bench full of waiting passengers and automatically straightened his back, pushed his bowler to the back of his head, lightened his step. There was an altercation at the ticket barrier and a young woman in a blue single-button coat, with a cloche right over her ears and a fringe into her eyes, hurried through. She reminded him of May; almost as fair, almost as blue-eyed, certainly slimmer around the middle. She came up to him breathlessly.

'Is it Monty?' She parted full lips and her tongue and teeth glistened visibly. 'I met my brother – you left your brolly in his taxi!' She produced an umbrella with a flourish. It wasn't his. He considered an umbrella made him look like a businessman instead of an actor. He said, 'You must be . . .'

'Sibbie Luker. May's erstwhile friend.' Sibbie laughed. 'Don't be frightened. I won't eat you.'

If it had been anyone else, Monty might have donned his man-of-the-world rôle. But Sibbie Luker was different. She had hurt May.

He said coldly, 'It's not mine. The umbrella.' He raised his bowler courteously. 'I'm sorry you have had an unnecessary walk. Good day.'

Sibbie stared at him, her mouth even wider.

'My God. You're cutting me. Aren't you? May's husband – cutting her best friend!'

'Good day, Miss Luker.'

'May would hate you for it.'

He turned and walked up the platform past the bench. She was one step behind him, talking still. Heads turned.

'It's no good. You can't get away from me. I didn't have a walk here. I had a run. And I do not run after men, they run after me.'

He was furious. 'Not this one, Miss Luker. I am May's husband.'

'Ah!' She stopped suddenly and her exclamation made him stop too. The people on the bench tried to look away. 'Ah,' Sibbie repeated. 'So. That is how you see yourself, is it? Of course you have no background of your own, have you? So May is not your wife first and foremost, you are her husband. Loyal. True. Good son-in-law to William and Florence Rising, brother-in-law to April and March.' She put a long gloved finger to her full bottom lip. 'What does that make our relationship, I wonder?' She held up a hand, palm facing him. 'Of course we have a relationship. I am half Rising, I have always shared everything with May—'

'So I heard,' he interjected against his better judgement.

'Ah, so you know about David.' She laughed, bending over, her hand now on her beautifully flat abdomen. 'But you don't know about the . . . other connection.' She straightened and sobered and considered him, narrow-eyed. 'I could tell you, I suppose. You wouldn't let on in case it hurt May. Maybe I will tell you one day, then you'd see that there is some relationship between us. But not now. Here's your train anyway.'

It came puffing in, filling the station with sooty smoke and heat. People got up and porters cantered nonchalantly alongside the running board. He went to an empty carriage and swung himself in. She was behind him.

'Look here—' he began angrily. Another passenger pushed in behind and Sibbie cannoned into Monty and held them both upright.

'Darling Monty. I really must go,' she said as if he were detaining her. 'Have a good journey. Are you sure about the umbrella?'

He hadn't felt such a complete ass since he'd been sent those damned white feathers in 1917. He shoved her to the door where she clung, laughing into his face. The man behind said jovially, 'Better close the door, lady! Give him a kiss quick!'

Sibbie obeyed, planting her open mouth over Monty's and flicking her tongue across his cringing lips before she turned and leapt gracefully to the platform.

'Goodbye darling. Hope you can sleep without me!'

She skipped up the platform and through the barrier, waving the umbrella like a sword. Monty sat down, hot and dishevelled and thoroughly out of countenance.

Once in London Road again, Sibbie's smile disappeared.

'One day it'll be different, my lad,' she murmured, making for the Cross where she would be able to see them leave the Cadena. 'One day I'll be head of that family. You'll see.'

It had been a long journey and they arrived at the tiny boarding house near the harbour very late, so there was no supper, not even a cup of cocoa. David undressed in the large draughty bathroom and put on his new pyjamas and the dressing gown he'd had in hospital and padded back down the landing. April peered over the top of the sheet, looking about twelve years old.

'Darling, don't look like that. It's late and we're tired. Go to sleep.' He wondered how he'd summoned the evil courage to marry her. He pulled back the covers to climb in beside her. She was naked.

'April!'

'Don't make me ashamed,' she whispered. 'I knew you'd say it was late. I knew—'

'Oh April. My darling girl. You don't have to. We've got all our lives—'

'I want to, David. I want *you*. Everyone saying I'm so young and thinking I just want you to look after me. It's so *funny*. Honestly, David, what I said back at the Cadena was true. I've wanted you – *wanted you* – since I was five years old.'

'It's a physical impossibility.' He began to stroke her body with his left hand, holding her with his right. He put his fingers lightly on her chin and followed an invisible line beneath it, down her neck, between her breasts, over her abdomen and back again.

'David. Please—' she said urgently.

'Plenty of time, Primrose. Plenty of time.'

She shivered and shook as if she had an ague. At last he slid his fingers between her legs and kissed her as she groaned in ecstasy. Much later he whispered, 'Is that enough, my darling?'

'I'm tired, David. I'm tired.'

'Then that's enough. Go to sleep, Primrose.'

'David, it was lovely. But why—'

'I told you. There's time. You were happy, darling?'

'Yes. Yes of course.'

It was true. But she also felt a faint shame. And something else. Was it fear? She turned over and pressed herself against his pyjamas and felt him wince as his leg hurt. She wouldn't tell him about Sibbie. Not now. Perhaps not ever. He held her and kissed her and told her he worshipped her. The shame went away. She slept.

Chapter Two

Fred Luker thought long and hard about March Tomms' repudiation of him at the wedding. In one way it suited him well; he was an ambitious man determined to make a great deal of money in the shortest possible time, and a divorce scandal would not help his business interests. If March had begged him to end the farcical muddle of her marriage to her great-uncle, he would have done so because he loved her. But he could love her just as easily while she was in the ambivalent position she was in now. Only he, Edwin Tomms her husband, and March herself, knew that her marriage was at an end. Edwin was a minor public figure in his home town of Bath and, ironically, wished to avoid a scandal as much as Fred did. Ostensibly March was paying a protracted visit to her old home to help her mother who was not strong; it was lucky in a way that Florence had not been strong since her last pregnancy sixteen years ago. Nobody thought it odd that although she had April, Gran Rising and Aunty Sylv to help run the small house in Chichester Street, she should also need her eldest daughter plus her first grandchild, Albert-Frederick.

Yes, the arrangement suited Fred Luker very well. He had March and her son under his eye without having to provide a home for them. It was March's attitude recently which was fast getting under his skin.

Fred had been obsessed with March Rising since he was sixteen years old. She had picked him up, dropped him, used him shamelessly; he had smarted and trembled and waited for her . . . until 1917. He had come home on leave after her brother Albert's death in the Somme, and found March changed for ever. The spiky independence he had loved had been beaten out of her by grief; she was withdrawn, half mad, contemplating suicide. She had turned to him then, thankful to be able to surrender her tortured spirit to someone who knew her as well as he did, who accepted her failings and loved her for them. And when he had returned from the dead last Christmas and driven down to Bath to take her – by force if necessary – from her marriage of convenience, she had turned to him again, giving herself to him with a joyful abandon that meant – that must have meant – she loved him.

And since then . . . what had happened? He had talked to her about his business prospects, not only in an effort to take her out of herself, but because he needed her interest and encouragement; she had been patently bored. He had asked her to contact her old employer, Mr Edward Williams, with a view to a loan. It wouldn't have been difficult, Bridget Williams was April's best friend. But she hadn't done it. He had wanted her to buy a typewriter so that she could use her skills in writing letters for him; she had shelved the whole idea. And now, when he had swallowed his pride yet again and asked her to spend a few days with him in Dean Forest, she had turned him down flat. He was back to square one: trailing round after March's favours like the love-sick oaf he had been before the war. And he too had changed since the war; since he had returned from the Silesian prison camp alive, *and* in his right mind. Yes, he was quite a different kettle of fish from the Fred Luker of pre-1914 who had tended his father's dray horse and tinkered with cars in his spare time and smelled accordingly.

So on the Monday morning following April's wedding, he drove once more to Bath, taking the same route he'd taken before when he'd gone to fetch March from her husband-uncle. His mood too was not dissimilar. There was a small, calculating smile on his normally rather set face, and his pale blue Luker eyes were narrowed in thought as well as against the strong June sunshine. He was almost certain he had found a way to kill two birds with one stone. He needed ready cash; and he needed to teach March a lesson. Maybe, with luck, the two went together.

He changed into second gear to take the long hill down into the heart of Bristol and his smile widened as the small, bull-nosed Morris edged its way around the drays and vans delivering in Whiteladies Road. Not so long ago he had driven his father's dray, sitting up behind the carthorse, catching the flies she flicked off with her tail. A servant: that's what he had been, no more than a servant. When he had bought the Army transport truck at the surplus sale in Aldershot, converted it into a charry and used it for outings and excursions, he was still a servant. His father insisted it was independence, no-one breathing down your neck, open air, your own master. But the fact remained, someone hired you, someone paid you. That made you a servant.

Now an entrepreneur . . . that was something different. Fred negotiated the cobbled dock roads and took the road for Bath and Wells. Entrepreneur. He had learned a smattering of the lingo when he was a prisoner and that's what Fritz had called himself as he negotiated sales between the Silesian coal-miners and the iron foundries, milking them both, courted by both during wartime shortages, touching his cap to no-one. And that was what Fred was going to do. He had promises from the pickle factory where Gladys his sister had put in a word for him; Bartie Hall, a warder at Gloucester Prison, said that if the price was right the prison governor would be pleased to buy from an old soldier. And he had been to the Forest of Dean and talked to the Freeminers down there three times already. They were a slow lot, but if he could flash some money under their noses, they'd agree to supply him.

The countryside levelled out alongside the dreaming Avon, so different from the turbulent Gloucester Severn. A signpost told him he was approaching the tiny village of Keynsham; he slowed, noting the huge chocolate factory on his left. Then he rolled down into the lovely basin of Bath itself.

Edwin Tomms was already a successful ironmonger when he married Elizabeth Rhys-Davies in 1868. He gave her a beautiful house in Bath, every comfort, her own carriage and two maids . . . besides four miscarriages. In the absence of any children of their own, Elizabeth – Aunt Lizzie – had taken a great interest in her orphaned niece's family. Florence had married far beneath herself, as had her poor dead mother, but William Rising had ambition and he was good-looking and a real family man. Lizzie liked him, loved and admired gentle Florence, adored the children. When Teddy was born and Florrie nearly died, she took them in for two months, and after that the links between the two families were strong.

But March was her favourite. March was darker than the other girls, more like the Rhys-Davieses than the Risings. March had aspirations and she loved to hear about her great-grandfather who had somehow been gypped out of his inheritance by something called an entail. And Uncle Edwin could see the Rhys-Davies in her too. He could see Lizzie as a young girl, as she had been when he first married her. He had coveted March when she was just a child and had bought her affection with presents. And after her darling Aunt Lizzie had died he had married her and been with her through the terrible premature birth of Albert-Frederick.

Then Fred Luker appeared last January and told him that Albert-Frederick was not a premature baby at all and was therefore not his child. Edwin thought he would go out of his mind. He determined to alter his will so that neither March nor her bastard son would get a penny. He waited to die.

But death did not come and neither did madness. He found he was saner than he'd been since Lizzie's death. Then he had lived in a half-world, convinced that March would come as Lizzie's successor. When she arrived on his doorstep that September afternoon, he had not been surprised. Lizzie had wanted March to have everything. Surely everything was Edwin. In fact March's arrival confirmed his madness and enabled him to live in it while she stayed with him.

Since her sudden departure he was able to understand why she had come to him and why she had stayed. Some of his egomania was dissipated forcibly. He saw that when Lizzie had begged him to give 'everything' to March, she had not included her husband. He saw that March had not been conceived and born simply for him. She was not Lizzie made young again. She was half Rising, and from somewhere deep in the Rising side of the family she had inherited a calculating nature. She had ingratiated herself with dear Lizzie just to get her worldly goods, and when Lizzie had died she had cut herself off from her uncle for over a year, and then suddenly descended on him when there was no-one else to save her from total disgrace.

His need for vengeance gave him energy. He had retired from the management of his three shops in Bath, but now he returned to them and interfered whenever possible. He became a pillar of the Baptist church where he and March had been married. He was on the governing board for three of the village schools in the area. And he waited.

Perhaps because he was so certain an opportunity for revenge would come, he did not turn Fred away when Letty announced him. Letty, a stout fifty now, had dropped a few sly comments about Mrs Tomms' prolonged absence from Bath, and sounded disappointed at a possible return.

'That Mr Luker's at the door, master. The one what took the missis back to Glawster with him.'

Shock held Edwin rigid for a moment, then he forced himself to say jovially, 'Ah, news of your mistress at last, Letty! Good. Show him in and then bring the port.' Edwin did not drink but he regularly produced port for his visitors. It was how he had got on the school boards.

Letty was disappointed at this reaction. From the look of the master's face when Miss March – Mrs Tomms in company – went off with that common chap last winter, Letty had hoped for a speedy scandal. As she said to Rose down in their basement kitchen, 'I can 'ear it brewing. Everythin' fine and dandy on top, and poison underneath!' Rose had said comfortably, 'Whoever got Baby Albert, got Miss March. An' I s'pose you en't suggesting that Master en't the legal guardian of that dear little lad?' That had silenced Letty. She dared not voice her suspicions, but she had them all the same. Albert-Frederick hadn't looked like a seven-month babby to *her*. But Rose worshipped the child to the extent that his whole background must be snowy white. So Letty showed in *Mister* Luker with a sarcastic little bob and muttered to herself as she went for the port that fine feathers never made fair lady, nor gentleman.

Edwin dropped his geniality with the closing of the door and did not stand up. He was sitting in the spoon back chair that had been Lizzie's favourite, then March's. It looked out over a railinged park where the summer leaves were jumping and jerking under a shower.

41

'Well? What do you want this time? You're not getting any of her things. And the child can die of cold for all I care!'

Fred grinned. He would rather a frontal attack any day. Nevertheless, in view of Letty's imminent return, he prevaricated.

'Nice view you've got from here. March was describing it to her mother the other day.'

Edwin looked at the straight square-shouldered figure outlined against the window. He was surprised it didn't collapse under the barrage of sheer hatred he was directing at it. But then, this upstart had survived other more tangible barrages quite recently. That was the trouble with the war. Servants thought they could be gentlemen.

Letty came into the room without knocking and Fred went on blandly, 'March is always talking of you. She is very homesick. But as you know her mother is not strong—'

'Will that be all sir?' Letty asked hopefully, putting the tray on a small table and clicking the single glass ostentatiously.

'Unless Mr Luker can stay for high tea?' Edwin asked, heavily sarcastic.

Fred resisted the temptation to accept. 'I'm booked in at a place in Almondsbury. Where March and I stayed last time we left here,' he said, watching Edwin for a reaction. Gnarled fingers curled slightly on the knife-edged thigh, that was all.

'Off you go then Letty. Remember I have the School Management Committee Meeting tonight, so I shall want my light grey top coat carefully brushed.'

'Yessir.' If Letty had been five stone lighter her departure might have been described as a flounce. She closed the door behind her with a click.

Fred leaned forward. 'So. You are still keeping up appearances. I'm glad of that.'

'Are you?' Edwin wetted his lips. 'What was all that nonsense about March being homesick?'

'Nonsense?' Fred feigned astonishment as he took a seat on the other side of the grate without waiting longer for an invitation. 'Nonsense? Did you really think poor March left here without a qualm? Naturally she has to be with her mother at a time like this. But just as naturally she misses her home very much.'

'Pity I'm in it, then she could come back. Is that what she thinks?' Edwin laughed unpleasantly. 'Well, she needn't think that. I've made a cast-iron will to keep her and the brat out of Bath, let alone this house!'

Fred lowered his head and did not speak for some time. Then he said quietly, 'I can understand, yes I think I can understand. But surely while you are alive that does not hold good? Surely you would allow her to come back here and see you?'

Edwin frowned, looking for the trap. 'I wouldn't give her house room here. She's a whore!'

'So you said before. I hoped that after a few weeks to reconsider you would see the dilemma March was in—'

'A few weeks? The girl has been gone for six months! And if I reconsidered for six years it would make no difference.'

'I raped her of course. You realize that I expect. She is very like her mother. Fastidious.'

There was a pause. Edwin's breathing became fast and audible.

'I had the devil's own job . . . certainly. You raped her, you say? How you have the gall to sit there and—'

Fred's head came up. 'Naturally I assumed you guessed that. After living with her for eighteen months.' He shrugged helplessly. 'I can feel sorry for the girl in a way. There she was pregnant and me presumed dead . . . besides, she wouldn't want *me* . . . beneath her. She turned to the person she loved best. You.'

There was a longer pause. At last Edwin said on an indrawn breath, 'Are you trying to tell me she wants to come back?'

'No.'

'Then what the deuce is this about?'

Fred smiled. 'Were you going to pour some of that port, sir?'

Edwin stared. Fred was not the sort to call anyone sir out of uniform. 'Not until I know what this visit is for,' he said bluntly.

Fred shrugged again. 'I wanted to see if you were keeping up appearances. Obviously you are, and with great success. School Management Committee, eh?'

'Naturally a man in my position – respected—'

'Quite. How long can you go on like this without . . . a visit at least from March?'

'Indefinitely I should think.'

'I shouldn't. Gossip. It might have started already.'

'I won't have that woman in my house!'

'Besides, if I were you, I would insist on my conjugal rights now and then.'

The pause this time was so long it seemed it would never end. Fred dropped his head again and studied his hands. They were short and blunt, a mechanic's hands. But a mechanic had to have sensitive hands as well as strong ones. Fred could almost feel his way around Edwin's mind.

The old man whispered at last, 'What you are saying is . . .'

Fred took a breath, sat up, stared ahead with his blue eyes as frank and open as they knew how to be.

'I am saying that you won't keep up this pretence of being respectably married if you don't have March here. And if you have her here you might as well sleep with her.'

The whisper was hoarse. 'She wouldn't let me. It was difficult enough before. But now—'

'I can get her down here. How you – arrange things – afterwards, is up to you.' Fred watched the old man lick his lips. 'She won't like it of course. But a great many wives don't like it. There's not much they can do about it.'

'My God. I could punish her for what she's done. I could make her—'

Fred closed his mind quickly to the thought of March and the old man and said, 'She wouldn't stay for long. You understand that. I could only persuade her into it for a short time. But that should be enough to establish that you are still respectably married. Very much married.'

'Quite. Quite. A great many people in Bath were

surprised when I took such a young wife. And when she produced the child—'

'Quite,' echoed Fred dryly, watching the old fool delude himself all over again. How easy it was. How pathetically easy.

'When could you – er – persuade her to come down?'

'Next week if you like. Or the one after. Any time.'

'Next week would suit me fine. I'll have to cancel my attendance at the Sunday School midsummer picnic. I wouldn't want to leave her alone. For a minute.'

'No. That would be unwise. I would bring her down and fetch her of course.'

'They will realize then that you are simply a messenger.'

'Quite,' Fred said again. 'A taxi driver. That's what I am.'

Edwin rubbed his hands nervously on his trouser legs, stared suspiciously at the young man, and turned to the port.

'Yes. March told me you drove a cab. Yes. Perhaps a small glass of—? Before you go back to Gloucester?'

'By all means. Won't you join me?'

'I don't.' Edwin poured and passed and watched Fred toss it back like medicine. 'I expect you . . . you must have regretted what you did . . . wanted to make recompense in some way . . .'

Fred put the glass in the grate. 'Regretted raping March, d'you mean?' He remembered for a sweet second her passionate acceptance of him in the stables of Chichester House that summer. Two years ago. He had battered down her grief, not her body. 'No, Edwin. I never regretted that. I couldn't regret something like that.'

The old man flushed up. 'I thought . . . I understood you to mean that you felt this whole thing was your fault. If March had not been pregnant surely none of it would have happened?'

'Oh, that. True. It wouldn't, would it? Which would have been a pity.'

'A pity? So much misery? Not only for me – you said March was unhappy.'

Fred shrugged. 'A little unhappiness never hurt anyone. And if none of it had happened, well, I couldn't have arranged this little reconciliation, could I?'

Edwin was not unintelligent all the time. He stared again, then his flush deepened to puce and having reached asphyxiation level, receded until he was yellow-white.

'What do you want?' he asked finally in a dead voice.

'Some of March's inheritance. Five hundred pounds.'

'She *is* a whore. So, she's willing to sell herself for five hundred pounds, is she? I could get a girl in Bristol for five shillings. Tell her that.'

'Don't be a fool. She knows nothing of this. Not even that I'm here. Don't you think what I'm offering you is worth five hundred pounds? That sum is nothing to you.'

'As I just said – you dirty, common criminal – I can get a woman just as beautiful and more amenable than March Rising for—'

'But you don't get only March for that money, Edwin. You get your name. And more. You get a reputation as rather an old dog. Young woman like March coming home for a week because she can't live without you. Good God, what's five hundred pounds in those circumstances? Think, Edwin. Think!'

Edwin thought, long and hard. It seemed to cause him a great deal of pain. While he thought, Fred revealed his supreme confidence in the final decision by going to the port bottle and pouring himself another glass and tossing it down after the first one.

Eventually Edwin controlled his breathing and said in a low voice, 'You are despicable. If she knew what you are doing she would hate you.'

'I'm willing to risk that,' Fred said. He went to the window. 'Looks like the rain has stopped. I'll have to get off. I've got people to visit tonight. Business. A cheque will do.'

'I shall tell her.'

'Tell her what you like.'

Edwin went heavily to a drawer in a side table equipped with silver-topped ink bottles. He withdrew a pen. 'How do I know she'll come? Your powers of persuasion might not be as great as you seem to think.'

'If she doesn't come, you've lost five hundred pounds,' Fred said carelessly. He came and stood over the table and his face lost its easy-going expression. 'Write it,' he said brutally. 'You've got no choice.'

Fred Luker left Royal Parade at three-fifteen and drove immediately to the branch of the West of England Bank in Milsom Street. He cashed Edwin's cheque, came out and went on over Pulteney Bridge, then turned and drove along the other side of the river, glancing now and then to his right where the view of the abbey was breathtaking. When he rejoined the Bristol Road he began to laugh. He thought about what he had done. The old man was right, it was despicable. March would be angry and outraged, she might even hate him for a time. But not for long. He threw back his head and laughed aloud and then decided it was his lucky day, so he swung the Morris in through the gates of the chocolate factory and asked a scurrying worker to direct him to the manager's office. He got in there without much difficulty and found what he called an 'officer type' sitting behind the desk.

'My name is Luker, sir,' he said, standing straight, almost at attention. 'I'm trying to start a coal business. Got relations with a small surface coal-mine down in Dean Forest. I'm selling what I can in small lots, but I reckon I could supply a place like this at a competitive price.'

The officer type surveyed him without pleasure.

'Your own business, eh? You chaps come out of the army with ideas above your station. We've got our own railway siding, man. Our fuel is delivered by a reputable Bristol firm.'

Fred let his shoulders droop. 'Thought I'd give it a try, sir. My job was gone see, when I got out. Parents . . . wife . . . you know how it is.'

The officer type frowned. 'Well. No harm in trying I suppose. How did you propose getting the stuff here? Long way from the Forest of Dean.'

'The mine is near Whitecroft, sir. We haul the coal

by dray to the coal siding there and train it into Gloucester and Stroud.'

'Sounds expensive. Three loadings. Stand at ease, man.'

Fred spread his feet obediently. 'We want the business, sir, so we keep our price down. We've got a couple of factories in Gloucester who are using us in a month or two. Trial period of six months. If the bills are less and the service good . . . who knows. I've got a possible market in Stroud – on my way there now.'

'And you came to Bath specially to see me?'

'Well . . . yes, sir. I heard you'd got your own siding, see, and I thought that would probably keep the cost down further. Like I said sir, I gave it a try. Sorry to have wasted your time.' He brought his hands from behind his back.

'How did you get here – er – Luker, was it? Train?'

'No sir. I drove. Car's outside.'

'Car eh? Thought you were penniless.'

'Had it before the war, sir. Morris. I'll have to get rid of it once I've scouted around for business.' He permitted himself a smile. 'I used to run a cab service in Gloucester. And the haulage. No call for it now – others got in while I was away. But I've still got the car and a dray and a cart-horse.'

'Hm. Enterprising sort of chap aren't you? What kind of prices are you offering?'

'Depends on the size of the order. The bigger it comes the lower the price. We do steam coal at a pound a ton for a train load. More than that – well, I'd work out a special price.'

The officer type stared at him, lifted his top lip and

very delicately gnawed his lower lip. 'Hmmm . . .' he said through his nose. 'Hmm . . . I'd have to talk to our accountant. Storeman. Those sort of chaps. Where can I get in touch with you – er – Luker?'

Fred put his cap under his arm and felt in his inside pocket for the card printed 'F. Luker, 17, Chichester Street, Gloucester'. His fingers touched the ten pound notes there and he smiled slightly.

'Right. My name is Porterman. Captain Porterman, though I don't use the rank now of course.' He stood up and came around the desk. 'I'd like to think I could give one of our chaps a chance. I'm not making any promises you understand, but I'll be in touch. How's that? Does it make the journey worthwhile?' He guffawed, quite certain it did. Fred let his smile widen into a grin.

'Gosh. Thanks sir. Thanks Captain. It's great to talk to someone like you. Gentleman.'

He got outside somehow before he laughed again. And he kept the laughter within limits until he was negotiating Bristol's narrow streets. Then all the way up Whiteladies Road and Blackboy Hill could be heard Fred Luker's raucous mirth.

May went to Helene's Hair Salon in Saint Aldate Street to gossip to her old friends and to use the telephone there to ring Monty in the Kilburn Music Hall. Madame Helene assured her that if she came back to Gloucester she could have her old job back, baby or no baby, and May dimpled and said she might well take her seriously. Amid the protestations May let her secret wish take voice. 'I – we – might well move back home,' she confided to Madame. 'Obviously now that we are having a baby we must have a home. I can't follow my husband around any more. And Gloucester is fairly central.'

Madame waved her hands as she believed Parisiennes did. 'My dear Miss May! Then I shall hold you to this! In six months – a year – when there is a vacancy here, I shall remind you of your promise.'

'Madame, no promise!' May laughed, blushing, knowing that it was all empty talk, but very pleasing to her ear. 'If . . . if . . . if . . . oh you know I should be glad to help you out.'

Later in the privacy of the tiny office with accounts and appointment books littering the shelf, she used the greasy wall telephone. 'May I speak to . . . is that you Monty? You beast, putting on that ghastly voice! You – what did you say ? Will I come to where with you? Bed? Oh *Monty*! You are incorrigible!' She spluttered into the mouthpiece, then caught sight of herself in a small mirror above the gas lamp. Immediately she peered forward and began to rewind her front curls on a finger.

'Darling, I'm so glad, full houses both nights? Well of course it was for you, Maud is no oil-painting you know, they'd hardly want an encore from her. What did you sing?'

She leaned back and tucked in her chin, studying her reflection for any sign of her neck falling in. At last Monty finished talking and she smiled into the mirror and said, 'Listen darling. I'm going to see some new houses this afternoon at Longford. Houses. *Houses*, darling. They're building some marvellous new ones at Longford. They're in twos so they're called semi-detached.' She made her smile into a grimace and looked at her teeth. She quite liked her teeth.

'Well Monty, we must live somewhere when the baby is born. Yes, I know we live somewhere now dear, but we can't bring up a baby in a bed-sitting room or theatrical digs. It didn't take you long to pop down here for April's wedding. I *know* it's further from Blackpool darling, but you're not at Blackpool very long.' She put her lips together and sighed audibly into the mouthpiece. 'What? Of course we'll have to talk it over, Monty. That's what we're doing now. Oh I *know* you don't buy a house like you buy a pound of potatoes! But you can get loans for houses. You remember Bridget Williams? Well, her father is an auctioneer and they are acting as agents for these new houses and they will arrange a . . . what did you say Monty? Well, we've got *some* savings haven't we dear? Surely. But we can't have spent all . . . nothing at all? I don't believe you. Darling I'll have to go, Madame is knocking on the door. Yes of course I do dear. Do you? Oh good. Oh Monty. Oh . . . goodbye.'

March found to her surprise that she was quite glad to see Fred Luker when he called the following Thursday evening.

Since April's wedding life at number thirty-three Chichester Street had seemed anti-climactic, to say the least. Will was always out somewhere 'seeing a man about a dog', Florence looked even more pale and thin than usual, and May was suddenly out of sorts. But it was Aunt Sylv who thoroughly got on March's nerves.

Sylvia was the one who had diagnosed her pregnancy while they were on holiday in Weymouth two years previously, and though they had never spoken of it since March slipped away to see her Uncle Edwin, Sylvia's wise, lizard eyes spoke much louder than words. Sylvia knew the truth about her marriage to Edwin; it therefore followed that Sylvia knew Fred had taken her from Bath practically by force, and she and Albert-Frederick were back in Gloucester for good.

It hadn't been so bad until now; April's sudden declaration on her seventeenth birthday that she was going to marry David Daker, had taken the family's attention well away from March and her baby son. But now April was gone. March devoted herself assiduously to Albert-Frederick, deliberately seeing in him her dear, dead brother, Albert, but she remembered vividly and constantly her battle of wills with Fred at the wedding. She hoped she had hurt him. But then if she had hurt him enough perhaps their peculiar relationship was at an end? Not that it would make much difference to her as things were; she was neither fish, fowl, nor good red herring. And it wasn't going to take much longer for everyone in the street to know that.

So, when March came downstairs that Thursday evening and found Fred chatting amiably to Florence and Gran in the kitchen, she could not help feeling a small leap of pleasure somewhere in her chest cavity. Fred's love for her was the only positive thing in her life, apart from her small son. He knew she was nervous, edgy, bad-tempered; he had told her he loved her with all her faults. He couldn't retract all that, not now.

He stood up as she came into the kitchen, watching her to see whether she was noting this refinement. He was shorter than Albert had been; his neck was thick and his shoulders were heavy and slightly bowed from the years of delivering coal. But his fair, slightly gingery hair and blue eyes were not unlike Albert's. She smiled at him. She was glad she had changed her blouse and re-pinned her own long chestnut-brown hair.

He said heartily, 'The very person I hoped to see. I was just saying to your mother that I need a little business advice, March.'

She couldn't resist parrying this blatant invitation. 'I know nothing of business—'

But he swept on smoothly. 'I wanted to ask you what Edward Williams would have done if he'd been faced with the sort of problem I've got at the moment. After all you were his secretary for ten years—'

'Nine,' March corrected. 'And he never discussed his business problems with me. I typed his correspondence. Inventories. That sort of thing.' She wondered why she was talking like this. She would like to walk up London Road with Fred now and listen to the late cuckoos on the Pitch. Florence rescued her.

'I don't know anything about business either, dear. But I do know that you need some air. And Fred has just asked me whether he can walk you down to the river for an hour to discuss this new contract he has got. Why don't you go? It would do you good.'

March sighed as if with martyred resignation. She

went upstairs to fetch her short jacket and to bite some colour into her pale lips; her face needed no help, two spots of colour emphasized her high thin cheekbones. She half-smiled at her reflection: she was excited.

With unerring instinct Fred led her across the road to Chichester House.

'We can't go in there—' March hung back, suddenly afraid. 'It's nothing to do with us any more, Fred.'

'Nobody's there now. Can't afford the rent or the upkeep of such a big place.' Fred grinned easily as he pushed open the door in the wall. 'Your April often walks here, didn't you know?'

The garden was the same: blackcurrants, gooseberries, loganberries, raspberries in the enclosure; giant rhubarb leaves, beds of mint, the rosemary and lavender bushes. They sat on the front steps and she began to feel the tension going out of her.

'Have you been to the Forest yet?' She tipped her face towards the evening sunshine and closed her eyes. The warmth soothed through her lids and into her head. She knew he hadn't gone yet; when he asked her again, she would go with him.

'No. I went to Bath instead.'

Her eyes flew open and she turned to look at him. 'To *Bath*?'

'Ever heard of the chocolate factory at Keynsham? One of these model places, like Bourneville.'

He began to tell her about Captain Porterman, making it sound much more definite than it had been. 'You see what this means, March? I've got to organize that rabble down in the Forest. Organize them properly. I need two train loads of coal every week.'

'So you're going down there soon – next week? I think I could come with you then actually.'

'Not this time, my love. It might be rough. Next time, certainly.' He sensed her incipient umbrage. 'I shall be going down often. I'd rather you and I were together when I'm not up to my eyes in work.' He lifted her hand to his lips. 'Besides I want you to do something for me next week. Something very important, March. Will you do it?'

'How can I do anything? I'm stuck in the house day after day with Albert-Frederick—'

'I need some money, March. Will you get it for me?'

'Don't be absurd Fred. You know I haven't got any money.'

'Your husband is a rich man, March.'

She took a breath and held it, looking at him. Then she let it go. 'You went to see Edwin,' she said with a kind of horror. 'You tried to get money out of Edwin.'

'I went to see Edwin with a proposition, March. As – as an intermediary if you like.' March liked long words. He held on to her hand and massaged the knuckles with his thumb; her bones were too near the surface of her skin. He felt a tenderness for her that almost undermined his intention. But March herself had set the pattern for their relationship: it had always been a duel. Only with her brother had March achieved an entirely loving relationship. And Fred did not wish to be March's brother-figure.

She was angry; bewildered too. 'What right had you to see Edwin without consulting me first, Fred? What have you done?'

57

He pressed her hand a little harder. 'I've every right to act on your behalf, March. As I told you last Saturday, in the eyes of God—'

'But without telling me? In the eyes of the *law* I am still married to Edwin Tomms!'

'Quite. You are in an impossible situation, Marcie. I felt I had to do something about it.'

The small flutter happened again inside her chest. There was only one thing Fred could have seen Edwin about and that was divorce. Divorce was a disgrace, it terrified her. But if Fred had actually managed it so that she was the innocent party . . . after all, the whole world could see that she had done her duty by her elderly husband . . . Fred was devious and clever, he might have arranged something. And then, one day, a long time in the future to give her time to recover from the past ten years, Fred would marry her. She did not even ask herself whether she loved him; it was enough now that he loved her.

She said again, all anger gone, 'What have you done, Fred?'

'Found his weak spot, Marcie. That's what I've done. His reputation in Bath – it's more important to him than hating you and Albert-Frederick. More important than hating me even!' He laughed and lifted her hand again to his face. It smelled of powder from the baby. His son, named for Albert Rising and Fred Luker; he still had to remind himself of that. He put his cheek to her palm.

'He wants to go on being respected – and admired as being a bit of an old dog for getting himself a young wife and a fine strapping son.' The hand was withdrawn and he said quickly, 'He's failing, March – he won't last long. If you'll do this he'll alter his will again in your favour. He knows as well as you do that it was your aunt's wish you should inherit everything—'

'What have you *done,* Fred?' The anger was back in her voice, and fear too. She couldn't face Edwin again; not after the frightful denouement last Christmas when Fred had arrived and told him the brutal fact of Albert-Frederick's parentage.

'Listen, Marcie. A week. That's all he wants. Just so that people will be convinced you haven't left him. Take a few drives with him – be seen around the town with him—'

'*No!* How *could* you *do* this, Fred? It was you who took me away from him – rescued me—'

'And it was you who told me only last Saturday that I hadn't rescued you at all. I'd smashed up your comfortable existence—'

'Oh God! I hate you, Fred Luker – I hate you—' She stood up, poised for flight. But he would not release her hand. He stood up too and pulled her to him. She was shaking violently but did not immediately pull away; she needed him, she needed his strength of will.

He said in a low voice, 'I thought you'd do this for me, Marcie. We planned so much – that night we spent at the George, d'you remember—' How could she forget that wonderful night when she had escaped from Edwin and given over to Fred the responsibility for herself, her son and her happiness. 'I told you I would keep that promise I made to you in the war,

59

Marcie. I want to keep it. But I can't do it without you, my darling. I want to be rich – successful – only for you, Marcie. We'll live in that house in Barnwood just as I said – we'll have a car bigger than the Williams' – we'll have tennis parties—'

'Fred – I can't – I can't—' But there was pleading now mixed with the anger and outrage. 'I can't face him!'

'Not a full week then, Marcie. Just a few days.'

'He won't change his will. And if he does he'll probably live for years!'

'Darling girl, he's seventy-six. And not much bigger than your mother!'

She stood there within his arms, still trembling, searching for a loophole. She found it. 'But you need money now – you asked me to get money for you now.'

'He'll let us have some on account, Marcie.' He felt her tighten and released her hand at last to stroke her hair. 'That's why I am so certain he will change his will, my dearest. We talked reasonably, he wanted to know how you were – and the boy.'

She wanted to raise her fists and pummel his chest; she wanted to tell him she did not believe him. But then she would have nothing. And he was asking her to help him; he was kissing her and the scent of the lavender was overpowering.

She whimpered, 'I don't know what to do, Fred. I don't know.'

'Then let me tell you what to do, Marcie. Let me drive you down to Bath for a few days – not quite the week – let Rose take Albert-Frederick off your hands for a while. You're tired. It will do you good to get away from Gloucester. Let poor old Edwin show you off to his friends. Let me bring you home—'

'I can't bear to say anything about money. You'll have to do all that, Fred.'

'Of course, Marcie. I wouldn't dream—'

'It's your responsibility. Your doing. If you think it's all right for me to go there again. And Albert-Frederick – don't forget *he's* your responsibility too, Fred.'

'I know. Oh Marcie, if only I hadn't been taken prisoner that summer. I'd've had compassionate leave and we'd have been married and probably been able to afford a little cottage somewhere—'

March leaned against his chest so that he had to continue his kissing on top of her head. She wasn't absolutely certain that a tiny cottage with Fred was exactly what she had wanted back in 1917, or now. Perhaps there had been some kind of rhyme or reason to the awfulness of that summer after all? And if there had, then Fred's idea wasn't quite so appalling.

She lifted her face and kissed him briefly.

'I'll have to go home now Fred. I don't want Mother running up and down stairs to Albert-Frederick.'

Strangely, she slept better that night than she usually did. If only it weren't for Edwin, she would quite look forward to returning to Bath. It was a city she loved, and a life-style she would have loved anywhere. Fred was right, Rose would take the baby right off her hands; and there would be meat or fish every day and twice a day if she wanted it. And it would just show Aunty Sylv.

Chapter Three

It was true May was out of sorts. She had been home to Florence several times since the beginning of her pregnancy and though she missed Monty when she was in Gloucester, she missed Gloucester even more when she was away from it. The two small rooms in Chestnut Grove just off the Kilburn High Street were pleasant enough. The garden backed on to the railway, but then the railway was only a stone's throw from Chichester Street. Kilburn High Street was quite as busy and interesting as Northgate Street; but Kilburn was not the sort of place in which May wanted to begin building a proper family life. She couldn't see herself hanging nappies in the garden there and pushing a pram down to the shops. She wanted to be among her own where she would be the centre of a small, admiring group of neighbours and friends; where she and March could meet in the park and thread the small streets on the other side of the railway into the Barton where April was, and go on down to the cathedral teashop or back to see Florence and Gran.

The *Citizen* were doing a feature on the new houses at Longford. Barely a mile down Worcester Street and there they were: a little village of them with black and white gables like Tudor cottages, and diamond-paned windows and quite some way from the treacherous flood area of Twigworth. But because there was that faint – very faint – risk, they were reasonably priced. Two hundred and fifty pounds; a deposit of £24 secured one of them immediately. May had let her imagination run riot until the phone call from Madame Helene's. She had wandered around the Northgate Furniture Mart and chosen a delightful round table for the dining-room; furnished the sitting-room with big squashy chairs upholstered in plush, and chosen a double bed for the front bedroom. She could see it. Cream wallpaper, a rose-coloured satin bedspread . . . and then Monty had been so unreasonable.

Naturally she had expected reluctance. He did not want her living a hundred miles from where he was. Naturally she had expected his caution about buying a property; the only people she knew who owned their own houses were the Williamses and Sibbie Luker – and Sibbie hardly counted. But that Monty didn't have £24 in the world was incredible. They spent hardly any of his money did they? And then, when he'd said that Gloucester was the last place on earth he'd want to live, it seemed practically an insult. How did he think she would feel if they settled in London and he went off to – to Timbuctoo? The concert party – the Happy Hey Days – were never long in one place.

She talked to Florence about it. Florence was sympathetic but adamant.

'Darling child, you know there is nothing I should like better than to have you near. But that is mere selfishness. Your place is with your husband. You don't need me to tell you that.' She smiled and her face was lit by love. May's heart contracted at its sallow thinness and she nearly said, 'I shall have Monty, God willing, most of my life, but you . . . how long shall I have you?' But she knew that no argument would sway Florence in this. Florence's list of priorities was immutable, husband and children always came first.

However, Monty would listen to Will and Will was more easily persuadable. But to May's surprise, when she tackled her father, he pursed his lips disapprovingly.

'Stay on? Here?'

'For a while, Pa. Until we could save enough to get this house I'm telling you about.'

Will thought about it. True, he would enjoy having Monty at weekends and when he was 'resting'. But if May was in Gloucester all the time there was more risk of her meeting Sibbie.

He said consideringly, 'Look here May, you know how your mother and me 'ud feel having you near. But you wanted this actor chappie and you can't desert him now—'

'Daddy! I wouldn't desert him for the *world*! I *adore* Monty – you know that. I've *explained* it to you.'

'Yes child. All right. But I don't quite see it like that. A woman marries a man's work in a way.' Will put his finger in his watch pocket and leaned back on his heels. 'Your mother . . . what should I have done without her?'

'I can't button-hole for Monty!' May cried, exasperated.

'But you can be with him when he has to go to these out-of-the-way places. It's all you *can* do for him. Imagine how he must feel – talk about lonely—'

'Oh Pa. I'm sorry. Don't make me cry, please. I can't *bear* to think of darling Monty like that. He *was* lonely till he met me. No parents. No family.'

So when she telephoned Monty next time at the Kilburn Empire, she was quite determined to fall in with whatever he wished. Nevertheless it was quite a shock to hear that he had left the Happy Hey Days.

'Left them?' He had been with the small concert party off and on since before the war. As he so often told her, they were his family.

'Darling, listen. So much has happened.' The line seemed to be under water and May blocked her free ear with the flat of her palm. 'You've heard of the Mincing Light Opera Company? No? May, they are *the* people to be with! Absolutely. Tophole orchestra, first-class singers . . . Came to the show last week and heard me sing . . . round to the green room afterwards . . . supper. My darling girl – a real opera supper. Can you believe it, May? '

'Darling, of course I can. I've always said you have the best light baritone I've ever—'

'Only snag was, I had to be ready by this Sunday. Opening at Scarborough on Monday.'

'Scarborough? That's where April—'

'So can you be back tomorrow sweetie? We'll have to pack up here and Maud wants to give a little party on stage after Saturday night.'

'Of course Monty darling. Of course . . . how sweet

of Maud. They'll miss you terribly!' May was smugly pleased about that. Maud Davenport's duets with Monty had always irked her. She added doubtfully, 'Darling, are you sure it will be all right for me to travel all the way to Scarborough? The birth is only six weeks away.'

Monty misunderstood her reluctance and rushed in with reassurance. 'Darling, you know it hardly shows! And they'll love it – it's supposed to be lucky to have a baby born on tour, you know.'

'But Monty, it's so far!'

'We don't have to change, sweetie. They shunt our coach off at Crewe and York and the next train picks us up and—'

'What about digs?'

'They send a man ahead. All arranged. Oh May, isn't it marvellous? It's an important little company you know. Mostly G and S. It's *Yeomen* and *Gondoliers* next week but they use the alternative titles *The Merryman and His Maid* and *The King of Barantaria*. Don't you think there's something rather top-drawer about that?'

'Oh yes darling. Rather.' May removed her hand from her ear and nibbled at the finger of her glove. It was much too early for a premature birth but supposing she got a giddy turn this evening? She couldn't possibly go to London tomorrow and then right on up to Scarborough the day after.

'So I'll see you tomorrow darling? Meet you. Paddington. The midday train?'

'Lovely, Monty. I'll be there. Unless anything really awful happens.'

It never occurred to Monty that anything could. His fair, delicate, ethereal May, once so prone to chesty colds, was as strong as a horse and had been since her visit to Bath in 1902.

May walked slowly down Saint Aldate Street, feeling herself being torn in two. Love and pride for Monty vied with her lazy unwillingness to join him and push her way through life again. Here, Pa saw to some things, Mother to the rest. Gran and Aunt Sylv were in the background, March and April available. It wasn't fair of Monty to expect her to leave such security just at the moment and struggle with luggage and porters and dirty trains. A voice broke through her thoughts.

'Well. Are you going to cut me dead then, May? You've been very careful not to go anywhere I might be, but I didn't imagine that if we met face to face you'd pretend I didn't exist!'

May's head jerked, puppet-like. Sibbie was standing before her, obviously about to turn into the tiny teashop on the corner. She wore a beautiful, semi-fitted coat with a single button fastening and long lapels; her hat was like a helmet and emphasized her vivid face with its rouged cheeks and bright red mouth and mascara'd eyes. May had seen such hats in London, but Sibbie must be the only woman in Gloucester wearing one.

She said, 'Sibbie! I – I didn't see you!'

'Didn't recognize me – is that what you mean?' Sibbie seemed very aggressive. Certainly it was the first time she and May had met since her self-exile to her bungalow by the canal, but April had run into her several times and insisted that Sibbie invariably smiled and waved.

May stammered awkwardly, 'You look very well, Sibbie.'

Sibbie eyed May scornfully. May pregnant was even more exquisite than May virginal, but she was not smart.

She said, 'You probably think I look like a tart.' She held up an elegantly gloved hand. 'Don't worry. I'm not offended. I like the way I look, and so do . . . others.' She smiled and brushed an invisible speck from her coat. 'Your husband for instance.'

May gasped. 'Monty? You've met Monty?'

'You couldn't be bothered to see him off two weeks ago. Someone had to!' Sibbie's smile widened. She reached for the door handle of the teashop. Inside, Will saw her, half stood up, spotted May and sat down again.

May repeated stupidly, 'You saw Monty off? But you don't know him!'

'I introduced myself. Your best friend. Told him we shared everything.' Sibbie laughed. 'So of course he let me kiss him goodbye.'

She opened the door and disappeared inside. May stared after her, glimpsed her father and would have run to him if Sibbie hadn't been there. She felt tears and panic threaten her. First David, now Monty. She clenched her hands and walked quickly down to Chichester Street and along to number thirty-three, hardly hearing Snotty Lottie's greeting or seeing the youngest Luker batting a ball against the wall of the Lamb and Flag.

Florence looked up from a blanket she was darning. 'Well May? How was Monty?'

May took a deep breath, looked at her mother's pricked fingers as they worked at the prison blanket Kitty Hall had brought round, and let her breath go again.

'He's got the most marvellous chance Mamma! With the Mincing Light Opera Company – serious singing at last. But I have to pack and go back to London tomorrow. We leave for Scarborough on Sunday . . . there's so much to do . . .'

Fred took the long way round to Parkend in the Forest of Dean because he wanted to call at Lydney railway station and enquire about coal trains going across the bridge over the Severn.

As early as 1917 Fred had investigated the possibilities of obtaining coal cheaply from the Forest Freeminers. During the wartime shortages it had been one way to keep his father's coal-delivery business going and Fred, on leave from his machine-gun nest in France, had enjoyed hammering the best bargain he could from the small, family-owned businesses in the ancient Royal Forest. Apart from the big Cannop Colliery in the centre of the seam, all the mines were tiny surface ones, needing no drainage pumps, no gas detectors. A pick, a shovel, a horse and cart – or even a wheelbarrow – were all that a man needed to dig his own coal. The trees had been there millions of years before the Crown annexed them as a hunting ground and to supply naval timbers. They had been packing their dead branches into humus, the humus into peat, the peat into sparkling black coal which was discovered as a side-line when the first miners dug for iron.

When Fred had seen for himself how casually inefficient that side-line was, he had spoken to the Freeminers of a co-operative; and had got nowhere. The Freeminers cherished their ancient rights, believing that only in them could they retain precious independence. Fred had cursed them for stupidity, but he had not forgotten them. During the long boredom of his incarceration in Silesia he had taken stock of his past life and future prospects, and the dream of being one of the new breed of 'middle men' had been born. He had dealt with coal in small amounts, he had worn a leather back protector and humped it all over Gloucester. There was money in coal, it was the heart of England. And the Freeminers of the Forest were waiting.

He did not let himself think about March. He had last seen her mounting the steps of the house in Bath, clutching Albert-Frederick over her shoulder and saying in a voice that Letty could not miss, 'Come for me tomorrow if Mother gets worse, mind, Fred.' He didn't want to remember that.

Now and then he had flashing glimpses of the Severn on his left and the presence of such a wide band of water between himself and March seemed to help him to separate her from himself in his thoughts.

The station master at Lydney was helpful and Fred turned north and drove up through Bream and Whitecroft to the tiny pub where he had taken half a dozen of the few remaining Freeminers several times before. The place was called the Gavellers Arms and boasted two rooms, both floors smothered in dirty sawdust and stinking of stale beer. Only one of the miners was present, a man called Danby, who had been spokesman for the others before. He rose from a seat in the window; he was dressed in leather breeches and collarless shirt. He held his cap in his hands and used it as a reason for not taking Fred's outstretched hand.

'Dun't bring no good news, Mister. 'Tuthers were for not putting in a face at all. But I said as we'd promised Luker to meet 'im 'ere and 'im bein' a prisoner of the 'Uns an' all, 'twere on'y decent to—'

Fred interrupted this rambling apology with upraised hand.

'Tell me about it when you've downed a pint, Danby.' He turned away immediately so that Danby could not see his taut face. He was ready to explode with sheer frustrated rage. The stupid ignorant fools had backed down. He'd got them to the point of being interested and assumed that he could carry the day and because he hadn't pressed home his advantage immediately with cash . . . well, he'd show Danby the five hundred. And then they'd bloody well pay for their own lethargy. He'd bleed them all white. He'd suck their blood until—

'Here we are, Mister Danby. Hereford hops. Nothing quite like 'em, eh?' He let Danby see his wallet as he paid for the beer. He asked for whisky himself. He sat down. 'Cold feet eh? Tell 'em it's all set up. The pickle factory in Gloucester. And—' He grinned tightly. 'And the bloody chocolate factory at Bristol. Keynsham. Ever heard of it? They bloody eat coal! Your chaps will have to dig twenty-four hours a day to keep them supplied! Paid in advance too, so I can let you all have some money.'

Danby picked up his tankard and drank deep. Froth coated his upper lip and he blew through his nostrils like a horse and cleared it.

''Sno good, mister. See, you dun't understan' the Forest. We'm in'pennant down yer. We got 'nuff to feed ourselves and our fam'lies. We dun't need no more, see. We . . . we'm in'pennant.'

Fred made a further effort to control his anger; he was not as tall as Danby but his shoulders were as powerful and they hunched forward as if holding himself in. His pale blue eyes stared hard at the face opposite him, despising it, hating it.

'That was one of the reasons I chose the Forest Freeminers. I could have gone to Coalpit Heath – any of the small mines around Bristol—'

'They 'ouldn't 'a lissened to ee, mister.'

Fred forced his shoulders back; this man was not quite so stupid as he had at first thought.

'You led me to believe you were interested.'

Danby made a movement that might have been a shrug and drank again. 'Us let 'ee go on. Aye. No 'arm in lissening.' He put down his tankard and looked keenly across the table. 'Lissen yer, mister. You get one to do it, the rest'll follow. That's all the incouragement I kin give you.'

'Well? Why not you then?'

72

'I got no sons to 'elp. I might dig ten 'undred a day. No more. Where'll that get ee?'

'No bloody where.'

'See?'

'Is there someone then? Someone who would lead the rest of the stupid sheep?'

Danby's expression hardened and he stood up. 'No, no-one.'

'Then why the hell did you just say—'

'Tellin' ee. Tha's all.'

The man shambled out without another word, either goodbye or thanks. Fred could hardly credit he had gone for good and waited, fuming, for a further ten minutes before investigating. Danby had gone. Like some animal he had left his watering-hole. The whole damned scheme was gone . . . down the drain. Fred drank his whisky and another. The landlord looked at him knowingly.

'Thought you 'ad 'em in the bag mi'boy, eh? Eh? Come down from Glawster throwing your weight about.' He laughed. 'Wait till you knows 'em like I knows 'em. You'll 'ave to squat yourself a bit o' land and dig the black stuff up with your own shovel. That's the only way you'll do it.'

Fred bought a third whisky and downed it. 'Squat?' he asked.

'Build. Draw smoke between sunset and sunrise and it's yourn.'

The old man laughed again. 'Make sure it's on a seam though, mi'boy. Make sure o' that. An' I don't reckon you'd know coal unless 'twere burning in your grate. Eh? Eh mi'boy?'

Fred licked around his mouth, tasting again the sharpness of the drink. He said slowly, 'No. No, that I wouldn't, Dad. That I wouldn't.'

He went outside and cleared some kids off the car. He got in and began to drive north towards Mitchel Dean, Longhope and Newent, towards where Will Rising had lived. And where Will's sister, the bovine Vi, still lived. Fred had never enjoyed feeling a fool, even in the days when he had known he was one. He was certain now that he was no fool, simply because he had emerged from the war unscathed. And he intended to show those ignorant Freeminers of Dean just that.

Edwin came into the sitting-room dressed in a pearl grey dust coat and carrying a cap. March was in Aunt Lizzie's spoon-back chair holding Albert-Frederick on her lap while she pointed out the waving trees in the park opposite the window. She looked up, coldly enquiring.

'I think we'd better take a drive.' Edwin did not look in her direction but went straight to the window, effectively blocking her view. 'The purpose of this visit is to show your world and mine that we are still married. It was our custom to drive out most afternoons.'

'I did not imagine you would have time,' she murmured. 'So many committees and functions—'

'Get your coat. And make ready your – your bastard son – and come!' Edwin's voice shook with rage. 'And if you think you can shelter behind him and Rose for the whole week, you had better think again, madam!'

March, who had shared Rose's bed next to the cot for the three nights she had been at Bath, stood up with dignity.

'I explained to you. Albert is used to sleeping with me—'

'Then his cot must be moved into our room! There is nothing else for it! What do you think Rose and Letty must say down in the basement?'

'I think they will assume that you are too old for—'

Edwin whirled round. 'Get your coat March! Quickly!'

March left the room.

The cottage on the Newent–Kempley Road was like a pigsty. Fred was used to near slum living; Hettie Luker cooked and washed after a fashion, she rarely cleaned. But this dirt was different. This was farmyard dirty. He was reminded of one of his rare conversations with Albert Rising in the coke yard at Chichester Elementary. Albert had been trying to describe the carefree enjoyment of life in the tied cottage at Kempley. 'Gran says they're as happy as pigs in shit,' he had laughed, flushing slightly, but knowing that Fred Luker of all people might understand. Fred had understood, but he still hadn't been prepared for the cottage which Vi Rising shared with her brother Wallie before he disappeared, and now with the four boys she and Sylvia had collected twenty years before. There was actually a pig asleep on the broken armchair in the kitchen and the smell was sharp and noisome.

Luckily the boys were all out working in the large

market garden that kept them in this state of filthy plenty. He knew they must live well, they were all as large as oxen.

'Just thought I'd drop in,' he bawled, shaking his head when Vi made movements to oust the pig from the chair. 'I wanted to have a chat with you. About old Forest customs.'

'Dun't 'ave to shout then Mister. I en't deaf. An' I dun't know nuthin' about Forest folk neither. We'm Newent.'

The way she spoke the Great Wall of China might have crossed the few miles between Newent and the Forest boundaries. And she must have very sharp ears indeed if she could hear a normal voice through the grunting of the pig and the cackling of the hens. He smiled propitiation.

'Call me Fred, Aunty Vi. I remember you when you came to Gloucester with Aunty Sylv after your father's funeral.'

'I never did. Never bin there till April's wedding. Never ast me. Wouldna gone anyway. Nasty noisy place.'

He swallowed and decided to come to the point. 'I thought you might know something about squatter's rights in the Forest. Talking to a chap in the Gavellers—'

'The Gavellers? Dun't want to go there Mister. Man was killed there back in 84. 'E was from Kempley and 'e smiled at one of the Forest girls. They shot 'im in the Gavellers. Sawdust is still stained they do say.'

Remembering the Gavellers Arms Fred would not have been surprised at anything.

'So you do know something about the Forest then?'

Vi scratched the pig's head gloomily. 'Only bad things. They buried 'im. Nuthin' were ever said.'

Fred frowned. 'Made an impression on you, Aunty Vi.'

'Ah. It did that. Pa used to tell us never to look at a Forest boy.' She scratched her head and added casually, 'It were Pa's brother what got shot y'see. An' nine months later Pa went down to St Briavels and brought Austen 'ome with 'im.'

Fred stared at her. Austen was another of Gran Rising's progeny and when the old home near Newent had been broken up after Grampy Rising's death, Austen and Jack had disappeared to the Rhondda coal mines.

He said slowly, 'Sounds to me as if Austen is your cousin, not your brother, Aunty Vi.'

She shrugged. 'Cousin, brother. 'Tes all the same when we wuz brought up under the same roof. Washed under the same pump. Ett off the same table. Slep' in the same—'

'So Austen was born in the Forest of Dean?'

Aunty Vi was suddenly cagey. 'I dunno about that. I never said 'e were my cousin neither. What for you so int'rested in Austen all of a sudden Mister? 'E wudn't one o' they conchies y'know. 'E were in a reserved occ'pation – the coal mines wuz jest the same as the army an' 'im and Jack 'ad bin miners since nineteen nought six!'

'Couldn't have done without miners, Aunty Vi, and that's a fact.' Fred forced himself to go over to the pig and pat its bristly back. It made a noise between a snort and a squeal and Vi smiled lovingly.

'No. I'm interested in this squatting business. Seems like if you can build yourself a house overnight you can claim the surrounding land. Something like that.'

'Thinking of living down in Dean then, are you? Dun't do it Mister, they'm a rough lot and no mistake.'

'But is it true? Does it happen these days?'

'Draw smoke twixt sunset and sunrise,' she incanted. 'Aye. I can 'member it 'appening. But for Forest folk. Not strangers.'

'And if your hearth – your fire – happened to be near a coal seam, could you mine that coal under the old Freemining laws?'

'If you're Forest. Yes. You got to be borned in St Briavels. That's what the mining law do say.'

He stared at her until she said uncomfortably, 'You can take some greens back with you. And some bacon. And there's a 'are what bin 'anging—'

He thanked her hastily and made his farewells. He could smell the cottage interior on his clothes; but he didn't care.

Edwin drove towards Bradford-on-Avon and stopped the car on one of the wooded banks. The river ran through green fields with a serenity and sparkle that reminded March vividly of Aunt Lizzie. She wondered how on earth that wonderful woman had been happy with this awful creature. Four miscarriages . . .

Edwin said, 'Is the child asleep?'

March glanced into the back seat and nodded.

'Good. Come here.' He made an ungainly grab at her, knocking her hat askew and hurting her breast. She gave a tiny, startled scream and held him off somehow. He grappled, panting furiously. He got his clawing fingers in the neck of her blouse and pulled hard; buttons flew everywhere and her camisole was revealed. He tugged at that.

'Edwin!' Her voice wobbled furiously. 'What do you think you are *doing*! Let me go this minute – d'you hear—'

'Whore!' he gasped. 'Harlot! You've been sold to me for five hundred sovereigns and you're not worth—'

'Sold?' Her voice wobbled up a register incredulously. 'What do you mean – sold?'

'Marital relations! That's what he said! And you promised to obey me – only two years ago – love, honour and obey! And I am *commanding* you now – commanding you!' He reared up behind the steering-wheel and flung the frail weight of his body on to her. The remembered smell of him almost made her vomit. She flung back her head and screamed at the top of her voice. Albert-Frederick woke immediately and joined his howls to hers. Like a scene in a farce, a courting couple hidden among the long grass on the river's edge also knelt up hesitatingly and stared at the rocking Wolseley.

March sobbed, 'Those people – my God – they can see everything!' Edwin glanced behind him and saw that they could indeed see everything. He whipped March's coat over her breasts. She immediately reached over her seat and took Albert on to her lap.

Edwin sat there, breathing fast, not looking at the courting couple. After a while they disappeared and Edwin got out and wound the handle. They jogged on to the sandy road.

Albert-Frederick stopped crying but refused to take his face out of March's neck. She said tensely, 'Edwin, I came here for the sake of your reputation only. If Frederick Luker said otherwise, he is a liar and a cheat.'

'You knew that already. You concocted this scheme together. I'm the donkey and you're the carrot . . . I accepted that. But I paid your – your *lover* – five hundred pounds to eat the carrot.'

She cried out at his coarseness and Fred's treachery. She imagined them talking together, working it all out. A carrot, to be bought and paid for and eaten. Not that the truth was much better. She might have guessed that in order to persuade Edwin to change his will in her favour, she would have to sleep with him. She hadn't used her intelligence; once again March Rising had been stupid. She huddled over Albert-Frederick's sunbonnet and was achingly silent.

It seemed to encourage Edwin, and he pulled off the road again. The car was silent; there was birdsong and Albert-Frederick's uncontrollable hiccoughing. He turned to her.

She said in a low voice, 'Edwin. Not again. I swear to you that if you lay a finger on me, I will let the Reverend Gough at the chapel know that we are living separately and that Albert is not your child. I swear that to you.'

'You have as much to lose as I have!'

'No. I shall go home. You will stay here.'

'I mean the money. I'll not pay any more to your fancy man. Not a penny more.'

'I should hate you if you did. Fred Luker can come and fetch me home but I shall not speak to him and I shall have nothing more to do with him. I swear that to you too.'

'Don't pretend you didn't know he had that money out of me. I won't believe you, March. After all, what was our marriage in the first place but a sale!'

To her own surprise, March began to cry on to Albert-Frederick's bonnet. 'Edwin, I made a mistake. I grant you that. Not just one mistake . . . I've done nothing but make mistakes. Ever since I was a child. All I can say is, I'm sorry. I'll stay for the rest of this week and save your face for you. If you want me to I'll come again on those terms. But there must be nothing else to it. I must be your great-niece again – never your wife.'

'He implied that when he needed money you would sleep with me—'

'He is nothing to do with me, Edwin. I don't care what he said. If I come to Bath again it will be of my own free will and because you have asked me. Nothing to do with Fred Luker. Now. Let us go home. Please.'

There was a long pause. Albert-Frederick buried his head in her shoulder and struck out behind him with a tiny fist. Edwin watched her slow tears and thought of the things he could say that would hurt her even more. But now he was tired and it did not seem worth it.

'Will you really come again? Sometimes?'

'I don't know – I can't promise—' She thought of Fred whom she had lost. Or never had. 'I expect so.'

'I will be an uncle to you, March. Just an uncle.'

He waited for her reply and when it did not come he got out again and cranked the Wolseley, and they chugged back slowly, just in time for tea.

March told herself she should be used to loneliness now, and anyway how could she be lonely when she had Albert-Frederick. But the tears would not stop and she pretended to Letty that she had a summer cold.

Fred had no difficulty in persuading Will to accompany him to the Lamb and Flag.

'Haven't got to see a man about a dog tonight have you Will?' he asked jocularly. Will shook his head and got into his new summer alpaca jacket. He did not much care for the way Fred Luker had started to call him Will instead of Mr Rising, and to turn his own little jokes against him. On the other hand Fred had shown him some of the money he now had, and Will knew he could be generous down at the Public.

The two men trudged down Chichester Street in the summer twilight and Fred explained briefly.

'If I can get hold of your brothers, I might be able to make our fortunes, old man,' he said, keeping up the jocular tone. 'Apparently the old custom still holds good in the Forest. And your Vi tells me that Austen is a St Briavels man. Couldn't be better.'

Will swung himself into the Lamb and Flag and went to the public bar.

'Two glasses full to the brim.' He nodded to Sid

Goodrich and Snotty Lottie. 'Don't be daft, Fred. Those old laws are gone and done for now. Some landlord 'ud soon come along and pitch you off his property—'

'It's Crown land, Will. All of it owned by George the bloomin' Fifth. Everyone's there with 'is permission. One more or less isn't going to make that much difference.'

'The miners themselves wouldn't stand for it. They're a funny lot Fred.'

'Don't I know it. Bugger me . . .' He took a breath and began to tell Will about that first visit to the Forest during his leave in 1917, then about the entrepreneur in the prison camp in Silesia.

Will said, 'Ah . . Silesia might be one thing. Dean is another.'

'Get one of them working and the others will follow. If Vi can remember her father talking about Austen's begetting, so will others. Don't you see Will, I've got a handle there. I'm not breaking any of their bloody laws – if Austen'll come in with me I'm using a Forest man to do my squat for me. And if there's any trouble we shall start digging around the Gavellers Arms – see if we can find any old skeletons.' Fred pushed money over the bar. 'Will, listen. I've got to get started quickly. If I don't I'm going to lose the contacts I've made. You've got to help me.'

'Me? What can I do Fred? I'm no miner—'

'Come with me to South Wales. Find your two brothers. Talk them into coming back and working for me. With me. A partnership if you like.'

'They wouldn't know the meaning of the word.

They're . . .' Will searched for words to describe his brothers.

'Like Vi?' suggested Fred. 'Then they'll work for me. Just find them for me, Will. I'll do the rest.'

Will laughed into his glass and drank. 'I'm not coming with you on any wild goose chase, Fred. When you came out of the army and bought that transport car you had the right idea. You can get another one – Henry's practically old enough to drive – and between you—'

'Will. You'd better come with me. Tomorrow.'

'What? Hey – who the devil d'you think you're—'

'Tomorrow, Will. Otherwise Florence might get to know about the man and his dog. Sorry . . . bitch.'

There was an electric silence.

Fred pushed a sovereign over the bar.

'Keep 'em going with that,' he instructed. 'I'm off, lads. I might have some work for you soon.' He touched Will on the shoulder and grinned when the alpaca jacket seemed to shrink away. 'Till tomorrow Will. Be ready early. Sevenish.'

He went outside. He had drunk too much and had too little food. He stuck his fingers down his throat and vomited into the gutter. Then he walked back down to number seventeen to see what Hettie had been cooking.

May had to admit that the members of the Mincing Light Opera Company were very friendly and definitely a cut above the Happy Hey Days lot. They gave her the seat next to the lavatory door because she needed to pass water rather frequently these days. Every time she went in and lifted the seat and saw the rails flashing by, down the long tube, she felt rather peculiar and had to pull out the small basin and hang her head over it for a few minutes. It worried Monty and she refused to tell him it was because of last night's party. She refused to talk to him very much at all. He had not noticed that, which was aggravating but not surprising, with one of the company an ex-Minstrel who still had his ukelele and insisted on playing 'Yankee Doodle went to London, riding on a pony . . .' because it was American Independence Day whatever that was.

Monty didn't know either, and when the day was explained, he said, 'I'm surprised it's a time for rejoicing. I should have thought the poor things regretted it more each year. To think they could have been part of our glorious Empire and they turned it down!' The ex-Minstrel laughed uproariously at this and so did one of the ladies, but the others nodded and of course May knew exactly what Monty meant; darling Monty, whose ideas and feelings ran exactly parallel with her own. She smiled at him fondly and then remembered she was furious and hurt and straightened her face. 'Dearest girl, have you got a pain?' he asked anxiously. She gave him a straight look from her very blue eyes and turned to look out of the window.

They were two hours at Crewe awaiting an engine to pick them up and take them on to York. The Company contralto, who had the biggest chest May had ever seen, got out a small meths stove and made tea and people came to their carriage and sipped it delicately from bakelite picnic cups as if they were in a drawing-room using bone china. The ex-Minstrel took a small mouthful of the remaining leaves, tipped his head back and made a horrible, gargling, choking noise. 'Helps to keep the tone gravelly,' he explained to Monty and May. There were other groups of coaches stationed in the same siding, and after the tea, Monty lifted May down carefully on to the ballast and they took a short stroll up and down while Monty read off the various Companies emblazoned on each coach.

'Reserved for North Company. *East Lynne.*' Monty sighed and squeezed her arm. 'This is Theatre my darling girl. Concert parties are all very well, but this is top-drawer.' He stopped suddenly and gazed at a compartment window framed in damask curtains where a gentleman and lady sat eating chicken drumsticks from napkins. 'Is that . . . is that Beerbohm *Tree*?' he breathed. May took great delight in saying shortly, 'Beerbohm Tree died during the war. Even I know that!'

'I thought he looked rather wooden,' riposted Monty immediately.

'Very amusing,' May acknowledged and had great difficulty in not laughing.

Fred waited until they had negotiated the narrow streets out of Bath before asking March any questions. She looked tired, her hair, normally glossy brown with lights everywhere in it, was simply brown. And she was so thin. She was wearing the jacket that her blasted brother had made her long before the war and she barely filled it out. He thought fiercely, 'Dammit all. I will make a pile somehow. The old man will die and I'll marry her and make her the greatest lady in Gloucester. Dammit, I will do it.' And he said aloud, 'This is the place. One of those model factories it is. I'll have to buy the first load on the open market but after that . . .' She said not a word and he asked abruptly, 'Well? Was it . . . unpleasant?'

She didn't give him a glance but held Albert-Frederick so that he could stand on her lap and look over her shoulder at the passing countryside.

He said impatiently, 'I can see you're in a temper. Shout at me if you want to. It was the only way I could get the old man to take you back and pay the money. Dammit all, you only had to open your legs! It's happened before, nothing to look deathly about!'

Still she was silent, and his words, perforce shouted above the engine note, seemed to hang hideously in the air between them. Albert-Frederick bounced joyfully, leaned forward and gave his mother one of his special, wet kisses. Fred saw from the corner of his eye a slow tear gather on her lashes. He swallowed. She never cried. March shouted and screamed and hit out in all directions. She did not cry.

He said, 'Go on. Tell me I'm a swine. Swear at me.' He waited and she said nothing. Albert subsided onto his well-padded bottom and she cuddled him down against her shoulder to go to sleep. On the top of his sunbonnet was a circular damp patch. Her tears? He drove on, giving her time, hoping that the sights and sounds of Bristol would take her out of herself.

As they approached Thornbury he said, 'Next stop Almondsbury. I'm going to buy you a lemonade and a sandwich. You need building up.' He felt a sudden tense quality in her stillness and added hastily, 'It's all right, I haven't booked us in at the George. I thought you should arrive back the same day I collected you.' She relaxed imperceptibly and he frowned. Twice – just twice – he had made love to March Rising, but each time she had wanted it.

He parked outside the George and fetched refreshments on a tray. Albert-Frederick slept soundly. Fred sat on the running board and drew at his beer, and his mood hardened as her silence continued.

'Look, you'd better know what's been happening in your absence. You need not make any comment, in fact I'd prefer you not to. Bit of a mess at the moment, but it's going to work out. I'm going to make it work out. Then perhaps you'll understand why I did . . . what I did.' He looked up. She was staring through the windscreen, an uneaten ham sandwich in her hand. He went on carefully, 'They backed out. The Freeminers. They thought I was an idiot with a big mouth and they listened to me as . . . as an entertainment. Like they'd have listened to Monty Gould. When it came down to it, they weren't there, so the money stayed in my pocket.'

He thought he heard a sound from her and glanced up again. She was as before. He drank again and continued. 'I heard about the old Forest custom – you probably know it. You build a fire grate and get smoke rising from it during the night and you can lay claim to a certain section of land. It was done a lot two or three hundred years ago. No reason why it can't be done again. But I need local men to help me. So . . . your

88

father and me, we went down to the Rhondda yesterday and found your uncles. Jack and Austen. They're over at number thirty-three right now, and tomorrow I'm taking 'em down to Whitecroft and Parkend – that's where most of the open-cast mines are.'

There was a definite sound from above him this time, and looking up again he saw on the immobile face what might have been an expression of scorn.

'I know I can't dig out enough to make it worth-while. I know all that, March. But once I can show the other pig-headed fools what I'm prepared to do . . . your father says it will mean a summons. He can't understand that the scale of business I'm prepared to do will make a summons worthwhile.' He counted on his fingers. 'There are at least a dozen Freeminers still pulling coal out of those seams. The mines drain down into the middle of the basin where the big Cannop Colliery pumps out the water. So the surface mines require no pumps. There's no problem with gas – no overheads at all. Each of those dozen Freeminers has a family who will help. They say they're not interested in money, but the sort of money I can make for them . . .' He put his glass on the running board and slapped his knee. 'Well, that's it March. I'm going to be working my guts out for the next year or two. After that . . .' He pushed himself upright and looked down at the top of her hat. 'Will you be all right over there with your mother for a year or two?' he asked roughly. 'There won't be much you can do to help me. Bit of typing perhaps. I'm going to get Sib to talk to Old Man William, so you need not worry about that.'

She spoke quietly, 'I'll be all right. It's what I want. More than anything in the world. To be with Mother.' She seemed to relax into her bucket seat at last.

He was embarrassed with her; just as he had been embarrassed as a young lad when she had been so far above him, so much in possession of that great mystery, herself.

He said, 'Be a bit crowded for a few nights. Your uncles . . . But I'll have 'em out by next week.'

She inclined her head and kissed the top of Albert-Frederick's sunbonnet. He got in beside her and drove carefully back through all the lovely Severn villages. He was this side of the river again now; not separated from March at all. Yet separated completely.

He remembered how she had been after Albert's death; withdrawn and hurt so badly he had imagined he had seen her body gently bleeding. That time he had forced her to put all her agony into sexual fervour, and – curiously – come to terms with both pain and passion. Now, glancing almost nervously at her, he wondered whether he might have done better to cook up some story for Florence Rising and book a night at the George.

But it was too late now. She would come round. Eventually.

Chapter Four

April had expected that sharing a home with her mother-in-law would prove very difficult at first. The shop and cutting-room facing the Barton were very small, the parlour and kitchen behind them smaller still. Mrs Daker, well known for her strange, cantankerous ways and her dislike of the Risings in general, had ruled the roost at 'Daker's' since her husband had died on the same day as April's own birth. On the other hand, during the frequent visits April had made to the shop as a schoolgirl, and because of her staunch friendship with David, ostracized by the rest of the Risings, the old lady had nurtured a soft spot for the harum-scarum girl with the cropped hair and hand-me-down clothes. April had an open, frank manner that ignored any awkwardness and permitted her to say such things as 'Lovely day, Mrs Daker,' when it was raining outside, and even 'I like to hear you sing, Mrs Daker – it sounds like hope.' So that, although the two women were wary still at sharing such close accommodation, there was careful circumspection on each side and a respect that might one day – with luck – develop into a kind of love.

What April had not expected was to find any awkwardness in the small front bedroom above the shop. There she had imagined a closeness with David that would be like the merging of their souls. She had imagined intimate looks that spoke a thousand words. She had imagined small and tender jokes, such as they shared long before marriage. April had looked forward to the day when she could give herself to David and he could give himself to her.

But she found that there had been more intimacy between them when they had not shared a bedroom. Nightly she gave herself to David, offering herself with a curiously innocent abandon which she shared with May; and because David did not give himself, there was always a small secret part of her that carried shame. He induced a physical ecstasy in her that she could not have imagined before, but because he did not share it with her she was reminded obscenely of Sibbie's words . . . 'he'll give you a good time'. Their love-making was something reserved entirely for the bedroom, it did not carry over during the day to be remembered in small smiles or even pretended archness. They had to work hard to resurrect their easy, tender friendship during breakfast; after supper they discarded that with their clothes.

They were . . . busy. During their honeymoon they walked the cliffs to Flamborough Head where the wind from Scandinavia made speech impossible. They went into the long fish sheds on the old quay and saw the lines of girls in their kerchiefs and big oilskin aprons gutting the herring so quickly it was difficult to follow their hands. David refused to swim because of his wound, but he sat on the beach and watched while April swam alone, lying on the water with her eyes closed against the sun while the ice of the North

Sea seeped through to her bones. When David towelled her dry, she said suddenly, 'Oh David, I love you so!' But there was bewilderment in her voice, and when he said, 'Do you my darling?' she was convinced it was her fault that he held back from her.

That night, as May got ready to attend the farewell party on the stage at Kilburn and March returned home from Bath, and Will and Sibbie cavorted in the wooden bungalow on the canal bank, and the uncles sat with Gran and Sylv and Florence and talked of the old days when Albert and Teddy had been alive . . . on the last night of their honeymoon, April wept and at last tried to talk to David.

'It's wonderful darling. Like heaven. But you're not there with me.' He kissed her and held her close.

'Don't say that, Primrose. You are my only hope of heaven.' His voice was deliberately light; his day-time voice. She tried to look into his face and could not.

'What on earth d'you mean darling?'

'If I present myself alone at those pearly gates, they'll surely turn me away. But if I'm with you—'

She was suddenly impatient. 'Oh David, be serious. Please. I know . . . I know what should be done. Tell me why . . . why . . . you won't do it!'

There was a silence. She pushed at his chest, wanting desperately to see his face in the frail light from the gas jet, but he held her to him fiercely. She whispered at last, 'It doesn't matter. I'm sorry—'

'No! It does matter – let me tell you. You must never think I don't love you with my whole self, April – that phrase, consumed with love. I know what it means.

It's like a fire, my love for you, and sometimes I think it will destroy me!'

She gave a small cry and encircled him with her arms, kissing his throat, holding him as if she expected his body to be ripped from her physically. 'I won't let it happen – I won't let it!'

'It's all right my love, my little love . . .' He found himself comforting her, stroking her hair. '. . . You are also my salvation, April . . .' He forced a laugh. '. . . As I said, my passport to heaven.'

She fumbled desperately with the problem of her husband. 'David, I do understand. When you came home first and nothing had changed . . . I mean, you had changed, your whole world had become hell and there we were – blind – not seeing what was happening. You could hear screaming and smell burning, and we just laughed and—'

He was amazed at her perception; he had known she felt for him, agonized for him, but that she *knew* and could find words to name something that, to him, had been nameless, was amazing.

He murmured, 'So you gave your beautiful hair to the Red Cross and went to work in the munitions factory.'

She clung harder. 'It was puny. I know it was stupid – you told me off, d'you remember? But I was trying to tell you that I wanted to be with you – I was trying to reach you—'

'In hell, Primrose?'

'Yes. In hell.'

'No-one can be with you in hell, my darling. That's what hell is. Isolation. If someone joins you, it is no

94

longer hell.' He kissed the top of her head. 'You did something much better than joining me, April. You forced me to think of someone else. Something else. That's why you are my salvation. Can you understand that?'

'I think so.' She rubbed his spine, feeling each vertebra with tenderness. 'That's why you married me. You saw it was selfish to keep me waiting any longer.'

'Oh Primrose. Sometimes you're as wise as a seventy-year-old crone! Then you say something like that and I am reminded that you are seventeen.'

'And you are twenty-eight, David! *Not* eighty!'

'I can be both. Like you.' At last he took her shoulders and held her away from him. 'Listen. It seemed right – it *was* right – at first, to keep away from you. Then there was Armistice night and I . . . you . . .'

'You realized that over half of me was grown-up, David.'

'Yes. All right. So then you pestered me unmercifully – yes you did – don't deny it—'

'I don't deny it.'

'And I was weak enough – wicked enough – to give in. But I made conditions for myself. You were seventeen. I could not bear to see you big with child.'

She whimpered a laugh. 'Big with child. Like the Bible.'

'Just like the Bible. A pact. A biblical pact.'

April was silent. She too had bargained with God. For David's life. For Fred Luker's life. For happiness.

He said at last, 'Now do you understand, April?'

'Yes,' she whispered. 'But I don't think you're right.

To make a baby together would be . . . would *be* heaven.'

'And then? To bring a child up in this rotten world? Wouldn't that be hell?'

She looked into his dark eyes and saw the bleakness returning, but still she tried. 'Does that mean . . . do you never want to have children, David?'

He answered her with a question that was a cry for help. 'Am I not enough for you, April?'

And she responded instantly. 'Always. Always and always, my dearest.'

She would have slept then, friendly in his arms. But when he caressed her, she felt she had to prove something. She moved against him, opening her mouth to his, responding to his touch like a finely tuned instrument. And the next morning their dual selves were waiting for them again, their dual intimacies which somehow could not be fused.

But if she had to prove something to him in the bedroom, it was as if he had to prove something to her in the shop. His uncaring attitude to the business disappeared on their return to Gloucester. True to his word, he made April a replica of her wedding frock in peacock-blue silk. He made her a blouse in shantung with enormous sleeves, like bat wings, called magyar sleeves because the Hungarian gypsies who went around with their hands permanently on their hips, wore them. He bought a wax model and draped it with one of the new up-and-down frocks and stood it in the window which had for so long displayed only gent's suiting.

People began to flock to Daker's. Sometimes they

stood in the Barton and gazed at the dummy and hid smiles behind their gloves. Sometimes they came inside for a reel of cotton to see April's latest creation. Soon they were ordering blouses and dresses for themselves. Will, forcing himself to go through the door he had vowed never to open again, said jokingly, 'You're going to put me out of business, April!'

She said quickly, 'It's nothing to do with me, Daddy. It's David. He's working so hard.'

Will nodded and said acutely and with regret, 'It's a new world, April. In my day I had my name on the window and that was all. Now, it's different. You put your goods in the window these days. David is showing off his work on a beautiful girl and everyone wants to look like you, my darling.'

She made a face. 'So I'm the goods in the window, am I?'

He laughed with her, but noted something in her eyes that made him think to himself: she'll soon be back home . . . she's not happy.

Florence spooned bread and milk into her grandson's rosy mouth and tried not to watch March over-anxiously as she sat at the table, her hands listlessly in her lap. Albert-Frederick tried to take the spoon in his own fat fingers and blew milky bubbles as it escaped him yet again. March did not laugh with her mother; she hardly seemed to notice her baby.

'March dear, I think this child could do with a walk this afternoon. He's getting bored with being in the house every day.' Florence wiped at the milky face and gave over the empty spoon. Albert-Frederick banged on the tray of his chair. Florence went on loudly, 'It's overcrowded here with Jack and Austen. Let's go to the park. We could walk along Spa Road, through the sunken garden and sit under Raikes' monument.'

March focused her, then took the spoon and stood up. 'Yes. All right, if you like.' Albert-Frederick yelled his frustration and she slapped at his grasping hand.

Florence could contain her anxiety no longer. 'Are you worried about poor Edwin, my dear?'

'No, of course not.' March widened her eyes like a frightened horse; very much as Florence had noticed April widening hers lately.

She said decidedly, 'Then you must be missing your sisters.'

March nodded gratefully. 'Especially dear April,' she agreed.

They put Albert-Frederick in the pushchair and lifted it down the steps, pausing ritualistically for him to point out the boot-scraper and Grampa's name on the window. And as they did so the telegraph boy's red bicycle turned into Chichester Street and bowled towards them. March put her hand to her breast; she would never forget the War Office telegram about Albert as long as she lived. The boy scraped the toe of his boot along the gutter and pulled up in a flurry of dust. Albert-Frederick sneezed.

Florence tore at the envelope and spread the paper. 'Can't see . . . glasses,' she said faintly. March took the flimsy sheet. 'It's all right. No reply.' She out-stared the boy who was standing there brazenly waiting for a tip, then turned to her mother. 'It's from Monty. It says "Victor has started his journey stop all's well stop more news later stop Monty."' She folded the paper and gave it to Florence. 'What a waste of money. However, May told me he was being paid twenty pounds a week! Twenty pounds – imagine it!'

Florence said, 'May, in labour. Oh March – oh darling – poor little May!' She turned. 'I really think we should go back inside and wait for the next wire.'

March looked determined. 'Oh no Mamma. You're not going to sit and worry for the rest of the day. There's nothing at all we can do about it. We'll walk to the park, then we'll come back down the Barton and tell April. By the time we reach the house, there might be some more news.'

Florence's black cotton gloves fluttered about her throat uncertainly. Then she nodded. The two women moved off down the street, stopping to let people speak to Albert-Frederick: Granny Goodrich, Hetty Luker, Daisy coming home for her half-day from Woodward's the chemist. It was like a royal progression.

They were in Manchester. There were fifteen theatres in the city, fifteen companies needing theatrical diggings. Mr Brockwell who went in advance and 'fixed them up', had allocated Monty and May to a house where there were already five children, on the grounds that the landlady must know how to deliver them. Mrs Turner put three saucepans full of water on the gas stove, and sent her five out to play. They ran up and down the back alley behind the house, shouting and screaming; she ran up and down the stairs flapping her apron and asking Monty where the doctor could have got to.

May was wonderful at first. She woke in the early hours to a strange, tearing sensation in her groin that was not too painful at all. When she got out to sit on the chamber-pot, she found her nightdress stained and she woke Monty excitedly. He went down and made tea and they sat up talking about the advantages and disadvantages of boarding-schools until Mr Turner went to the iron foundry at six o'clock. May could still feel objective about the lump in her abdomen, and after Sibbie's disclosure or boast or whatever it had been, she had come to wonder whether she might have let Monty feel neglected. He had told her once that he was the only baby she must have, and it was true she had practically seduced him when he was drunk on Armistice night. So she seriously considered letting Victor go to one of the new kindergartens when he was three. Or four. Or perhaps six. But that was before he was actually born.

At midday the tearing sensations had a clawing quality to them and extended around her back and down her legs. They made her feel terribly tired, yet ensured that she could not sleep. She told Monty he had better go for the doctor and send a telegram to Chichester Street. 'Make it amusing,' she instructed. 'Mother mustn't worry.'

But by the time Monty returned, May was writhing at regular intervals, and as she writhed, beads of sweat appeared on her upper lip and tears of fright came into the corners of her eyes. It was then that Mrs Turner began running up and down the stairs and the screaming of the children suddenly seemed unbearable.

In between pains May gripped Monty's hands desperately.

'Darling boy, I don't want you to see me like this, but I can't manage without you . . . Could anything be wrong d'you think? Surely a little pressure from inside couldn't be like this? He's been kicking and moving about for ages now and there's been no *pain* . . . oh – oh Monty it's coming again . . . oh dear God . . . oh Mamma . . . Mamma!'

Monty tried to cradle her and was amazed at her strength as she pushed him from her to reach up and grab the brass bed rail and pull her contorted body up as if she could draw it away from the pain.

The doctor arrived, young and raw, and insisted on Mrs Turner's presence while he examined his patient. Mrs Turner, veteran of five births, had not actually seen one. She held her throat with one hand, her stomach with the other and very obviously fought against heaving.

'By no means dilated,' the doctor said nervously. 'Try to relax a little Mrs . . . er . . . Gould. You are working against your contractions.'

He lacked the simple language and the authority of a midwife and May ignored him and thrashed about helplessly.

Mrs Turner gasped, 'Hot water . . . downstairs . . .'

Monty hovered at the top of the landing. 'Isn't there anything you can *do*? She can't go on like this. My God, if I'd thought – we'll never have any more. Just get us through this and we'll never—'

The doctor said, 'Ether tends to slow things down, of course.' He bit his lip as May choked a scream behind the door. 'She could do with some nursing care.'

'Anything. We've got cash. When – who – where—'

'I'll send someone.' The doctor couldn't wait to get away. He edged past Monty and went down the stairs in a rush. Monty hesitated, listening to him speaking to Mrs Turner, then went into the bedroom.

Fred turned out of Northgate Street and bounced down Mews Lane to the stables where his younger brother, Henry, was currying the big dray horse which was all that was left of old Alf Luker's livery business. It was six weeks since his abortive meeting with Danby in the Gavellers Arms, and he was ready to make his bid to 'squat'. Austen had come with him on his furtive search for a site with a likely 'coal dig' as he put it, and when he had found it, Fred had gone to great lengths to conceal their tracks. Since then he had quietly supplied the spot with enough food and equipment to keep them going for a week if necessary, and tonight was the night. Somehow they had to comply with that ridiculous law and build a fireplace, a skeleton dwelling around it, and a chimney.

He parked the small charabanc within reach of the outside tap.

'Good wash Henry, soon as you can.' He climbed out stiffly and stretched himself, then plucked a sovereign from his jacket pocket and spun it in the air towards his brother. 'Oddfellows' dinner at Cheltenham Town Hall. Made a collection for me after. It's yours.'

Henry, prepared to be resentful and sullen, caught

it and grinned delightedly. 'Right business to be in, Fred,' he said cockily. 'Dunno why you waste so much time down in the Forest.'

'I'm not wasting my time, boy, don't worry about that.' Fred slid out of his jacket and folded it over one arm; his shirt was stained with sweat; it was a hot day. 'Going to be gone for a few days this time. I want you to take over the charrie. Right?'

Henry glowed. He was still sixteen and had only driven the charabanc while Fred sat critically next to him.

Fred went on, 'Our Glad has got the booking list and she'll tell you exactly when to leave and what to do. You listen to every word she says, our Henry. D'you hear me?'

'Ah. An' I won't be familiar. An' I'll change me shirt and wear your jacket and touch me cap and say wanna wipe y'r feet on me ass kind sir – and—' He dodged Fred's hand and went to the tap. 'An' why is our Glad doing all this booking bizz then, our Fred? What happened to the true romance story with you-know-'oo?'

This time Fred went after him and got him by the top of his right ear. Henry yelped and danced.

'You will never talk about Mrs Tomms disrespectfully my lad unless you want to feel the full force of my—'

'I didn't say nothing 'bout March Rising, our Fred—'

'Then you will say nothing in future either!' Fred sent him spinning back to the tap, dusted his hands and continued. 'Gladys doesn't enjoy the pickle factory any more than our Sib did. If we can get her interested in the business we might keep her off the streets.'

Henry rubbed his ear ruefully. 'You en't got a very high opinion of your fam'ly, 'as you, our brud?'

Fred picked his jacket up from where he'd dumped it on the bonnet of the charabanc. 'I haven't got much of an opinion of anyone, Henry. Anyone at all,' he said. And went to change into his working clothes.

By the time he had picked up the two uncles, Jack and Austen Rising, it was four o'clock. He packed them into the Morris together with overalls and beer bottles, and drove to the Cross, then turned down Westgate Street and headed for Newnham-on-Severn. Florence and March, returning along Eastgate Street from a call on April in the Barton, saw them and smiled at each other, thankful that the house would be theirs at tea-time. They had both searched unobtrusively for Albert's name on the new War Memorial at the park, and finding it, had felt the usual terrible pang.

Monty said wildly, 'My God, it's four-thirty! He promised he'd send a nurse – you can't go on like this my darling!'

May became rigid yet again, fighting a pain, then suddenly sat bolt upright clutching at herself. Terror held her face still.

'Monty – Monty! Something has happened – oh my darling, I've lost it – I've lost it!'

He pushed back the clothes. May's nightdress was saturated. He ran to the door and shouted for Mrs

Turner and she stumbled up the stairs, yellow-faced and apprehensive.

''Tis the waters missis. They'm broke, that's all. Should be a mite easier now. More room like.'

Monty was inordinately grateful to her, especially as it seemed she was right about the pain. May lay exhaustedly on the pillows and sipped tea and could be held to his shoulder.

'It's still there . . . Monty, it will come back. I know.'

'Not so badly, sweetheart. The nurse should be here and she will help you. Try not to—'

'Monty, I can't bear it.' May lifted her ravaged face and looked at him. 'I simply can't bear it. I've tried to be s-s-sensible – not to say anything – but you shouldn't have *kissed* her! If you love me how can you look at another woman?'

'Sweetheart, are you delirious? What do you mean?'

'S-s-sibbie said – she said you'd kissed her. After April's wedding. On the station platform.'

He was aghast. 'I *knew* something was between us! She is a wicked evil woman, May! And you believed her – oh my darling girl, do you think I could ever *see* another woman when I have known you?' He was so distressed he began to weep. 'Oh May – beautiful May. You cannot think so poorly of me that you really think—'

May pulled his head to her breast as she had done so often and he wept there like a child. Then a pain came upon her suddenly and she closed her eyes and bit her lip till it bled so as not to disturb him. The midwife came upon them in that pose: wife in the midst of a contraction, husband weeping all over her. She clapped her hands like an angry schoolteacher and thrust Monty from the room. Then she was out of her coat, into her white apron and starched headgear, hot water was sent for and poured into ewer then into basin – May always wondered why – hands were washed, scolding instructions begun. May thought of Snotty Lottie who had delivered all Florence's children with the well-known twisting emergence for which she was locally famous, and prayed that this woman had the same expertise.

Fred turned the Morris carefully off the Blakeney road into a track which skirted the Forest School at Parkend. He ordered the Risings out into the ankle-deep bracken and loaded them with the beer and clothing. Then he led them straight into the Forest along an unmarked way which, it seemed, he knew very well. They stumbled after him for over half an hour, rolling on unseen logs, slipping on leaves that were damp even in the height of summer. Jack and Austen kept up a steady stream of curses.

''Ow much bluggy further then Fred-lad?' bawled Jack at last, as he went down on one knee over a hidden stone. 'Sodd'n' 'ell, din't expec' this sort o' caper. Ee said ee wanted our expert 'elp. Not a bluggy forced march!'

'Nearly there,' Fred said briefly over his shoulder. 'And keep your voice down for Christ's sake. This is supposed to be secret.'

'No need for language,' Jack said mildly, picking himself up and shouldering his sack of beer bottles.

'Christamighty, we could've stayed in the Rhondda and 'eard clean talk at least.'

'Shut up, our Jack,' Austen advised. 'We cum this far . . . I've seen it, remember. 'Tis good coal.'

They emerged into a glade filled with sun and dissected by a tiny crystal-clear stream. In front of them the packed leaves rose sharply into a solid wall of oaks. Near the stream was a large tarpaulin-covered heap.

'Good.' Fred went around the dell like a sniffing dog. 'No-one's disturbed a thing. I left one or two traps around.' He got back to the tarpaulin, removed some stones which weighted it and flung it back. A pile of stores was revealed, tinned food, shovels and picks, candles and tobacco, camp beds, blankets. He grinned at them above the glorious jumble. 'Think I did my bit all right then? It's taken me a dozen trips to supply this, *and* I never took the same route twice. Did *you* remember it, Austen?'

'Bluggered if I did Fred-lad,' Austen grinned, stepped over the stream and dug his hand into the leafy loam. 'Come and look at this, our Jack. Ever seen anything like it?' Among the handful of loam, coal dust sparkled wickedly.

'Christamighty,' breathed Jack. ''Tis there. 'Tis just *there*!'

Fred grinned again. 'No tunnels, no gas, no floods. You just dig the stuff out. And it's ours if we can get up some sort of shack before tomorrow morning and light a fire.'

'No-one can see us, Fred. 'Oo's to know whether we does it or no?'

''Tis the Forest law,' Fred announced righteously.

'And we're not going to start by breaking any laws!'

He watched sardonically as they cavorted about like schoolboys, grabbing shovels and starting to dig willynilly, jumping the stream in their cumbersome boots, slipping on the bank, falling in the water. Then he walked into the sun and started to mark out a rough foundation with the heel of his boot.

It was Sylvia who broke the silence as they sat around the empty grate that evening long after Albert-Frederick had gone to bed.

'It would be tonight of all nights the men are missing,' she grumbled. "Twould 'ave taken our minds off our May if they'd been cluttering up the place like usual.'

Will said good-humouredly, 'Don't I count as one of the men then? Or perhaps I'm not cluttering the place up quite sufficiently.' He sprawled out in his chair and Sylvia laughed obediently. Florence glanced at March and spoke almost apologetically, 'We do tend to take a long time in labour, Sylvia dear. I don't think we need worry unduly.'

But Sylvia had lost her baby girl in this very house, and she still considered May to be delicate.

'I just 'ope 'er man will remember to send another wire,' she fretted. 'These actor fellows are a flighty lot when all's said and done.'

'Monty's all right,' declared Will stoutly, thinking of his other two sons-in-law. 'He'll just be coming off stage now.' He had acquired one or two professional terms and liked to air them occasionally.

Sylvia looked across the room disbelievingly. "E

wouldn't go on and do his songs tonight, surely? Not with his wife in labour?'

March spoke for the first time. 'Why not? May won't want him hanging around, I assure you.'

Sylvia thought of her husband, Dick Turpin, waiting outside her bedroom door, suffering the agony with her. They thought they had fine feelings, these in-laws of hers, but when it came down to it they could be a cold lot.

Will looked at his watch; Sibbie would be waiting, but he couldn't leave them like this. 'Where's our April? I thought you said you'd called in to tell her this afternoon? I did think she'd be down with us.'

Nobody answered him.

David said, 'Darling, I expect you want to walk along to Chichester Street for news. I'll get my stick.'

'No. I don't want to do that, David.' April had a strange set and stubborn look to her normally mobile face. 'I want to go to bed.'

David glanced at his mother, glasses on the end of her nose, reading that night's *Citizen*. A small smile lifted her inverted mouth.

'Very well dear. You go on up. I'll be with you in a moment.'

He made a show of locking up and putting out the breakfast cups and saucers. He was trembling with desire. The shop door pinged against its lock as he had one foot on the bottom stair. Cursing under his breath he stumbled through the dark room and unbolted it. A dark figure, vaguely familiar, stood there.

'Manny Stein – by all that's holy! What brings you here?'

David backed in and Manny followed. His stilted courtesy, his black hat which he constantly raised and lowered, his bag . . . all proclaimed him foreign.

'I was nearby . . . had to look you up . . . your charming wife . . .'

Mrs Daker became very Jewish and pressed him into her own chair. David called April. She came downstairs, her blue eyes black with pupil, the summer dressing-gown wrapped around her thinness revealing almost as much as it hid.

'Mr Stein – all right then – Manny—' She held out a hand and he took it in both of his. It was very hot and damp. David, watching, saw his reaction; the awareness in his dark face. April sat down quickly.

Manny Stein said, 'I have a job in your line. In London it is called the rag trade. Here it has more dignity—' He gestured towards the shop where the window announced bespoke tailoring.

'Welcome, welcome to the business, whatever it is called,' David said in a dry voice. 'We shall have to share ideas. April is a great one for innovation. Perhaps you should talk to her.'

'Don't be absurd, David.' April tinkled a laugh. 'Manny deals with ready-made clothing I dare say.'

'Yes. Certainly. But my wholesaler also supplies embroidery materials. Tapestry stands. I see you have a haberdashery line . . .'

'You're selling? At this hour?' David's brows went up. Manny Stein flushed.

'No. I had business in Cheltenham. And I thought—'

'Mr Stein must stay with us this night!' Mrs Daker brought in tea. 'He can have my bed with pleasure. I hardly close my eyes now.'

'I wouldn't dream of it, Mrs Daker. I have in any case reserved a room at the Bell Inn, but my train leaves at eight o'clock tomorrow.'

They looked at him anew. The Bell Inn. David said, 'You sound prosperous, old chap. Is it a sign of the times?'

'Indeed yes.' Manny nodded briskly. 'Always after a war there is a boom in fashion – luxury trades in general. And the new modes for ladies are very easy to copy.' He smiled at April. 'As your sisters knew when they made their wedding gowns.'

David waited for April's comments and when they did not come he said, 'Is there any possibility of you staying till a later train tomorrow, old man? I'd be interested to see anything you have.'

Manny suppressed a smile. 'But certainly David. For a friend, anything.'

April stood up. 'If we're seeing you tomorrow, Manny, will you excuse me now? I'm very tired.' Her cheekbones beneath the huge dark eyes looked unusually prominent. He scrambled to his feet and bowed ridiculously from the shoulders. She smiled tightly and avoided David's eyes as she went to the stairs. There was a short silence, then the voices droned on beneath her.

Angry and shaking she lay between the sheets, hours from sleep. At midnight she heard chairs scraping and David came up the stairs. He crept into their room, closed the door softly and began to undress by the light from the bead of gas in the popping mantle.

'I'm not asleep. Turn up the gas, David,' she commanded levelly.

He did as he was bid and looked down at her with the half-smile that always twisted at her heart with its strange mixture of love and sadness.

'Still awake, baby? Did we disturb you with our talk?'

'I have not been to sleep yet. And I am not a baby.'

He paused in the act of pulling off his tie and his smile became cajoling. 'I knew something was wrong. You were stiff with irritability.'

'I told you, I wanted to come to bed.'

'I know. We were going to bed if you recall. And Manny arrived. He was my best man at our wedding, Primrose.'

'He is a salesman. He came for business.'

'It crossed my mind. But . . . there is friendship too.'

She burst out furiously, 'He convinced you with that tale of the Bell! I could tell – you and your mother – you believed him!'

'Hush darling. He is still downstairs.'

'I don't care if he is here! In this room with us! He was laughing at you!'

'What does it matter, April? Surely you are interested to see some of his lines? It could be good for *our* business – which seems to absorb you fairly thoroughly!'

'Sometimes. Yes. Certainly. Now – tonight – I was interested in something else!'

His smile appeared again and he began on his shirt

buttons. 'Darling girl. Did you think for one moment that I put Manny Stein before you—'

She bunched herself into a corner of the bed, clasping the clothes around her. 'Don't come near me, David! I mean it – keep away—'

He stood there, braces dangling. 'I thought it was what you wanted. April, what on earth is the matter with you tonight?'

'Don't you know? There was a time when you would have known – instinctively you would have known what was the *matter* with me! That man . . . looking at me . . . making me feel . . . I don't want to be looked at, David! I don't want to be the goods in your shop window! My sister is having – has probably had – a baby! Tonight!' She was panting with anger and her voice was loud. 'I want a baby! I want a *baby*! D'you hear me?'

He continued to remove his trousers. 'I imagine most of the Barton heard you, Primrose.' He reached for his nightshirt. 'Manny is probably enjoying it very much. I don't see how he could help looking at you when you came down in that ridiculous dressing-gown—'

'I hoped he might take the hint. That we were going to bed – together. Like husbands and wives do!'

He picked up his trousers and put the legs seam to seam with great care. 'I thought you understood how I felt about you, April. And about children. We talked at Scarborough—'

'I'm too young and the world is too wicked! That was it, wasn't it? But I'm not too young. And it's up to us to make a world fit for our children. And if my sisters can—'

He looked up, suddenly angry. 'Do you have to copy May in everything?'

He had missed the point again. She almost stammered with rage as she searched for words to wound. Then she said, 'You didn't object when I picked you up after she'd dropped you!'

He finished smoothing his trousers over the bed rail. She sat up straight and held out her arms. 'I didn't mean that, David. I'm sorry.'

He turned and looked at her. As before, she was naked, her body thin but perfectly formed. He said through his teeth, 'Are you tormenting me deliberately April? Are you?' He grabbed at her and pulled her against him so that they were eye to eye. She said something in a gasping voice which he did not hear and he put his mouth on hers and forced her down again. She cried out against him and twisted to free a trapped leg. He pulled up his nightshirt and rammed into her furiously.

So for a few seconds of frantic activity. Then he collapsed and lay with his face in the pillow. And she stared at the gas globe until her vision starred.

Then, slowly, she closed her knees together and straightened her legs into the bed; next she turned on to one elbow and put her hand on David's springy hair where it grew into the nape of his neck. She leaned down and kissed the top vertebra in his spine. Stroked and kissed. Whispered into his ear, 'David. I love you. I love you, my darling. And you love me. That is all that matters. Without that I would want to die.'

He let her murmur for a long time, then, not looking up, he put an arm across her and lifted his head onto her breast. She held him, stroking, kissing, murmuring; far into the night.

All the way home from the theatre Monty prayed it would be over. It couldn't have happened during the performance because one of the little Turners had promised to run round with the news; but it might have happened in the last half an hour while he took off his make-up and wended his way through the streets of back-to-back houses, forcing his steps to slow each time they involuntarily quickened.

The light was on in the front bedroom.

Of course the light would be on; May would be waiting for him, wanting to show him the baby and kiss him and tell him never again. And then, like a blow across his face, came the scream.

He took three more paces to the next gas lamp, and hung on. The scream appeared to have been unheard by anyone else; the street remained deserted and uncaring; even the dust and smell of compacted humanity had been blown away by that single note that held the depths of exhaustion in its basic pleas. Monty muttered, 'Please God ... please ...'

Nothing else happened. It could have been the birth scream. He listened for the cry of a child. Nothing. He remembered the ex-Minstrel who was called Frank O'Rourke saying jokingly, 'Don't let it get the better of you, old man. It's always worse for the father!' Certainly Monty would infinitely prefer to be bearing this pain rather than listening to May bearing it.

He pushed his hat to the back of his head and laid

his forehead against the cast-iron lamp post. 'Please God . . . please God,' he muttered again. Then he straightened, marched another six paces to the front door on the street, found it, unlocked and let himself in to the cabbage smelling hall. Mrs Turner appeared at the other end of it, silhouetted in a square of light from the kitchen.

'Is it you, Mr Gould? I hoped the doctor . . .'

'You've called him again?' Monty hurried down the passage, divesting himself of hat and coat as he went.

'Twice sir. She's real bad. Weak, see. Seems she's very narrow – I noticed it myself when you arrived. Too much in front and not enough at the sides I said to my Bert.'

'Who is with her now?'

'Midwife. Reckon the doctor will want her in 'ospital.'

'Oh my God. My God.'

The front door opened again and the young doctor came in with a rush and went straight upstairs. Monty returned to the newel post and hung on to it.

It was very dark in Dean Forest that night. Fred worked stripped to the waist and gleamed whitely with sweat; the others eyed him askance and left their braces over their vests. They could have been mistaken for the wild boar that had once roamed these parts, grunting and digging and snorting and smelling. As one of them barrowed stone from a convenient ruined wall nearby, another shovelled and slapped at a big board of mortar and a third spread and sludged and bedded carefully. Occasionally they would stop one by one and reach for the bottles stacked in the stream. They spoke no word.

At three-thirty, Monty sat on the stairs and put his head on his knees. The doctor was still with May but all sounds had now ceased and Monty was certain she was dead. He tried to pray and could not. He tried to recall her face and it wavered behind his lids, a blur of angel-blonde hair, creamy skin and blue blue eyes; the intrinsic May was not there. Desperately he tried to instil his image with a persona; if he could not then she really was dead. He could keep her alive by force of will, but he must *see* her.

Mrs Turner said, 'Cuppa tea sir. Come on now, drink up.' He was angry with her for interrupting his concentration and gestured the cup to the step by his right leg. 'Gawd, what a night,' she went on in a half-moan, half-whisper. 'You en't going to forget this night for some time to come, are you sir?'

He did not reply and after a hesitant moment she backed down the stairs and disappeared again into the kitchen. As if at a signal the bedroom door opened and the doctor, shirt-sleeved, sweating and not quite so young as before, appeared on the landing and signalled him to come up. He kicked over his cup, ignored it and scrambled up the stairs.

'The position is – ' the doctor looked completely done up '– forced to anaesthetize to alleviate the weariness . . .' How could he use such long words at a time like this? 'Now we need her to be alert in order to . . .' She wasn't dead. May was alive.

'No time for fainting spells, man!' The doctor was

extremely unsympathetic, he jerked Monty upright. 'You have a part to play!'

His words could not have been better chosen. Monty listened hard to the producer of this particular drama and knew it was the part of his life. He took a deep breath and went into the bedroom.

He was prepared for blood, for smells, for disarray; there was none of that. Each time May disturbed the covering sheet, the nurse straightened it. Later she untucked the bottom and rolled it up for the doctor to examine his patient. There was no sign of blood and the smell was of strong antiseptic. But if Monty was disappointed, May's thin face, 'pale and peaky' as Florence always insisted, her damp-dark hair, her half-closed drugged eyes were drama enough.

'Monty . . .' Her voice was a thread of distress.

'It's all right my darling.' He crouched by the bed and took her hands in his. His eyes filled with tears.

'I don't want you to see . . . Please.'

'The doctor—' they didn't even know his name – 'he wants me to be with you for a few minutes, my sweetheart. That's all.' He kissed her knuckles. 'May. You have to start bearing down, darling. Next time you must bear down as hard as you can.'

'I know. She said that.' May let her eyes roll towards the nurse at the end of the bed. 'I can't. I can't do it, Monty. I'm too tired.'

'Of course you can do it, my beautiful. You've had a nice sleep.'

'They think I slept. But I didn't.'

Monty smiled at her. 'You'll be all right now I'm here. We'll do it together, May.' He made his voice confident. 'I'm going to hold your hands and they will hold your feet and we'll work really hard.'

The nurse said in a low voice, 'I think it's now.'

She rolled back the sheet expertly and exposed May's distended abdomen. Monty glanced over his shoulder and nearly shrieked in horror. The smooth white belly he knew and loved, suddenly had a life of its own. Grotesquely it contracted and convulsed and at the same time May gave a soft moan and closed her eyes as if trying to leave her body to manage alone. The doctor and nurse took a leg each and crooked it expertly and the doctor said, 'Now. Now if you please Mrs Gould. *Now!*' They pressed hard on the slim, race-horse legs and Monty averted his eyes, his part forgotten, his hands already slackening their hold on May's limp fingers. The doctor snapped, 'Come on Mr Gould. A little encouragement—' and the nurse cut across him with a single loud command, 'Push!'

Monty's voice rose to a trembling crescendo, his 'part' forgotten in sheer terror. 'May? May, wake up darling. Please wake up. May ... please ...' The transparent eyelids trembled and he shook her hands with frantic fussiness, like a pestering child. 'May! It's Monty. Open your eyes. You have to—'

The eyes opened and looked at him, first with puzzlement, then with the automatic reassurance they always brought to him. The doctor's voice stated his requirements once again with careful precision; the nurse repeated ringingly, 'Push!' and Monty stared at her, frightened, his clear brown eyes like Teddy's eyes when he was in trouble. Darling Teddy and darling Monty. Always wanting help . . . She gripped his hands in her long fingers, braced her heels on she knew not what and began to work.

The trees seemed to wake up slowly that morning of August the twelfth. It was going to be hot again and the leaves of the oak that had supplied so many navies sheltered one beneath another, very still, conserving their strength for the parched day ahead.

The small dell, which had been so beautiful in the evening sun the night before, appeared completely desecrated in the first of that morning's light. The banks of the stream had been broken down by trampling boots and the thick pad of leaves covering the right-hand bank had been churned into an open wound of fern roots, brambles, broken stone, dollops of cement, discarded timbers, empty bottles, even clothing. The strange construction overlooking this waste in no way resembled a hovel, let alone a cottage; it might have been a giant clothes-horse set about a miniature blacksmith's forge. And the men still moving around in a trance of weariness were feeding the forge with pathetic offerings of bracken and twigs.

Fred straightened his back.

'Right. The matches.'

Jack lumbered over to the trampled tarpaulin and grovelled through some loose candles, balls of twine and an assortment of cutlery.

'Austen!' he growled out of the side of his mouth. 'You 'ad 'em. Where b'ist?' Austen shook his head, incapable of speech. 'You were lighting the bluggy lantern—' Jack scrabbled futilely again and Fred galvanized himself into action, leapt through the open timber frame and snatched at the box of lucifers protruding from the tobacco tin.

'Christamighty,' he grumbled, setting light to the kindling. 'Lose the lot if I relied on anyone else wouldn't I? Sun will be coming through them trees any minute now—' As he spoke, one single piercing ray came through the tangle of waist-high fern behind the tin chimney, shone across the stream and spotlighted the point where Austen had shovelled out the coal-grit. Everyone looked towards it and seemed to stop breathing. Then there was a crackle, a spurt of flame, and a steady line of smoke, unwavering in the still air, rose steadily upwards. They watched it, tipping their heads until it surmounted the trees around them, a banner for anyone to see.

They looked at each other. They didn't have the energy to cheer.

And in Manchester, at number eleven Jubilee Walk, May gave the final push that expelled Victor Gould from the safety of her womb. And Monty did the classic thing, and fainted. May did not worry. Relaxed and instantly recovered, she lay back and watched with a little smile as the doctor saw to Monty and the nurse to Victor, and her eyes were oftener on Victor than on Monty. When they gave her the small wrinkled bundle, she was glad that Monty could not see her. It was a moment that excluded him completely. She looked at her son and knew how Florence had felt at Teddy's birth; how March had felt at Albert-Frederick's. *This* was what life was about. This was the ultimate fulfilment. There was no need for more. She was indulgent when Monty came to her, pale and apologetic and completely adoring.

'Darling boy. It must have been simply dreadful for you. I won't let it happen again, I promise.'

The nurse looked at her sharply. Monty, who had been about to beg her never to have another child, was taken aback and murmured, 'You might change your mind, dearest.'

She kissed him maternally. 'Don't worry baby. I won't. Two babies are quite enough for me.'

The nurse said, 'Mr Gould has been a tower of strength, Mrs Gould. An absolute tower of strength.'

May smiled, unable to explain that it was Monty's final weakness that had called forth her own strength. 'Yes. Yes, he would be,' she said.

Monty kissed her and let them usher him outside while they 'made her beautiful'. As if you could improve on perfection. He frowned, remembering how his 'part' had slipped away from him in those final minutes, then just as suddenly felt glad. It had been one of the rare times of his life when he had not been acting, when he had been utterly sincere.

Nobody connected with the Risings had attended the Victory Parade of the previous month in London, yet four weeks later they did indeed celebrate their personal victories in a variety of ways. Victor William, child of the Armistice, was born. Fred squatted on his coal seam and named it Marsh Cottage after March. And David triumphed over his own dark soul and let April see his final weakness.

Chapter Five

By 1923, when April was twenty-one and had been
married for four years, an enormous change had
somehow occurred in the Western world which was,
sometimes pathetically, mirrored in the microcosm of
narrow provincial life in Gloucester. Suzanne Lenglen
was not only winning every singles match at
Wimbledon, but she had brought the new fashion for
freedom in women's clothes to its peak. April, who
had joined the Hucclecote Tennis Club with her old
friend Bridget Williams, wore a bandeau on and off
court, and in the short skirts her husband made for
her, worn with pale lavender stockings and long,
cuban-heeled shoes, she had become one of the leaders
of the social set in the city. She smoked her cigarettes
in a long jade holder and blew perfect concentric
smoke rings for her young nephews. David too was
well-known, not only as a designer of women's
clothes. He lectured at local church halls and institutes
for the Worker's Educational Association. His
subjects were diverse but not unconnected: Fabric and
Design was closely linked to the Political History of
the Industrial Revolution, and his art students left
their course with a thorough knowledge of conditions
in eighteenth-century weaving sheds.

Meanwhile their marriage had settled into a

pattern which both thought completely secure and immutable. April accepted that – for whatever reason – David did not want children, and she continued to demonstrate nightly that he was all in all to her. And David, still 'fighting his demons' as she put it, encouraged her to lead the city's social set from a long way in front. They were both conscious that there were limits to their undoubted happiness. David especially knew that beyond those limits was a precipice and a bottomless pit. So they worked at establishing their secure pattern and keeping within its boundaries, and a small incident that summer showed them how important those boundaries were.

March and May continued their patterns along very similar lines. May and Monty had acquired a house at last in a London suburb; and officially March still shared a beautiful home in Bath with her husband. But both girls preferred to spend most of their time at the shabby old terraced house in Chichester Street, where Florence, thinner still, conducted life with a gentle baton and provided just the right mixture of love, tenderness and asceticism that the varied Risings needed.

March, the pain of Fred's treachery scabbed over with bitterness, worked hard towards some sort of reconciliation with her uncle-husband in the hope of a solid reward after his death. She had visited him five times since that fateful week in 1919; the third time he had spoken of asking Mr Hazelbank to call. Mr Hazelbank was the Tomms' solicitor. He mentioned the proposed call each time March left him now, as if to ensure her return; but Mr Hazelbank had not come.

May was, as usual, enjoying life thoroughly. Victor

was handsome and lively and very intelligent; Monty was as devoted as ever; the new house was fun and they led a hectic life there, so that it was good to return to Gloucester now and then for a rest and to give Victor a taste of ordinary routine. May had the best of both worlds. Just as her father had.

May and March never discussed current affairs; their father and April did, though separately and at great variance. April, at home with David and her mother-in-law one evening that early summer, held forth with only surface objectivity.

'No. Actually I don't particularly mind I haven't got a vote. Most girls of my age aren't capable of making an intelligent choice. March will have a vote next year and she'll vote for Mr Baldwin's party because he looks like Papa!'

David, busy with his sketch-pad near the kitchen window, grinned appreciatively at this remark, but said gently, 'I didn't ask whether you minded, Primrose. I asked whether you considered it a fair arrangement. Men at twenty-one and women at thirty?'

April made a face. 'Of course it's un*fair*,' she agreed. 'But then, everything is, isn't it?'

David glanced up, pencil poised, wondering if April meant anything personal by that unusual cynicism. Mrs Daker sighed as if she was in front of the Wailing Wall, put down the evening edition of the *Citizen* and removed her glasses.

'President Wilson has lost,' she announced. 'America does not join the League.' She lifted her shoulders to her ears. 'It is in any case doomed.'

'But Mother, it is the hope of Europe!' April took up new cudgels, glancing at David for support in this at least. He treated the present as if it were already history and therefore merely interesting. But David narrowed his eyes, measured her – or something – with his thumb on his pencil and continued to draw.

Mrs Daker shook her head. 'Mr Wilson had no place for a Jewish nation in his plans,' she said.

'That might have come later, Mother. If only we can have a long enough peace, anything can be worked out. Negotiated.' She watched David irritably as he went on drawing. 'Well. What do you think?' she asked at last.

He flashed her an amused smile but did not stop work. 'I think the Dough boys and girls know what they're doing,' David said. 'They're a practical people, dealing in actualities and not hopes.'

'But the League is a practical idea!' April protested.

David shrugged. 'The concept of a re-formed Europe is asking for trouble. This new Czechoslovakia for instance – how many races – three, four? Rumanians, Slovaks, Germans. And as for the Polish Corridor – a red rag to a bull.'

'If you mean Germany is the bull, you must see you're wrong. They're a beaten nation.'

'They weren't beaten, Primrose. We made a peace treaty with them and it's not the same thing.' He grinned. 'Come and look at this and tell me what you think.' He showed her his sketch, putting the tip of the pencil on the knob that was the head of his figure. 'This is what the cloche hat does for design – incorporates the whole body, head and all, into one long line.'

'Ugly,' pronounced Mrs Daker. 'The female frame is not meant to look like a snake's. It is composed of different . . . features. The hat sets off the head. Then come the shoulders and the bosom.'

'But Mother, this is fashion!' April turned her enthusiasm into a channel where they could all agree. 'You have a genius for a son – David, if you make the hat even deeper – bring that tiny brim right down over the ears—'

David whooped with delight as he sketched in two short strokes at the top of his drawing. 'Mother, you have a genius for a daughter-in-law!' he declared.

'Of course there must be no sign of hair,' April mentioned.

'The shingle is the thing by which we catch the market . . .' David petered out helplessly and April finished for him.

'By which we catch the market with a zing!'

They clutched each other, laughing, and Mrs Daker said with a smirk, 'I have two lunatics for a son and his wife. That is what I have!'

Will, on the other hand, was perfectly satisfied with the state of things. Contrary to David's prediction, he thought America ought to keep out of their affairs from now on, even to the extent of forgetting the national debt.

'The least they could do,' he grumbled over his stout in the Lamb and Flag. 'Coming into the war when it was practically over—'

Lottie looked into her empty glass, then over the wall of the snug to where Will, Alf Luker and Sid Goodrich were putting the world to rights.

'Time to toast young April then, is it, Will?' She put her glass onto the counter. 'I did bring her into the world, so let me join you. I wouldn't mind a drop of gin if it's a special occasion.'

Will, quite used to her gambits, was undisturbed. 'First I've heard about it then Lottie.' But he signalled to the landlord all the same. His geniality had not abated since Armistice Day; Sibbie brought him business as well as pleasure, and life at number thirty-three was pleasant with just himself and the women. And young Albert-Frederick of course. What a nib, into everything.

Lottie feigned astonishment. 'Nothing in the oven yet?' she asked with her usual coarseness. 'How long she bin married then, Will?'

'Four years.' April was the one small speck in the clear blue sky of his content. She had not come home yet. March was still there most of the time; when Edwin was ill she always went to nurse him but it was never for long. April, on the other hand, called for an hour at a time and was always anxious to get back to David Daker. He passed Lottie her gin and looked into her knowing eyes. 'Maybe they won't have any family,' he said defiantly. 'It's not unknown these days.'

'Ah,' she agreed. 'Young April's spreading her wings and that's a fact. Them dresses she wears! And she smokes like a chimney!'

'They all do. She's a modern girl, Lottie.'

Lottie wiped away her dewdrop with the back of her hand and stuck her nose in her glass. When she surfaced she said lugubriously, 'It's not the life your

April wants, take my word for it. Made for mother-hood that girl was. Made.'

Will felt a pang at his heart. The thought of April with David Daker was still horrific to him; he had been almost relieved when Sibbie told him what the shrapnel wound had done to him. But the alternative of April being deprived of a child and trying to forget her need in what he called 'flapping' was even worse. He growled unguardedly, 'I always said that young Daker wasn't right for her – always said that.'

Lottie's eyes brightened, this was much more like it. She decided to roll up her sleeves metaphorically and chance her arm.

'Don't want to take too much notice of Sibbie Luker, Will,' she advised. 'David Daker wasn't the first one she'd sampled, and he won't be the last neither. I reckon most of the good citizens of Gloucester 'ave 'ad a conducted tour around that young lady, so 'tidn't no good holding it against David Daker.'

She watched with enjoyment as a dark flush spread up Will Rising's neck and into his face. She liked Will well enough and had felt sorry for him in the past married to the Rhys-Davies purity, but it wouldn't hurt him now and then to be reminded that he was in no position to be smug about the way he'd arranged things.

He muttered, 'Sibbie Luker is like her mother. Honest and straightforward as the day—'

'Casts their light over everyone d'you mean, Will?' asked Lottie innocently. 'Ah, I reckon you're right there.' She had gone far enough and subsided onto her seat again to talk to the dull but worthy Granny Goodrich from the dairy.

After a pause Will turned heartily to Granny's widower son, Sid, and told him what a good chap Baldwin was.

'It's his pipe,' he stated didactically. 'Shows him to be a regular Englishman. Not to be hurried or rushed into anything. Steady. That's Stanley Baldwin. Steady.'

'Ah. We need someone like that at the helm.' Sid nodded over his own pipe. 'D'you know, I had someone come in the shop the other day and ask me if I wanted to join the International Labour Party. What d'you think of that, Mr Rising?'

'Damned cheek,' Will exploded. 'Artisans like us –' he included Sid in the term – generously, as he was only a shopkeeper – 'our own men – that's us. Even before Lloyd George did away with the workhouse!'

'I reckon we did ought to band together though,' Alf Luker said into his tankard. 'D'you know what? All those young 'uns what fought for King and country, lot of 'em en't got no jobs and if they en't got anyone to fight for 'em they don't allus draw any money.' He supped deep. 'I reckon we ought to band together.'

'Unions you mean,' Will said scornfully. 'Get over to Russia if you want that sort of thing, Alf. Christamighty, your Fred en't doing so badly on his own.'

Alf's rheumy eyes went from his beer to the stained counter top and up along the roll of honour on the wall behind the bar.

'Our Fred's different,' he said at last. 'Dunno where 'e gets it from – not me nor 'Ettie. 'Im and Sib, they's the same. Determined. 'Ard as nails. They'se a union all to themselves an' tha's a fac'.'

They were back to Sibbie again. Sometimes Will thought everything began and ended with Sibbie Luker.

But he wished Lottie hadn't said what she'd said. Sibbie might have been a naughty girl before she took him, but since then – five years almost – she'd not looked at another man. Surely.

May was on one of her frequent visits to Gloucester. She brought presents for everyone, although it was less than a month since she'd scattered her largesse before. There was a steam engine for Albert-Frederick who was displaying an inordinate interest in all things mechanical. There was perfume for March and April, a box of dates for Gran and Aunt Sylv, ridiculous lace hankies for Florence, an enamelled daisy brooch for Daze, tobacco for Will. May was dressed, not entirely in fashion, in trailing silk, Victor was handsome and stalwart in velvet. May was no penny-pincher, Monty was still getting good parts in the kind of operettas that were all the go now, and she spent whatever he gave her.

But the news she brought with her now was of the house.

'My dears, it's absolutely delightful. Practically inside Bushey Park – not far from Hampton Court, April, which you'll just adore. We have to be near London, you see. All the big shows are there.' She snatched four-year-old Victor from the floor where

Albert was accusing him of 'interfering' with the new steam engine. 'Baby, you wouldn't like it anyway.' She kissed the protesting child. 'Well then, Mummy will buy you one all for yourself.'

'You spoil him, May,' March disapproved. 'He's not really interested anyway, it's just because it's Albert's.'

May said, 'And as Albert won't share his toys, I'll have to buy Victor one of his own.'

April put her cigarette in an ashtray and knelt on the floor. 'Darling, let's show Victor how it works, shall we?' she cajoled her older nephew.

March too knelt down. 'You will share the toys that Aunt May brings you,' she told her son tightly. 'Give the engine to Victor.'

May instantly regretted her small dig. 'Oh don't be silly March. You're right. Victor isn't really interested.'

'I am! I am!' Victor shouted.

'He'll break it,' Albert looked up at March defiantly, then saw her expression and repeated without hope, 'Mummy, he'll *break* it!'

He hung on to the steam engine and March gripped it and forced it from his fingers and passed it to Victor. Albert did not cry. He watched with all his eyes as Victor turned the small brass model over and over. May slid him to the floor.

'Listen. Girls. I've had the most marvellous idea. How about if I ask Mamma to look after Victor – you do the same, March – and we three go up to London together? Just for a weekend. Monty is up at Harrogate until next week and we could have a wonderful time, just the three of us. You'll love the house and I can take you into town and show you the sights . . . oh do say yes!'

April sparkled immediately. 'It would be rather marvellous,' she agreed. She had her hand casually on Albert's left shoulder blade and she pressed it as she turned to him. 'You'd love having Grandma all to yourself, wouldn't you Albie?'

'Don't call him that please April.' March levered herself back into her chair. 'And I'm not sure that Mother is up to looking after two children.'

'Aunt Sylv will do most of it,' May said. 'And Mother would *adore* to think of her three chickens painting London town red!'

April squatted by Albert, picked up her cigarette and blew a thoughtful ring. 'What do you say, March?'

'We'll see what Mother thinks.'

It was as good as an enthusiastic agreement coming from March. April released Albert and hugged May's knees and May tickled Victor's velvet stomach until he doubled up with giggles, dropped the steam engine on to the floor where the flywheel snapped off.

'What a good job Uncle Fred can mend that sort of thing.' April smiled at Albert and handed him her cigarette holder. 'Here darling. See if you can make a smoke ring like Aunty April.'

He looked at March and shook his head dumbly, his mouth drawn in to bottle a sob. May was telling everyone that darling Victor hadn't meant it and March was ignoring the steam engine and frowning angry disapproval at April.

133

April jumped up and put the engine on the mantel-piece. 'For Fred,' she remarked, then went to the gramophone.

'Let's hear that song again, May, shall we? Albie – come and dance with me—' She wound furiously and placed the needle. The strains of Kern's 'Look for the Silver Lining' filled the old bandy room. She took Albert in her arms and sang the words to him significantly. He encircled her neck with his thin arms and smiled at her adoringly.

Later Florence joined them with a tray of tea things and May sat at the piano and played the latest craze, 'Kitten on the Keys'.

And at the Midland Hotel in Manchester, the leader of the resident dance band, a young man called Henry Hall, played the same number as his solo, and received no less applause. Music, Modes, and Money were the new vogue. And the Risings were dabbling in all three.

Fred heard of the proposed London weekend from his sister, Sibbie, and was not a bit pleased.

'A few years ago neither Will nor Florence would have permitted them to go up there alone! I'm surprised at that sop May calls a husband. As for Daker—'

Sibbie lay back in her chaise-longue and laughed raucously.

'Hark at who's talking! My God our Fred, I've heard about you! No woman is safe when you're around and you've got the cheek—'

'You know how I feel about March.' He looked at her coldly. He had never confided in her because he didn't trust her an inch, but she had been living at home all through the years when March Rising had occupied his every waking thought. 'The other women . . . they're nothing.'

'Then they should be.' She stopped laughing and went to the mantelpiece to pick up her cigarettes. 'You think I waste my time with Will Rising, but I don't spend my life with him. I've got other . . . contacts. Contacts who are very generous. You could make certain that your – er – ladies – are just as useful to you.'

'It's different for a man.'

'Rubbish. Some of these rich bitches are on permanent heat for someone like you. Instead of blackmailing me into getting concessions for you from my poor old alderman, you should be looking around for bored wives with rich husbands.'

He shrugged. 'Maybe.' He took the gold automatic lighter she offered him and lit her cigarette with ill grace. 'Meanwhile, can't you have a word with Will? Make him see what folly it is to let those girls loose in London on their own?'

'I want Will to be happy.' She blew smoke through her nostrils. 'Funny. Nobody believes that. Even Ma thinks I do it for some kind of revenge.'

Fred watched her curiously as she rearranged herself on the sofa. Her movements were automatically sensual now; she couldn't help herself.

'Do you love him then? Are you trying to tell me you love a man old enough to be your father?'

She gestured widely with her cigarette, tipped her head back and studied the ceiling. 'What the hell is love, Fred? Do *you* know? I certainly don't. I wanted to belong to the Rising family. I tried to do that by sharing what was May's. Her sandwiches at school, her soap, her love affair. When that went wrong I had to think up something else. And there was Will. He was unhappy, Fred. Now he's happy.' She lifted her head and looked at him. 'Is that love?'

He shrugged again. 'I wouldn't know. I meant the other thing. Bed.'

'Oh. Is that all? I enjoy it well enough. And he – he adores it!' She laughed her harsh laugh again. 'I enjoy it with anyone, Fred. But he . . . that's why if you ever tell him about the others, I'll kill you.'

He pulled down his mouth in mock terror. 'You do the small things I ask of you, Sib, and he'll never know. It's up to you.'

She laughed again, drew on her cigarette and stood up.

'I adore being blackmailed,' she said and came to stand very close to Fred before blowing out her smoke.

He stood his ground. 'Talk to Will then,' he said.

'I might do.' She put her hands on his shoulders and kissed him slowly. 'Yes, I might do.' She let her hands slide across his back until her glowing cigarette touched his ear lobe. He sprang back, cursing. And she went to the window and stood looking out at the sluggish waters of the canal. 'Yes. All right.'

But Will's adjurations came too late to baulk the plans of his three daughters. David, always encouraging April to enjoy herself, was all for the weekend, and March and May, devoted mothers though they were, began to look forward intensely to two whole days without their offspring. They went up by train on Friday afternoon, arriving at the suburban terminus of Hampton Court in the red glow of a perfect May sunset. A taxi took them through Bushey Park to the row of villas – amazingly like the ones at Longford – on the other side. May conducted them through the rooms with housewifely pride and for the first time since her return to Gloucester, March felt a pang of envy for her sister. She had imagined that the joy of caring for a lovely home had been stamped out of her by the unhappiness she had known at Bath. For four years now she had been in retreat in the shabby old-fashioned terraced house in Gloucester which did not even belong to her father. Now in May's small house she saw all her heart's desire. She could imagine herself and Albert in something similar, entertaining friends, working in the garden. Almost timidly she asked May whether she could cook supper in the laboratory-like kitchen. May agreed happily. April laid the table in the dining-room where French windows led on to a lawn; May collapsed in an armchair in the 'lounge' and shouted instructions to her sisters.

The next day she spent an hour on the telephone, 'rallying the forces' as she put it. As a result, a taxi arrived just before lunch and disgorged a young man who introduced himself as 'Eugene'.

'You're May – I've heard all about you. I was with Monty before the war in a juggling act. Has he told you? I'm in the chorus line now my dear – the very best I could do I'm afraid. But I'm not wanted this evening so—'

'It's most awfully kind of you.' May had actually

spoken to Frank O'Rourke, the ex-Minstrel of Mincing Light Opera days. She felt confused and a little bothered by the arrival of this stranger. After all she was responsible for her sisters. And might darling easy-going Monty object? She said, 'I thought Frank might squire the three of us around the sights . . . you know.'

'I do indeed.' Eugene eyed March and April appreciatively. 'Frank mentioned that you were a corker, Mrs Gould, and I shouldn't have thought it possible that there were any more at home like you. I'd have been quite wrong of course.'

April had met young men like this at the tennis club. But there she was always with David – or they knew about David. They knew she belonged to someone else and therefore their banter was permissible. Bereft of David, she felt unsafe and very vulnerable.

Eugene said he would take them 'out on the town' and bundled them all into the waiting taxi. They went through countless suburbs and into Hill Street while Eugene put May at her ease by countless familiar reminiscences.

At Hill Street he found he did not have enough money for the taxi, which did not surprise May in the least. She dug into her handbag and turned to follow her sisters into a very dark house lit by shaded lamps and impregnated with incense fumes. People were everywhere and it was necessary to slide around the walls in order to reach the small tables loaded with food. Armed with a finger of toast topped with pâté and olives, April found herself propelled forward into a central clearing. Sitting on a chair remarkably like a throne was an Indian princess. A lady-in-waiting crouched at her feet. They both wore gold embroidered saris and were hung with jewels.

Someone enquired April's name and murmured an introduction. A man said, 'I am the Maharanee's aide-de-camp. She would deem it an honour if you drink with her.' Champagne was poured into a glass and topped with what April knew to be *crème de menthe*. Someone said, 'You must meet Captain Mahbou.' And her hand was taken between dark fingers, pale at the ends. Suddenly there was an opening in the crowd at the end of which was a grand piano. The Maharanee clapped her hands with childish delight as a young man in evening clothes and white gloves appeared and bowed very low. The ADC gave some orders and more joss sticks were lit and twirled their smoke gaily into the heavy air. The young man sat at the piano and removed his gloves. May appeared behind Captain Mahbou and whispered, 'That's David Plunkett Green,' and the next minute the huge reception room was filled with the minor wail of 'Harlem Blues'. There was dancing. A girl in a silver dress did a shimmy alone before the throne. Eugene said, 'Time to go. How about tea on the river somewhere?'

They went outside and there was another taxi. Eugene got in, so did Captain Mahbou and someone called Rupert. April found herself sitting on Captain Mahbou's large, whitish, greyish palm. She shifted hastily and said, 'I am married you know.' He smiled like a hungry wolf and said, 'I am married several times. It is of no account.' March said firmly, 'We are all married. And it is of great account to us!' Rupert seemed to find this an unusual statement. He called March 'Goddess' and spoke to her of someone called Rose Marie who was on in Leicester Square. Her silence went down very well with him and by the time they reached Maidenhead he was on his knees before her, elbows in her lap. May and Eugene continued to chatter theatre shop, exchanging gossip like Gran and Hettie Luker in the wash-house on a Monday. And April thought determinedly of David, and how she would make all this into a very funny story for his entertainment when she got home. And how she would never leave him again.

They left the taxi at the Dumb Bell hotel and went in for tea. There was dancing to a three-piece band and Captain Mahbou took April around the floor in a sort of crouching run, holding her so close she could scarcely breathe. They left the Dumb Bell and took Eugene to the theatre and they stayed until the first interval. There were no seats; they stood at the back of a box and Rupert held March's hand to his face and murmured 'Goddess' occasionally. Captain Mahbou put a protective hand on April's bottom again and smiled widely at her every time she looked at him. His white teeth in the darkness of the box quite dazzled her; she was not used to White Lady cocktails, nor champagne and *crème de menthe*.

May, a little disconsolate without Eugene, wanted to go home when they left, but the men protested vehemently.

'It's only nine o'clock!' Rupert was appalled. 'Let's go to Wembley Fun Fair!'

They stopped en route to drink more cocktails and

as the ground then seemed unsteady beneath their feet, it was a natural choice to take a boat at the River Caves which was luckily the first sideshow they came to. They sprawled about on the hard duckboards and floated through dark caverns past scenes from various nightmares: Orpheus and the Underworld, the Bottomless Pit, besides various gibbeted bodies and writhing chained prisoners on an island. Here, Rupert decided they must land and release the captives. He leapt ashore and held the curved prow of the skiff while the girls scrambled out, followed ponderously by the Captain. They spent half an hour chopping at the papier mâché chains with the Captain's sword, and, sweating and triumphant, returned to the water to find the skiff had floated away. Furious shouts came from the entrance.

Captain Mahbou said, 'It will be bad for the Maharanee if I am found.' April whispered, 'Take off your shoes everyone. Quickly, follow me!' She waded into the knee-deep water and as the lights went on and the hunters stamped through the river maze, she led her small band around the back of the island and past the single amazed attendant at the gate. 'Quick – run!' she ordered, setting a good example. They all ran in different directions and April found herself on a road she had never seen before. She leaned against some railings and put her shoes on and a taxi cruised to a halt near her.

'Selway Gardens. Next to Bushey Park,' she ordered.

The driver looked at her bedraggled state. 'Got enough money, miss?'

'Of course,' April replied haughtily. 'I am a personal friend of the Maharanee of – of—'

'Ah.' The taxi driver nodded. 'I thought I knew that smell.'

May had reached home before she did and was making cocoa in the immaculate kitchen. They waited anxiously for March and when at last she arrived, they stared at each other incredulously.

'Did it really happen?' asked March. 'I can't believe it.'

May apologized. 'I didn't know, girls. I mean usually when Monty rings up friends, we have a meal or go to the zoo with Victor. Are you all right?'

'Of course,' said both girls in unison.

April recounted her conversation with the taxi driver and they sniffed each other and began to giggle.

But the next morning they felt awful. Eugene telephoned and brought a subdued Rupert for afternoon tea. They walked slowly through the park and caught a bus to Hampton Court. It was a day of fitful sunshine and the ancient house held occasional hollows of sheer menace within its golden walls. April felt again the sense of being a mere dot in the enormous wheel of time; from the utter meaninglessness of yesterday, she viewed the equal meaninglessness of her present life with David. She wasn't really helping him. Four years they had been married; the business was prospering well, they were inseparable, yet he was still lonely.

'Darling, what is it?' May asked anxiously. 'Do you feel sick?'

April looked at her two sisters and said, 'It seems

so pointless sometimes. I wish I could die . . . now.'

May was horrified. Rupert said, 'It's a hangover, old fruit. I wish I could die with you.'

Eugene shuddered. 'It's this place. Let's stroll over to the Wick and have some more tea. And ices.'

But March took her arm and held it close against her side. 'I know exactly what you mean,' she said in a low voice. 'But there's no way out. You have to keep on and on.'

April felt tears flood her eyes and she held tightly to March as they walked back to the gatehouse.

'We should have tackled the maze. That would have cheered us up,' said Rupert.

'April could have rescued us again.' May tried to rally her sister. 'She was marvellous last night, Eugene. Really marvellous.'

They sat around a small iron table and Rupert lifted his tea cup solemnly. 'I'd rather have a hangover with you than with anyone else I know,' he said.

It raised a wan smile all round.

But the weekend in London had a lasting effect on the three Rising girls. They had sampled the delights of the jazz age and found they left a sour taste as well as a rocking insecurity.

March continued to receive letters from Rupert for some time, and his ridiculous adoration reminded her yet again of Fred Luker's treachery and the arid years that had elapsed since then. She thought of Edwin, bed-ridden but still alive at eighty, promising her that if she kept visiting him he would make a new will in her favour. She thought of Albert-Frederick growing less like his uncle and more like his father every day.

And she wished that Rupert could be older and more serious and be wealthy as well.

April told David of her 'conquest' and wished she hadn't when he looked at her searchingly as he laughed.

And May, inexplicably and quite simply, wanted to go home.

Indirectly it had its effect on Fred Luker also. Over the past four years he had tried again and again to win March back to their passionate and sparring relationship. At first his failure to do so had hurt him, then when she continued to visit Edwin in Bath, he was angry and frustrated: if she had resented his arrangement so much, why did she continue it? But all the time he had known that between Gloucester and Bath she was safe; safe for him when he had 'made his pile'.

Then two things happened at once. Captain Marcus Porterman informed him almost casually that he had arranged to take future coal consignments from the Welsh collieries. Someone he had been in the army with had bought a controlling interest in a mine and officers must stick together. And on the same day, Fred heard about March's trip to London.

There was nothing he could do about that other than approach Sibbie, and that proved useless. He was tired of feeling guilty where March was concerned, so he chose to see her trip – alone and unchaperoned by Albert-Frederick – as disloyalty. Simmering with rage he went to see Porterman to suggest a compromise: a half-and-half arrangement perhaps. The weekly coal train to Keynsham made Fred's business very profitable indeed; without it he would just make ends meet, maybe not even that. He had more enemies among his band of miners than friends. The Freeminers of the Forest of Dean did not take kindly to his arrival, nor to his bland assurances that he had observed all their laws. When he introduced Austen Rising to them at the Gavellers Arms, he noticed one or two of the older men exchange glances. He smiled as he told the younger men that Austen was 'St Briavels born'. Then he turned to the others. 'Isn't that so, gentlemen? We don't want to hang out any dirty washing, but I think you will bear me out?'

He had had no more difficulties and within a month he was fulfilling the contract he had made with Porterman and with the pickle factory besides half a dozen local hauliers. But they did not like him for his veiled blackmail and they would enjoy seeing him go down, even if it meant losing the good living he had given them.

Captain Porterman said, 'Look here Luker, I made my position plain in the letter. I didn't expect to see you two days later. I'm sorry about it, but Fawcett Jones was my commanding officer and he approached me personally.'

'You gave the contract to me, Porterman, and now you're backing out. That's all I know.'

The good Captain coloured angrily. 'No need to cut up rough, Luker. Nothing was signed.'

'A word of a gentleman. I thought it was binding.'

'No place for gentlemen in business, old man.' Porterman tried to sound genial. 'Wife's having a party at the weekend for Fawcett-Jones. Perhaps you'd like to pop in and put him wise as to tonnage and price?' He saw Fred's expression and swept on, 'These place cards – she asked me to drop them in to the house this morning and I rather overlooked them. You pass it on your way back to Bristol. Think you could drop them in for me? Just give them to the maid, no need to see Leonie.'

Fred was about to tell him what to do with his place cards, then checked himself. Leonie. Probably a fancy name for a stuck-up dowager with a moustache as luxuriant as her husband's. On the other hand, it was worth a try – he had nothing to lose.

'No trouble at all, old man,' he said with a familiarity that was insulting. 'A pleasure, in fact.'

Leonie Porterman was nearly forty, childless and bored. She had married above herself socially, but Marcus Porterman was her inferior in everything else. When her maid told her that Mr Luker wished to see her on a personal matter, she was immediately interested.

'I've heard about you, Mr Luker. My husband admires your business acumen very much.'

'And I've heard about you.' Porterman had never mentioned her before today. She was a short, thickset woman, very dark; but no moustache. 'I didn't imagine you could be so . . .' He let his voice die, swallowed visibly, took her hand and bent his head to it with deliberate clumsiness.

She didn't pull away. They stood holding hands in front of the low fire. There were twin windows either side of the chimney breast; outside, willow trees and lawns, inside, flock paper and armchairs like big boxes.

She tinkled a laugh. 'I've read about people like you. Isn't it called animal magnetism?'

He roughened his voice. 'I don't know. I've never felt like this before. God . . . you're beautiful. I'm sorry – I don't know anything about women.'

She smiled delightedly. 'You must let me teach you. I know quite a lot about them.'

He thought of all the women he had known: he thought of March, remote and aristocratic. He risked saying, 'I don't want to know about other women. Just you.'

She drew a little breath but did not turn away. 'You'd better sit down, Mr Luker. I'll ring for tea. Or would you like something stronger?'

'Whisky. Neat please.'

'My God, you're very direct. Could I have my hand back please?'

'Oh . . . must you?'

'Not really.'

They walked together to the side table containing decanters and glasses. She poured some whisky into a glass, drank from it and gave it to him. He managed to toss it back without taking his pale blue eyes off her.

She said in a low voice, 'Stop looking at me like that, Mr Luker.'

He whispered, 'Why?'

'Because I like it rather too much.'

He couldn't believe it would be this easy. He had imagined getting a foot in; inviting her to meet him at a roadhouse somewhere. He had been here exactly ten minutes.

He didn't have to pretend any more; desire flamed

147

in him quite suddenly as it often did. He put his finger in the whisky glass, wiped it across her lips and put his mouth to hers. When he lifted his head her eyes were closed and she would have fallen if he hadn't held her.

'God . . . this is marvellous.' She looked at him. 'I've dreamed of this sort of thing. Dreamed. Have you read any Lawrence?'

'No.'

'Good. I want it to be natural. You're so natural, Luker. Earthy.'

But it was she who slid her hand inside his baggy trousers and found the opening in his pants.

'My God,' she whispered.

'Yes,' he whispered back.

They lay on the rug in front of the summer fire and he was rough with her because he knew instinctively that was what she wanted.

Afterwards they lay quietly side by side and he trailed his fingers languidly across her breasts.

'I wish . . . I wish . . .'

'What do you wish, my gorgeous Luker?'

'I wish this could go on for ever.'

'I don't see why it can't. With pauses for meals and things of course.'

He lifted his head. 'Didn't you know? I've finished here. The Captain has given me the old heave-ho.'

She propped herself on one elbow and stared down at him. She was no fool, this woman. Fred held his breath.

She smiled. 'I think he'll retract that, Luker. He'll be pleased I've found myself a friend. I get bored, you know, and that worries him. So . . . while we're such good friends, I think you'll find that Captain Porterman will buy all his coal from you.'

He held her gaze for a long second, letting her read whatever she wanted in his face. Then he reached up and took her head in his hands and kissed her, rolling over on to her as he did so.

'What, again?' she asked.

'We've only just started, Mrs Porterman. And we've got a long way to go.'

He drove home slowly and unsmiling. He had saved his business and he had somehow scored over March, but it gave him no pleasure. And then he found the forgotten place cards in the map pocket on the door. At last he began to laugh.

Chapter Six

In the spring of the following year, when Mr MacDonald had struck a Lab–Lib pact and formed the first Labour government, April and David moved to a new shop in fashionable Eastgate Street, almost opposite the market. Manny Stein called himself a partner now, and brought them large orders from London, besides plenty of ready-made stock. It was the most exclusive shop in Gloucester and second only to Jaeger and County Clothes in Cheltenham. In an upstairs workshop with a skylight overlooking the work going on in the new Kings Square, David designed and cut his couturier outfits. In the big sitting-room with its armchairs, ashtrays, gas fire and a view of the busy street outside, they entertained their many friends and acquaintances. Would-be politicians and intellectuals gathered to discuss the work of Albert Mansbridge, the Webbs, Dr Marie Stopes, besides who was what in Gloucester, the clothes they wore, the things they said.

It was after one of these evenings that Tollie Hall joined the International Labour Party. And Bridget Williams suddenly spoke of women's rights and meant nothing political at all, as most of the young men present soon discovered. And it was during one of these evenings, when May was home for Easter and March had left Albert-Frederick with Florence, that an amateur photographer snapped the three girls laughing together against a background of cut flowers from the shop. The picture appeared in the *Citizen* the next night under the heading 'Daffodil time again. But these Gloucester daffodils are with us all the year round.' They were all old married women now, but collectively they were still known, with much admiration, as 'the Rising girls'.

Albert-Frederick sat on the coke pile in the playground of Chichester Street Elementary, and dreamed of his aunt. He had adored April for as long as he could remember and had been passionately in love with her since last year when she had danced with him and sung 'Look for the Silver Lining' and had understood so exactly how he felt. Whenever he had a spare moment, he deliberately thought of April and her short golden curls and her smoke rings. He thought of them running away together and living in a very sunny place with fruit to eat and a real stream and a model railway. He knew that was what she wanted. He knew that she was unhappy.

A voice said, 'Oy! What you doin' up there? You're not allowed up there!'

It was one of the huge boys who would be leaving in the summer. Albert-Frederick slithered off the coke pile quickly and stood before him, looking at the ground.

'Well? What were you *doin*'?'

'Thinking. I was thinking.'

'Filthy little sod. I can guess what you was thinkin' too. Get up in that corner.'

He shoved Albert around the coke pile and behind the boys' lavatory. Albert began to whimper in terror.

'Come on. Take off y'r jersey!' Hands seized his new grey jersey knitted by Gran Rising, and tugged. 'Down with your breeches!' The hands snapped his braces to his knees. He felt his pants pushed down. He began to scream and squirm unsuccessfully; his trousers were trapping him around his knees. The next minute, horny fingers were shoved brutally up his back passage; he screamed in earnest like a stuck pig.

'What the hell—' A new voice cut through his terror. His captor was removed from him very suddenly and there was a scrabbling crash of body on coke. The voice said tensely, 'Get out! Go on, get out you little swine! If ever I catch you interfering with – with anyone – again, I'll make you wish you hadn't been born! Understand?'

The big boy was whimpering now. 'You broke me arm! You rotten . . . let me *go*! Yes – yes, I understand – course I understand . . . but they got to know 'oo's boss! You dun the same, Mr Luker – I 'eard about you! 'E's a soppy little bugger – 'e's got to learn—'

Fred Luker said tensely, 'Just get out. Clear off.'

There was a moment's silence and Albert knew they were alone together. He continued to cry.

Fred said sternly, 'Stop that. Pull up your breeches. Make yourself presentable. And come with me.'

He marched Albert into Miss Pettinger's office without pausing to knock. The headmistress, in the midst of collating the school bills for that term – including the pile of coke in the yard – did not look up.

'Outside,' she said calmly. 'And knock. Then wait for me to tell you to come in.'

Fred took a moment to admire this leathery woman whom the years merely made stronger. His hands and backside recalled her ministrations of twenty years ago; he would have liked Albert to stay with her. But it was not to be. What had been good enough for Fred Luker was not necessarily good for his son.

He said, 'Sorry. No time, Miss Pettinger.'

She looked up at that and managed a wintry smile. 'Oh, it's Fred Luker, isn't it? Have you come to offer me some cheap coal?'

There wasn't much she didn't know, this one. Fred wondered what else she might guess after this interview.

'No miss. I've come to say that I'm taking young Albert Tomms home to his mother. And if she takes any notice of what I say to her, he won't be coming back.'

Miss Pettinger looked at the hiccupping boy, then at the grim-faced man. She put down her pen and laced her fingers.

'Now we will stop that crying and be quite quiet.' She waited again and Albert's breathing became normal. 'Good boy. Sit down while I talk to Mr Luker.'

Albert looked around for a chair. Uncle Fred was standing right in front of the only one besides Miss Pettinger's. It was unthinkable to disobey, so he sat on the floor. Miss Pettinger did not look at him.

'Are you complaining about my school? Or about my pupil?' she asked gently.

'I am complaining about another pupil, miss. No names, no pack drill. No tales. He was interfering with this boy.'

'You witnessed the interference?'

'Yes.'

'Then you must tell me the name of the perpetrator. And I will deal with the matter. Your duty is done, Fred. I thank you.'

'Sorry miss. I'm taking Albert home.'

'Don't you think that amounts to interference too?'

Fred felt himself flushing. 'I'm a friend of the family, miss. I'm very fond of the boy.'

'I don't doubt that. He is a likeable boy. But you have no right—'

'Sorry miss. I'm taking him home. You can't stop me.'

'Probably not. I don't intend to try. But I think you will find that Mrs Tomms would prefer to see me on this matter.'

Fred nodded curtly, took Albert's flaccid hand and pulled him to his feet. He walked the length of Chichester Street knowing that in this as in so many other things, Miss Pettinger was right. March would tell him to mind his own business and she would take Albert straight back to whatever he had to face next time behind the coke pile.

But Fred knew nothing of the first Albert's ordeal at the hands of the bishop many years ago. Fred knew very little indeed of the bargain that March had struck with her Uncle Edwin when she had been only four-teen, to free her beloved brother from the excesses of being the bishop's page. All Fred knew was that March had barely spoken to him for the past four years and would certainly oppose him on principle.

He found the household in its usual state of calm and quiet routine. Sylvia Rising and the old lady were out at their scrubbing jobs, Florence sat in the dining-room button-holing industriously for Will who was in the workroom making a suit for one of the younger Council members. March was 'doing upstairs'.

Florence, who answered his knock, led the way down to the kitchen. She did not ask unnecessary questions; it was obvious that Albert was upset about something but unhurt physically. Automatically she boiled milk for cocoa and put a hand on his shoulder in silent sympathy.

'A bit of an upset in the school yard, Mrs Rising.'

Fred had long ago joined the conspiracy to shield Florence from worry. 'But while I'm here I'd like a word with March.'

'She's polishing in the bandy room, Fred. Do go up. Albert and I will have some cocoa together and be happy and chatty.' She picked up a postcard from behind the tea caddy and put it on the table in front of the boy. 'Look darling. A card from Victor. It's Charlie Chaplin, isn't it?'

Albert forgot his troubles on the instant. 'Victor 'ud rather go to the pictures than play with his toys,' he commented, peering at the clown in his bowler hat. 'Bet he couldn't read what it says.' He spelled out laboriously. 'Comic Cuts.'

Fred, hearing this as he closed the kitchen door, felt a surge of unusual pride. Dammit, Albert was only six years old and he could read. His son.

March looked up from the piano with a fine mixture of expressions on her face. Guilt because she was looking through sheet music rather than polishing, wariness because it was a man's step and men were not frequent visitors in this house, then baleful aggression.

'What do you want?'

Fred held out a pacific hand. 'Listen, March. I've brought the boy home from school—' He hung on to her physically as she made for the door in a surge of panic. 'He's all right. Drinking cocoa with your mother. Quite all right.'

'Then why—? What business—?' She backed to the piano again as she snapped questions.

'It's not the right place for him, March. That's why. And it is my business as you very well know.'

'I haven't noticed you making it your business over the past six years.'

He shrugged. 'I thought I made it very much my business when I brought you home from Bath.'

For the first time she spoke of that second visit to Bath. 'You forfeited any rights you had – to me or to Albert – when you sent me back there.' She seemed to regret her words and made a dismissive gesture. 'That's all over anyway. Why have you brought Albert home?'

'It's not over. Not for me. I still love you, March.'

She looked at him and put a hand to her throat. Then she whispered, 'Why have you brought Albert home?'

156

Fred said deliberately, 'He was being buggered by a thirteen-year-old.' He thought how Leonie would have enjoyed his words. March did not. The effect on her was frightening. The colour drained from her face, her mouth opened as the skin tightened around it, her eyes pulled sideways, oriental fashion.

He went to her and put his arms around her and she did not pull away. 'You don't know what I'm on about darling, do you? One of the jack-me-lads had the boy's trousers down and his fingers up his backside. Nothing to worry about, it's happened to all of us, but I couldn't stand there and see—'

'Nothing to worry about?' Her eyes were glazed. 'You don't understand. Oh Fred . . . he's downstairs?'

'Yes. And he's all right. It's something boys do—'

'I know! Oh God, I know!'

She was shaking like a leaf and he held her very close, her remembered smell bringing his old feelings for her back with a rush. He had schemed for the moment when she would turn to him again, now it was here he was unprepared. He murmured, 'It's all right now, March . . . all right,' not even thinking of Albert-Frederick any more.

She said wildly, 'It's not all right! He can't go back there – I won't let him – but what else, where else – oh God, it can't happen again – it can't!'

'What can't happen again, Marcie?'

'Edwin. I can't ask him again—' It was Edwin who had saved her brother Albert from similar ignominy, and though Fred did not know that, he realized with her words that he had the key to March's gratitude and therefore . . . love. What a fool he had been not to see it before.

He said strongly, 'Of course you can't ask Edwin, Marcie. There's no need. I can look after my own son. He shall go to Marley – it's got a good reputation.'

'Marley?' Her trembling abated. 'Albert at Marley? They have a uniform. And they learn French.' She became very still. 'It's an expensive school. Very expensive.'

'The money's nothing. Only the best is good enough for Albert-Frederick.'

'Oh . . . Fred. He would love it there. He's never liked Chichester Street – he's like my brother Albert, you see. A bit lonely.'

'If he doesn't like Marley, he can try somewhere else.'

She moved away from him to stare into his face. 'You've done that well? I mean, I wouldn't want you to risk your business or anything.'

'Why not? Parents do risk their businesses for their children.'

'Oh Fred. You've hardly . . . looked at him.'

'I thought that was what you wanted, Marcie. But I have looked at him. And wanted to help.' He held out his hands and she put hers into them. 'I'll give you the cash. Then you can pay the fees yourself.'

She gazed at him. Her transparent brown eyes held an expression he hadn't seen for some time: hope.

She said, 'Thank you for – for bringing him home, Fred.' She dropped her gaze. 'I'd better go down to him now.'

'All right. But tonight, when he's in bed, will you come for a drive? Not far—'

'I'm playing tennis with April. At Hucclecote.'

'Then I'll take you there. And bring you home.'

They both remembered that the first time Fred had taken her anywhere it had been to Bridget Williams' house at Hucclecote. They shared so much. She smiled and nodded.

May was restless. Over Christmas and New Year Monty had been in pantomime at the Fortune, and their lives had been as nearly regular as they had been since their marriage. It did not suit either of them and when the season finished Monty made no attempt to get another part. They went to parties, taking Victor with them, and afterwards lay in bed till midday. Their money dwindled rapidly. Monty discovered the delights of the racecourse. He was lucky at first and they lived the high life. At not quite five years old, Victor could order a lunch running into four courses and a wine to go with each course. He could interpret the semaphore of the tic-tac men and knew how to place a bet. He was quick, intelligent and lively, and the bond between him and his mother was so deep as to make outward show rarely necessary. They could exchange a small smiling glance that excluded the whole world, including Monty. He was aware of it and was jealous, and did not know it.

They had a row.

It was Sunday and they woke at eleven and made indolent love until they heard Victor going downstairs to feed his goldfish. Immediately May prepared to get out of bed. Monty detained her.

'Not yet Mamma . . . Monty wants Mamma . . .' It was their usual way of talking but May wriggled free and reached for her satin negligée.

'Don't be silly darling. Victor is about.'

'Monty wants—' He giggled, still drunk from the night before, made a grab across the bed and pulled her down again. She was suddenly angry.

'Monty! You're hurting – don't be so ridiculous! I want to cook a proper lunch today and take Victor for a walk in the park – *Monty*—'

She tore free and retied her negligée. Monty sank back in the pillows pretending to cry. It had always worked before.

'Stay there then baby.' May made an effort. 'I'll bring you a nice cup of tea in bed. How's that?'

She left without waiting for a reply. It was with conscious pleasure that she joined Victor in their modern lounge and watched the goldfish surface for their ant eggs. The child looked up briefly and smiled.

'When we go to Grandma's next, may I take Pipsqueak and Wilfrid?' He followed the swimming fish around the bulbous tank with interested eyes. 'I want to show Albert that toys are silly.'

'Darling. You don't really think toys are silly, do you?'

'Not silly. But not important. Albert thinks they are important. He's never been to the races. Nothing.'

May reflected that perhaps Albert was a good influence on her precocious son. She nodded. 'Of course you may take Wilfrid and Pipsqueak to

Gloucester, if you can think of a way of carrying them.'

'Easy-peezy,' Victor said airily. 'They can go in your flour jar.'

'What about my flour?' But May was laughing as usual. Teddy had rhymed words just as inconsequentially as Victor did.

He smiled cockily. 'Throw it away,' he advised.

They were both laughing when Monty came into the room. He stood swaying for a moment, holding the door jamb, naked and unnoticed. The laughter abated somewhat and he announced pathetically, 'Monty *needs* Mamma!' He came behind his wife, undid her negligée with a wild flip of his hand and cupped her breast, trying unsuccessfully to get his mouth to it. She staggered back, caught her heel in her satin hem and sprawled onto the sofa. Monty fell on top of her. She screamed and he laughed and began to kiss her. They struggled and fell to the floor. It was like a scene from one of the silent films that were all the rage, except that the hero should then have charged in and removed the would-be rapist with a well-aimed fist. Instead Victor leapt onto his father's bare back, dug his nicely manicured nails into the base of the slim neck, pushed his sharp knees into the kidneys and braced himself with eyes shut and teeth bared. Monty sobered very suddenly and got off May. He then reached around and tore at his son and held him up at eye-level.

'What the *hell* d'you think you're doing?' he yelled furiously.

'I hate you!' shouted Victor. 'You were hurting

Mummy – you took off her clothes! I hate you!' He began to scream.

Monty shook him like a puppy and the child gathered breath and spat vigorously. Monty then dropped him and aimed a swipe at his head which missed. Meanwhile May had gathered herself and her trailing negligée together and joined in the general shouting match. As the full impact of Monty's aggression was realized she launched herself at him, a she-cat in defence of her young. Monty recoiled, fended her off by the simple expedient of pushing her back on the sofa, turned and left the room with what dignity he could muster.

May and Victor calmed down gradually and an air of embarrassment seemed to settle between them. Outside the bay window, the people next door were returning from church; a middle-aged couple with grown-up children. They eyed May's rather smeary windows curiously and talked in high, unnatural voices as they walked up their own garden path and let themselves into their house. The sun poured into the cheerful little room, glinting off the fish bowl, the fireplace with its chrome companion-set, the oval bevelled mirror. It was just as always; yet it was as it had never been before. May thought she could not bear it.

'Mamma . . .' Victor whimpered. 'I'm frightened.'

May wanted to say, 'So am I darling,' but of course did not. Instead she smiled warmly. 'How ridiculous! Whatever is there to be frightened of?' She stood up and held out her hand. 'Come on. Breakfast and lots of tea. Then we'll go upstairs and pack.'

'Where are we going?' wavered Victor.

She pretended astonishment. 'I thought you wanted to show Pipsqueak and Wilfrid to Albert? We're going to stay with Grandma of course.'

Victor was instantly comforted. 'Oh . . . yi pee-pipee!' He held her hand and they went into the kitchen. 'Ackcherly Mummy, Albert is my favourite cousin,' he said.

'Actually, he's your only cousin,' May said, laughing.

Monty, listening from the bathroom, felt a terrible aching gulf where his stomach should be. It was partly because he was going to be sick, and partly because he knew he had lost a little piece of May.

Somehow they managed to organize a picnic by the river. It was August Bank Holiday and Fred's mystery tour for the Gloucester Indian Club Swingers had been cancelled, so he took them to Rodley. 'Rodley on the Mud' Will Rising called it, and Gran grumbled incessantly. 'Why we 'ad to come 'ere when we've got the park right under our noses I'll never know.' But they were there because the uncles, Jack and Austen, could join them from the opposite bank; and the children could swim and scream; and Fred could see March in a swimming-costume.

Aunty Sylv and Florence, Hettie Luker and her Gladys, Kitty Hall and Tollie, unpacked the food under half a dozen strategically placed umbrellas. Inside the coach the girls changed into their bathing-dresses and hats and put on rubber shoes to wade and slide through the mud to the turgid water. April turned

163

to survey the back of her bathing-dress and remarked, 'Good job Captain Mahbou can't see this,' and March giggled and said, 'It's barely decent,' and was glad that Fred would see her in her modest affair. May laughed gaily, she was very gay this holiday, and said she just wished Eugene could see them all as he would go absolutely tollymollary. Bridget Williams, fresh from her training college, with a job at a school in Tuffley, wore a brief, pleated tennis skirt and over-shirt. 'I know it's not a bathing-dress,' she said coolly. 'I want to look human, thank you very much.'

They emerged from the charabanc amid applause. Will leaned his head on Florence's knee and tipped his bowler to shield his eyes. Sibbie possessed what she called a one-piece which she wore to swim from the canal bank. He wished she could have been here today. David kissed the end of April's nose and told her she was a credit to the firm; April replied quickly, 'Good job you can't get in the water darling – you wouldn't be safe with me!' Fred murmured to March, 'You're beautiful . . . beautiful . . .' She said, 'I can't swim very well . . .' and he replied, 'I'll keep you afloat.'

Tollie flicked his quick eyes over the three Rising girls and then let them rest for a little longer on Bridget. He wondered when she would decide to marry him. Not for a while . . . she enjoyed having him on a string with a dozen others, and her excuse was that in Gloucestershire married women were not permitted to teach. He couldn't imagine his life without his mother or Bridget to tell him what to do, to wear, to eat, to say. But nobody could tell him what to think. Jack and Austen rubbed their hands as they dived into the charabanc to change into their ancient costumes. They made the most of the Forest girls, but their own family had 'class' and could be cuddled and kissed quite freely up to a point which limited avuncular behaviour. And Gladys Luker wasn't exactly family anyway.

The men all followed Jack and Austen and the girls began to scream their way through the oozing slime. Here the Severn flooded every winter and the water meadows yielded their rich alluvium annually over thousands of years. However hot the summer, only a thin crust dried on top and this broke like a biscuit under the rubber bathing-shoes. The Rodley mud was supposed to be very good for the skin and was heated and used on the faces of many wealthy ladies who would pay money for it. In its natural state, now and then disturbed by the frantic escape of a browsing eel, it was rather too plentiful to be inviting. Sinking to calf depth at each step the girls assured each other in piercing shrieks that it was medicinal, but their groping feet still cringed at their unsteady hold, and when Gladys wailed, 'What if we disappears? Like the man at the Picturedrome in *The Sinking Sands of Assam?*' May gave a shriek and led the retreat.

They were too late. Coming towards them at full pelt were the males of the party, Victor and Albert-Frederick in hot pursuit. Fred led the way. They followed him in flat dives from the low bank, crouching and launching themselves off like seals on to the already churned mud. Fred aimed himself at March, caught her around the knees and brought her down on top of him to continue into the river. Austen and Jack carried Gladys off; Albert and Victor claimed May and April. The river churned and swirled as if with a shoal of elvers. Albert and April dived and surfaced again and again; Victor splashed with his mother in the shallows; Gladys screamed and clutched at her bathing-suit and Austen's raucous laughter could be heard practically down river to Bristol.

Fred said, 'March, I love you. I want you. I can't go on like this. Come away with me, please darling.'

They did the new side-stroke so that they could face each other in the water; the current took them quickly away from the rest.

'Oh Fred—' March's open mouth shipped water and she coughed and spluttered. He took her head on his chest and drew her into the bank. They held on to a willow branch and laughed. It was as if their long four-year estrangement had never been; any awkwardness had been lost in the old awareness.

She said gaspingly, 'Fred, it would get about – these things always do. It was bad enough when you brought me back from Bath that time, but that's forgotten now—'

He interrupted. 'Listen, Marcie. You've never seen Marsh Cottage – I named it for you, you know. We've moved out of there – Jack and Austen are with a chap named Danby now. I sometimes sleep there – use it as an office. Come down with me next week—'

'Fred, I'm going to Bath next week.'

'To that old man?'

'You know why I go. I've explained. He's promised to change his will again. And he's over eighty now.'

'And has he done it yet?'

'No. But—'

'Exactly. He'll be dead one of these days and he still won't have changed it. Can't you see he's got you on a string? We don't need him any more, March.'

Her face became serious beneath the close-fitting cap.

'I thought . . . I thought you might want to marry me because of that money, Fred.'

He released the branch and took her round the waist. She too let go her hold and they sank beneath the water. When they surfaced he was kissing her. She spluttered again and reached for a handhold on the bank. They lugged themselves up on to the grass.

Fred kissed her again through her spluttering and her protests.

'Listen woman,' he panted. 'It's you I want. You—'

'All right – all *right* Fred!' But she was laughing again, glowing like the carefree girl she'd never been. 'All right, I'll come with you. Yes – yes – I promise! Yes, I do love you – I do!' She softened suddenly, 'Oh Fred . . . I do . . .'

He kissed her slowly, then began to tell her how they would arrange their trip to Marsh Cottage. She nodded.

'Darling, I think we'd better go back. Edwin doesn't matter but I wouldn't want Mother or Dad to think there was anything between us.'

Fred smiled, thinking of Will Rising and Sibbie. But he said, 'All right, Marcie. We'll go back and swim with the others.'

In the event March did not want to get in the water

again, so they walked along the bank to where April and May were towelling the boys. Fred felt a triumph that effervesced into schoolboy tomfoolery; he suddenly leaned down, whipped April's rubber bathing-shoe from her foot and ran with it back to the river. Once there he hurled it to the middle of the stream. It became the object of a game they put on for the entertainment of the others. April ploughed through the mud again, laughing and calling him names; he brought her down with a flying tackle and rolled her in the ooze until she looked like one of the popular nigger minstrels. He spat mud and went for her again in the shallows, then they both set off for the shoe, which was bobbing blearily in mid-stream.

April was an expert swimmer. She had for a time belonged to the Ladies Swimming Club at Barton Baths – when she had needed an excuse for looking into the shop window at Daker's – and had learned the new Australian crawl. Fred, less expert, scrambled through the water without finesse but at a good rate. His strong grip wrenched the shoe from her scrabbling fingers and he held it aloft with a gasping cry of triumph while she squeaked and pushed herself out of the water like a leaping salmon. 'Race you for it!' he panted and set out for the opposite bank.

The stage was taken by Bridget and Tollie who swam around each other warily. When Gladys left the river, shouting abuse at Austen and clutching her bathing-dress to her, Bridget suddenly dived. The next moment Austen disappeared with a shout of surprise. When he surfaced, blowing like a whale, Bridget was already up and announcing to the world that he had left her no modesty whatso*ever*! She too clutched her sodden shirt and it was plain to see someone had ripped it from her shoulder. Eyes sparkling, she screamed at Tollie to defend her honour. Austen began to shamble out of the water circumspectly. Bridget said, 'Oh never mind darling.' She encircled Tollie's neck and presented her legs on top of the water. 'I'm too tired. Carry me out.' Tollie crooked his arms and complied.

On the other bank in another mud bath, April surrendered too.

'Keep the shoe . . . drown me if you must . . . I'm exhausted!' Her laughing gasps ended in a long-drawn-out moan as she threw herself supine on to the warm slime, arms stretched above her head, eyes closing against the burning sun.

'Poor little April Rising,' Fred mocked, squatting by her, lifting one limp foot, beginning to shove on the mud-filled shoe. 'Poor helpless little April Rising—'

'April Daker,' she corrected lazily. 'I'm a married woman now remember, Fred.'

'Poor little April Rising. Pretending to be a married woman—'

Her eyes opened, her smile died. 'What do you mean by that?'

He knelt over her, a supporting arm either side of her head. His own pale blue eyes grinned into her darker ones. 'I mean you're still the schoolgirl. That's what I mean. You might be taller than most of us, with a missis to your name and fancy frocks on your back and your own bank account and your silver cigarette case—'

She relaxed, grinning back. 'Oh shut up, Fred Luker. Businessman of Gloucester. Sharp as they come – hard as nails—'

He lifted a casual hand and plopped a dollop of mud onto her face. She refused to flinch. 'Delicious,' she said, licking it daintily from her upper lip. 'Chocolate flavoured if I'm not mistaken.'

He collapsed on top of her, laughing again 'Oh you're beautiful! Lovely! The best of the Rising collection. Come on. Move. Albert's halfway across the river and March will blame me if he gets swept too far downstream.'

She was up immediately, searching the water anxiously.

'Stay there darling!' she called to the dog-paddling boy. 'Aunty April's coming for you!'

She plunged into the river, Fred forgotten. He watched her admiringly, still smiling. He wanted March more than any other woman in the world, but he knew his teasing words just now had been right. Somehow the goodness of Florence, the passion of Will, the discrimination and sentiment of March, Albert and May, the daring of young Teddy – somehow they had been perfectly combined in April. She was the best of the Risings.

He glanced at the opposite bank and saw David Daker's eyes on her. Then he looked further and saw March watching Albert. April reached him and they began to cavort together. March subsided and let the gaze move to Fred as he stood there, caked in mud, like some primeval being. She didn't smile.

He gave a roar like a lion and dived into the water.

She was jealous. She was actually jealous. Almost as jealous as David Daker.

Albert had been immediately happy at Marley Close school, but he was even happier when his cousin joined him 'for a week or two'. Like April and Teddy before them, the two boys discovered that their family connections earned them special attention from the untrained teacher who owned the old house on the Twigworth Road and strove to keep it intact by running one of the new-fangled kindergartens. Arnold Baxter was the second son of a second son; his brother had died at Ypres, his father in a TB sanatorium. His uncle was a solicitor in Gloucester, pompous and not very successful, and there were many sons who would inherit his money.

Arnold, shell-shocked and unqualified for anything, huddled in the big four-square Georgian house at Twigworth for nearly a year. Then, like a gift from heaven, a French nurse who had met him at the field hospital in Armentières visited England and looked him up. She had read of the work of Froebel and judged very shrewdly that English opinion was swinging towards German intellectualism in a kind of reaction from the four years of forced antagonism. She also realized the potential of the big house and grounds near a city which provided scantily for its infant population. In any case she was fond of Arnold and very sorry for him, and there were no prospects for her in France. She was nearly forty and he was twenty-two, but he was grateful to her for marrying him. They were happy, and the children in their kindergarten were happy. By 1924 it had a preparatory department with a growing reputation, enhanced if anything by astronomical fees.

'To play is to learn,' trilled Mrs Baxter in her accented English as she led a trail of six-year-olds to clean the lawn of daisies. 'To learn is to play,' echoed her young husband, not entirely inaccurately, as he tinkered with the boiler in the basement, shadowed by Albert Tomms whose grandmother was a Rhys-Davies.

Victor dismembered his daisy during rest-time that afternoon.

'The whole *thing* is called the calyx,' he told his cousin knowledgeably. 'Each separate piece is called a sepal.'

'You mean petal,' corrected Albert, lying on his back and dreaming of driving an engine.

'No I don't. These are petals.' He sprinkled white scraps over Albert's face. 'You ought to listen to Mrs Baxter, Albert. She tells you about real things.'

'Engines are real things. Arnold was in one of the tanks in the war. They're real things.'

Victor didn't give up. 'Have you ever seen your Mummy without any clothes on?' he demanded. The thought of Aunty March without clothes was so funny he began to laugh.

'No. And neither have you.' Albert turned his head to grin back. Sometimes Victor was so silly he had to laugh.

'Yes I have. And my Daddy. His thing was as long as this.' Victor spread his arms wide. He saw the success of this confidence and went on boastfully,

'And my Mummy's chests were as huge as balloons.'

Albert's laughter was checked. When he had swum with Aunty April in the river he had noticed that her chests floated on the water like balloons. He said unguardedly, 'I'd like to see Aunty April without any clothes on.'

Victor said, 'Easy-peezy. I'll ask her if you can.'

He was rewarded by a faceful of torn-up grass and a red-faced Albert saying, 'I didn't mean it! Stupid little idiot!'

Sibbie Luker had never liked March. It was unfair of her because if March had not vacated her job as typist to old Alderman Williams, Sibbie would not have got it and then would never have owned her own bungalow and been her own mistress. Perhaps a natural antipathy had been exacerbated by guilt; whatever it was, Sibbie made no secret to her brother that she did not like March Rising and was not happy that he was friendly with her again.

'What difference does it make to you?' Fred asked, surprised to see her in the tiny office he now had in Kings Square. 'And how do you know we're friendly again?'

Sibbie jerked her head to the window; Gladys had tactfully 'gone for her grub' when Sibbie arrived. 'Gladys told me what you were getting up to at the picnic.' She paused while he gave a few opinions on family gossip, then added, 'It wouldn't be seemly if anything permanent came of it, Fred.'

'Seemly? What the hell do you know about seemliness?'

She said with dignity, 'I know about it even if I don't appear to be seemly.' She sat down on Gladys' typing stool and faced him squarely. 'Look here Fred, I mean it. You can't marry March and that's that.'

'Out of it, Sib. Go on. Out. I'm not discussing my affairs with anyone, let alone you.'

She sighed patiently. 'Fred, I don't like discussing my affairs either. But as it's you . . . when Florence Rising dies I'm going to marry Will.'

'You . . . what?' He stared, then leaned back in his chair and laughed uproariously. 'Pull the other one, Sib. Go on, here it is—' He stuck his leg out accommodatingly and she kicked it.

'Shut up Fred. I mean it. She's older than him and the next bad winter will take her. I shall marry Will and all those girls will be my stepdaughters. That amuses me a lot. But it won't amuse me one bit to have you as a stepson.'

'Why not?' He went on laughing, holding out his arms and mewling 'Mamma' at her in the most infuriating manner.

She stood up and pulled her hat down over her ears. She could have killed him.

'You don't understand, do you . . . you oaf. I've always wanted this – to be head of the Risings. You'll spoil that if you've married into them first—'

'I thought you only wanted to make Will happy.'

'So I do. But I want this as well. Oh it's no good talking to you, Fred. This is for all of us – Ma went to bed with Will long before I did and then he dropped her and it nearly broke her heart. This is for her as well – and for me – and for you and Glad and all the poor

174

bloody Lukers who have been down there somewhere—' She stabbed a gloved finger at the torn
oilcloth.

He said slowly, 'You're mad.'

'If you want to call me mad, all right. But can't you
see that you mustn't marry March?'

'No. I can't see that at all, Sib. And if you think Will
Rising would marry you – put you in Florence's place
– you really are mad.'

'He loves me!'

'He might do. But he worships Florence.'

'When she's gone he'll worship me. You'll see.
Everyone will see.' She turned and went to the door.
'One more chance, Fred. Promise me you won't marry
March Rising. Take her to bed if you like. But don't
marry her.'

'Clear off, little sister,' Fred said briefly.

She left. And made straight for Chichester Street.

It was not so hot as it had been on the day of the
picnic and Albert and Victor were playing with
Teddy's old iron hoop up and down the pavement.
Sibbie marched straight past them and knocked on the
open door of number thirty-three.

Victor, suave man of the world, but still intensely
curious, said, 'May we help you? The lady of the house
is resting.'

Sibbie could easily have thoroughly disliked him
but he was May's child. She leaned down. 'I'd like a
word with Mrs Tomms. Could you ask her to step
over the road for five minutes? Tell her it is very
important.'

She did not wait for an answer but ran across to the

garden door of Chichester House and let herself through. Very quickly March's head appeared, her eyes startled and full of enquiry. She flushed angrily when she saw who it was.

'You!' March was not one to bandy words, she turned immediately and would have gone except that Sibbie said quietly, 'It's about Fred. And you'd better listen.'

March hung on to the door against her instinct. And in that time Sibbie did her work.

'Before you get any friendlier with my brother you'd better hear about him. He's had plenty of girls in his time – you probably knew that. But now, there's a special one. And you won't be able to break it up. He'll tell you it's a business arrangement, but he enjoys his business as you know. Her name is Leonie Porterman and she lives at Keynsham.'

Again March looked at May's old friend, a fleeting glance that told Sibbie she had heard the name Porterman before. Sibbie did not overplay her hand. She stood there staring back at March, convincing her with silence. March seemed to droop, then again she turned to go. Something made Sibbie start forward. 'It wouldn't have done, you know, March. Not you and Fred. You're not matched – not matched at all.' Then the heavy door clunked shut.

March told herself she should be grateful she was saved from making a complete fool of herself all over again. She did not write to Fred or get in touch with him, but the day before they were to have gone down to Marsh Cottage, she left for Edwin and Bath. As the train drew out she and Albert waved through the window at May, April and Victor getting smaller and smaller on the platform.

'We'll be going back to Grandma and Grampa soon, won't we, Mother?' Albert asked anxiously.

'Of course, son. Of course,' March said and smiled at him. Rose had written that Mr Tomms did not come downstairs any more, so it could not possibly be long before he died. But she would not leave him now until he did, whether he changed his will or not. At last she would keep her wedding vows: for richer or poorer, till death do us part.

A wire came from Monty in his usual extravagant vein.

'Please forgive me and come home stop I love you and always will stop cannot live without you stop broken-hearted Monty.'

May put it with the others, but knew she couldn't hold out much longer. Nobody understood her any more like Monty. She was thirty, a married woman with a growing son, the young soldiers who had flocked after her in Chichester House were gone. There were no Eugenes or Ruperts in Gloucester. She needed Monty's adulation.

She decided to leave Victor with her mother for a few days and have a second honeymoon in the semi-detached house at Bushey. She half-closed her eyes and pictured the bright, neat lounge, the bathroom, the modern kitchen. It would be heaven to be home. She and Monty could lie in bed all day and maybe she would become pregnant again. She thought of her words at Jubilee Road after Victor's birth, and smiled.

Of course there must be more children. Pregnancy suited her.

She sent a wire saying, 'Meet me Paddington two fifteen' and caught the ten forty-five from the Great Western Railways station. It was October the tenth. She wore a new coat, thin blue wool with a single button fastening and lapels down to her abdomen, and a blue straw cloche chosen by April, cream gloves and low-heeled court shoes. Cloche hats did not suit her, she still had her long hair which was too thick to be contained neatly; her feet and ankles were so narrow they needed more support than the cut-away court shoes and before she had walked the length of the platform she had raised a blister on her right heel. Crossly she settled herself into a corner seat. No-one had come to see her off and she suddenly felt very hard done by.

However, May loved travelling and by the time the snorting engine pulled past Old Oak Common, she was smiling again. It would be lovely to see Monty. She wondered whether he would be wearing his new plus-fours. He looked marvellous in them, he had such well-shaped legs. He would hold out his arm and they would walk down to the lawn at Paddington and people would turn and stare at them and wonder who they were. She simply must not limp, it would spoil everything.

He was wearing plus-fours and a terribly sporting sort of cap. She put her arms around his neck and kissed him for a long time, standing on one leg with her blistered heel waving in the cool air. When she drew away she was horrified, and thrilled, to find his eyes swimming with tears.

'Monty . . . baby . . . Mamma's back.'

'Oh my darling. Oh my wonderful girl. What have I done? I love you – insanely – you must believe that.'

'I believe it, darling.' She kissed him again. 'Oh I've missed you so much. I didn't realize how much till I saw you standing there looking so beautiful—' She kissed him again. People were looking and smiling. 'Baby, have you got a part yet? You didn't mention in your wires—'

'No. No, I haven't. I'm getting too old for the younger parts and they say I'm not mature enough for—'

'Baby, don't *worry*! Panto rehearsals will start soon.'

'They've started, May.'

'Oh . . .' She kissed him. 'Mamma's poor baby then. We'll find something, don't worry. Let's go home and go to bed. We can have supper there. Like we used to before Victor. D'you remember?'

'Oh May. Oh God, May—' The tears were running down his face. She glanced nervously at the audience and reached in her sleeve for a handkerchief. A pang of uneasiness clutched her diaphragm.

'Darling,' her voice became urgent. 'Please. Let's get home. Never mind the underground. A cab—'

'May, it's no good. It's no good.' He seized the handkerchief and coughed into it. 'You'll have to go back, darling. There's nowhere . . . nowhere at all . . .'

She said sternly, 'Monty, tell me what has happened.'

'I thought . . . money. It would please you if I

won a lot of money. Epsom . . . I went to Epsom. And greyhound racing. And car—'

'We've lost money before, Monty. We'll win it next time.'

'It wasn't money exactly.' He looked at her and gripped her hands. 'May, don't hate me. Please don't hate me.'

'I could never hate you, Monty.'

'I lost the house. Our house at Bushey Park, May. It's gone. Lock, stock and barrel. I'm staying with Maud Davenport and her mother. There's no room . . . nowhere. You'll have to go back to your mother, darling – thank God you didn't bring the boy. May – I'm so sorry – don't look like that—'

'It couldn't . . . not the house.'

'I had to, May. I'll explain—'

'I don't want to listen. What about Victor's toys? Our things – my clothes – that lamp we bought—'

'Darling, it had to go as it stood. A debt of honour is not like . . . it's not a legal debt—'

'Well then—'

'It's collected by people who don't care how they get it. They knock you about, May—'

'And you just let it *go*? In case they knocked you about?'

'May, try to understand.'

She understood only one thing. She turned and walked back to the ticket barrier. 'When is the next train to Gloucester?' she asked in a high voice. The audience dispersed. The show was over.

*   *   *

It was at this time that the newspapers published a letter by a certain Comrade Zinoviev containing instructions to British Bolsheviks in their work of subversion in Britain. The following General Election returned Mr Baldwin's 'plus-four boys' with unprecedented relief. Tollie Hall said to David Daker, 'It was too soon anyway. In another five years it will be a different story.' He dreamed of a revolution and a new Britain; it made the office at Williams Auctioneers just bearable.

Chapter Seven

In November that year, Monty Gould came to live with his wife and son in Gloucester. He was in debt, depressed, and resentful of his 'luck'. Luck was a word much in use that year; most people were down on theirs. May made him promise to give up gambling on the grounds that it would upset her mother. She went back to work with Madame Helen and passed on all her tips to Monty. As he never had any money, she had to assume he was breaking his promise. She went to see Mrs Baxter who agreed to take Victor on special terms as he was almost a Rhys-Davies. She told Monty she would never forgive him; but privately she thought that next summer when she had saved up £24 which would secure one of the Longford houses, she might try very hard to 'take him back'. A little punishment wouldn't hurt him now.

April flipped the curtain of the changing booth and presented herself to David and Manny. Her dress was like a fringed lampshade hanging from beneath her armpits. Her curly hair had been slicked down into the nape of her neck; the sides brought forward on her cheeks in two rigid curls.

'What do you think?'

It was David's latest creation, the hair-style as well as the dress.

Manny Stein moistened his lips. 'Good. Very good.'

'David?' April was not interested in Manny's opinion. She stood close to David and deliberately batted her lashes.

He grinned. 'It'll do.'

She pouted. 'It's supposed to drive you mad, darling.'

'Wicked woman. Go and change this minute.'

She flipped back through the curtain and behind her heard Manny Stein say, 'It drives *me* mad.'

David ignored that. 'The thing is, can you sell it?'

Manny said, 'I could sell a gross if April would come and model it.'

She waited, unconsciously holding her breath. Then David said smoothly, 'Sorry old man, that's not on. I couldn't spare April.'

Manny Stein said resignedly, 'Well. I think I can still sell a gross!'

April's joyous laugh rang out over the curtain. 'Darling David. You're such a spoil-sport. Manny might have got quite a price if I'd gone with the frock!'

Neither man returned her laugh to her and she looked at the pier glass in the booth and made a face at herself. She was nearly twenty-three and she and David had been married for a long time. She shouldn't be always trying to look for reassurances of his continued love.

Sibbie opened the door to Fred and sighed as she recognized him in the early twilight.

'Look Fred, if you've come to have another go at me about March clearing off to Bath, just leave it, will you? I've had a trying day and I'm not in the mood.'

'Oh?' He shouldered past her into the neat sitting-room. Will's pipe lay in the hearth. He picked it up. 'Careless. Not like you, Sib. Or are you trying to get the feeling that he's already your husband?'

She snatched the pipe from him and put it on the mantelpiece. 'I'm serious Fred. I don't want you needling me any more. I had nothing to do with March's leaving Gloucester and I don't know anything more about it. At a guess I would say March had news that her uncle was dying and dashed off to get her hands on some cash. You know what she's like as well as I do.'

He did. And it was possible. He would never completely understand how March's mind worked. Maybe his foolery with April had upset her that day and she was trying to punish him. He had decided to let her stew for a bit; but it was nearly Christmas. Surely she'd be home for Christmas.

He said, 'Nothing to do with March, little sister. A lot to do with you. I want you to have another go at Edward Williams.'

She sighed again, this time with exaggerated patience.

'I've told you, Fred. I can't. Not while his father is alive.'

'Why not?'

'Charles Williams is my benefactor after all,' she said with Victorian primness. Fred laughed scornfully.

'No well, seriously Fred, Edward Williams knows about me and his father. He's not likely to—'

'In other words, you're good with old men. The younger ones see through you.'

Her face tightened. 'You really are a swine. The point is that Edward is a good man – yes, there is such an animal, Fred. And though he's got that awful wife, he's still faithful to her. And if he changes his mind he doesn't want to follow in his father's footsteps.'

Fred grinned. 'I can think of another way of putting that, Sib. Anyway your other old man – Will Rising – didn't seem to mind going from mother to daughter.' He leaned easily away as Sibbie aimed a swipe at him. 'Pull yourself together, girl,' he advised. 'Charles is practically senile now. Edward will be an alderman one day like his father. I want him in my pocket. I've got other interests now and I need someone in the Council Chamber behind me. He'll be at the Mayor's Masked Ball at Christmas, and I know the alderman always takes you, so go to it.'

Sibbie sat down suddenly in front of her bright fire. She said, 'I'll make a bargain with you, Fred. You want Edward Williams. I want Monty Gould.'

He did not take her seriously at first. 'Wrapped for Christmas?'

'How you like. Bring him round here one night and I'll have another go with Puritan Edward.'

He went to the fire and kicked at a coal. Ash fell into the hearth and she leaned down immediately to sweep it up.

He said slowly, 'What about May?'

'We've always shared everything, May and me.'

'You bitch,' he said.

'Aren't I just?' She smiled at him, cheerful again. 'We'll see how I manage with younger men, Fred. Shall we?'

The new flat above Daker's Gowns was vast compared with the huddled living quarters in the Barton. When the shop was closed April was often very conscious of the emptiness below them; she was glad that the entrance via the fire escape into the alley behind Eastgate Street did not take them through the ghostly, carpeted showroom with its papier mâché models gleaming in the reflected street lamps. Next to the flat was David's big cutting-room and on the other side was a gap in the roofs and then the living quarters of the Bishop family who owned the Bon Marché. In the freedom that such private isolation gave them, April sometimes did outrageous things. She hardly knew why she did them. At the back of her mind she had a vague idea that she must 'hold' David by such ploys. Now she undressed very slowly while he lay in bed, his knees crooked to support a book. She was wearing the very latest French knickers and stood fiddling with the button, waiting for him to look up. He did not. She recalled the enormous awareness that had existed between them when she had been just a child.

'Did I put out the gas?' she asked rhetorically and flitted into the big living-room which May called a lounge. The gas was out. She walked between the big square chairs and the ashtrays on stalks and into the tiny hall, then through to the cutting-room. The

186

uncurtained skylights were full of stars. She went to one of them and looked through and down. She could see the new Post Office and the plane trees which lined the cattle market. It was bitterly cold. She shivered and put her hands over her bare breasts. How long must she stay here before David came to investigate?

He said behind her, 'What are you doing out here like this? You'll freeze.'

She turned, her face lighting. 'David. Darling. Come and look at the city just before Christmas. I think it might snow.'

'Come to bed. Ridiculous child.'

'Don't you like my new knickers?'

'I adore them. I adore you. Now come to bed.'

'Hold me David. I'm cold.'

He came to her and put his arms lightly around her waist. 'You're not in the least cold.' He kissed her nose. 'D'you know something, Primrose? You're growing up into the most frightful flirt.'

She pouted. 'Only with you. And that's allowed.'

'No. With others. Poor Manny—'

'Poor Manny indeed. When I think how he wriggled his way into the business—'

'And Fred. We all know Fred belongs to March but the way you annexed him at that picnic in the summer! I thought May would scratch out your eyes!'

'Oh *David*! Fred's practically my brother!'

'And this man you met last year in London? Captain wotsit?'

She was reduced to giggles, leaning her forehead on his chin. 'I wish you could have seen that.' She looked up, pretending shock. 'Maybe you're right though, darling. D'you know what Victor told me?'

'What's that, Primrose?' He was as indulgent as an elderly uncle.

'He told me that Albert wants to see me without any clothes on!'

'You didn't—'

'David, of course I didn't! He's six years old!'

'I wouldn't put it past you, April.' David smiled, black eyes gleaming with amusement. 'What did you tell the little so-and-so?'

She looked prim. 'I told him I take my clothes off in front of Uncle David *only.*'

He held her to him quite suddenly, looking into her eyes without laughter or indulgence.

'Darling . . . darling Primrose . . .'

Immediately her hands went to his head in reassurance. 'It's all right, David. All right.'

'I want – I want—'

She stared at him, one hand stroking his dark hair down into the nape of his neck. 'What do you want, David?' she whispered. 'You've got me . . . you know that.'

'I want to make you pregnant.'

The words, simple enough in themselves, were shocking between them. The wish had been spoken by April five years before and never mentioned again. Their sex life had been erotic and sterile. It seemed to her she had to work constantly to eradicate her spoken wish from their lives, and she had done it by changing herself. By becoming the decade's innocent and outrageous symbol – a flapper. To hear now that her wish was also David's was cataclysmic. It was a sudden wrenching-away of the superficiality of those five years. She forgot her nakedness and the provocation of her French knickers. She went on holding his head, stroking it, and gradually on her face a smile dawned. She let it grow until it seemed to engulf the two of them in the sheer radiance of her happiness.

'Then . . . then you will,' she whispered. 'Oh my dear David.'

His voice shook uncontrollably. 'You know it's not . . . the shrapnel . . .'

'That you want to – it is enough.'

She meant it then. But afterwards as he lay face down beside her, his hands clenched on the pillow, she knew it was not enough for him. She pretended not to know that he had failed and kissed his ear, murmuring, 'Good night darling, it was perfect.' Then she lay very still on her back. She had read in a medical book by Dr Marie Stopes who was all the rage, that even an invisible speck of semen could fertilize a baby. When she was certain David was asleep, she pushed her pillow beneath her buttocks in an effort to encourage that speck into her womb.

Edwin had a relapse just before Christmas, so there was no question of March going home even if she had wished to. Rose made up a truckle bed for her in his room and put Albert into the other double bedroom on the first floor. They shared the nursing between them, and Letty took and fetched Albert from the small school in town which did not associate play and learning in any way at all. A week before Christmas when Rose crept downstairs to start on the grates, March crawled even more exhaustedly in by the side of her son to get two hours sleep before dawn. He curled against her, warming her with his body.

'I don't like it here, Mamma,' he whispered.

Somehow she controlled herself. 'You'll enjoy it after a while, darling,' she whispered. 'Bath is a beautiful place.'

'But you're busy with – with Papa – all the time. And Letty is very boring.'

She said sleepily, 'Your Uncle Albert called her Petty Letty.'

Albert giggled. 'I'll tell Victor that when I get home.'

Home. It sounded like heaven to March. And of course heaven was barred to her. If only Edwin would send for Mr Hazelbank. If only . . . so many things.

She whispered, 'We'll stay for Christmas, darling. Try to make your uncle – I mean your father – happy for Christmas.'

Albert saw nothing odd in this. A mixture of the Baxters' freedom of thought and his old-fashioned Sunday School, he said self-righteously, 'Yes. We have to make sacrifices at Christmas for Jesus Christ's sake.'

'Amen,' said March, and fell asleep.

Florence went down with the Spanish flu and had to take to her bed and resume her daily meal of raw chopped liver. Gran creaked up with a pan of coals from the range each morning for her fire; May put a clean cloth over the card table near the armchair and brought in a dainty breakfast tray. Florence surveyed the tiny glass of snowdrops flanking her poached egg, and smiled. 'Oh May. Where on earth did you get them?'

'We grow them in pots along the window sill. At the salon.' May poured tea and set the teapot in the hearth. 'Now darling, I'll be home at five. Promise me you'll eat your liver at midday. Aunty Sylv says that yesterday you dithered with it.'

'I promise,' Florence croaked through her raw throat. 'Now darling girl, wrap up warmly. These bitter winds will go to your chest.'

May smiled gaily as she went out, but that night her face was gloomy as she collapsed onto the bed in the attic which she shared with Monty.

'We're so *busy*! I know you think hairdressing is a pleasant pastime for me, but it's frightfully hard work. I'm on my feet all day, then when I get home half the time Jack and Austen are sprawled out in front of the fire.'

'Only at weekends darling. Come on, let me undress you and put you to bed. Like I used to.'

'If that's all the help you can suggest, never mind!' May said, exasperated. 'You could undress Victor if you must undress someone!'

'I do enough for him, May,' protested Monty. 'It's the most awful drag out to that wretched school. I don't know why you don't let him go to Chichester Street. And I've had to go out shooting with your father most of the day.'

'Oh my God.' Will hardly ever visited his rabbit shoot on Robinswood Hill. 'Oh my God, you *have* had a hard day!'

Monty was not used to sarcasm from beautiful May. 'Darling, please be kind to poor Monty,' he said, kneeling down to slip off her shoes.

She moved her feet away. 'I've told you. I'm tired.'

'We could have another baby,' he suggested.

'What? When we haven't got a home for ourselves? You must be mad!'

Monty flushed. 'I think I'll go down to the Lamb and Flag then. It's only half-past nine.'

'You do that. Let me get a decent sleep for once.'

'I might not come back,' he threatened childishly.

She went to the dressing-table and unpinned her hair. 'I think I could spare you for one night. Quite easily.'

Monty left the room and banged the door and Florence heard him go past her room like a whirlwind. She had become very fond of her son-in-law since his terrible misfortune last autumn. It seemed to make him so much like her own Will during the war when he had been so down on his 'luck'. She hoped that in the quiet routine of Gloucester life he could find his old happiness again. Just as Will had.

Fred was in the Lamb and Flag. He tried to think about Edward Williams and how he could use him in the future. He needed to expand. His activities as an entrepreneur had proved very rewarding: Fred had a gift for manipulating people and then organizing them, and then making sure they were grateful to him. There seemed no reason why he could not extend his particular talent. The only trouble was, thoughts of March constantly got in the way. He kept remembering her at Rodley, clinging to him, laughing and making him laugh. Hell's teeth, surely she hadn't cleared off to Bath in a fit of pique because he had rough-housed with April?

When Monty Gould came in, eyes glittering and face flushed, Fred recognized his mood only too well.

He bought him three drinks in quick succession. Monty had drunk a great deal in London and had been almost permanently and happily intoxicated. Tonight, drinking whisky 'medicinally' as he put it himself, he became more morose by the minute.

'Something must change m'luck pretty soon, Fred. One horse – one decent bet – that's all I need.'

Fred swilled his beer in his glass, staring down into it as if all the answers were there. 'A man makes his own luck. You have to take life in two hands and twist it the way you want it to go.'

These were words Monty wanted to hear but his voice was still plaintive. 'How can I do that down here, old man? That's what I want to know. Don't expect me to start digging coal or gravel or whatever it is you're digging now, do you? I'm an actor, Fred. I want to act.'

'Exactly. That's what I'm saying. Act a part to get a part. Who could help you?'

'Maud could help. Maud Davenport. The Happy Hey Days are booked for a summer season at Blackpool. Maud could get me my old place. But May . . . May won't let me go and ask Maud. Never liked Maud.'

'There you are. You've got to act two parts. One for May. One for Maud.'

Monty giggled. 'One for May. One for Maud. All for Monty!' He sobered. 'I'm not going home tonight, Fred. Show her. Can I come over . . . stay with you?'

Fred grinned. Sometimes Fate played right into his hands so neatly it was unbelievable.

'Sorry, old man. But I know where you can go. Relative of mine.'

He led Monty out of the pub and down Northgate Street. Like a lamb to the slaughter.

Sibbie opened the door of the bungalow wearing her new eau-de-Nil satin nightdress; Monty recoiled and so did she.

'You din't say, Fred – you din't say it was your sister. I can't – May's tole me about you!'

Sibbie recovered immediately. It was lucky she had no-one else with her that night – very lucky. She pretended terror. 'What on earth has happened? Fred, what are you doing here with May's husband? Is something wrong with May? Oh my God – that's it, isn't it? May's ill and she needs me with her—' She backed into the warm, well-lit living-room as she spoke. Monty, nudged by Fred, followed.

'Nothing is the matter with May, Miss Luker,' he said with what he hoped was dignity. 'Your brother offered me a bed for the night and I suppose this is his idea of a joke.'

She rounded on Fred. 'How could you, Fred? Do you think I have no feelings? Do you think Monty has no feelings? I have already tried to befriend him once and was rebuffed—' She hurled herself on to the chaise-longue and burst into tears.

Fred said stiffly, 'I had no idea you two had met

before. Monty needed somewhere to sleep and you have a sofa. I couldn't take him home with me – you know what it's like over there. Sorry I've put my foot in it.' He jerked his head at the door. 'Come on. We'll go. You'll have to make it up with May.'

'We can't leave her like . . . like this . . . old man . . .' Monty felt unsteady on his feet. It was very warm in the room and very cold outside. It was a long way to walk back to May's anger and all the problems of thirty-three Chichester Street. He cleared his throat. 'Miss Luker, it would seem I owe you an apology.'

Fred said, 'Well, I'm off. You're over twenty-one. Please yourself.' He opened the door, slid through it and closed it quickly behind him. Monty looked helplessly down at the shaking satin shoulders.

'Please Miss Luker . . . please . . .' he stammered, out of his depth. He was too drunk to choose a rôle and much too drunk to realize that Sibbie had already chosen one for them both.

She flung herself upright and dashed away her tears. 'I'm sorry,' she said bravely. 'I really am. I suppose Fred thinks it's a joke but – ' she looked up at him through drowned eyes ' – you see Monty, I really was part of the Rising family and this sort of thing really hurts.'

'I'm sorry,' he repeated miserably. 'Everything seems to have gone wrong lately . . . everything.'

She got up slowly and went to a chiffonier glittering with cut glass. 'I heard about the house. Last autumn. If only things had been different . . . I could have helped.'

'You?' He stared at the back that was so like May's. Even their movements were identical.

She shrugged. 'I have some money. I don't want it. You could have had it.' She carried a drink to him. 'Here. Drink this and sit down for five minutes. You look all in.'

'I am. Completely.' He collapsed and allowed her to crouch before him with the drink. 'I don't know which way to turn.' He could see down the front of the nightdress. He seized the drink and tossed it back. She was still there. 'It's generous of you to suggest . . . it was an enormous debt.'

She shrugged again and the nightdress did a shimmy on its own. 'You can hold them at bay with small payments.' She grinned. 'I know about things like that.' She stood up just before he fell forward on to her. She refilled his glass and put it in the grate. 'That's a nightcap. Drink it then go to sleep on the sofa.' She went to the door of her room. 'And remember, if you need help in the future and you can bear to ask me—' She disappeared in the midst of his prot-estations. He looked at the door, heard her moving about inside and tried to curb his imagination. He drank the whisky, helped himself to more, paced about the room, held the mantelpiece and leaned over groaning. He wanted to be sick. Was there a bathroom? Where was the kitchen? He blundered into her room. She held his head over the chamber-pot and wiped his face afterwards.

'I smell terrible,' he groaned, hating himself.

'Poor baby,' Sibbie crooned. 'Come into bed and let me get you warm.' She drew off his trousers and jacket and wound herself around him, holding his head against her breast like May always used to, but never did now. He slept blissfully and when he woke at eight o'clock the next morning they were both naked. He did what she wanted him to do, groaning aloud with the pain in his head, forgetting it only momentarily as they shared a brief orgasm.

But Sibbie was blindingly happy. She had felt triumph when she had first slept with Will Rising on Armistice night, but nothing compared with this. As Monty Gould grunted guiltily on top of her, she smiled blindly at the ceiling. 'We're together again, May,' she whispered ecstatically. 'Together again at last.'

Chapter Eight

April, Bridget, Tollie, David and Manny Stein went to one of the Cadena's famous tea dances. David did not dance but he wanted to enjoy watching the impact of April's lampshade dress. He was not disappointed. William Bishop, who was rumoured to be about to expand his Bon Marché into most of the new Kings Square, approached him with an enquiry. David led him through the tables to walk around the balustrades and look down on the Saturday shoppers in the restaurant below.

Tollie held April gingerly as they fox-trotted unadventurously.

'What you don't seem to understand, April,' he said, 'is that if only there are enough Labour members – prospective members that is – they are bound to be voted in. Now that the working-class man has a vote he will obviously return a working-class representative.'

'There's no guarantee of that,' April said without much interest. 'They've only got to look at what happened before. Mr MacDonald couldn't make it work even with the help of the Liberals so—'

'It wasn't the time,' Tollie said eagerly. 'But now . . . things are getting worse. Baldwin is hopeless. Did you read all that drivel about the Coal Commission last year? You see, if it goes on like this there'll be an uprising in less than twelve months.'

April opened her eyes wide. 'D'you mean a revolution? Like in Russia?'

'The same.'

'Oh Tollie. This is *England.*'

'Exactly. A land fit for heroes.' He laughed. She looked at him uncertainly and laughed too.

Bridget held him very tightly indeed. 'I saw you laughing together Tollie, don't try to deny it. April is my best friend. My very best friend, but if you think you can play fast and loose – even with my best friend – *especially* with my best friend—'

Tollie said wearily, 'Do you ever think of anything but sex, Bridget? Anything at all?'

'Yes. I think of your advancement. Daddy says he needs someone for the antiques. And I told him—'

'I wish you wouldn't, Bridget. I'm not interested in antiques. I'm not interested in the auctioneering business at all.'

'What are you interested in, Tollie? Apparently it's not sex. So just what is it?'

'Politics. I'm going to go in for politics. Socialist politics.'

If he thought he might put her off, he was wrong. She was silent, staring at him while they circled the floor again. Then she said, 'Darling. Of course. It's absolutely you. And I can help you. I know so many people. You'll be one of the intellectuals like that man with the funny name.'

'Chiozza Money,' he supplied glumly.

'Do you know him, Tollie?'

'Not personally.'

'You will. You'll know them all.' She threw back her head triumphantly. 'And what is more my dear, they will know you.'

Tollie felt his heart like lead inside his chest.

Manny Stein drank his tea and put down his cup to take April's fingers in his. She tried to free herself and could not.

'April, listen to me. David will return in a moment, I haven't long. Leave him. Come away with me. You know I love you and I can give you anything you want.'

She drew in her breath and horror widened her eyes as Tollie's threat of revolution had not. She might have 'flirted' with Manny as David had said, but that she had pushed him to this point appalled her.

'Manny. You don't know what you are saying. Truly. Please let us forget it – you did not speak.'

He did not release her hands. 'I knew of course you would try to put me off. You are besotted with David. It is a childhood passion which is meaningless now, April. You are a woman, not a child. You do not love him – perhaps you do not love me either. Yet. But I can love enough for both of us—'

'Manny, please don't say any more. You make me hate myself.'

That surprised him. His dark, covetous eyes sharpened. 'You? Hate yourself? That is ridiculous, April—'

'I have teased you, Manny. I know it, and you must realize it now before you say any more. I did not mean to hurt you, to make you believe there was anything more than affection on both our sides.'

200

'My darling. I have loved you since I saw you first. There was never mere affection on my side. And if there is that much on yours—'

She tugged furiously at her hands. 'I am going to leave you now. Where is David? I want to go home.'

Manny restrained her with difficulty. Over Bridget's shoulder Tollie raised his eyebrows. Manny said quietly but with great force, 'Listen to me, April, and think over what I say. This is a shock to you. Yes. But I have known about you and David from the very beginning. I heard your argument that night, not long after you were married, when I called at the Barton shop. Do you remember?'

'I remember. Oh God—'

'David cannot give you a child. I can.' She tugged again, half standing, scraping her chair. 'I will release you now, April. But I want you to think over my words. You are the toast of Gloucester. I can make you the toast of London and a mother also.'

She jerked and was free. David came to meet her as she ran between the tables. He took her arm and felt her tremble.

'Bridget will bring your coat, darling,' he said smoothly. 'Let us go on and make some tea, shall we?' The shop was across the road; even so it was odd to walk through crowded Northgate Street on a Saturday afternoon in January in a dress like a lampshade. David made nothing of it. They went straight through the showrooms where the assistants hurriedly stood up from gilt-backed chairs and pretended to be sorting through the ready-mades. David did not let go April's elbow till they were at the top of the stairs, then he turned her to face him. His expression was tense.

'What happened, Primrose? Did Manny make a pass?'

She tried to laugh and to control her shaking. 'Yes. I suppose that's what it was. Forget it, David.'

'What did he say?'

'Nothing. Absolutely nothing. Really.' She put her face on his shoulder, unwilling to meet his eyes. She thought of Manny Stein at the bottom of the narrow stairs in the Barton, listening. She shook.

'My God. I *told* you. Before Christmas I told you that you were leading him on—'

'How?' Her voice was a sob. 'That's not fair, David. I don't like the man – never did. But he was your best man – your friend in hospital—'

'What did he *say*?'

'I can't even remember. Nothing much. I'm being silly.' She turned her face into his neck, willing him to put his arms around her.

'I'll chuck him out. There's nothing binding in the partnership, it's a sort of gentleman's agreement.'

'David, I won't hear of it. If I did encourage him – without meaning to – it's so unfair!' She forced herself to straighten and look at him directly; he made no attempt to hold her. 'I've choked him off now. There'll be nothing else. You can't send him away because I've got the heeby-jeebies. I'm sorry darling.' She turned and went into the sitting-room. 'You see, he won't come over with the others.'

But he did. He crouched by the gas fire with a toasting-fork looking more like Mephistopheles than usual. And when April glanced at him he smiled as if they shared a secret.

She went into the bathroom and splashed her face with water. If only . . . if only . . . she and David could have a baby.

It was March's thirty-second birthday. Dr Maine came in the morning and pronounced Edwin fit enough to partake in 'suitable celebrations'. March smiled and clenched her hands behind her back to stop them from clenching around Edwin's scrawny throat. It had occurred to her several times that it might be possible to hasten his end, although poison had been in her mind rather than physical violence. Not only had he kept her running up and down stairs all day and all night, but Mr Hazelbank had still not been summoned.

She said smoothly, 'Rest now my dear. When Albert comes home from school there is a special cake.'

The two men chortled like silly children. It was as if Edwin knew that his good health and careful nursing depended on Mr Hazelbank being always in the offing, as it were. Every day Albert pleaded, 'Mother, when are we going home?' And March replied impatiently now, 'For goodness' sake Albert! When we can – just as soon as we can! How many times must I tell you!'

She saw the doctor out and went down to the kitchen for Edwin's hot chocolate. It infuriated her to see Letty sitting doing nothing. 'You can come up with me and fetch the night's linen, Letty,' she said.

'Laundry. Rose's job,' Letty said insolently.

'Not today. Rose has been up all night—'

'She's younger than me!'

'So am I. And I pay you to do what I say!'

'*You* don't pay me, Miss March!'

March fumed. So soon this woman would have the last laugh. But not yet. 'No. But I can soon stop you being paid, Letty. So come on!'

They went upstairs in mutual dislike. Edwin, on the other hand, seemed livelier than usual. He sipped his chocolate and put it on the tray. 'Ah Letty. When you fetch Master Albert from school, do not take him for a walk. There is a special cake for tea – ' he looked archly at his wife ' – we'll have a little party. You and Rose must come up—' He stopped speaking and closed his eyes. They stared at him, puzzled; he whined and whimpered but was rarely abrupt. His head settled into the piled pillows, a pulse throbbed in his neck and was still.

March rushed at him furiously and felt for his heart; there was none. She shook him. 'Edwin! Edwin – wake up this instant! Do you hear me?' She went on shaking him until Letty removed her hands.

'It's no good, Miss March. He's gone. Lovely way to go too, with the both of us by him and him so happy.' Tears spouted from her eyes. 'Don't take on so,' she said to herself as well as March.

March crouched by the bed sobbing noisily. If Letty hadn't known her as a child in one of her tantrums, she'd have thought the girl really was frantic with grief. March looked up.

'I can't bear it! I can't *bear* it, Letty! Get Dr Maine

– quick, quick, there might be a chance! The silly fool said he was better – get him!'

'Don't be silly, Miss. Come on now.' Letty got March up on her feet, feeling a twinge of sympathy in spite of herself. 'We'll go and have a cup of tea and send Rose for the doctor and someone to lay out. Come on now. It's been expected long enough.'

March suddenly felt very tired. Whatever she did turned out to be wrong. She might have guessed this would, too. She allowed herself to be led out of the room.

Fred sat one side of his desk and looked at Leonie Porterman sitting on the other side. Her hair was shingled so short it was like a man's; her make-up was heavy. It was March's birthday and she had not even come home for that; he thought he hated Leonie Porterman, yet he knew that he would sleep with her tonight.

He said, 'I will not have you coming to the office to see me, Leonie. I've told you before. I've got friends in Gloucester – good friends – but if you continue to flaunt our relationship to the skies, they will have to drop me.'

'Oh stop being such a Filthy Luker!' She smiled at her oft-repeated pun. 'Everyone knows about us anyway. D'you know, when Marcus and I had our last row he told me that we're known as "Three in a Bed Unlimited"! That's rather good, don't you think?'

'I don't suppose Marcus thought so.'

'He says he'll buy you out. Killing, isn't it? He'll pay you money not to see me again. If you could push the offer high enough, Luker, we might elope on it!'

'Oh shut up Lee, do. And clear off, there's a good girl. I'm going down to the Forest in a minute.'

'I'll come with you. I like that place down there. It's earthy. Reminds me of the gamekeeper's cottage in *Lady Chatterley*. Did you read that book, Luker?'

'Yes, I did.'

'What did you think of it?'

'Filth.'

'Exactly. Your sort of book!' She laughed uproariously as she lifted her skirt to adjust a suspender. She added, 'Shall we go in my car or yours?'

'Go? Where?'

'Marsh Cottage. You just said—'

'Leonie, I am going alone. I am selling the cottage to one of the miners and I can't have you tagging along.'

She pulled down her skirt and surveyed him through narrowed eyes. 'You'll be coming to Keynsham tonight I hope, Luker. It's Wednesday.'

Was there a hint of menace in her voice? He said levelly, 'I'm busy tonight, Lee.'

'Very. Same here. As usual.'

She wasn't going to let him off; and it was March's birthday. He couldn't bear the thought of Leonie Porterman on March's birthday. He stood up and reached for his jacket on the back of the chair.

'Right. I'm off then.'

'Don't be late tonight then, Luker. I wouldn't want Marcus to get his coal from *anyone* else now.'

He watched her sturdy figure go past the window. Yes, she had been threatening him. He went to the small mirror that Gladys used and struggled with his collar stud, nearly choking himself with his suppressed anger. The sooner Sibbie delivered Edward Williams to him, the better.

While Fred talked to Leonie Porterman, April went for a bath. She rarely bathed during the day, but David had promised to take the afternoon off, hire a car and drive her to Bath to wish March a happy birthday. Like Fred, April had assumed March would be home, first for Christmas, then for her birthday. When her weekly letters to Florence contained no such news, April planned this surprise visit.

She sang as she wallowed in scented water. Gracie Fields' record of 'Sally' was still very popular and the only way to imitate those clear soprano tones was to use the steamy acoustics of the bathroom. She was into the second verse, wavering slightly as she descended the scale for '. . . don't ever wander . . . away from the alley and me . . .' when the door knob rattled, the door opened, and Manny Stein stood there.

April was shocked. She relied on the isolation of the flat to wander around half-dressed and leave the bathroom door unlocked. She had avoided Manny since that day in January and when she could not, her manner had been heavily repressive. Before then she might have laughed as she grabbed her face-cloth to hide her upper parts; now she did not. What was worse, he did not move.

'Get out!' she snapped. 'How dare you—'

He said, 'I knocked first. I didn't realize you were taking a bath.'

'Now you do. So go.'

'David said you were upstairs. He did not seem to object.'

'*Go!*'

'I simply want to know whether you have thought about what I said eight weeks ago in the Cadena.'

'It was absurd. Ridiculous. Get out!'

'April, you cannot dismiss my – my declaration—' He smiled slightly at the word. 'You cannot dismiss *me* like that. My love for you is absolutely consuming. I look at you lying there and I hardly know what to do.'

'I'll scream.'

'And no-one will hear.' He took a step inside and closed the door behind him. 'Let me talk to you. Explain. Please take away that face-cloth.'

She felt her outrage turn to fear. There was something crazy in his face, in his quiet request.

She forced reasonableness into her own voice. 'Listen. Manny. I can't talk like this – I simply cannot. I shall panic and there will be the most frightful scene and we shall never be able to meet again. Go into the living-room and sit down. I will be with you in three minutes.'

'April, I dream of you. Every night. And all day long. I am obsessed.'

'Two minutes. I promise you, Manny—'

The door opened again and David stood there. He saw his wife sitting in the bath, precariously modest, talking smilingly with a man.

He said tensely, 'Stein. It's you. Get out of this flat. This building. And don't come back.'

'I must talk to April. Surely you understand that? Surely you—'

He got no further. David caught his arm and swung him through the door, hooked his gammy leg around the immaculate ankles and felled him in the tiny hall. April screamed with fright, leapt up, grabbed a towel and crowded behind David. Manny picked himself up with difficulty. He had hit his head as he went down.

He said, 'I thought you were lame. Or is it an excuse you use when it comes to impregnating your wife properly?'

David hit him open-handed across the mouth. He began to bleed. He dabbed it with his handkerchief and laughed.

'For someone who professes to abhor physical violence, you are doing well this afternoon, my friend.' He stared at David. 'My friend,' he repeated. He looked beyond the open door and smiled slightly. 'Adieu, fair April. I shall be waiting. If ever you need me.' He left.

April sat on the edge of the bath, not knowing whether to laugh or cry or be sick. She let concern for David overtake all three emotions.

'Darling. Are you all right? Your leg—'

David surveyed her without any expression on his face. 'My leg is very good for ejecting suitors. As that one pointed out. What is more important – are you all right?'

'Of course. But I don't quite know what might have happened if you hadn't arrived when you did.'

'I think I know. He would have – what was his word? – impregnated you.'

'David!' She stared up at him, dismayed. The towel had fallen and she retrieved it fumblingly, embarrassed to be naked in front of him. 'It wouldn't have come to that!'

'Wouldn't it? Surely it's what you want? Oh, you might have put up a bit of a fight, of course, but—'

'*David!* Don't talk like this – please.'

'Why not? You're a passionate female, April – face up to it. Erotic too. D'you know, some of the things you've done – and let me do – have shocked me. Does that surprise you? A soldier with two years' experience in French brothels, shocked by a schoolgirl in his home town.'

She was weeping. He said savagely, 'Get into the bedroom. Go on. Now.'

'But David . . . we're going to Bath to see March . . .'

He pulled her up and shoved her ahead of him into the bedroom. She lay on the bed on her side, watching him in horror as he pulled off his clothes. There was no tenderness. After less than three minutes she felt something eject into her. She had never felt that before. He got off her and stood at the side of the bed, his anger still burning in him almost visibly.

'There! Are you satisfied? Have I *impregnated* you now?'

She held her crutch fiercely, her eyes like stars. 'David – there was something! I felt something!' She lifted her buttocks slightly. 'I *knew* Sibbie Luker was wrong all the time! I knew—'

His hands ripped hers away. 'What do you mean – Sibbie Luker?'

'Nothing—' She flinched from the anger in his eyes;

it had been hot, now it was frozen. 'Nothing, David!'

He pulled her upright and shook her hard. 'Tell me! Tell me what you meant. You've been discussing me with Sibbie Luker. Just as you discussed me with Manny Stein!'

'No! No, David. Darling – really—'

He pulled her on to the floor and she fell to her knees.

'Tell me now! Otherwise you can get out of here and go with him!'

She sobbed. 'I hate him, David. I always have. But he's Jewish and I thought if I showed my dislike it would hurt you and your mother! After the Cadena – in January – I thought you understood!'

'You know me better than that, Primrose. That's the trouble with you, you've always known me – seen through me. And you talked me over with Sibbie – comparing notes, was that it?'

'No! Never!' She hung from his hands like a drooping flower. 'David, please let me lie down to let the semen—'

'You fool! Don't you realize that's happened before? Twice before, to be exact. Just twice in six years! Christ! Surely you told Sibbie *that*? Surely you used one of your wonderful long words – impotent – that's the word, April. That's what they call it in those books you read – impotent!'

He flung her hands from him and she collapsed against the leg of the bed. There was a long, sobbing silence. He went to the window and looked out.

She said, 'Sibbie found me in the garden of Chichester House. The morning we were married. She said there would be no children. That is all. I didn't listen.'

He took a long, trembling breath. 'You should have. Anyway, you know by now. Six years this June we've been doing our stuff, April. You and me. Some stuff, eh? We could give lessons.'

'Please David . . .'

He turned and went to the door briskly. 'Look. I don't want to see you again today. Maybe not for a week or two. Is that clear? If you want to stay away for good, that's OK with me. I shall understand. Obviously. If you want to find Manny . . . well, that won't be difficult. He's waiting over the road. I can't say *that* will be all right by me, but I suppose it's what I deserve.' He went out, shutting the door carefully behind him. She heard the door in the hall close similarly, then his muffled footsteps on the stairs. Slowly she stood up and began to dress. It was difficult because she couldn't stop crying.

Dr Maine was kind.

'Please don't distress yourself any more, Mrs Tomms. Your husband was a very lucky man. I understand entirely why you spent so much time with your parents.' He smiled knowingly. 'Sick mother, certainly. Also a very demanding husband, yes? Mr Tomms was very fond of boasting, you know . . . yes, boasting. But when you were needed you returned to look after him. And of course he took advantage of that too.' He patted her shoulder. 'I hope I may continue to be of service to you.'

March stared stonily ahead. 'I shall have to go home

after the funeral, Doctor. I cannot afford to live here.'

'My dear, you will be a wealthy woman. A very wealthy woman.'

The front door bell rang and she stood up. 'I believe that will be the undertaker. You will excuse me.'

'Don't forget I am always ready to attend you, my dear Mrs Tomms.'

'I won't forget.'

March wondered how long he would remember. Once the will was read everyone would be only too anxious to forget 'dear Mrs Tomms'. She ushered him out. Rose was keening in the basement and Letty had gone to meet Albert from school and take him for an afternoon tea at Kunzels. She dealt with the undertakers. She thought bleakly that if Edwin weren't already dead, she really would kill him now. With her bare hands.

Fred thought of Leonie and March and his strangely empty life and wondered what had gone wrong. When had the intricate and marvellous business of making money turned sour? Had it been when his manipulation of people had rebounded, like twisted elastic, and he had found that one trick – just as one good turn – deserved another?

He gritted his teeth with annoyance as he drove over the Cross, swerving to avoid some stupid girl wandering along in a dream. Then he saw it was April. He pulled up the car outside Dentons and jumped out.

'April?' She turned and he saw fear in her face. 'April, what the devil is the matter? Where are you going? It's not that warm – where's your coat?' He had a moment of panic. Something had happened to March. Life would never be the same.

But she relaxed and smiled. 'Sorry. I thought it was . . . someone else. Sorry. I didn't mean to . . . sorry.'

April rarely apologized. And there were smudges on her face; no rouge or mascara, just smudges.

He repeated, 'Where are you going? D'you want a lift?' A bicycle came close and he took her arm and held her flat to the Morris. She was shaking like a leaf. 'You're cold. Get in. There's a rug on the back seat. I'll take you home.' Which was ridiculous. The shop was just around the corner.

But she got in and when he reached back for the rug, she huddled herself in it as if she was ill. He realized that must be it; she was ill. A dray pulled by two horses lumbered past them, full of beer kegs. He drew out behind it but could not pass.

'I'll go down College Green and into Northgate that way,' he said.

She shook even more. 'No. No, I don't want to go home. I – I don't know where to go.'

He glanced sideways. 'Are you ill, April? Have you got a chill?'

'No. I'm cold. But it's warm in here. The sun comes through the windows and . . .' Her voice trailed away. She was crying.

He said, 'I'm going to the Forest. Come with me.' He saw her nod and freed one hand from the wheel to clutch hers. 'Don't cry, little April. I can't do anything about it while I'm driving.'

She went on crying. 'That's what's good. I didn't want to be alone. But I don't want . . . I don't want . . .'

She hiccupped mightily and tried to laugh. 'Oh God. Daddy used to call me little April. Even when I was taller than he was. Oh I wish I was little again. Oh Fred, I don't want to be grown-up.'

'Well, I don't want to be a kid again, thanks very much.' He pulled out and overtook the dray at last. The gypsy encampment down on Westgate fields smoked sootily ahead of them. 'I got plenty of beatings when I was a kid. I remember Miss Pettinger beating me for swearing. And Pa leathered me regular for one thing and another. Don't wish that on me again, April.'

She hiccupped another obedient giggle. 'All right Fred.' She found a handkerchief and wiped at her face. 'Thanks for picking me up. Am I going to be a nuisance? Are you going to do some of your coal business?'

'No. I'm going to hand the key of Marsh Cottage to one of the Freeminers. You haven't seen the cottage we built have you, April? Me and your uncles.' He grinned at her. 'The architect's nightmare, we should have called it. Tell you what, I'll take the Newent road. That will take you back to your childhood.'

'Oh, Fred. You are good to us all. D'you remember when you collected Teddy and me from the infirmary when we had our tonsils out? You and Sibbie and Gladys were like our family.' She inverted her mouth apologetically. 'How is Sibbie, Fred?'

'Flourishing. She talks about the past too. She—' He grinned again, ruefully. 'She still thinks of herself as part of your family.'

At Lassington he stopped the car and they got out

and looked at the famous oak tree, already propped in ten places. As they walked back to the car, Fred suddenly dived into the hedgerow and came up with a daffodil bud. 'The first of the Newent daffs,' he said, presenting it to her. 'We got here before the gypsies.' She held it against her face and he knew she was near tears again. 'Come on. Across country to Bulley and then to Mitcheldean.'

He drove slowly, pointing out landmarks as if to a child. 'Westbury over there – Rodley the other side of the river. We'll have another picnic there this summer, shall we? Down that road is Flaxley Abbey and Speech House. The Forest is like a little country in itself.'

'They mined iron long before coal,' April mentioned, trying to make an effort. 'And the oaks went to the Navy for years. David's got a book about it.' Her voice faded again. She sniffed the daffodil pushed through the button-hole of her blouse and her eyes filled up.

Fred said matter-of-factly, 'You and David have quarrelled. Quarrels are soon mended, April.'

'Yes. Yes, I know. But . . . the cause of this one will always be there.' She straightened her back and took a deep breath. 'Never mind. We'll manage.'

Fred felt a definite urge to murder David Daker. He said shortly, 'If the cause you are talking about is my sister, forget it. It doesn't matter.'

She glanced at him and then gasped a little laugh. 'It's a good job I know about Sibbie, Fred, otherwise you could have just put your foot in it.'

He laughed too. 'Sorry. Didn't think of it like that. You'd have to know about Sibbie, I suppose.'

'Yes.' She didn't want to talk about Sibbie. Her unguarded remark to David about Sibbie had revealed much more important secrets: the secrets of David's mind. She said suddenly, 'Did I flirt with you at the picnic last summer, Fred?'

He was going to say yes. Then he saw her white knuckles on her knees. 'No. We were like a couple of kids. Does David think you flirted with me?'

'Not just you. Others. You see . . . Manny Stein made an absolute fool of himself this afternoon. David found him. Us.'

Fred frowned and turned into the track leading to Marsh Cottage. He switched off the engine and leaned back, letting the silence wash into the car like a balm.

He said at last, 'So. David was rattled by what he saw, and because he was rattled, he accused you of flirting with everyone, and you had a row.'

'More or less. I suppose that's it. Yes.'

The simple definition had its effect; he watched her lean back too, wind down her window, comb her fingers through her hair.

She tried to laugh wryly. 'David said I was erotic. Me!'

He shrugged, determined to take it all very casually. 'Like your father, I suppose.'

She turned at that, startled. 'Like *Daddy*?'

He could have bitten his tongue. 'Your father had five children after all, April. And he always seems to me . . . affectionate. In some ways he was more of a mother to you kids than your mother!'

She laughed more genuinely, knowing what he meant. 'We were lucky he was always *there*. It made us very close. Like David.' She swallowed. 'Perhaps it is possible to be too close.'

He got out and helped her from the car as March had taught him to do so many years ago. She kept the rug around her shoulders and declined his helping hand over the rough parts. She jumped lightly from log to log in the marshy places. When they came to the dell she exclaimed with delight, slipped out of her shoes and paddled down the stream.

There was no sign of Danby. They went into the house and he let her look round while he lit a fire. She was entranced with everything.

'It's like playing at house! Those beds along the walls – and the table and chairs. Oh Fred you were so clever – you deserve to make a fortune!'

Nobody had given him such unstinted praise. He found himself telling her about the treks to the dell to supply what had to be one gigantic endeavour. He told her about that first trickle of smoke which had climbed along the first sunbeam and was his public claim to the land. He couldn't explain about Austen's irregular birth and the way he had used it to lever the other miners into working for him, so she saw him as entirely romantic, entirely idealistic. For the first time he did not enjoy deceiving another person: even when he had tricked March into the Bath visit he had felt a certain pleasure because he had scored off her. So he took one of the palliasses from the bunks and threw it down by the fire. 'Come on, sit here while I make tea. You paddled in your stockings – ridiculous girl. Take them off and dry them.'

She did so and he watched her from the corner of

his eye, marvelling at her unselfconsciousness. Was this what David called flirting? She had the natural, clumsy grace of a colt, all legs and arms and a certain lack of co-ordination. He brewed the tea, opened a can of milk and stirred it in. She had had army tea with David. She sipped, stretched her long, bare legs, sipped again, and without warning, put her cup down and began to sob as if her heart would break.

Fred said, 'Now come on, old girl. Out with it. What's been happening exactly?'

She put her head in her hands and rocked to and fro like Mrs Daker did. It seemed to help. She blurted suddenly through her fingers, 'It would be all right if we could have a baby. Oh Fred, if only we could have a baby! I'd give anything – do anything – to give David a baby!'

It was all clear. He remembered something Sibbie had said once.

He said uncomfortably, 'You're still young, April. You'll start a family soon.'

'No.' She rocked again. 'No. After this awful business with Manny he . . . we . . .' She shook her head and started again. 'I thought we might then. But he said it didn't mean anything. He said because of the shrapnel he can't . . . he said he's impotent. Oh God, Fred, if I had a baby I think he'd be all right. I think the demons would go away for ever. I think he might be whole again!'

He let her get on with it for five minutes. She rocked a bit more, and was still again, weeping quietly.

At last he said, 'Let's get this absolutely straight, April. This afternoon David made love to you.'

She was silent for so long he thought he had got it wrong. Then she said, 'Made love. I suppose you might call it that.'

'Well, did he or didn't he?'

She looked at him and smiled slightly and sadly at his directness. 'We had intercourse. There was no love in it.'

'Has it happened before?'

She answered again as if he were a doctor searching for a diagnosis. 'Twice.' She made a face. 'Just twice.'

'But this time . . . you might be pregnant. That would prove him wrong, wouldn't it?'

'Of course. That's what I've been at some pains to explain to you.'

He said severely, 'Don't take that tone with me, girl. I was the one who held you when you were sick after your tonsils, remember.'

She puffed a helpless laugh. 'Oh Fred. Be serious.'

'I was never more so. If you find out in a couple of months that you are pregnant, he will know it was because of this afternoon. Am I right or not?'

'You are right. But if it didn't happen before—'

'Then obviously, you make assurance doubly sure.'

He looked at her and she looked back at him quite blankly. She did not know what he was talking about.

He said carefully, 'A donor. You need a donor. This new artificial insemination thing – you've heard of it? The semen is taken from a donor.'

'My God, Fred. What the hell are you suggesting?'

He grinned easily. 'Hang on to your hat, girl. I'm suggesting something that might make you run out of here very quickly. I am suggesting that I could be your donor.'

She was silent, staring at him, assimilating what he had said. She was not shocked, but she was adamant.

'No. I'm not going to run, Fred. I'm honoured – if I follow you correctly then I really am honoured. But you see . . . I couldn't.'

'Then that's all right. Let me pour you some more tea.'

He did so and she drank it. The middle of the fire fell in and he crawled towards it and threw on two logs. It crackled comfortingly.

She said, 'You must think me ridiculous. One minute I say I would do anything to help David to get over . . . this. And the next . . . I could agree here and now, Fred. But when we actually . . . when you . . . I should fight you off. Instinctively. Can you understand?'

'Of course. I'm not hurt, little April. I shall go on loving you as a brother, and I hope you will go on loving me as a sister.' He sat very still, frightened to disturb her. 'But, if ever you change your mind . . . well, it wouldn't be disloyal – not with me as the donor, would it? I'm a brother but not a brother. Can *you* understand?'

'Yes. Yes, I can. And you're absolutely right. Absolutely.'

He sat on, wetting his lips carefully, watching the shining length of her shin bone as it splayed into the arch of her foot.

She said, 'Would it work the first time? I mean . . . we couldn't do it more than once.'

He nearly told her that it worked first time with March, but did not. He shrugged his shoulders just enough so that she could feel it.

She took a deep breath. 'Your . . . your Freeminer is a long time coming for the key.'

'Yes. He won't come now. I'll have to drive by his place and drop it in.'

'Oh. Then we ought to go.'

'We'll have to wait till this fire goes down.'

They were silent again, looking into the heart of it. April said very quietly, 'I'm frightened, Fred. I'm sorry but I'm really frightened. There's so much to think of and no time.'

'What is there to think of? It's a solution. Which you can either take or not take. That's all.'

'David . . . oh, David would be so *happy*.'

'Perhaps that is the answer. David's happiness.'

'But it would be a trick. A secret from him.'

'A secret, yes. A trick? I'm not sure. You see, April, if it really did happen this afternoon, how will you ever know whether it's a trick or not? Whether it's David's—'

'Then I ought to wait and see.'

He was silent and it was she who eventually said, 'But – if he's right and there's no baby, I might never have another opportunity.'

He moved away from her, propped himself on his hands and spoke consideringly. 'What you need to realize, April, is that the baby, one way or another, is yours. If it has been made by David, then that is fine. Wonderful. If by a donor, then that is all he is. A donor. Do you see what I am saying? A donor is not the same as a father. The baby is yours in any case. You choose the father. And your choice will always be David because half of you is David anyway.'

He heard her quickly indrawn breath and knew he had said the right thing and wondered where the words had come from. He leaned forward, shook some leaves and dirt out of his turn-ups, got up and went to the window above the yellow sink. It was getting dusk, but dusk came early in this tree-filled land. He did not want to look at his watch; it must be past five o'clock. Danby wouldn't come now. But how long before David began an official search?

He turned and looked down at April. She was clutching her crooked knees now, still staring at the dying fire. She glanced up, met his eyes and gave a small, sickly grin. He saw she was incapable of making that final decision. He walked briskly to the door, bolted it, found an old newspaper and pushed it over the window.

She said, 'Fred, listen. Must it be now?'

'Yes. You know it must be now. Or never.'

'Fred, I can't take off my clothes. I couldn't bear that.'

He wanted so much to laugh. To hold her and kiss her all over and make her enjoy it. He was almost certain he could.

He said, 'It might be difficult, little April.'

She half-smiled to oblige him. 'You know what I mean. Only my knickers. You mustn't . . . look.'

'All right.'

She wriggled about and did something, then lay down on the palliasse. Her face was set. He slid out of his jacket and waistcoat, slipped his braces off his shoulders, stepped out of his trousers. She averted her eyes. He knelt between her legs.

'I – I'll try not to push you away, Fred,' she gasped. 'But if . . . you will understand, won't you?'

He couldn't help grinning down at her then. 'Darling, it's not that serious. Really.'

Tears formed in her eyes. 'Probably not for you, Fred. For me it's more than just serious. It – it's damnation.'

The words did not have impact for him then. He was very gentle, very careful, propping himself on his elbows and watching her for any sign of revulsion. He kept up a steady, insidious rhythm, and saw her being absorbed into it, fists unclenching and holding his shoulders, lips relaxing and parting as her breathing quickened. He knew it could only happen once for her and he timed the whole operation with an objectivity which did nothing to lessen his enjoyment.

But then, when it was indeed happening, she flung her arms above her head suddenly; her body arched to his; she tipped her head far back and her eyes opened and stared at the wall behind her with a terrible intensity.

'David!'

The cry was hoarse and cracked; it was a plea, but there was no hope in it. Fred found himself glancing up at the wall, half expecting to see David there, turning from them in disgust. The wall was of course empty; but he knew it had not been empty for April. She had chosen damnation.

He thought she would be inconsolable afterwards;

he expected tears and despair and remorse and an endless need for justification of her decision. But there were no tears and hardly any words. She lay quite still, her knees crooked and firmly together as if holding herself in while he dressed. Her eyes were open and followed his movements curiously but without any resentment; she looked friendly still.

He knelt by her head. 'I dug some latrines up in the bank, April. I'm going there now. There's a bucket under the sink if you want it.'

She smiled and shook her head and lay very still.

'Are you all right, my dear?'

'Yes. Yes of course. I must stay here for a few minutes more, Fred. You go on. I'm perfectly all right.'

'April. Please don't feel guilty. You *know* you weren't unfaithful. I know about infidelity. You weren't unfaithful to David.'

She smiled again, kindly, as if to reassure him. 'Like going to the doctor's, Fred?'

'Well . . .'

She laughed. 'Go on Fred. I'm all right.'

He went. When he returned she was ready to leave, the rug around her shoulders, the fire damped out, the room already cold and empty and dark. She had put her stockings and shoes back on and combed her hair. Without her usual make-up she looked as she had looked on her wedding day; a schoolgirl in adult clothing.

He held the door and they looked around them, knowing they would never come here again. She went ahead of him along the track. She did not jump from log to log this time, she went very carefully indeed. He tucked her into the car and drove on to Parkend and Danby's cottage. He pushed the key through the door; he couldn't see the burly Freeminer now and haggle with him. Anyway he didn't want anything for the cottage now; it was above price.

As the words came into his mind, he knew that there was the answer for him. What had happened was above price. April's act this afternoon had been for love; nothing more, nothing less. He looked at her as she sat waiting for him in the car and felt a pang of pure envy. He would never know love as she knew it, as David Daker must know it.

He slid in beside her and she gave him that smile again. She said, 'So. It's gone, Fred. Marsh Cottage – your cottage. I'll never forget it. Thank you for taking me there.'

He shrugged. 'It could have been anywhere. The place doesn't matter.'

'Oh, it does. It couldn't have been anywhere, Fred. Any more than it could have been anyone. Only you, dear Fred. Only you. And only the place which you built yourself with your own hands.' She leaned across and kissed his cheek. 'I'll never forget . . . never.'

He drove away towards Lydney. There were tears on his face because he felt he had shared that love.

Fred dropped her in Westgate Street so that she could walk through to the cathedral. He kept asking her if she would be all right and in the end she promised that at eight o'clock that night she would light the lamp in the bedroom which looked into the Northgate.

'Will you go out especially to see it then, Fred?' she asked.

'Of course. David might . . . you don't know what might happen. If it's not lit I shall come straight up. Is that clear?'

'Quite clear.' She put her hand through the car window and he shook it formally. Then she walked down College Green and into the Cathedral Close. She kept her thighs as close together as she could. The west door was standing open and she slipped into the candle-lit nave and stood very still, surveying its magnificence with new eyes. So often she had come here: when Albert was singing a solo; when she had been confirmed; when she had wanted to pray especially hard for David. And now, when she was pregnant.

She walked with her funny gait up the central aisle, staring at the massed organ pipes above her, feeling the old tombs beneath her feet. She felt in perfect communion with the universe. There was no need for the complication of words which would entail pleas and supplications and explanations. She existed in space and there was a place for her; she wasn't lost or overlooked; she had an essential importance.

She reached the roped-off chancel and knelt where she had knelt for her confirmation. And that was where David found her half an hour later, as he made the rounds of her special places for the tenth time that day.

He knelt by her and put his arms around her and his head on her shoulder.

'Will you forgive me?' he asked.

227

She wasn't surprised to see him. Such a perfect moment had to be shared with him. She turned her body towards him and told him what she had learned that day. 'There's no need,' she whispered. 'I am never going to ask your forgiveness for what I have done, David. You must not ask me for mine. We must put our faith – entirely – in our love. There is no other way.'

David, the intellectual, the wisely objective, held his young wife and could not speak. When his voice returned he said very humbly, 'Can you tell me what you mean, darling?' He looked at the high altar. 'I think I understand. But is it the same understanding as yours?'

She smiled at him, an ordinary everyday smile that had nothing ethereal about it.

'Oh David, how could you? You know I'm hopeless at explaining things.' She sighed. 'I think I mean that we – you and me – are imperfect. Very imperfect. We can't rely on one another. That sounds awful David, but we must accept it, mustn't we? It is . . . possible . . . for us to betray one another—'

'No!' he whispered. 'I promise you that—'

She put her hand over his mouth; her voice became stern. 'You must not make any promises. And I won't either. That doesn't – mustn't – matter. Promises. What we do and why do it. What does matter is our love. So long as we've got that . . . so long as we can hold that above water . . . there need be no misunderstandings, no need for forgiveness. There. Have I explained it properly?'

'Yes, April.' He helped her to her feet. Then asked

with a dry mouth, 'Did I . . . back there this morning
. . . did I drown our love?'

'No.' She began to walk back down the nave,
leaning heavily on his arm. 'Did I?'

'No.'

They emerged into the darkness. For the first time
April could remember, there was no physical awareness between them; they clung to each other and
hardly felt movement and limbs. Perhaps because of
that, they were closer than they had been since their
wedding day.

Chapter Nine

The next day April went to Bath to be with March.

David drove her down and they parted with a sense of fitness that had some relief in it. The intensity of that communion in the cathedral was impossible to maintain, and the new relationship which they must now find was just out of their reach. A pause was necessary. They had not been parted since April and March had gone to London to stay with May. April needed to assimilate what had happened and to come to terms with it. Once in Bath with March she put aside her own concerns; she placed the whole problem squarely in the lap of God. If she was pregnant, then only He knew . . . anything. And if she wasn't pregnant, He had decreed it and she must accept that too. David left her fearfully. He knew that she had had some sort of revelation during their day of separation and he assumed it to have been entirely spiritual. He wondered – when she came back to earth – whether she would still want to be married to him.

April did not go with March to the funeral. Letty and Rose, who had lived with Edwin so long, went to the ceremony at the chapel and supported March to the graveside. April stayed behind to look after Albert. He was just seven years old and had given up hoping that they would ever return to Gloucester and Marley School and Victor, but with April's arrival he realized that the old man he'd had to call Papa had really gone for ever and they would be going back to Grandma and Grampa soon. He simply could not understand his mother's irritable gloom; he knew she had been as bored as he had with Edwin Tomms.

He helped April put parsley around the plates of bloater paste sandwiches and risked a few questions.

'Aunty April, why is it called funeral meats? It's fish paste sandwiches and cake.'

'Ye olde custom,' April informed him with exaggerated lugubriousness so that he knew it was all right to laugh. 'And probably all your poor Mamma could afford with the money tied up right, left and centre.'

Albert ate a sandwich reflectively. 'Mummy says we'll be like church mice. D'you think we will be?'

'I don't know, Albie. It won't matter anyway. You'll come back and live with Grandma and Grandpa. You won't mind that, will you?'

'I'll *love* it!' Albert raced around the big dining-room table blowing crumbs from his mouth indiscriminately. 'I'll be so hap-hap-happy!' He jumped knees first onto a chair. 'And Victor loves mice! He'll put us in a cage and keep us safe!' He laughed hysterically and for the first time in a week.

April picked him up and hugged him.

'I can smell bloater on you. Here, chew some parsley.'

They both chewed parsley and giggled. Albert kept his arms around his aunt's neck and snuffled into it.

She smelled delicious; even her hands which were definitely bloatery.

'I wish we could go away and live on an island,' he said. 'Just you and me.'

She sobered, thinking about it. She said, 'D'you know, Albie, so do I.' She kissed him. 'The awful thing is, I couldn't live without Uncle David. And you couldn't live without Mummy. But I know exactly what you mean.'

He let her put him down and give him another sprig of parsley. For a moment he felt a pang of sadness; but it was a happy sadness because he shared it with his aunt.

March stared at Mr Hazelbank as if he had gone mad. 'Are you sure that is Edwin's last will?' she asked.

'Certainly, Mrs Tomms. Unless you have found something in the house, that is the last will and testament of your late husband. Everything is yours unconditionally. It is only to be expected surely?'

April leaned forward. 'Are you all right, March? You are so pale my dear.'

March said faintly, 'But the date . . . it's only just after Aunt Lizzie's death.'

'Darling, you know it was Aunt Lizzie's wish. That you should have everything. And there has been no need for Uncle . . . for Edwin to change that, has there?'

Dr Maine, who had been assiduously attentive during the proceedings, picked up March's clenched hand and encircled her wrist with his fingers.

'Shocked condition . . .' he mumbled, fumbling in his waistcoat pocket for his watch.

March wrenched her hand away. 'I'm perfectly all right thank you, Doctor!' she snapped. 'It's just that . . .' She looked at Mr Hazelbank. 'I rather thought Letty and Rose . . . they've been with him – us – for so long.'

Mr Hazelbank smiled. 'I dare say your husband knew they could rely on your generosity, dear lady.'

March heard the unction in his voice; this was the first time any of Edwin's contemporaries had called her 'dear lady'. It confirmed, more than anything else, that she was rich. Perhaps rich was too precise a word – comfortably off. She looked around the dining-room at the table where Aunt Lizzie had lain in her coffin and Uncle Edwin had claimed his niece.

She put a hand on April's arm. April was the ugly duckling who had turned into a swan. Was March going to be the church mouse that turned into a well-fed, purring cat? Had it all been worthwhile after all? The shame, the indignities, the sheer boredom and drudgery at the end – if she could emerge from them independent of everyone – *everyone* including Fred Luker – wouldn't it be worthwhile?

She said cautiously, 'There *might* be another will – something more recent – around the house—'

Mr Hazelbank's smile became indulgent. 'I rather doubt it, dear lady. Your late husband consulted me in all his affairs, I do assure you. But if you should find . . . send for me immediately and I will act for you. As I shall be delighted to act for you in all things.'

March inclined her head and stared down at her

lap. First Dr Maine, then Mr Hazelbank; professional men, touting for her patronage. She wouldn't be in the least surprised if Fred Luker proposed to her the minute he heard about this news. She must start spring-cleaning the house, and do it alone. If there was a later will, and surely there must be, then she must be the one to find it.

April was all sisterly concern.

'Darling, you really do look done up. Now just sit there – wasn't it Aunt Lizzie's favourite chair? Put your feet up and let me look after you for a bit. You've obviously been run off your feet . . .' She fussed and grumbled and asked about Albert's school and told March about Florence's illness and May's job, anything to divert her mind. Still March continued to stare blankly before her and April concluded contritely, 'I never thought you would be so frightfully cut up when Uncle Edwin – sorry darling – *Edwin* – died. How stupid I was. As if love has limits. *I* should know that! Oh March, you must have hated leaving him so much to look after Mother.'

March stood up and went to the window. 'Not really. There were difficulties.'

April, with all her new knowledge, understood. She said, 'Come and sit down, darling. Let me look after you for once. Please.'

'I can't. I must be doing something. Don't worry about me, little sister. It's my way.' She turned resolutely. 'I'm going to start on his room. No – I want to do it alone.'

'But March, not now darling! It's getting dark and you've had such a trying day.'

234

'Don't worry, April. I'll be an hour. No more. Go downstairs and look after the old girls, will you? I can't seem to bear the sight of them any more. And – and April.'

'Yes darling?'

'In an hour can you call me? And can we sit here and have bread and milk together?'

·'Oh March . . . of course.'

They both remembered the days when Florence had sent them ailing to bed with bread and milk.

That spring and summer Sibbie Luker reached a new height of well-being that made her almost beautiful. She did not make the mistake of approaching Monty again; she guessed that guilt would sour any future meeting she might engineer. But she had possessed him, however half-heartedly, and the confidence she gained from the brief encounter swept her on to conquer Bridget's father, Edward Williams, with ease.

In May, 'young Mr Edward', as he was still called at the auctioneering firm in King Street, took his seat in the City Council Chamber. Fred immediately thumbed through Leonie's many acquaintances in his mental notebook, chose one with a large gravel quarry in the Cotswolds and contacted him with a proposition. He was a reserved man, another war survivor who was a defeatist, and had inherited the gravel pit when it was thriving, since when he had sat back and watched it decline. His name was Walter Lanyon, he had been in the same regiment as Marcus Porterman and he seemed to come to Leonie's parties to get a good square meal. He disapproved strongly of

Fred's blatant association with Leonie, but when he heard his terms he realized he might afford a small-holding with the profits and he could then live as he wanted to; as a recluse.

So in June Fred Luker secured a contract to supply materials for the new council estate being built to the south of Gloucester, known locally as the White City. The deal was made on a friendly basis; Edward Williams had a high opinion of the Risings and had always encouraged Bridget's friendship with April. And he was aware that the Lukers were almost an off-shoot of the Risings, deplorable though his wife considered that connection. When Edward succumbed to Sibbie's charms he offset guilt and self-disgust with the undeniable fact that Sibbie did not 'do it' only for money. Like his father before him, Edward discovered that Sibbie brought real affection with her. After thirty years of sterile marriage – apart from Bridget's conception – Edward Williams thought he might be falling in love again. So he listened to Fred's application sympathetically and swayed his fellow councillors with him. Had he not done so, Fred would not have hesitated to threaten him. But it did not come to that.

Meanwhile Sibbie bloomed like a flower. If the Rising girls were likened to daffodils, she could be likened to something hardier and brighter, a buttercup, maybe even a dandelion. She took no money from Edward because old Charles Williams paid her a regular income and other men who flocked around the small bungalow were more than generous. She had achieved the sort of power she had always wanted; she was making two men very happy – Will Rising and Edward Williams; and she was helping her brother Fred. Life that summer of 1925 was very sweet for Sibbie Luker.

Indirectly her seduction of Monty helped him too.

Terrified that he would meet her again, ashamed of facing Fred, unable to look May and Victor in the eyes, he left for London after a few weeks. There was a room for him at Maud Davenport's, as there always had been, and he let her comfort him. He told May that he was looking for work and it was not long before Maud secured a niche for him with Happy Hey Days again. This time he did not have a solo act; he was Maud's accompanist in one spot, and during the finale he was permitted to sing a duet with her. They had a summer season at Bournemouth, but he thought it was best if May kept her job at Madame Helene's. Just until he got himself settled.

April stayed with March until all the Bath business was settled up. This took longer than it might have done because March refused to sell the house until she had personally dusted every corner of it. Eventually they returned to Gloucester in June, a huge pantechnicon of furniture going ahead of them to be stored in Stayte's furniture repository in Arthur Street until such time as March could buy her own house in Gloucester. Letty and Rose were pensioned off and in an excess of gratitude for the many 'keepsakes' from the house, came to see them off at the station.

March hung out of the window, trying to shield Albert's eyes from possible smuts.

'You'll write to me, Albert?' Rose's eyes swam

with tears. 'You won't forget old Rose, will you?'

'Not likely. Nor Petty Letty,' Albert said with unaccustomed cheek, simply because he wanted to report that particular *mot juste* to Victor. Letty decided to smile.

April said, 'We'll come and see you anyway. Take care of yourselves—'

'Rose, we're leaving.' March tried to disentangle Rose's arms from Albert's neck. 'Your skirt in the running board—' Rose dropped back and was enveloped in steam. March collapsed onto her seat. 'Well that's that. We shan't see them again. Albert, come in and pull up the window please.'

April slid out of her hip-length cardigan, rolled it up and put it on the sagging rack. 'They're not that old, darling. And Bath's not that far away.'

'I shan't go there again, April. That chapter is closed. Albert, come in this minute.'

'Then another one is beginning,' April said rallyingly. 'Cheer up darling. Everything is going to be marvellous for you now.' She smiled. 'I'm beginning a new chapter too. You're not alone in that.'

March tugged at the back of Albert's pullover. She was practically certain Edwin had not left another will, and she felt quite different now about the last eight years. Edwin, after all, had honoured Aunt Lizzie's wishes whatever he might have implied; and he had been motivated by fear, probably, just as she had. Fear of being old alone, dying alone. She was glad now that she had stayed with him, almost regretful at the ending of that chapter.

'Yes. A new chapter. It frightens me in a way.

238

Albert, will you come *in*! The wind is blowing my hair all which-ways.' She opened her eyes at April. 'And you too? Of course you've been ages away from home and I know what that means to you. You and David are so close. Closer than Monty and May. Closer than Ma and Pa even.'

'I suppose that's what I meant. Yes.' She was certain about the baby now, but David must be the first to know. She stood up and hauled Albert in by force. 'Albie, do as your mother says!'

He looked round at her in surprise, but then sat down in the circle of her arm. Everything in Albert Tomms' world was absolutely and completely all right.

David had written to her almost every day. His letters made no reference at all to their terrible day in March; that physical cleft followed by the spiritual reunion transcended mere words perhaps, but she was conscious that he was frightened to mention it. His letters told her of daily events in the workroom and the shop; Manny had obviously gone for ever with all his contacts – though again this wasn't mentioned. David had been to London himself but he was no salesman; amid the witty observations and asides she gathered that he was retrenching. The Eastgate Street shop would provide them with a comfortable living; the original tailoring premises in the Barton, now a haberdashery, provided Mrs Daker with an interest and an income. But some of their plans would have to be abandoned; a chain of exclusive gown shops in the south-west, as Manny had foreseen, would remain a dream. And the house in the country, where they could entertain their less fortunate friends, must be shelved. 'Obviously Gloucester, which spawned us, is not going to let us go,' he wrote wryly.

April read his letters in the privacy of her room overlooking Bath's beautiful gardens, and sometimes she laughed aloud. His comments on Bridget and Tollie Hall's strange courtship, his vignettes of Florence and Kitty Hall sitting in the small back yard at Chichester Street drinking tea sedately, Aunty Sylv and Gran trudging home from their scrubbing jobs, May and Victor at Marley School's sports day . . . they were touching and funny. He ended one letter: 'Sometimes I ask myself why the confines of this narrow-minded city are not only acceptable but welcome, like a comfortable jacket that unexpectedly looks well too. Then I know why. Because every small incident, every sight, every harsh vowel sound, is illumined and made beautiful by you.'

It was the nearest he came to declaring his love. He did not visit her during the three months she was absent. He very carefully exerted no pressure on her at all, giving her breathing space, a chance to reassess their marriage; even to end it.

She wrote back just as obliquely. She saw the spring and summer literally unfold in Bath and she described it leaf by leaf, pigeon by pigeon, as each tiny symptom of her pregnancy revealed itself. And the nearest *she* came to declaring her love and announcing the baby was: 'The narrow confines of home are what we both need now, David. Our lives are going to be quite different and we shall have to have dependable old life-lines to guide us.' She did not realize how abstruse she was being; she thought he must read between the lines and know.

He met them at the station in a cab driven by Fred's brother, Henry. The luggage was strapped on to the boot-flap and Albert permitted to sit next to the driver. March sat between David and April.

'How is Victor? Has school finished for the summer? How is Grandma? I've got ten engine numbers and a number one Meccano set.'

David said heartily, 'Everyone is very well. What about you three?'

'We're OK. Will Uncle Fred help me with my meccano, Henry?'

March said, 'Do not use that abominable Americanism please, Albert. And Uncle Fred is much too busy to help you with anything.'

Henry said easily, 'You're right there. Up to his eyes he is, fixing deals for the council now, would you believe it.'

'The city council?' asked March in spite of herself.

'The big time, that's what it is,' Henry said cockily. 'Everythin' 'e touches turns to gold. Gladys says it's only 'cos o' the Portermans. Lose them and 'e loses the lot *she* says.'

March sat up very straight. 'I see.'

They drove past Clarence Street and around the long sweep of the cattle market. The plane trees were immobile in the summer sunshine and the smell of dung and vinegar drifted reassuringly into the cab. As they dipped into the low road beneath the London

Road railway bridge, Albert hung out and shouted his name and had to be dragged in and reprimanded again.

He turned a sunny face to his mother. 'I just wanted to tell Gloucester I was back,' he said. 'Did you hear the echo? That's the reply, you see.'

April and David exchanged a smile across March.

They left her and Albert and most of the luggage at Chichester Street and went straight home. April had intended staying with her mother for an hour but suddenly she had to tell David as soon as possible. She had to take that anxiety out of his dark eyes.

The flat was meticulously tidy and clean.

'Your mother's been,' she said, walking round, touching familiar objects, looking out of the window and exclaiming at the new buildings in Kings Square, then the sweet familiarity of Eastgate market.

'No. I've kept it like this in case you came back unexpectedly.' He smiled at her again. 'I'm getting finicky, I keep dusting and polishing every blasted thing.'

He wouldn't let her into the kitchen; he had a meal in the oven.

'You're nervous,' she said. 'Stop it, David. I had to stay with March – she's been working herself silly – but I'd have come back after the funeral if I could.'

'You said our lives would be different. Of course I've been nervous – *am* nervous. I don't know what the hell you've got in mind, Primrose.'

'Didn't you guess?'

'You want to go to London and sell our lines? I

remember you said something about it once – a year ago now I expect—'

'Idiot. How can I go to London when I shall be so busy here? How can I be any kind of shop window for selling your designs when my shape will be all wrong?' She looked at him and swallowed fiercely; he trusted her so, that was what hurt. It would never occur to him that she could betray him. She whispered, 'David, we're going to have a baby. Next December. I thought you must guess.'

He stared at her for so long that she thought she must be wrong, he must have known about Fred all the time. And then he held out his arms, still silent, and his black, guarded eyes filled with tears. She had never seen him weep. She stood within his embrace and kissed his ear and his neck, and then led him to a chair and sat on the arm with his head on her breast.

At last he spoke in a muffled voice. 'I'm sorry darling. It's just that . . . I wanted so much to give you a child and I thought I never could.'

She whispered, 'And I wanted to give *you* a child, David. That is why I did it.'

He hardly heard her words, and if he had would not have questioned them. It was not the moment for questions. They held on to each other for a long time and when at last they parted, smiling almost sheepishly, they still constantly touched each other as if for reassurance. Everything was sweet and poignant, every action significant. They ate David's meal and washed up. They sat together talking far into the night. David's happiness shone from him unreservedly and April was sure that his dark places were lightened for ever.

But when they went to bed at last and he began to caress her, she drew away.

'Forgive me darling, do you mind? We've waited for so long for this baby, don't let's risk . . . anything. You do understand, David? You're not hurt?'

'Primrose, how could you hurt me? How could you *ever* hurt me?' He took her hand and held it between them. When he slept April stared into the darkness and prayed earnestly.

'Please God, make it his. Please God . . . please . . .'

Fred heard of March's return to Gloucester with mixed feelings. It was almost a year since the picnic at Rodley when they had been so close, almost a year since she had deserted him. He had been forced to see it as desertion because there was no other explanation. No letter, nothing. Sibbie's interpretation was the only one: March had heard that Edwin was failing and had decided to play the part of the devoted wife in the hope of getting some cash out of him. In a way he understood her. After all, for almost as long as she could remember, the Bath inheritance had been her birthright. Her Aunt Lizzie had made no secret of that. But that she had gone on the day before their trip to Marsh Cottage and without a word . . . that made it the sort of rebuff she knew he would understand. More than a rebuff, a deliberate insult.

His pride made him stay away, stay silent, immerse himself in work, degrade himself with Leonie Porterman. And then April had turned to him.

April was a new dimension in Fred's life. He had always taken her for granted: the kid sister who had a crush on David Daker. He had been 'fond' of April. At the Rodley picnic he had admired her. At Marsh Cottage he had loved her, yet had known humbly that his love fell far short of hers for Daker. If her love was a model, then his for March came nowhere near it. But then . . . nobody else's did . . . nobody else's could, dammitall.

Maybe that didn't matter. Maybe he and March were as much in love, in a different way. A sparring way. Often an angry way. What they lacked in tenderness, perhaps they made up for in a kind of total awareness. Fred shook his head angrily, unused to introspection, simply knowing that his feelings were confused and it was April's fault. He had to see March and he had to see April and he did not know which he ought to see first. It would make a difference, somehow he was certain of that. He wanted – almost desperately – to know whether April was pregnant or not. If she was, in a peculiar way his pride would be restored . . . or rather, wouidn't matter any more. He would feel he had helped to make April happy again; he had redressed some of his wrongs . . . Monty . . . March . . . even Marcus Porterman. He could go to March and tell her he understood her damaged soul as no-one else would ever understand it; he could tell her he loved her and wanted her and they had been meant for each other always. He could almost borrow some of April's tenderness and woo March yet again; but differently this time. Without anger; without challenge.

He would see April first.

But he needed to see her alone to find out whether she was pregnant, and she never seemed to be alone. He went into the shop twice, pretending he was choosing a birthday present for his mother, but she was never there. Neither was David. Presumably they were closeted together idyllically upstairs. Did that mean she was pregnant or she wasn't? She had been in Bath for three months and as far as he knew David hadn't visited her there; they had a lot of leeway to make up. The fact that they were inseparable now could mean anything. Anything at all. And time was passing; twice he had seen March walking down Chichester Street with Albert and his heart had contracted at the sight of her. But she hadn't seen him; or worse, she had seen him and pretended not to. It was like that other time all over again; the time when he had tricked her into going to Bath and she had not spoken to him or looked at him all the way home, and Albert's sunbonnet had grown wet with her tears.

Then, over a week after March's return, he left the car outside the King's Street office and walked round to see his mother at midday. It was Saturday and Victor and Albert were scuffling together in Mews Lane, just outside the Chichester House stables where Albert had been conceived. Fred hovered by the rear entrance to number seventeen and watched his son.

Albert was tall for seven and superficially very much like his dead uncle. Only Fred knew that the fair gingery hair and blue eyes came from the Lukers and not the Risings; it was a secret he would have to keep all his life and for the first time it irked him. He would

246

be proud to claim this boy as his flesh and blood; proud to go to the Marley School sports day, as May had done to see Victor, and make deprecatory jokes about Albert's undoubted prowess. 'Takes after me for running – I had to scarper out of trouble often enough!' Victor might be witty and clever beyond his years, but Albert could have laid him in the dust any time he wanted during their mock fight. He just didn't want to. Fred conveniently forgot the difference in the boys' ages and wondered fleetingly where Albert had got his gentle streak from. Maybe there was something of the Rising in him after all. April Rising.

Victor was spluttering helplessly with laughter, making no attempt to return the volley of light slaps from his cousin, sheltering behind upraised elbows and reeling dramatically every time Albert's fingers touched him. Albert too was grinning from ear to ear as he practised the fancy footwork of the great Jack Dempsey as seen at the Picturedrome with April and David that week.

'Mouse eh?' he panted. 'Do I feel like a mouse then, Victor Gould or Mould or whatever your name is? Does this feel like a mouse? Or this? Or this?'

Victor yelped and crouched and cried out, 'Mercy – mercy, great mouse – yowps! – I mean *church* mouse! Quite different, old man – I mean old mouse – cripes alive, mercy on us!' He reached the ground and knelt there as if in obeisance, checking his laughter to say, 'Church mice is nice!' then exploding again uncontrollably.

Albert folded his arms and surveyed his victim severely. 'That's better. I might be poor as a church mouse but I'm still older than you, bigger than you and sensibler than you!'

Victor looked up. 'Did you say smellier than me, oh great mouse?' He gathered himself up and ran, laughing and yelling again, with Albert in fist-shaking pursuit, through the gate of Chichester House and into the derelict, overgrown garden.

And Fred went in to see his mother with a considering frown on his face. He was frowning as much at himself as at this new aspect of the March problem. Had he really forgotten the business of the money? Or had he assumed that March had got something, if not everything, of her inheritance? He frowned again because he could not answer his own questions. Then he wondered if that was answer enough; if the money – or lack of it – simply did not matter.

This thought was surprisingly comforting, as if some of April's feeling was already rubbing off on him. So-called Christians were eternally assuring each other and everyone else that money did not matter. He'd never believed them before.

He couldn't wait to get over to March and tell her this. He was glad she was as poor as a church mouse because now she would know he loved her entirely for herself. He imagined himself telling her this and her melting into his arms. If he could catch her alone, in her room, he could undress her then and there – he was expert at that because it was one of Leonie's rituals – and they could wedge a chair under the door handle and lie together on her bed and the years would evaporate with all their bitterness and wasted time. And it occurred to him also that he could get news of

April over at number thirty-three. Two birds with one stone.

Henry had told him about Albert's precious meccano; on the way back to the office he bought a more advanced set and spent the afternoon making and un-making the suggested models to ensure it was all intact. He called at number thirty-three that evening at seven-thirty when he was fairly sure Albert would be in bed.

He was a little too early. May and March were in the kitchen with their sons, feeding them a supper of bread and milk.

He greeted the boys. Then May. Then March. 'And how is your mother?' he asked formally.

May replied because March had turned the tap on at the sink.

'The same. She says she is well but I doubt she weighs six stone.'

Florence had never looked heavier than six stone to Fred. He said, 'And how are you, March? And Albert?'

March made no reply. He ached to tell her that he understood how she felt; the last ten months wasted on that old man. Albert said, 'We're OK.' And March said in a withdrawn voice, 'I have asked you before not to use that silly word, Albert!' And Fred thought of the last time he had been with her on the river bank, cradling her in his arms, wet, bedraggled in that ridiculous swimming-dress. He felt suddenly powerful; at last he was in the position he had always promised himself; and so incidentally was March. He had money and influence and March had none. Neither of them were tied legally; he could rescue her properly this time; give her all the things she so badly wanted.

May collapsed into a chair and put her elbows on the table. 'I can tell you it's marvellous to have them back. What with going to the salon every day, fetching Victor from school, worrying about Monty and Mother . . . it's just too much for me.'

Fred ignored that and addressed March's back. 'It's been a sad time for you. You must have been thankful to have April. How is she?'

March made no reply and Victor giggled into the quietness. 'Aunty Ape. Aunty Ape played a jape!' Albert clattered down his spoon, leaned across the table and aimed a swipe at his cousin. May intervened with horror.

'Albert! We do not hit each other in this house, *if* you please!' She put an arm round Victor. 'Did he hurt you, darling? '

March came to life.

'Of course Albert didn't hurt Victor. Now come on, boys. Into the dining-room to say good night to Grandma and Great Grandma and Aunty Sylvia.' She glanced at May. 'I'll take them up, May.' She did not look at Fred.

May kissed Victor and sat back, indolently toying with the spoon in his empty dish. 'Well Fred. And how is the big business tycoon?'

Fred noted the antagonism and knew it was linked with Sibbie. May and Sibbie had been like sisters, which must now make their estrangement worse. He hoped it was that; he hoped that fool Monty hadn't felt bound to confess.

He stared at her. 'Flourishing thanks, May. And how is Monty?'

She pushed at the spoon moodily but she did not flush so it was all right, she didn't know about Monty and Sib, thank God. He went to the door. 'I'd better go. You didn't answer just now, is April all right?'

'Fine. Radiant actually.'

He looked over his shoulder. 'What does that mean exactly?'

The defences went up; May did not trust Fred. 'Nothing in particular. She's glad we're all together again I expect.' She got up and went to the sink, dismissing him, and he closed the door behind him and stood in the passage for a moment, considering. If April were pregnant he was so much part of the Rising family that he could take March by storm; force her if necessary. But surely May would have told him just then? May was usually so frank and open that she seemed almost simple.

He took the stairs quietly, two at a time. Albert and Victor were sharing one of the attic rooms and he looked in just as Victor had lifted his nightshirt at Albert and March had caught him a resounding slap across his buttocks.

'I'll teach you to stop those dirty tricks!' she said furiously as the child subsided onto his bed with a yelp of surprise.

'Now now—' Fred entered and scooped Victor under the clothes, grinning privately at him to show it was all good fun.

March said, 'What are you doing up here? The boys have already said good night—'

Fred interrupted smoothly. 'I missed Albert's birthday.' He produced the flat box from inside his jacket. 'Here you are, old son. Instruction book with it. It's slightly up on the one you've already got—'

Albert was delirious. 'How did you know I'd got one? Oh Uncle Fred – it's corking marvellous – honestly! Look at the *tools* – oh cripes—'

'Don't swear please Albert!'

'My birthday in seven weeks, Uncle Fred,' Victor mentioned helpfully.

'You've thoroughly unsettled them, I hope you know!'

He looked at March and wondered whether her hectic flush and general tension were good signs or bad ones.

'Let them look at it, March.' He took her elbow and got her out on the landing. 'Might as well go in here – your room, is it? I want to talk to you anyway. When we've . . . finished . . . we can slip in and tuck them up. How's that?'

She pulled away. She was visibly trembling now. He felt her anger and wished it were not there. He was used to it; sometimes it was good, a sign of passion in her. But for now, tonight, he longed for a quiet acceptance of their love; their eventual good fortune which had been so long – so very long – in coming.

She made no move so he pushed at the opposite door and went inside. The room was like a cell, white honeycomb bedspread over an iron bedstead, a single worn rug on the highly polished oilcloth, thick lace curtains and a black blind half unfurled against the low-level sunshine. A virgin's room. An old maid's room.

March spoke from behind him. 'Just what do you think you're doing, Fred? This is my *room*!'

'Yes. Yes, I see.' He walked slowly to the window and looked down on Chichester Street. He said, 'March, I'm sorry.'

He heard her draw in a breath and hold it. 'Sorry? How do you mean?' She sounded tentative, almost hopeful.

He gestured around the room 'This,' he said vaguely. He turned and grimaced to hide the fact that for two pins he could have burst into tears like a soppy kid. 'It's been awful hasn't it, Marcie? Over seven years of it. Tied to that mean old swine in Bath. Putting up with Christ knows what in the hope of softening him up. And all for nothing.'

She frowned, puzzled rather than annoyed.

'Hardly for nothing, Fred. Surely that's why you're here?'

They stared at each other uncomprehendingly. Fred made one of his flat-handed gestures as if trying to wipe a slate clean. 'I'm here to ask you to marry me, Marcie.'

Colour came into her pale face. Her eyes burned at him. He saw her swallow before she said very carefully, 'Why didn't you come sooner, Fred? We've been home well over a week. You knew that. You saw me in town the other day with Albert.'

'Of course I knew. I wanted to give you time to unpack!' He couldn't meet her feverish eyes. 'Dammit all Marcie, I'm asking you to *marry* me! We've had to wait all this time, what does a week matter?'

'It might matter a great deal. A great deal.' He thought for a moment she was going to cry and he hoped she would. He could comfort her then, he could call on the new tenderness inside him. But she clenched her hands into fists at her side and went on, 'It would matter if during that week you had heard that my circumstances had changed.'

He saw his opening and blundered in. 'That's what I wanted to talk to you about, Marcie. When I heard the boys larking about this afternoon—'

'Larking?'

'In Mews Lane. Victor was teasing Albert about, well, about your changed circumstances – and it came to me quite suddenly that you and I have been wrong all along. Money doesn't matter. It really doesn't, Marcie—'

'Not a bit. Not when you've got enough.'

'Well . . . yes, all right then. And we have.'

'So you didn't come to ask for my hand when I returned from Bath because you thought Edwin had left me penniless.' March spoke very clearly and next door the boys fell silent. 'When you discovered that was not the case you couldn't wait to come over here and tell me that money doesn't matter. How touching.'

Fred said quietly, 'Drop your voice, Albert is listening.' He brushed past her and shut the door then faced her again angrily. 'Listen Marcie. I don't know what you got from Edwin and I don't care any more. He's dead, that's what counts. We can get married – legally. We've been married in the sight of God for—'

'Please don't keep bringing God into this, Fred. You don't know what you're talking about. Be honest and admit it's Edwin's money you're interested in, not me.'

'That's not true, Marcie. You might not believe me but I honestly thought you were penniless.'

'And you were sorry for me?'

There was no pleasing the woman. He did what he should have done in the beginning: took her by her upper arms and held her very hard while he kissed her. It was like kissing his mother's clothes-post. Yet he knew she wanted to respond; he could feel her holding back deliberately.

'What is it, Marcie? What's the matter?'

She closed her eyes in a gesture of surrender, then opened them quickly. 'I don't trust you, Fred. I can't trust you. Ever again.'

He shook her slightly. 'Trust me? Trust me to do what, Marcie? You know me and I know you. So we both know what we can trust and what we can't. That is enough. It has to be enough.'

He kissed her again and felt her tremble against him. Desire flamed in him and he forgot resolutions of tenderness, mutual forgiveness, and began frantically on the row of buttons that ran from the neck to waist seams at the back of her sloppy blouse. Just for a second he thought he had won; she gasped and fell against him and his hand slid expertly beneath her bust-bodice and reached under her arm. And then she tightened in a kind of instinctive reaction against his expertise. Her head jerked back and she stared wide-eyed into his face six inches from her own. Whether she saw ardour or just plain lust, he never knew, but she thrust against him hard and held him literally at arms' length, looking for something she obviously couldn't find.

At last, when he reached for her again, she shook her head.

'No Fred. I suppose that is what trust boils down to. Knowledge of someone. And I don't know you. Not any more.'

'Christamighty, March. You know enough. You know that we should be together. You knew that at Rodley. Then you pulled back – just like you're pulling back now.' He put his hand under her outstretched arms and cupped her breast. 'Come to me, March. Now. Like you did before in Chichester House stables. And at the George—'

She slapped his hand furiously. 'My name isn't Leonie Porterman, Fred! I don't come running every time you beckon!' She turned her back and went to the window. Her open blouse sagged between her prominent shoulder blades; she was much too thin. She made an obvious effort to control herself and said in a quiet voice, 'Leonie Porterman is the reason I don't trust you, Fred. Don't know you. That's why I'm not sure whether you asked me to marry you because you thought I was poor. Or very well off.'

He was shocked into a temporary silence. The passion which had sparked between them, died. After a while he said softly, 'When did you hear about Leonie?'

She sighed deeply. 'After Rodley. Why do you think I stayed in Bath? There was nothing for me here.'

'And there was something in Bath?'

'Edwin needed me. He was dying. You might not believe me but I'm glad I stayed with him to the end.'

'Especially as it appears you got what you wanted all along. His money.'

He could not seem to goad her. She lifted her shoulders and let them fall. 'He never changed his will as he told us he would. After Aunt Lizzie died he left me everything, just as she wanted. He never changed that.' She glanced at him quickly. 'That's why I'm glad I stayed. He did what she wanted. He saw that if he punished me for what I had done, he would also punish her. When I realized that, I also realized that he – *he* – could be trusted.'

There was another silence. He said, 'Who told you about Leonie Porterman?'

'Sibbie.'

He heard his breath whistle in his mouth and cleared his throat.

'What I've done . . . it's always been for you, Marcie.'

'What you've done, and what you've made me do too?' she asked bitterly. She rounded on him. 'Fred. I thought I needed you. Ever since Albert died I believed that. You told me it was true and I believed you. Now . . . now I don't need you—'

'You still want me. I could tell – just now—'

'That – that's disgusting! I don't want any of that ever again!'

He said steadily, 'I won't see Leonie. I won't touch a penny of your money. I'll never interfere between you and Albert-Frederick—'

'You certainly won't!' Her eyes were very wide and

clear. 'You can break two of those promises and I could bear it. But I cannot risk you breaking that one, Fred. Albert-Frederick is all I have. You must not come between us!'

'I have a right to see to his upbringing, March.'

She heard the threat in his voice and it was the final straw. He tried to retract. 'I didn't mean—' But she was already pushing past him to get to the door. He grabbed at her arm, but the time for physical persuasion had gone. She paused on the landing and reached behind her in a frantic effort to re-button her blouse; he made a move to help her and she left it, running down the stairs uncaringly just to get away from him.

He stood in the doorway for a moment feeling, for the first time, completely defeated by March's stubborn nature. Then he turned and went back to the window and tried to recapture his former sense of her courage and pathos. But the tenderness had gone and as he searched for it, consciously trying to force it back into being, he realized that next door the boys were quarrelling again. Someone fell on the floor with a bump, then Victor's voice said shrilly and without its accustomed humour: 'He only gave it to you because he wants to be your mother's new sweetheart!' There was another bump and Albert's reply, muffled, but still audible, came through the wall. 'She only wants me. She told me so. Uncle Fred always gives me presents at Christmas and birthdays. So sucks to you.'

The last of what Fred privately called his 'softness' went from him. Grimly, he was glad that when it came to serious matters Albert-Frederick did not allow Victor to get the upper hand. Even more grimly he planned his next move: he would pay a visit to Sibbie and give her the thrashing of her life.

And then he would console himself with Leonie Porterman.

Chapter Ten

A few days later, another proposal of marriage was made and turned down, though not so irrevocably as Fred's.

After the Zinoviev letters, Tollie's political interests had taken a severe bend to the left. He received certain instructions from the British Communist Party, all of which advised him to conform, to melt into his background, to support the present regime, and to wait for the Day. Tollie obeyed without difficulty, but when the next instruction came he had the strangest feeling of being hoist with his own petard. It was obvious the Party had been doing some investigating; this was disturbing but it was also a compliment because it meant they were taking him seriously. They had found out about Bridget; her father; her grandfather; her ambitions. They thought she was the perfect cover for their latest recruit and it turned out that by 'cover' they meant 'wife'. He must marry as soon as possible and produce a large family.

He had long resigned himself to the fact that one day he would marry Bridget, but that day never seemed to draw closer because for one thing Tollie was afraid Bridget might swallow him whole once she was married to him, and for another Bridget herself was having far too good a time to tie herself down to one man. The other problem was that she had oft stated that she had no intention whatever of producing 'brats'.

However, Tollie took the project seriously. He used the office telephone to ring Bridget and suggest a picnic after work. An hour later she was in King's Street, a large wicker basket of food on the dickey seat of her three-wheeled Morgan.

'Where shall we go?' she asked gaily. Her school, small, private and very exclusive, closed early for the summer, and three months stretched deliciously ahead of her. 'You demanded the picnic so you must choose!'

Tollie had never demanded anything in his life, but lately he had found it expedient to share Bridget's fantasy.

'Just drive up to the Cotswolds and let's see where we get to!' He climbed in beside her and kissed her cheek. 'You smell nice.'

'You smell of the office. I'm going to tell Daddy to give you some decent jobs. I don't see why you can't get out and about a bit now. You must know all the background.'

A few months ago he would have deprecated. Now he said, 'I'd like to specialize in the books actually, Bridie. Any chance d'you think?'

She flashed him a sideways glance, surprised and pleased. 'Of course. If that's what you want, that's what you'll get.' She sighed dramatically. 'You always do get what you want, Tollie Hall, don't you?'

Tollie thought wryly of the first time Bridget had seduced him. He had been fourteen to her sixteen.

Obediently he leaned across and began to nibble her ear lobe. She screamed and swerved the car around a vegetable cart, then took it very fast over a level crossing. They bumped madly. He knew better than to protest. He just laughed into her ear.

'You're incorrigible darling,' she panted, enjoying herself very much. 'Just wait till we find a quiet place, will you?'

He knew it was hopeless to talk about the book department of Williams' or even Bridget's school. He directed her carefully up Robinswood Road, through Painswick and past Bull's Cross towards Miserden. At a certain point they turned off into the ferny woods. She would have thrown herself on him immediately but he kissed her, held her off and suggested a walk.

'Darling . . .' She pouted at him. 'Couldn't we walk later?'

'No. Now. Come on. I know what I'm doing.'

She was surprised again, but not entirely averse to his new masterful manner. They wandered through the fern until they came to the lip of an enormous quarry. It was empty with a strange, cathedral beauty of its own. Tollie had come here with April and David Daker after a political meeting at Cheltenham and he had earmarked it for future solitude. It was the ideal spot for a proposal.

They sat down and surveyed it.

'It's a bit awesome, isn't it?' Bridget shivered. 'Hold me, Tollie, I'm frightened.'

Bridget had been frightened only twice in her life; once when March blackmailed her when she was eight years old, and a few weeks later when Teddy Rising had died and it had been her fault. But she knew full well when a really feminine girl should be frightened, which was almost the same thing.

Tollie held her tenderly.

'Marry me, Bridie, and I'll look after you,' he said.

She was unmoved. 'Well of course you will, darling. It will be marvellous.'

He drew away. 'Then you will?' He fumbled with one hand for the ring.

'Will what, Tollie?'

'Marry me. I just asked you to marry me, Bridie.'

'Oh darling, you are so funny. We've always known we would get married one day.'

'Not one day, Bridie. A definite day. Next month – isn't July a specially good month for weddings?'

'No. June, my sweet idiot. June brides. Surely you've heard of June brides? What's that you've got there darling – a ring! Tollie, you've bought a ring – you're serious!'

He slid it on her finger. 'When?'

She spread her hand admiringly; it was a single small diamond.

'A solitaire,' she said dramatically. 'It's beautiful, Tollie. How sweet of you darling. Not that I can wear it publicly of course. I'll put it on a chain around my neck.'

'What d'you mean? I want everyone to know we're engaged.'

'Don't be silly darling. You know married teachers are taboo.'

He did know and it had always been his safeguard.

263

He said stubbornly, 'Then you must leave teaching. If we're going to get married next month, Bridie, you can't keep it a secret.'

'Next month? Who said anything about next month?'

'You did. July, you said.'

'Don't be absurd darling, of course I didn't. We can't get married for ages yet. We haven't got any money – anywhere to live—'

'Bridie, we can't go on like this.'

'Why not? It's marvellous, Tollie.' She snuggled up to him, still holding her hand above their heads so that the sunlight caught the diamond chip.

'No Bridie!' He wrested her away. 'No more of that till we're married.'

'Don't be ridiculous darling. Why ever not? It's 1925!'

'It's still wrong.'

'No such word. Don't be cruel to your Bridie. Feel how my heart is hammering away—' She slid his hand beneath her blouse. He pulled it back as if he'd been stung.

'No, Bridie.'

But she was adamant and he had never stood against her. She fumbled in her bag, handed him a packet so that he could 'take precautions'. Tollie turned his back on her and did his own fumbling, and then had a brilliant idea.

'Ready, darling?'

He turned to find her naked among the fern. Shielding himself with one hand he crouched by her.

'Ready, Bridie,' he whispered.

After all, he had his orders. Everything was fair in love and war, and this was both.

Fred got no satisfaction at all from his punishment of his sister. He dared not risk bruising her too much in case repercussions from Edward Williams rebounded on him; anyway, her brazen frankness on being found out matched his own.

'I had to stop you somehow darling,' she said, nursing her arm where Fred had twisted it savagely behind her back. 'You'd have done the same if I'd got in your way.'

'How the hell you can see March and me as a stumbling-block to any of your plans—'

'Well, in the end it wasn't even that.' She slid the bodice of her dress off her shoulders and supported her arm above her head. 'It just wouldn't *do,* Fred. You and March. Oil and water. She's a prude and you're not. You *need* Leonie Porterman.'

He hit out at her head in frustrated rage. She swung with the punch and her shingled bob hung over her bare uplifted arm in an attitude of complete surrender.

He ground out, 'You know nothing about me – nothing!'

She looked at him through her hair and smiled. 'You're a man, aren't you?' She extended her arm. 'Kiss it better, Freddie. Kiss it better for Sib.'

He slapped the arm away. 'Save that rubbish for your old men.'

Her pale blue eyes were challenging. 'I wish you weren't my brother, Fred. I wish you were one of my men. It would be so . . . relaxing.'

'Relaxing?'

She laughed. 'You're such a wicked man, Fred. You'd make me feel innocent again. Dammit it, compared with you, I am innocent!'

He looked at her. Her petticoat was satin and strained across her breast provocatively; her mouth was open on her laugh and he could see the separate pearls of her teeth and the redness of her tongue. He understood her sexual attraction.

'You . . . you bitch!' And then he had to laugh with her, because, after all, they were two of a kind.

So he could not sublimate his anger and disappointment at March in thrashing Sibbie; there was still pleasure to be found with Leonie but she never failed to remind him of the hold she had over him. The gentleness that had seemed to be softening his life, had gone. He hardly knew what he wanted any more.

He heard of April's pregnancy from Will one night in the Lamb and Flag, and immediately his spirits lifted. He bought a whisky for Will and watched the ginger beard flip to the ceiling as he tossed it back. The old man plonked his glass on the bar and grinned like an excited schoolboy.

'I was delighted about Albert. And Victor of course. Florrie and I . . . we were both delighted. But this . . . little April . . . after all this time!' He leaned confidingly towards Fred. 'Kept a very soft spot for little April, I did. Jealous as a snake when she married Daker – well, you know I didn't care for him o'course. You know most things about us Risings, don't you Fred lad?' The grin developed into a laugh. Then Will sobered. 'I was glad at first . . . no babies . . . shrapnel in the groin y'know. Then. Well. She's like Florrie, a natural mother. Loves her nephews. It didn't seem right that she should be married to someone who couldn't . . . I mean . . . you know what I mean, Fred.'

'I know,' Fred agreed, grinning himself because he was the only one who did know. He and April. 'I'd like to see her. Congratulate her. And Daker, of course.'

'Why not?' Will spread his hands expansively. 'We'll go round now my boy. Take a bottle and wet the baby's head, eh? That the idea?'

'No.' Fred knew suddenly what he wanted to do. He wanted to see April alone. He wanted to reassure her. Be the big brother. He wanted to tell her that if she ever needed him, he would be there. 'No, we won't intrude, Will. I shall run into April some time. It's late.'

'Quite right. Consid'rate. Long evenings made me forget . . . prob'ly already in bed. Like we should be. Eh Fred? Eh?'

'That's right Will, that's right.'

But it wasn't that easy. April was surrounded by family and friends and rarely seen without David. Fred finally had to make his own opportunity.

One hot Sunday in July, Tollie called for April and David and drove them out to Barnwood to watch the tennis. Fred followed them at a discreet distance, paid his entry fee and lurked in the club house, peering out of the windows now and then to check on her presence. It was like an oven in the wooden, tin-roofed building. He sweated, tore off his tie, removed his hat and wiped his forehead and wondered what the hell he thought he was playing at.

At four o'clock tea was served and the ladies began to move discreetly to the wooden lavatories set well away from the courts. When April emerged, holding her hat and lifting her hair to catch a faint breeze, Fred was waiting for her.

'Fred! I didn't know you were here! Come and have some tea.'

She seemed genuinely pleased to see him, yet at the same time very anxious to get back to the others. He shook his head, smiling to put her at her ease.

'No tea thanks, April. I hoped we could talk for a few minutes. Alone.'

She swung her hat by the brim, fanning herself exaggeratedly. For the first time it struck him that he might not be welcome; that her practically sequestered state since her return from Bath might have been engineered to keep him at bay.

He said quickly, 'I want to talk, April. Just that.'

'Of course.' She glanced at David. He was sitting in a steamer chair, his bad leg supported, his head on one side as he listened to Tollie's political jargon. 'But won't they – everyone – think it rather odd if we stand here jawing on our own?'

'Walk down to the church with me then. The cars are parked there. You can tell David you needed some shade.' She still hesitated and he said, 'You owe me that much, April.' And then immediately wished he hadn't.

'Of course,' she said again. She fell into step by his side, still swinging her hat, and as her arm brushed the thin material of her summer frock the slight swelling of her abdomen showed for an instant. Fred had a crazy impulse to put his hand there, gently and tenderly to feel the outline of his child.

He said abruptly, 'I understand I can congratulate you.'

She looked at him and gave him a brief smile, then studied her white, low-heeled slippers again. 'You can congratulate both of us please, Fred. David and me.'

He drew a long breath and stood back while she took a narrow turn in the ancient footpath. Aspen leaves hung limply above them and the smell of warm foliage was heady. They came to a stile and she put her elbows on it and surveyed the old grey church beyond. She seemed hardly conscious of his presence, let alone his part in this baby.

He said deliberately, 'What about me? Aren't I to be congratulated too?'

She became very still. He looked at the back of her neck where the short hair curled into the nape and wanted to touch there too. He had hardly put his hands on this girl; he had been decent all the way through. Now he wished he hadn't.

She said quietly, 'Fred, we made a bargain. This is David's baby.'

'That remains to be seen, surely?' He heard the sharp edge on his voice and wondered what he was doing. He had come here to talk peacefully with April about the baby, to show his pleasure, to cement their trust and friendship. He was ruining everything.

She pushed herself off the stile and stood very straight.

'Is your car parked over there? We'd better say

goodbye now, David will wonder what has become of me.'

He flushed at such an obvious dismissal.

'I'm sorry, April. But what do you expect when you hide from me like you've been doing? I can't publicly announce anything, but I thought privately – between ourselves – we could acknowledge the fact that—'

'This is David's baby!' She lost her cool-cucumber dignity and turned to him, as flushed as he was. 'Can't you see that any sort of private conversation between us is out of the question! That had to be part of the bargain – I thought you realized that.'

'What happened to the brotherly feeling? You were my sister if you remember and I—'

'What we did couldn't have – have happened other-wise, Fred.' The flush made her beautiful. Luscious. Practically edible. Her eyes were violet, dark with huge pupils. 'But when we decided to do that, Fred, we stopped being brother and sister. Surely you see that?'

'What did we become? Lovers?'

There were tears in the eyes; tears of anger. She paused, then spoke cuttingly. 'You've done plenty of deals, Fred. Has love ever entered into them?' She saw the pain in his face and made a dismissing gesture with her hat. 'Oh Fred . . . listen. If you'd given me money for some reason, you wouldn't *mention* it again. Don't you see? A gift is just that. A gift. There is always gratitude, but it must be unspoken.

'I told you how I felt . . . then. That day. I can't speak of it again, ever.'

'Is that why you've been avoiding me?'

'Have I?' The tears came to nothing; she couldn't even be angry with him for long. She frowned, thinking about it. 'I don't think consciously I've avoided you. But obviously I haven't sought you out—'

'You never sought me out, April. I didn't seek you out either. But we met. Often. That day in Westgate Street when I nearly ran over you in the Morris . . . if that happened again . . . if you have another row with David and I see you, will you get in the car with me and let me drive you to the country?'

Momentarily the frown deepened, telling him his hypothesis was in bad taste. 'Of course not. That would be practically . . . a conspiracy.'

'Was it a conspiracy before?'

She blurted, exasperated, 'It . . . *happened,* Fred! Nothing was planned! But I . . . we have to forget it now. Can't you understand that?'

He said levelly, 'All I understand is that you're going to go on avoiding me. I had a sister – a friend. I'm not going to have her any more.' He thought, first March, now April.

She said nothing but she turned her face away from his slightly, unable to meet his eyes. He had a view of her profile, so much less austere than March's or Florence's, less fine than May's. A hand seemed to have gently brushed the nose and upper lip towards the wide forehead. She was imperfect in a perfect way.

He said, 'So this is goodbye then, April?'

She made a small negating gesture. 'Not quite so dramatic as that, Fred. Just—'

'I've got nothing to lose,' he went on as if she hadn't

spoken. 'I'll say goodbye the way I want to say it.'

He took her firmly by the shoulders and turned her to him and kissed her. In a way it was like kissing March. A clothes-post. In another way it was quite different. There was nothing in April that responded to him. Nothing at all. He let her go.

'Goodbye then,' he said, as if his kiss had been merely brotherly. He leapt the stile in a way that David never could and grinned at her over his shoulder. 'One thing, whether you want to or not, you can't very well forget me, can you?' He let his gaze slide to her abdomen, then he didn't look at her again. Damn all the Risings . . . at least the Rising women. He could do without them.

Tollie Hall and Bridget Williams were married in September of that year. Both families had been resigned to the match for some years and Edward Williams had always accepted Tollie, as he had the Lukers, as an extension of the Rising family. But Alice Williams thinned her mouth to an invisible line for the ceremony and made no effort to smile at anxious little Kitty, let alone the upright Bartholomew Hall, warder at Gloucester Prison.

April went back to the sumptuous house in Barnwood to help Bridget change into her going-away outfit, and felt that she too was saying goodbye to a way of life. It was doubtful whether she would ever enter this bedroom again where she and Bridget had talked and laughed and wept. Bridget had consoled herself after Teddy's death with his best friend, Tollie, but April had never realized Bridget felt enough for

Tollie to actually marry him. Yet here they were, married.

April sighed. 'It's a funny old life.'

'My God. You sound like your Aunty Sylv. What's funny about it? You try to make it fun, yes. But it always catches up on you in the end.'

April made a face at her friend. 'Wedding day talk?'

'I don't know, I've never been married before. Your wedding day was different, April. I've never seen anyone so happy. You were transported somehow.'

'Surely you're happy, Bridie?' April was suddenly anxious.

'I suppose so. I'm being sick all the time at the moment, so it's rather difficult to decide.'

'You're . . . Bridie, you don't mean—?'

'Of course I mean. You don't think I'd be getting married yet if I weren't pregnant, do you? I'm having a marvellous thing with Maurice Foster at the tennis club at the moment. He dances like an angel. I suppose in a month or two I won't be able to get around the floor. Oh well, never mind, you and I can get together and swap symptoms!'

April forced herself to kiss her friend and smile congratulations and only as they went downstairs did she say, 'What about Tollie?'

Bridget snapped, 'What about Tollie? He tricked me – I swear he arranged the whole thing so that I'd have to give up teaching and marry him.'

April hung back and watched as Bridget received admiration from the guests for her red dress with the dropped waistline and matching silk coat. Bridget knew, as well as April did, that Tollie Hall would never trick anyone. Besides, somehow April had always had the impression that Tollie was rather a reluctant suitor.

In November of that early winter, a new department was set up at Williams'. It dealt with rare second-hand books. It was run by the young Bartholomew Hall, who was something of a scholar and had a quiet yet confident bearing that was well suited to the impoverished gentry he mostly dealt with. The firm bought him a small car and he went to all the sales in the county. People liked and respected him. He had married Mr Edward's daughter and got her in the family way immediately, which was another feather in his cap. She had always been a bossy, wild sort of a girl; he would be good for her.

It was in November too, that March moved into her house. A house of her own, just as she had always wanted, just as Fred had promised her. And she had done it without Fred.

March had listened hard to the idle gossip that abounded between Gran, Aunt Sylv and Hettie once Flo had retired to her room. Hettie saw no reason to be ashamed of the way Fred used his liaison with Leonie Porterman to further his own ends. She hinted at Sibbie's comfortable position with a kind of defiance, but it was different for a man. She giggled unashamedly that Fred had to eat the icing before he could get to the cake. March heard and understood. Fred could have given up his scandalous association with Captain Porterman's wife and returned to number thirty-three with another proposal. He chose instead to continue the affair quite flagrantly. It was his way of showing March that not only did he not want her money, he did not want her either.

March hardly dared to admit to herself how hurt she was. She looked back over her life and saw that when she had given in to pain, she had usually leaned on Fred. And each time that had happened, he had let her down. When she had fought back and taken her fate in her own hands, she had found some kind of solution. She decided to fight back now.

The house was only twenty minutes' walk from Chichester Street. The three girls went to see it one grey afternoon with Florence on April's arm, each imagining she was helping the other. April wore an olive green hip-length jacket, very full, with a matching beret; she managed to look like a Parisian artist. March was severe in a tailored costume. May wore a tweed coat with a big fur collar. Florence knew how gaunt she looked and had pulled a veil over her cloche hat and under her chin.

They walked slowly up London Road to the top of the Pitch, down the other side to Barnwood Road, and there, just off to the right, was a quiet cul-de-sac of spacious houses with their own large gardens, called Bedford Close. March had seen the discreet For Sale sign back in the early autumn and had fretted and fumed for six weeks while the Bath house was sold and the estate settled up. Florence assured her that there were plenty of houses to be had that were just as nice, but March wanted that one. It was on the way to the Williams' place at Hucclecote and it had its own tennis court, yet it was close to Florence and Will. No other house would do. The Rising women walked around its big empty rooms on November the fifth, with a kind of awe.

'Albie could have one of the upstairs attics for his train set,' April discovered with delight, panting as she reached the second floor.

'This room is big enough for a grand piano,' May exclaimed, breathing deeply on the stale air in the sitting room, and admiring its french windows looking on to the garden, and its beautifully moulded cornice.

March said, 'I must get Jack down for a few days to sort out the tennis court. We can have tennis parties next summer, girls. Won't it be wonderful?'

May marvelled, 'The kitchen is so light. Of course the gasometer takes all our sunshine, but this one is particularly bright.'

'It reminds me of Chichester House,' Florence nodded.

It was the final seal of approval.

Even so, it was to Bridget's old-fashioned flat in Wellington Square that the young marrieds of Gloucester flocked that winter. Bridget armed her guests with paint pots and brushes and dared them to do their worst on her high walls and ceilings. Afterwards they would play charades until the small hours, even hide-and-seek in the railinged gardens in the square. A new and daring card game called strip poker was introduced, and the residents in Brunswick Road were shocked to see Maurice Foster running past their windows just before Christmas, dressed in just his shirt and combinations. Then, quite suddenly, Bridget lost her figure and her interest in parties.

April's baby was late. It was due on 23 December and she was still on her feet through Christmas and its aftermath.

'He wants to be a 1926 baby,' she said in reply to the many exclamations of 'Are you still about – you must be so fed *up*!'

Sure enough on the last day of December, at midday, her waters broke without warning. She was determined that her baby would be born without fuss, and kept going for an hour afterwards without calling down for David, but then she was forced to lie on the bed because her legs would no longer support her. There were plenty of old wives' tales about dry births, and she tried to dismiss them from her mind as her contractions became more grindingly painful. David called young Dr Green whose father had brought Teddy into the world, and he said she was 'nowhere near' and to call him the next morning. So Florence, frail as a cobweb, came to sit by the bedside and tell David not to worry.

As the hooters in the docks blared out for the New Year, April sweated and panted and twisted on the bed in the flat above the new Kings Square.

'Darling, hang on. Is it very awful?' David asked, looking in agony towards Florence.

'Yes,' gasped April. 'And I'm enjoying every minute of it. D'you hear? I'm having a baby! I'm having your baby, David! It's the most wonderful thing in the world!'

Florence took her hands and remembered her own

lonely births where the pain had not worried her so much as the indignity. And David gathered April to him and whispered, 'D'you think I care about that any more? It's you, April . . . you're the one. Just be all right!'

Grey dawn did not break until past seven on the first of January, and showed that there had been a fall of snow in the night. April asked her mother to go to the skylights in David's cutting-room and fetch her some. Florence brought it in a saucer and together they examined the transparent crystals just as they had when April was a small girl. Then another contraction dragged April into her own special no man's land and she clutched at her mother's hand so that the snow slipped onto the pillow. Both women ignored it but when the pain had passed, April rolled her forehead in its icy coldness and seemed to gain some relief.

David was busy with callers. Will came every hour, his expression accusing each time he glanced at David. Tollie was at Tewkesbury, but Bridget risked driving her Morgan over the icy roads to bring grapes and a bottle of gin. March left Albert with Aunty Sylv and came to sit anxiously by the bed, remembering only too well how it had been for her eight years ago. When she returned to Chichester Street, it was the turn of Gran and Sylv to trudge round under their black umbrellas. May arrived after Helene's had closed at six, expecting to greet her new nephew or niece, and was horrified to find April still 'nowhere near'.

'This is longer than I was!' she said to her father in the living-room as he tried to get a light from the gas fire for his pipe. 'Shouldn't the doctor be here by now, Daddy?'

'He's looked at her twice. Something's not dilated, whatever that means.' The pipe would not draw and he looked pathetically at his middle daughter. 'May, she's going to be all right isn't she? We were so close and this blasted husband of hers—'

'Dad, of *course* she's going to be all right! As for David – that's all water under the bridge!' May paced irritably, tired as usual these days. 'I suppose the doctor knows what he's doing?'

'His father saw your mother through Teddy. And that was the worst thing I've ever known.' Will stared gloomily at the gas radiants. He jerked his head at the bedroom. 'She's like your mother. Won't cry out.'

'Oh God. What can we *do*?'

Will sat up. 'Snotty Lottie. That's what we can do. She'll know if there's anything wrong.' He hustled to his feet, his pipe rolling unheeded to the floor. 'I'll go for her. She'll be in the Lamb and Flag. Bridget Williams brought some gin. Get it open for Lottie, our May. Have a sip yourself, you look done in.'

May screwed up her face and did as she was bid. She felt so much better that she had another glass with Lottie, then with her father. Unable to stand, she sprawled in one of the box-like chairs; she hadn't felt like this since she and Monty had lived it up in their lovely little house in Bushey Park. She looked at the empty glass on the wide arm of the chair and saw again Victor's fish bowl and the oval mirror and the thick, thick carpet. Tears came into her eyes.

David stood in front of her.

'She's going to be all right, May. Don't cry, please don't cry. Lottie says she's going to be all right.'

She couldn't stop crying. She wanted Monty; she wanted another baby and all the fuss and attention that went with it.

David said, 'Don't go out without something to keep out the cold. Have some of this gin . . .' She had some more and staggered down the fire escape more adroitly than she would have done sober. She realized that it was very late, everywhere was closed, even the public houses. She skidded grandly around the Cross and started down Northgate Street. There was a cat in the road and she called 'Rags?' and then remembered that Rags had died on Armistice night and wept more tears. The snow built up on her fur collar and melted against the warmth of her neck. She was so tired; always tired these days. The opening of Saint John's Lane loomed on her left and she wondered how she would ever reach the railway bridge and the turning into Chichester Street.

A voice called, 'May! Is that you, May?'

She turned, thankful for any diversion. A snowy figure hurried towards her from the Cross, at first looking so much like April that May gasped, then materializing, galoshed and hooded, as Sibbie Luker.

'May, what's happening? Your father has been with April most of the day and when I tried to enquire, March opened the door and told me to mind my own business!'

May drew herself up to her full height. 'And so you should, Sibbie Luker! April is our sister. Nothing to do with you.'

Sibbie drew back and her muffled figure seemed to harden, black against the snow. She barked a laugh. 'You know better than that, May! Rising business is my business!'

But May, belligerent with gin, was not embarrassed or cowed. 'David is married to April please remember, Sibbie. He wouldn't look at you now, believe me!'

'Perhaps I'm not talking about David Daker! Perhaps I dropped David Daker when you did, May! Yes, I think I did. I wanted a bigger share of your family. And I got it! What concerns Will Rising, concerns me, and don't you ever forget that again!'

May stood erect and magnificent for a few seconds longer while Sibbie's words seeped into her fuddled brain. Then she sagged, her beautiful neck sank between her shoulder blades, and the snowy collar met the snowy hat. In between, as out of a helmet, May's small face glared, pinched and disbelieving.

Sibbie glared back briefly, still rigid with the anger that May's unexpected attack had sparked; then common sense prevailed and she realized she had made a tactical error. Will would be deeply hurt and angered by what she had done. It might spoil . . . everything.

She drew nearer to May. 'Oh May, surely you don't begrudge me an interest in your family? You never used to. We shared everything, don't you remember? Your banana sandwiches and your darling mamma's umbrella and – and – I've always looked on your father as – as a kind of uncle—'

May took a step away and nearly slid over in the snow with her own uncertainty. Had she

misunderstood? That day Will had been in the teashop
. . . had he been meeting Sibbie?

Sibbie laughed sympathetically. 'Darling May.
D'you know, I do believe you're the slightest bit tiddly.
That's why you seem so strange, isn't it? You've been
drinking April's health, has she had the baby? What is
it? Is she all right?' Sibbie purposely raised her voice
to the one she had used as an excited schoolgirl; her
consonants disappearing as her accent slipped into
broad Gloucester.

May was partially reassured. 'Oh Sib . . . of course
I'm not tiddly! And April – poor little April – forty-
eight hours—'

'Well, you were a long time weren't you, May?
Gladys told me it was terrible for you. And among
strangers too. At least April's got her family with her.'

'That's true.' Incredibly May began to feel as she
had felt in the old days, with Sibbie like an echo by her
side. 'But of course, I had Monty . . .' She caught
herself up in case Sibbie should mention that
disgraceful – and hurtful – incident when she had
forced a kiss on poor Monty. Sibbie must not share
Monty in any way whatever. Monty was entirely
May's.

'Of course you did,' Sibbie said in her oddly
persuasive burr. 'I've never known a man so devoted
as your Monty.' She smiled, and in the lamplight her
teeth looked very white and pointed.

May said, 'I must go. Victor will be wondering . . .'

'Yes. I'll walk round with you, dearest May. Call in
on Mother.'

'There's no need . . .' But Sibbie had taken her arm

and was helping her along the high pavement beneath the railway bridge where the drips from the ballast above were forming long icicles already. It was surprising how easy it was to cover the distance with Sibbie's hand beneath her elbow. When they reached number thirty-three she hesitated, and Sibbie seized the moment to embrace her fondly as in the old days.

'Darling May.' Her hands, suddenly ungloved, slipped warmly under the icy fur collar and around May's damp neck. 'It's been so long, and I've missed you so much.'

May felt tears gather in her eyes again. 'Oh Sib . . . so long . . . we're getting old . . .'

'That doesn't matter. We shall get old together.' Frozen cheek touched frozen cheek and May put her arms around her old friend and held her close. In spite of Monty so far away, in spite of poor April in the throes of childbirth, in spite of *everything,* she felt comforted.

Young Dr Green said, 'I'm afraid it will be a forceps job. Lottie – you can boil them up for me if you will. Kindly wash your hands first.'

Lottie used her sleeve, her nose dripping freely as it always did in times of stress.

'No need for them things, doctor sir. The 'ead be crowned ben't it? Let me 'ave a go. C'mon now. No need to worry. If I can't do no good, you can tinker around as much as you like.'

The doctor remembered tales his father had told, and stood over the ancient crow-like woman while she washed her gnarled hands. There were so many cracks and crevices in the palms it was absurd to hope they could ever approach sterility, but at least a token show for the sake of his reputation . . .

Lottie left the soap on her hands and sat confidently on the end of the bed. 'Next time, little April. Next time. Just do your best and old Lottie 'ull do the rest.'

The voice came through faintly to April's consciousness and the rhyme reminded her of Teddy. It was as if he were here in the room with her, just as he had been so often when they were ill together. She tried to tell Florence and no words would come. It was infinitely reassuring when her mother leaned close and said quietly, 'I know, my darling. He's been with us all the time.'

She did not feel Lottie's expert hands, nor hear the grunts of satisfaction coming from the old woman as the bent fingers touched tiny temples, but she obeyed the command as best she could when the time came, and with the last atom of her strength she bore down. Lottie did not waste her time or the baby's strength by useless tugging. Young Dr Green watched, fascinated, as the fingers slid further and hooked beneath a minuscule armpit. And then he witnessed Lottie's famous twisting action come into its own. The baby corkscrewed and slithered on to its waiting rubber sheet; April groaned her trembling relief; Lottie wiped her nose and pushed the shoulder blades in one action; air pumped into new lungs and the baby cried.

Florence whispered, 'She's perfect, my darling. A perfect little girl. You've got a daughter, April.'

It was as if Teddy was laughing somewhere and April laughed with him.

'Davina,' she whispered to Teddy and her mother. 'David's daughter. Davina.'

Florence said, 'Of course, darling. Davina. Little Davie.'

And Teddy, who of course must know everything, went on laughing.

The next day, suffering badly from a hangover and the emotional business of welcoming a girl into the male ranks of the younger generation, May decided that her life could not continue as it had for the past year. Monty came to Gloucester once a month with chocolates for Florence and tobacco for Will and flowers for May herself. They were wonderful weekends, he spent enough money to keep them all for a week, and Victor was invariably sick on the Monday after a visit from his father. But May had been brought up in a household where man and wife lived and worked together. Even now, when her father was so often out on business, he was still there to deal with the daily round in a way that most men were not.

He got in the coal each morning and chopped Flo's liver for her lunch with just the right amount of onion to make it bearable. When she had been recovering from last year's influenza, he had carried her downstairs every day and back to bed every night. May was not to know that his tenderness towards his wife was in direct proportion to his physical feeling for Sibbie. Nevertheless a hint of threat stayed in her mind after her meeting with Sibbie on the first night of the New Year, and strengthened her determination to change her own way of life. She wrote to Monty who was in pantomime at Bognor and told him to find a flat suitable for the three of them. Victor was openly rebellious.

'I don't want to leave Gramp and Gramma!' he screamed at his mother. And he certainly did not want to leave Albert, so recently returned to him from Bath. But May was inclining to the view that Albert was a bad influence on her young son. March had complained several times that Victor was 'rude'; May knew of course that Albie, eighteen months older than Victor, was the real culprit. The boys saw far too much of each other, both back at Marley where discipline was lax, sleeping together until March moved out of Chichester Street then half the time insisting on exchange visits. They were babies, but they would grow up.

The reunion was doomed from the start. Monty was used now to having a companion who fed him his cues. In the old days May had fulfilled that role and others besides. He would have died for May and enjoyed watching himself do it. But then Victor had been born, and Monty had gradually realized that his son was superseding him in May's order of priority. When Sibbie had held him closely, he had felt again the warmth that appreciation always gave him. He had repaid her – albeit guiltily – the way she obviously wanted, and though he had not been able to face her again, the warmth lingered. He needed more of it.

Maud Davenport supplied it.

She did not require a companion in bed; she required what she had had from him before May appeared on the scene. He ranked alongside her at rehearsals; if there was any altercation Monty was automatically on Maud's side; he chaperoned her everywhere. In return he was treated like a favourite son. His tie was tied for him, he had a cup of tea in bed every morning, baths were run and towels were heated.

She was inconsolable when he landed a tiny part in the panto at Bognor. He felt the same. But the dame of the panto was an elderly clown called Desmond Oakfield. Monty had diggings with him and two other unattached men. But Desmond favoured Monty.

'My guess is, my dear – ' he used a lorgnette to emphasize his words ' – you have sung in opera. Am I right? Just don't tell me I'm wrong.'

Monty smiled charmingly and admitted it.

'I knew it. When you sang that chorus with me, I could hear it. There's training there. Don't tell me I'm wrong.'

Monty had never had formal training; he made deprecating sounds. Desmond tapped him lightly with his lorgnette.

'Mock modest. You need someone to blow your trumpet for you, dear boy. May I volunteer?'

'Too kind, Mr Oakfield,' Monty murmured.

'Desmond. The name is Desmond.'

May interrupted this partnership brutally. She arrived at the theatrical lodging after curtain-up. She was tired, Victor was tired, they were both homesick. She was used to theatre landladies and when she rang the bell she arranged herself suitably, her bag on one side, her good-looking son on the other. When Mrs Townsend opened the door she saw a frail, rather

Edwardian beauty, golden hair escaping in tendrils from her hat; she recognized her instantly as a Wronged Wife.

May held out her hands. 'Mrs Townsend! I would know you anywhere from my husband's letters! I want to thank you for looking after him for me while I was detained – at my parents' home.'

Mrs Townsend was overcome at being part of this drama. Obviously this beautiful lady knew nothing of Desmond. She did not suspect she was a wronged wife. Mrs Townsend ushered her into the front room which doubled as sitting and dining-room for 'the theatricals'. A fire was burning and a kettle was on the trivet for them to make their own cocoa, the usual late supper was laid on a cardboard-stiff cloth. Mrs Townsend gestured widely and said she would get Townsend to take the cases up. Then she whisked herself away to sort out the sleeping arrangements. Both Desmond and Mr Gould had double-bedded rooms and had been tactful enough to rumple the bedding each morning. She flung back the sheets and investigated thoroughly, then breathed a sigh of relief. Maybe she had been wrong.

Wrong or right, May was having none of it. The next day was Sunday and she had Monty and Victor out of the diggings ten minutes after breakfast. There had been no joyful meeting the night before; May and Victor had already retired when Monty and his fellow actors returned, and they announced their arrival only by a note propped against the cheese dish. They were firmly asleep in the middle of the feather bed and Monty had had great difficulty in squeezing himself

288

alongside Victor. The temptation to tiptoe along the landing to Desmond's room was almost over-whelming. The atmosphere at breakfast was completely artificial. May would have liked to fire a great many questions, but she had discovered before that it was very difficult to carry on any acrimony in the company of actors.

Desmond made a great fuss of Victor, keeping him on his knee while May fitted his coat over his shoulders and calling him 'my pretty' and 'baby bird' in a way May found revolting but which Victor exploited to the full. He showed May half a sovereign as they walked along the promenade looking for house-agents that might be open on Sundays. 'He'll give me another one if we go back to tea, Mummy,' he said. 'I don't want you to have anything to do with that man!' May snapped, cold and hungry after her sketchy breakfast. 'He's not a nice man at all!' And Monty, not knowing whether to be pleased or sorry at the sudden arrival of his family, said uncomfort-ably, 'He's not bad, May. Heart of gold.'

She did the best she could, but she hated every moment of her first month in Bognor and wondered why on earth she'd come. Monty tried to 'keep in' as he put it, with Desmond Oakfield, which meant that they did in fact see plenty of him and his lorgnette and his half-sovereigns. The only decent school for Victor would not take him until his seventh birthday, which was not until July. May could have enjoyed herself with Victor on his own; she could have striven for a renewal of her old relationship with Monty on his own, but as a threesome they no longer jelled.

After a particularly wet day in February, the sheer ennui of their situation came to a head. In front of Victor the bickering crescendoed into something more.

'What exactly do you want from me, May?' Monty said with more weariness than anger. 'I've begged your forgiveness over and over again for losing the Bushey Park house. But you're determined to punish me for the rest of my life—'

May was aghast. 'That's not true, Monty! Surely you haven't felt that all this time? Oh my dear . . . ' She turned swiftly to Victor. 'Darling, please go to bed now. Daddy and I have to talk.'

Monty, with a parental attitude far ahead of his time, put out a restraining hand. 'Let him stay. We're together in this problem. He might as well know what is happening and why.'

'He doesn't understand, Monty!'

Victor said, 'I do. Mummy and me want to live in Gloucester and Daddy doesn't.'

His parents were temporarily silenced. They had not realized themselves how simple the problem was.

Victor said, 'We could live with Grandma and you could come at weekends. Like before.'

Monty glanced at May. 'We ought to be together more than that, Victor. That's why your mother brought you down here last month.'

May said, 'Well . . . we are a *family*. That's how families live. Together.'

'We don't have to be a replica of your family, May.'

'I know . . . I know.' May wandered to the window and looked out helplessly. The lamp lighter was doing his round; it was nearly time for Monty to go to the theatre.

She said, 'I think I'm fed up with you being an actor, Monty. It's too uncertain. When you've got a job, the money is marvellous but we spend it as we get it, then when there's no job we have to rely on Mother and Dad—'

'I know.' Monty came behind her and touched the nape of her neck. 'I hate that too. But what's to be done?'

'You could give it up surely? Fred would get you a job in Gloucester and we could rent a little house—'

Monty laughed. 'Oh May. Can you imagine it? Digging coal with Jack and Austen? Or even helping Gladys with the books nine till six and a half-day on Saturday—'

Victor said with innocent acumen, 'Daddy couldn't act that part!'

Monty picked him up and sat him on his shoulders; it was a rare union between them. May, looking at them laughing together, felt suddenly isolated. And from that feeling was born an absolute determination to woo Monty away from the theatre and into a permanent home in Gloucester. She went to them and circled them with her arms. It wouldn't be so bad. She would work on it slowly, going home with Victor for long periods, joining Monty when she thought it . . . necessary. Something had gone out of their marriage, but she could put it back. She was certain of that.

Tollie was pleased, and not really surprised, at the way the birth of his first child paralleled the political situation. The first day Bridget felt movement inside her, the government withdrew their subsidies to the coal industry. Tollie watched, fascinated, as his wife swelled in time with the escalating problem. As the mine-owners one by one declared that reduced demand required lower wages for the workers, so Bridget grew rapidly like an inflating balloon. Maurice Foster stopped calling and at the same time Mr MacDonald warned that if the miners came out on strike so would the railways and the engineers. As Mr Baldwin assured the country that no-one would starve, Bridget went into labour. And when the news came through on their cumbersome crystal wireless set that the fields in Durham and Wales were no longer working, and that – as the Lord Mayor gloomily put it to Councillor Edwards – 'the balloon has gone up', so Bridget's balloon also went up and she produced a baby daughter.

She was on her feet, or rather on her *chaise longue* in time for Tollie to join the ranks of the 'plus-four boys' who were to break the national strike with which he so ardently and so secretly sympathized. In a week it was all over and would have been without Tollie driving the tram from Longford to Worcester Street, but he took on himself some of the blame for its failure. He remembered the successful 'putsch' in Berlin six years before, and cursed the jolly phlegm of the English.

Four weeks later when only the miners hung grimly on to their principles, Bridget asked querulously, 'Darling, what are we going to call it?' She measured her waist with her hands and wondered how soon her milk would dry up and her breasts return to their normal size. 'What about Marianne? Or Jacquetta?'

Tollie walked over to the new perambulator being rocked proudly by his mother, and looked into it. He had remained curiously detached from this child of his; she had been a means to the end of obeying his instructions from the Party and that was all. He had been pleased when her carrying had meant there were no more calls from Maurice Foster and no more all-night parties in the flat, but he had had little interest in Bridget's symptoms. Now, reflected in Kitty's face, he saw the protective love and tenderness which had umbrellaed him all his life and had been extended to Teddy Rising and Teddy's mother and all the Risings. He remembered the enormous influence this love brought with it, and he looked at the tiny, bonneted occupant of the baby carriage with sudden interest. Could such a love influence this child as it had influenced him? Was this where his teaching could begin?

He said, 'Let's call her something real, Bridie. None of your fancy modern names mean much.'

'Oh God.' Bridget looked bored to death. 'Is it to be Martha or Mary?'

'No. No, let's call her Olga.'

The harsh unusualness of the name pleased Bridget. She considered it, her lower lip thrust provocatively forward. There was no way she could match the charm of Davina. But Olga had a distinction of its own.

'Olga Hall,' she murmured experimentally. 'Olga Hall.'

Kitty clinched it. 'It's such an ugly name. I've never heard it before.'

'I like it,' said Bridget. 'Olga she shall be.'

April came home from her first visit to the tiny Olga Hall. She was amused at the baby's amazing likeness to Tollie.

'The same quiet brown-ness – d'you know what I mean David?'

David grinned. 'Exactly.'

'There's nothing of Bridie about her at all. Tollie has always been so self-effacing.'

'Don't let him fool you, April. Underneath that quiet, subdued exterior is a banked fire.'

'Oh David. I grew up with Tollie Hall, remember.'

'Nevertheless . . . How did Bridie seem? As unbearable as ever?'

April smiled. 'You never liked her, did you?'

'Not very much. She tried to be so damned overbearing, but if it hadn't been for the Risings she'd have been invisible.'

'Oh David,' April repeated, laughing helplessly. She stood up and smoothed her thin voile dress. She was as slim as ever, her hip bones showed through the thin material.

'I must go and feed Davie. Then I'm going to bed. This hot weather makes me so tired.'

David frowned his concern. 'Don't you think you should put Davie on a bottle now, Primrose? It's a bit much for you surely?'

She dropped an apologetic kiss on to the top of his head. His hair was getting sparse and unexpectedly she felt tears of tenderness clog her throat.

'I just love doing it darling. But I expect you're right. I'll talk to Dr Green.'

She trailed into the bedroom, stepping out of her shoes and unbuttoning her dress as she went. She loved the summer, she always had. It must be the breast-feeding that was making her feel like a piece of chewed string.

She leaned over Davina's crib. The child was beginning to stir, her innate rhythm telling her it was time for her ten o'clock feed. She had been a model baby, placid and content, with none of David's restlessness. April stared at her, seeing again the baby's complete dissimilarity from David. Many babies had fair hair and blue eyes, but it was now obvious that this baby was not going to change. And David was not like Tollie Hall, he was a strong, dominant character who surely should have stamped some of his characteristics on his child.

Davina stretched delightfully and opened her eyes at her mother. She clenched her fists and gurgled recognition. It was such a recent accomplishment that April momentarily forgot her sadness and laughed as she picked her up and settled them both on the bed.

'Mamma's been to see Olga Hall,' she said as the baby sucked busily. 'She'll probably be your best friend later on. You'll be a bit older than her but that won't matter. Her mummy was two years older than me and it didn't make any difference.' She felt the tears collecting again and cleared her throat angrily. 'And her daddy is the same age as your Uncle Teddy. But you'll never know Uncle Teddy.' Suddenly she bowed over the tiny blonde head and sobs racked her body.

David came in like a whirlwind.

'What is it? What is it, my darling girl?'

But she couldn't tell him. She couldn't tell herself. She had to pretend it was the heat. Or the breast-feeding. Or remembering Teddy. That was what it must be, after all. That was what it had to be.

David took the baby and changed her nappy expertly. As usual she burped obediently and curled on to her side preparatory to sleeping the night almost through. David came back to April and put out a hand to stop her buttoning her dress. He knelt on the bedroom floor between her knees and put his head between her breasts.

She stroked his hair lightly. 'David. Darling. I'm all right now you know. It was just . . . the heat.'

He slid his hands around her waist and massaged the base of her spine. 'We'll buy a bottle tomorrow, darling. Don't worry about it. Relax.'

She took a breath and held it while his thumbs moved into her groin. 'David . . . please. Not while I'm still . . . David, no.'

'Yes, Primrose.' He moved his mouth over her breast and into her neck. 'We've been apart too long. Much too long. No more feeding, no more worrying.' Expertly he straightened his wrists, pulling her dress and knickers over her buttocks. She was filled with panic and fell back on the bed, digging her elbows into the counterpane and dragging herself away from him.

'David . . . David, I'm frightened!'

'I know.' He spoke calmly but he followed her on to the bed and began caressing her naked body insistently. 'I know, my darling. It's strange, isn't it? I was the one who used to be frightened. And your love – your physical need for me – forced me to hide that fear. To pretend. To simulate. Oh April...' He moved his hand behind her shoulder blade and held her to him while he kissed her. The combination of tenderness and adoration was too much for her. Tears poured down her face.

Still he would not release her.

'Listen, darling.' He ignored her weeping and put his mouth to her ear. 'Listen. I'm not frightened any more. Because of Davie. Surely you can understand that? I can admit to you now that if I try to make love to you, I might – I probably shall – fail. It doesn't worry me any more, April. I want to go on trying. Surely you won't let your fear come between us, April?'

'You don't understand – you don't – ' She tried to stop her blubbering in case it disturbed Davina.

He said, 'Is it because the last time – when Davie was conceived – I took you in anger? Is that it, April?'

'No. Oh no David.' She clung to him suddenly, burying her wet face in his neck and kissing him frantically. 'Never think that. I knew – even then – I knew it was love. Darling, I can't explain.'

'You think that because I succeeded last time and made a baby inside you, it will hurt me all over again if next time I fail.'

'I suppose so,' she agreed miserably. She did not let herself remember Davina's actual conception, but contrarily, the absolute sterility of the experience was with her still. In her agony of conscience in Marsh

Cottage, she had hardly been conscious that Davie had been made without love; now the sheer irony of it seemed to freeze her soul.

He lifted her chin from beneath his and kissed her gently. 'It won't,' he whispered. Then he kissed her again. And then again. Gradually she responded, unfolding for him in a kind of half-remembered dream. And this time he did not fail.

Much later he murmured, 'Darling. It's so soon. Perhaps I was selfish. If you're pregnant again, your health . . .'

She rolled over and kissed him. 'Don't worry, David. You're quite right. It's much too soon. I couldn't possibly get pregnant when I'm still breast-feeding. It doesn't happen.'

He chuckled sleepily. 'You've been reading your books again, Primrose.'

She almost contradicted him, then let her head nod on his shoulder. He roused himself when she was silent and leaned on an elbow to look at her.

'There will be other times, darling. I'm not saying it will be all right always, but there will be other times.' He grinned at the silent crib. 'Davina is living proof of that.'

She met his eyes and forced herself to hold his gaze.

'D'you remember when she was being born, David? You said all that mattered to you was . . . me.'

'You know I meant it, darling. Do you doubt it now?'

'No. No. But it's how I feel. You are everything to me, David. Even now – even now that Davie is actually here – you are *everything*. I don't want more children. I don't want another baby, David.'

He stared down at her, his black eyes searching her face for a clue to the enigma he thought he had always known. There was no clue save for a desperate intensity to be believed.

He smoothed her hair and cupped her face protectively.

'Don't think ahead, April. Just let us be thankful we have each other. And Davie.'

She held his hand where it was and turned her face to kiss the palm. They held each other and eventually slept.

April was not in the least surprised to find a few weeks later that she was not pregnant. It seemed to her that love and the conception of children had very little to do with each other.

Chapter Eleven

Davina Daker was four years old. It had snowed
during the night and snow nearly drove her mad with
the sort of suppressed pleasure that in other people
erupted as excitement. Davina's excitement made her
grin from ear to ear incessantly, so that her cheeks
looked ready to burst. Her father called her his 'little
apple' and she did indeed have the rounded goodness
of that fruit.

Her grandparents were giving her a party, and at
her own request they were walking the long way
round to Chichester Street. Everything looked so
much nicer with its covering of snow. The dustbins in
the alley behind the Hippodrome were fat white mushrooms, and the trees in the cattle market were lacy
against the black of the auctioneer's shed. David lifted
her onto the wall to walk along its length and make
footprints in the fresh snow there, and April ran ahead
over Northgate Street and threw snowballs at them,
missing each time to make them laugh. Davina knew
she was the happiest person in the world because it
was simply impossible for anyone to contain any more
happiness than was inside her. She couldn't even call
out when they were beneath the railway bridge; she
stood stock still and listened while her parents did it
for her and the echo bounced back from the icicled

roof. 'Dav . . . eeena! Dav . . . eeena!' There were a few other people about and they looked and smiled at her.

They went straight into Will's workroom as arranged. Will lifted Davina onto the cutting-table and Florence began to unbutton her leather gaiters with the button-hook. 'Your fairy dress is ready,' she said conspiratorially. 'Shall Mummy and Daddy have a cup of tea while we dress you?'

'Yes,' said Davina, shining-eyed.

Florence slid her feet into her black dancing shoes with the elastic that criss-crossed up her legs over her white socks. Then she began to fix a crêpe paper tutu around the tiny waist. In the corner the wings waited, fashioned on thin wire.

Will was in his element, once again head of a big family, surrounded by eager children. He insisted on fixing Davie's crown and bowing low to her. He glanced at Flo to exchange proud smiles. Flo was like a girl again, as arrow-thin and aristocratic as when he had first set eyes on her at Kempley churchyard back in the eighties. He did not see that her dark hair was iron-grey and her back bent; happiness had given Will rose-coloured spectacles.

He said, 'How's that then, Davie?'

Davina nodded her head experimentally and the crown did not fall off. 'It's luvverly,' she breathed.

'And so are you,' Florence said. Will nodded. This child had none of the Daker darkness in her, body or soul; she was all Rising, just as April had been at her age.

'We're lucky,' he said, reaching for Florence's hand. She smiled. 'Haven't I always told you that?'

David sat at the kitchen table and drew the early edition of the *Citizen* towards him. He had not really known the Risings until their move to Chichester House, and this kitchen had no memories for him. He held the paper up and watched April over the top of it. She moved around preparing the tea with a mature grace that he was now accustomed to, but which struck him anew in these different surroundings. He tried to date the change in her from girl to woman.

'Four years,' he murmured. 'Four years ago.'

She lit the gas and turned to smile at him, the match still in her hand. 'It seems incredible, doesn't it? I can hardly remember a time when we didn't have her. What did we use to *do* all day, David?'

'You'll burn your fingers.' She blew out the match and threw it on the range. He grinned. 'I'm glad you're not entirely sensible!'

She looked at him in astonishment 'Sensible? You've never called me that, darling. I don't think I like it. It sounds very dull.'

'You're never dull, Primrose. But you have changed. You are different. I can't put my finger on it.'

She reached cups and saucers from the dresser, turning down her mouth humorously. 'You're trying to tell me I'm getting old.' She shook her head. 'One minute I'm a child-bride, the next an ancient wife.'

He rustled the *Citizen* dismissively. 'Stop fishing for compliments, Primrose. Whatever age you are, I am going to be eleven years older. Always.'

'Poor old man.' She poured tea and placed his cup squarely on the page in front of him. He sighed.

'That *is* childish.'

'You weren't reading. You were watching me.'

'Admiringly.'

'No. Like you watch some of your students. Objectively. Clinically. It makes them squirm.'

'It didn't make you squirm.'

'No.' She met his eyes above her teacup and saw there everything she had ever wanted to see in David's face. No more secrets. No more demons. Davie had done that.

She said breathlessly, unable to sustain the moment, 'If I've changed, what about you? University tutorials in Cheltenham, Gloucester and Bristol – now *that's* what I call sensible!'

He recognized her mood. It happened often; it had been happening – as he said – for four years. He laughed and reached reassuringly for her hand. 'You call it sensible, I call it education, Tollie calls it politics and my mother calls it getting above my station.'

She laughed too, then suddenly lifted his knuckles to her lips. 'Oh David . . . I knew it always. You're a very clever man.'

'Not clever. No. Otherwise we would be wealthy and I would understand you.'

She chose to ignore the last half of his remark and held his hand to her cheek consideringly.

'You know a lot. You read everything in the news-papers and you listen to the wireless, then you sort of stand back and fit everything together like a jigsaw puzzle. And when it doesn't fit you know it is wrong. Somehow.'

'It's called forming an opinion. Everyone does it. You do it.'

'No. Not in the same way. I feel things are wrong or right. And often I don't feel . . . correctly.'

He watched her again and she thought she might squirm at any minute. Then he said abruptly, 'And what do you feel about us, Primrose? You and me?'

'I feel we are the luckiest people in the world. We are indivisible.'

There was a long pause. Then he released his hand and put it flat on the newspaper in front of him. She frowned.

'David, what is it? Don't *you* feel we are indivisible?'

'Of course.' He smiled. 'I'd like to lock the door and make love to you in front of that range.'

'Oh David. It's Davie's birthday party.'

'Four years ago you couldn't have spoken those words . . . we are indivisible. You would have come round this table and kissed me. That's what I meant when I said you had changed.'

She laughed, stood up and went round the table. She made the kiss long and lingering but then she straightened with a businesslike sigh.

'I'd better go upstairs darling. Really. We'll be together tonight.'

'Yes.' He touched her fingertips with his mouth. 'Yes. We're together every night, Primrose.'

He watched her go through the kitchen door, then return to blow him a kiss. 'Don't stay too long reading. Davie will expect you.'

He nodded and turned back to the paper to skim the headlines about the young Prince of Wales, who seemed set to follow his illustrious grandfather's example as far as ladies were concerned. David sighed and reached for his recently acquired spectacles in order to scan the small print. He was confronted by a list of wills and bequests which reminded him obscurely of something April had said a long time ago. Davina had been given to them by God. He frowned . . . a trite belief doubtless shared by every mother. But April was wont to make bargains with God on a strangely personal basis. He remembered her before the high altar in the cathedral that ghastly evening in 1925; he remembered her calm certainty and assurance. Had she in fact fretted and prayed herself into a conviction that if she were pregnant, it was a special, never-to-be-repeated dispensation?

David gnawed his lip and shoved his glasses higher up his nose. It was hard to pinpoint the change in his beautiful wife. There was a barrier – a flimsy veil of a barrier – between them. She had been an impulsive girl; now she was a mature woman. Just as loving, just as responsive. But . . . He drew in a breath and straightened his shoulders. The impulsive young girl had so often seduced her older husband. He remembered her skipping around the flat in french knickers and nothing else, deliberately provoking him. She no longer did that. Of course there was Davie to consider. But she no longer seduced him; he seduced her.

His eye was taken by the last will and testament of Alderman Charles Williams. He saw that Sibbie shared a large slice of his inheritance with Edward Williams. Sibbie was wealthy in her own right. He smiled grimly and wondered what she would do with her money. He hoped she wouldn't succeed in buying

Will Rising at last. It would hurt April unbearably.

Upstairs, April stood inside the door of the bandy room for a few minutes, surveying her family and friends with smiling affection. She was unconscious of any barrier, however flimsy, between herself and David; the instinctive survival element in her subconscious had successfully shifted any barrier there might have been away from the small, secure Daker trio, and firmly entrenched it around Fred Luker. It had been the only solution to an impossible situation for April. She no longer had a brother; David, Davina and April were one unit, Fred was an outsider. Every time she looked at Davie and saw the Luker element in her, so she turned her back more firmly on Fred. She had no idea that this attitude had altered her feeling for David, unless it had deepened and strengthened her love still more. She was unable to look at her problems objectively and fit the pieces together 'like a jigsaw puzzle'. She felt her way intuitively.

Fred could not be completely ignored or forgotten; apart from his physical presence in her life and the local gossip about him which was rife, he had . . . perhaps . . . saved her marriage. So although he was thrust as far away as possible, he was a constant reminder of . . . betrayal. The woman who had lain with Fred Luker could not be quite the same with the man she loved, the man she had betrayed. She could respond to his ardour as she had always done, but she could not initiate it.

But as she stood there watching the inmates of the bandy room, she knew nothing of this. She fiddled in her handbag, got out her cigarettes and holder and began to smoke as usual. Davie was still downstairs being dressed by her adoring grandparents; the rest of April's world was here, secure, at least for the moment.

There was May, on one of her frequent visits home, sitting between the brass candlesticks of the piano, letting her hands stray over the yellow keys in an improvisation of her own. May had been involved in long-drawn out negotiations with Bridget and Tollie over the past few months in an effort to get Monty a job at Williams'. Looking at her now, April could see her sister's yearning to be home for good; to give up following Monty around the country and settling Victor into new schools. May was beginning to look ... not old ... matronly ... her hair a more silvery blond. She must be thirty-six this year. April felt a small qualm at the passing of time. David was almost forty.

March, on the other hand, was thinner, with none of May's soft outlines. Her hair was still chestnut dark and very glossy, her movements quick and precise. Her eyes went constantly to Albert-Frederick, kneeling on the sofa with Victor, looking out of the snowy window towards the cathedral spires. Her glances were not overtly affectionate, she seemed to be checking up on him. It was as if she could overhear their murmured conversation, though had she done so she would not have been merely watching.

April kissed her two sisters and grinned at the boys. Victor was saying quietly, 'She used to be my mummy's best friend and now she's a kept woman ...' Albie coloured as he met April's eyes, and Victor stopped his words with a hand over his mouth. April put an arm around each shoulder and said softly, 'If it's one of your naughty jokes you'd better keep it to yourselves.'

She went on to greet Bridget, pregnant for the third time, overweight and a little blowsy. Olga and Natasha sat on the floor at her feet, fighting over their dolls. Bridget was full of complaints as usual, looking strangely complacent at the same time.

'It's heartburn time, my dear. Did you suffer that way?'

'I think so. I can't remember really.'

'No. It's a long time for you darling, isn't it? Tollie says pregnancy suits me but of course he doesn't have to put up with it, does he? I hate him sometimes.'

'Bridie. You know you love being pregnant and you love dear Tollie.'

'Dear Tollie indeed. Bossy Tollie perhaps.'

'Bossy? Tollie?'

'You don't know him, April. He's very masterful.' Bridget's eyes sparkled and April chuckled and shook her head at her friend.

'You don't change, Bridie,' she said almost scoldingly.

She smiled across at Aunt Sylv, pouring lemonade into an assortment of glasses on the card table. Gran, nearing eighty, had chosen to take to her bed for the afternoon. The children would visit her in turn later, and she would receive them as Queen Victoria had received her grandchildren, with a kind of gracious disapproval.

The door opened and Will appeared, signalling to May. She began to play a triumphal march and in came Davina, angelic in white crêpe paper and tinsel. Davina's grin looked nearly painful, her fringe stuck out from her silver crown and she shouldered her wand like a soldier's rifle. Everyone clapped. Bridget snatched up Natasha and said, 'Look baby, look at the fairy queen.' And Olga said enviously, 'It's only Davie Daker.' Victor, enthralled and uninhibited, yelled, 'Three cheers for the Risings!' And May, proud of her handsome son who always said the right thing at the right time, laughed delightedly and called out, 'Take the fairy queen for the first dance then, Victor dear – the polka!'

April took Davina's wand from her and watched smilingly as Victor led her out with much aplomb. Then Albert was before her, bowing low. 'Aunty April, will you dance with me?'

Will and Flo passed them, dancing with exquisite ease. Will had tried to do the one-step with Sibbie to the music of her gramophone but nobody suited him like Flo. She was as light as a feather, quite literally. He glanced down at her, frowning slightly. It didn't mean anything of course, she'd always been light and after Sibbie who had plenty of flesh on her, she was bound to seem frail. But Flo . . . Flo who had been to death's door once in their lives together and had returned to him . . . if anything happened to Flo, he couldn't live on. He was quite certain of that. He could not bear to lose Flo. Nor Sibbie. He could not bear it.

Albert studied April's mouth, just level with his eyes. He wondered if he was going to swoon.

'I've been eating parsley,' he said abruptly to her throat.

She laughed. 'So. You didn't forget my words of wisdom! Now why would you be eating parsley? Is it bloater paste again?'

He was so pleased she remembered, he almost swooned again.

'I've started smoking. Properly. I've got a holder like yours and I can blow rings like you do.'

'Wicked child. If your mother finds out—'

'I do it in the attic. When I'm fixing my train set. Nobody comes up there, it's strictly private.'

Aunty April laughed again, flinging back her head like Grandpa did, exposing the white column of her throat where it plunged down into the neckline of her woollen dress. Albie felt the sweat cold under his arms.

The door opened and Uncle David appeared. Surprisingly, behind him came Fred Luker. Albert opened his eyes wide and looked for Victor to test his reaction. It was a long time since Fred Luker had been Uncle Fred to the boys; Victor referred to his wealth as 'ill-gotten gains' and told Albie lurid stories about his private life. Only Grandpa still called him Fred and went with him to the Lamb and Flag and laughed indulgently when Albert's mother pulled her disapproving face.

Aunty April's hand tightened suddenly and Albert forgot the intriguing arrival of Fred.

He blurted, 'I love you, Aunty April!'

'Do you darling? How marvellous. I say, can we sit down a minute?'

They sat down almost behind the piano. It was as if she wanted to be alone with him and Albie felt his heart flutter with a kind of panic. She was so beautiful; her legs so long, the swellings beneath her woollen jumper-thing so perfectly proportioned. He still dreamed of seeing her without clothes.

He said passionately, 'I'd do anything for you, Aunty April. Anything in the world.'

She looked at him properly and her dark blue eyes smiled warmly. She picked up his hand and sand-wiched it between her own.

'Dear Albie. Thank you.' She considered, her head on one side. 'All right then. Will you look after Davie for me, darling?'

Coldness touched him. 'Are you going away, Aunty April?'

'No. I don't think so. But sometimes mothers can't help their own children. You wouldn't understand that—'

'Oh I do. I do.' There were links between him and March forged of steel, but she was rarely able to help him.

'Then will you keep an eye on her, Albie? If anyone seems to frighten her or—'

'I'll kill them, Aunty April,' he promised.

She laughed. 'Well, you need not go as far as that.' Unbelievably she leaned towards him and he knew she was going to kiss him. The reddened lips were a perfect Cupid's bow, and he anticipated how they would feel against his, very soft and slightly sticky. He couldn't bear it. He really would swoon.

'I have to go to the closet,' he said and stood up quickly, nearly hitting her chin with his shoulder.

David had to leave early to see to the shop. He was surprised when April, helping him with his coat and muffler in the narrow hallway, decided she would come with him.

'Primrose, you can't. Davie will feel deserted.' He held her by her shoulders. 'What has happened? Has Albie made a lewd suggestion?'

'Oh David. You are *ridic*ulous! I just want to be with you.' She scooped his hands away and pressed herself against his cold overcoat, then stood back, laughing. 'I'm being silly. Of course I can't leave Davie. I'll see you in an hour or two anyway.'

'True.' He poked his head and pecked at her and she clung again, but without passion. With a kind of desperation; as if they were shipwrecked and about to be torn apart. She stood at the door and waved to him, shivering in the cold. He gestured her to go inside, then tramped around the corner into London Road. The barrier – whatever it was – had suddenly become thicker, and she was trying to force herself through it. But what the devil could it be?

Sibbie Luker was taking advantage of a whole day without Will, to entertain Edward Williams. She put a pan of chestnuts beneath the fire and cooked a leg of pork with turnips.

'Barton Feast?' He was referring to the traditional meal served at the annual hiring fair.

'I have to celebrate my feasts when I can.' She had never tried to hide anything from Edward; he had known of her from his father and her long association with Will Rising had been part of her attraction. Edward Williams admired all things to do with the Rising family. She fished out the pan of chestnuts and swept the hearth again. The bungalow was kept impeccably.

'Isn't it strange, Edward – ' she removed the chestnuts one by one, blowing on her fingers ' – so many men say they love me, yet at Christmas and Easter, Bank holidays and Barton Feast, I am always on my own.'

He reached for her. 'Ah Sibbie. That won't always be.' He held her on his lap, protectively. He had endured a frigid wife for thirty years now, and his adored only child, Bridget, had grown away from him. This child-woman was just that: mistress and daughter to him. The meal was ready and waiting on the table but she did not push him away; she had never pushed him away.

He whispered, 'I've asked Alice for a divorce, Sibbie. I want to marry you.'

She drew away and stared at him. Sibbie was never shocked, but at that moment she was close to it.

'She wouldn't agree to it,' she breathed.

'Not yet, no. But I shall wear her down eventually.'

'But . . . she will cite me as co-respondent.'

'Yes. Would you mind very much? I shouldn't care a button.'

'But darling. You're a councillor. You'd have to resign – you don't know what it's like to be – to be—'

'Ostracized? No, I don't. I'm looking forward to it. It will set us apart. Isolate us. Together.'

Sibbie said nothing. She let him kiss her repeatedly until his passion was thoroughly aroused. She let him undress her and lie her on the hearth rug and she watched the glowing fire out of the corner of her eye and groaned occasionally and wondered whether she was pleased or not. What about Will? And what would Fred say if he knew he was in danger of losing his best 'contact'?

But . . . it was the first marriage proposal she had received and she couldn't help feeling a small thrill.

He said, 'Our dinner will be getting cold, my darling.'

'I love cold pork.'

'So do I. And cold turnips.'

'And as for cold roast chestnuts . . .' They laughed together and made love again. Edward Williams was only five years younger than Will Rising, but he had fought in the war with Sibbie's generation and she never thought of him as old.

Fred could almost smell himself smouldering with resentment. He managed to corner March alone in the kitchen and as he shut the door on the two of them, he had a glimpse of April Daker kissing her husband in the hall as if her very life depended on it. Fred decided he had had more than enough of being treated like the plague by the Rising girls. Two of the children here today had been fathered by him so he had a perfect right to come to the birthday party of one of them. He had been sorely tempted to stand in the middle of the bandy room and announce the fact to all and sundry. But Davina was so sweet and shy, and Albert-Frederick so tall and serious, and the peculiar tenderness generated all those years ago by April Daker in Marsh Cottage had nourished itself on the two children until it was the only thing that mattered to him. Making money . . . Leonie Porterman and the other women . . . they were appetites which he gorged in sporadic bursts and then forgot. Albie and Davie and his right to be near them, caring for them, that was what mattered.

March was making tea for the women. She had an enormous tray loaded with cups, saucers, spoons and was bending down to check that the gas was lighted beneath the kettle. She actually jerked upright and put her hand on her breast like Hedy Lamarr. She wasn't unlike Hedy Lamarr. Well, he could put on the drama too if necessary. He leaned his back against the door and surveyed her.

She visibly swallowed, then said tensely, 'What do you want? Why did you come here today?'

Fred wished he could tell her the real truth; he told half of it. 'Your father asked me. I accepted because I wanted to see my son with the rest of his family. When I bump into him accidentally in town he's awkward with me—'

'What do you expect? Everyone knows now – I'm surprised my father asked you – anyway, what do you mean you wanted to see . . . I don't understand.'

'You're supposed to be intelligent, March. I wanted to check up on Albert-Frederick. My son. Make sure he is happy.'

315

'He is not—' She whispered the denial hopelessly and did not finish it. He felt a pang of pity for her.

'March. Listen. Four years ago I asked you to marry me. Whatever you thought at the time you must know now that it wasn't because of your money.' He waited. She shrugged, still with that hopeless look about her. He went on carefully, 'You've got exactly what you always wanted, March – what I promised I would get for you. Do you remember? The house in Barnwood, the money. You hire a car when you want it. You help your mother out. You buy presents for your family. Everything. You've done it on your own and I know you well enough to be sure that gave you a great kick. Didn't it?' Still she said nothing. Almost automatically she turned off the gas and poured the contents of the kettle into the teapot. He let her finish. Then he said in a low voice, 'Is it enough, March? Are you satisfied?'

She caught hold of the handles of the tray but did not lift it. She said, 'I . . . manage. Very well.'

He remembered the sterile old maid's bedroom that had been hers in this house. For all her money and fine house was her new bedroom very much different?

He whispered, 'Such a waste. All that fire and passion wasted. Drying up. Shrivelling.'

Her head came up furiously. 'How dare you speak to me like that, Fred Luker! What right have you got to come here and insult me – try to wound and humiliate and—'

'Because I'm the only man you've really given yourself to, March. I'm not the only man you've loved. I know that. I know that I must always come second to your blasted brother . . . a corpse. But I'm the only man you've wanted. The only man—'

'Be quiet!' She really was outraged. She came around the table and gestured angrily for him to move from the door. 'Let me out! This minute. All you can think about is – is – lust and – and carnal passion and—'

He caught her flailing arm and held it hard. 'Will you marry me, March?'

She was still. Like a wary half-tamed animal.

'Marry you?' Her clear tea-brown eyes flicked over his face and then down to his hand on the sleeve of her dress. 'Why?'

Her wariness was infectious. He tightened his hold; he must say nothing about Albert-Frederick. If she thought he wanted to have any kind of say in the boy's upbringing, she'd be threatened, just as she'd been before.

He said, 'The usual reasons. Love.' But love was only one reason. The main one was that he and March were meant to be married. She was going against their destiny. His voice was flat, unemotional. She did not believe him.

'You mean you want another bedfellow? Isn't that Porterman woman enough for you?'

'March. Leave her out of it. We're talking about you and me—'

'How can *I* leave her out of it? You won't. You're still seeing her—'

'No.'

She was childishly triumphant. 'You are. Victor saw you both go into the Bell Hotel last week. He went

317

in and asked for your room number. Told the man you were his uncle and she was his aunt. Gave the name Luker. The man told him there were no Lukers registered in the hotel and the lady and gentleman he had just seen were Mr and Mrs Smith!'

Fred felt himself go cold. He twisted her arm fiercely. 'Now you're lying. He'd never have told you that cock and bull—'

'I heard him telling Albie. He's a dirty little monkey. But he doesn't make up things like that.'

'He told Albert?' Fred felt his heart contract painfully. He brought March close to him and stared into her eyes. 'You let him tell Albert? You denied it, I hope.'

'Of course I didn't deny it. I knew – it was true. Everyone knows—'

'But *Albert* . . . Godamighty, March . . . my son—'

She pushed against his chest and suddenly there were tears in her eyes. 'I knew that was why you asked me again to marry you. Your son. That's what's gnawing at you now, Fred, isn't it? Love . . . you don't love me. You probably want to take me to bed again. But you don't love me. Otherwise you'd have given up Leonie Porterman four years ago when I first told you I knew about her. Better still, you would never have got entangled with her in the first place—'

He shook her angrily. 'Did you put Victor up to following me?'

'Of course not. He does things like that. He's an underhand child. Devious.'

'Albert wasn't with him? You're sure of that?'

'I told you. He was whispering to Albie—'

'Why didn't you shut him up?'

'Why should I? Maybe – in this case – it was better for Albie to know the truth.'

'You bitch, March.' He altered his grip, took hold of both her wrists and clamped them behind her back. They were chest to chest. He could smell lavender and Pears soap and see the lines of discontent around her mouth. He said, 'Listen. You're to talk to Albert. About me. You're to put this – this piece of gossip – right. Do you understand me?'

She was breathing quickly, almost panting. 'I understand what you are saying. Yes. But the – the *gossip* – is true. Isn't it?'

He missed the near-pleading in her voice and heard only the disgust. His resentment flared into a defiance that he *knew* was absolutely justified.

'What d'you expect? A monk?' He used a term that Leonie had coined. 'A Lukerian. Is that it?' He laughed. 'You know – of all people – you know I'm not like that, March. Besides, Leonie Porterman is business. She has her husband in her pocket, and I need her husband. It's as simple as that.'

'That might have been true in the first place, but not now. You've no need . . . now. You're your own man now. You – you *like* her!' The tears had gone but her eyes were very bright.

He did not release her hands, but used his arms so that he was supporting her rather than imprisoning her. He whispered, 'You went to Edwin Tomms from necessity at first, March. But later . . . you told me . . . it was different.'

She said nothing and there was a long pause while

they gauged each other's breathing and being. Then his head came down to hers and she did not move away. The next moment the door opened hard against Fred's back; he jolted March two steps backwards and into the table. The teapot, balanced precariously on the edge of the tray, fell to the floor and smashed. March freed her hands, twisted, saw it, gave a sound between a moan and a scream and swung back to hit Fred hard on his left ear.

Aunt Sylv came in.

She surveyed them calmly, her lizard eyes uncondemning.

'You two up to your shenanigans again, are you?' she asked. 'I'll clear that mess up and leave you to it.'

Fred gave her a look of dislike, turned and left the kitchen. March said furiously, 'You always have to *interfere*!' and began to hurl broken china into a bucket. She remembered dissipating her temper in this very kitchen over thirty years ago by banging her head against the table leg. But her brother Albert, who had been the cause of it then, had understood and had not left her to erupt alone.

By the time she went into the hall, Fred had left. She went into her father's workroom and watched him through the letters in the frosted glass. He ploughed through the snow; over to number seventeen. He was not wearing a hat or a coat. She put her forehead against the cold glass and let the tears come.

It was bedtime; the party was over. May stood behind her mother's chair and brushed the long greyish hair over one hand, gathering it and returning it to the brush with a slow soothing rhythm. Florence closed her eyes. Will was seeing a man about a dog, Victor was in bed, Sylvia was reading the *Citizen* aloud to Gran. It was a time of complete peace.

May said, 'I suppose Fred would have given Monty a job. But that sordid business with Captain Porterman and his wife . . . Monty hates anything like that.'

'Of course darling. Monty is so open and honest.'

'But if Tollie really will need an assistant soon, that will be ideal. Bridget says he never has a spare minute. Although – ' May giggled naughtily ' – he must have some time with her by the look of things.'

'Really . . . May,' Florence protested weakly.

'Yes. Sorry Mamma. Anyway I don't think Monty could possibly have any objection to being Tollie's assistant. Do you?'

'Will it mean a financial loss to him, dear?'

'Not really. The salary is wretched of course, but Monty doesn't have many engagements now. We shall save a lot of money by living in Gloucester.'

Florence was watching herself in the mirror as her favourite daughter expounded more plans. There she was, looking dishevelled with her hair down, and there was darling May, frowning slightly, brushing and combing and brushing and talking and not realizing that her mother had gone away from the small vignette and was watching it from elsewhere. And as Florence watched, so she saw the tiny hiccup that jarred the mirror-image, then the froth of redness at the lips. She saw May drop the brush and scream and reach for something – a pillow-case – then the picture tipped back as if the mirror was falling over, and it was gone.

May sobbed, 'Mother – Mamma – my little Mamma please, please come back.' Florence had collapsed like a broken doll and May lifted her bodily and put her on the bed. Blood flowed from her mouth and gurgling sounds came from the nose. She wasn't dead.

Sobbing, May ran to the landing. 'Aunt *Sylv*!'

Sylv appeared from the wing room and broke into a lumbering trot. Halfway along the landing another door opened and Victor appeared. 'Mummy?' he said on a panic upward inflection.

'Get back to bed!' she screamed. 'Go on, I'll come in a minute!' She pushed Sylvia ahead of her into the front bedroom and watched as the big hands turned Florence on to her side. The blood flowed faster still.

Sylv panted, 'It's got to come away, she'll choke on it else. Christamighty 'ow 'ave she got so much!' She mopped desperately. 'Water – wring this out in the basin. Oh Christ . . . Jesus Christ . . . come and 'elp us now.'

May was crying loudly and despairingly. Gran appeared in the doorway. 'Go and fetch Lottie,' she rapped out, moving to the bed and supporting the limp body with her ancient one. 'Go on. Then see to your boy. He's near histry-errics.'

May ran as she was, home-made felt slippers and all, straight into the Lamb and Flag and bundled Lottie out.

'Nuthin' I kin do about lung flux,' grumbled the old woman, her shawl flapping around her in the bitter January wind. 'Jest got to let it come away—'

'Come and see, Lottie – just come and see,' sobbed May.

But it was over when they got back upstairs, and Florence was coming out of her faint and looking at them in some surprise.

'Am I going to die?' she asked weakly when she saw Victor shivering by the door. 'I'm not frightened, but I would like Will to be here.'

Someone had made tea but she couldn't drink it. Sylv said doubtfully, 'I'll go and look for 'im, Flo, but I en't sure . . .'

Victor tugged at May's hand and whispered in her ear. She glanced at him sharply and took him on to the landing. He told her Will's exact whereabouts. She felt the last dregs of reality slipping away from her.

'How do you know?' she breathed.

'Albie and me. We followed Gramps one night. Sorry Mummy.'

It was the first time she had hit Victor. He crumpled where he stood, holding the side of his head but not whimpering, somehow understanding why she had to do it.

'Sorry Mummy,' he repeated.

'Get back to bed. Go on. Now. I'll come and see you later.'

'Are you going . . . there?'

'Never mind.'

'But are you? I know the way.'

'So do I. Go to bed.'

It was a long walk down the Bristol road to the swing bridge and the small lane alongside the canal, and it was made longer by the wet snow underfoot.

May was tempted to call for April, but April was Will's favourite child; she couldn't do that to him – or to her. Besides, Sibbie was her friend, which somehow made it her responsibility. She ploughed on, tears warming her frozen face. She should have known years ago.

No lights were on in the wooden bungalow. She hammered at the door, then kicked it. Even when the gas was lit in the room beyond she kept kicking and hammering and crying. When the door swung back and light framed Sibbie, she could hardly speak.

'Tell him . . . tell him . . . oh tell him his wife's dying and needs him! Tell him that – go on!'

She turned and ran back the way she had come, unheeding of Sibbie's shouts. But she was exhausted after her long tramp and Sibbie was fresh. She caught May up long before the bridge.

'Wait. Oh wait May, please. You don't understand – I tried to tell you that night! I tried, my love – my only love – but you were drunk and you didn't – couldn't – understand. It's you, May. It's always been you. Please believe – believe—'

May tried to brush her aside, but she stood her ground. She was barefoot, her nightdress scarcely decent. Already she was shivering uncontrollably. Will came blundering up.

'Godamighty our May, what's up? Is it your mother?' His concern was such that he forgot his own position. He had pulled galoshes on to his feet, his hair was on end.

'She coughed blood. Pints of it. Lottie says she'll be all right, but she wants you. Oh God . . . Pa . . .'

He was recalled to the present. 'I'll explain all this

later, May. Come on now, rally round, girl. We've got to get home quick.'

He scooped May away from Sibbie and sloshed them both down the lane. Sibbie stayed where she was, keening like Mrs Daker.

'May . . . May . . . don't leave me. It's you, May. You . . .'

'She's deranged,' Will said briefly. 'I've been trying to help her. Deranged.'

'Oh Pa . . .' May did not know what to think or say or feel. Poor Pa, poor Sibbie, poor May. Or was it wicked father, even more wicked Sibbie, and stupid, silly May? And what about Sibbie's arms around her neck, Sibbie's bare feet blue in the snow, her body all too obvious in the satin nightie pressed to May's coat?

Will said, 'Forget all that. Tell me about Flo. Is she really going to be all right? I can't live without her, May. You know that. None of us can live without her.'

May nodded. That was true at any rate. That was real.

But again Florence rallied. White and shaken, she took to her bed once more and lay looking at the map of Norway on her ceiling and eating her raw liver. Dr Green had a quiet word with March and suggested perhaps she could take her mother to Spain or Italy. Terrified, yet fascinated, March began to make tentative plans. April would look after Albie for her. It could be arranged.

But March had planned – years ago – to take another dear invalid abroad to recuperate, and her plans had come to nothing. And March had been born under an unlucky star.

Chapter Twelve

As soon as Florence took to sitting in her chair, May flew back to Monty. It was the sort of half-and-half life she had been leading for the past four years while she paved the way towards Monty changing his life-style, but before the discovery of Will's perfidy she would have used Florence's illness as an excuse to make a protracted stay in Gloucester. Now she couldn't wait to get away from everything she held dear. Even in far-off Harrogate, surrounded by people she did not like very much, she could not throw off the horror of that night. She would sit by herself gazing out of the window in their rented rooms and shuddering convulsively.

Amazingly, Monty was not in the least surprised.

'Your father had to have an . . . outlet,' he said uncomfortably. Something made him explain this to May; she needed to know that men had to have that something. 'I know Florence is a wonderful woman, May, but you must realize they haven't slept together for years.'

'It's horrible. Horrible.'

Monty flushed. 'I'm sorry you think so.'

'I don't mean *that*. I mean Sibbie.'

'But you knew about Sibbie already, May. We've

talked about it before. Everyone in Gloucester knows about Sibbie.'

'Yes, yes of course. But with my *father*. She's my best friend—'

'She was your best friend, darling. Twenty years ago.'

'But underneath . . . oh, you don't understand.'

She didn't understand herself. Could it be that she was jealous of her own father? Victor, precocious child that he was, had to air his views with the same brand of innocence as his mother used to have.

'When I saw her through the window with Gramps, she looked like Marlene Dietrich. And that's enough to give anyone the shudders!'

May drew in her lips, hating the thought of Victor spying and seeing – what? But Monty fed his precocity as usual by roaring with laughter and swinging mock punches at his son's shoulders. The next minute they were all over the furniture and the landlady's aspidistra was on the floor. May was glad about their male rapport in one way. In another, it excluded her. She shuddered again. She needed someone. She needed . . . Sibbie.

April and March sat in the beautiful sitting-room at Bedford Close, admiring the first daffodils in the garden and discussing the proposed trip to Nice, which was as far south as they thought Florence could stand. Albert, true to his promise to 'keep an eye' on Davina, had taken her upstairs to his private domain to watch his train and locomotives making their complicated circuit. May was sitting by an open window of very second-class theatrical diggings in Harrogate, watching Monty and Victor play cricket in a small back yard. She would smile and clap and then return to the letter in her lap which was from Bridget Hall, née Williams.

For most of the letter Bridget described her latest pregnancy symptoms; her third baby was due any day now; but in the final paragraph she said that if Monty would like to write a formal letter of application to her father, a place might be found for him in the firm. 'Tollie badly needs some help with the rare books and Monty has a certain air about him. Get him to quote a bit of Shakespeare in the letter, Daddy loves Shakespeare. And he loves the Risings too and Monty is a Rising really, isn't he.' May smiled at that but decided not to show it to Monty, he wouldn't like it at all.

Outside another run was clocked up and she clapped obediently. She wondered how she could 'get' Monty to write a letter to Edward Williams, the idea of him being an assistant to Tollie had been all hers. And in any case did she particularly want to go back to Gloucester now? Knowing what she knew, it would be difficult, if not impossible. Suddenly she crumpled Bridget's letter and threw it in the empty coal bucket, leaned out of the window and called, 'Shall I score? You're doing so well . . .'

At number thirty-three Chichester Street, Kitty Hall was telling Florence that Bridget had in fact gone into the nursing home in the early hours of the morning.

Florence smiled rather anxiously and Aunt Sylv got her ponderous weight out of the chair and went to put the kettle on. It was one of Will's business days and the women prepared to relax and discuss the younger generation.

Edward Williams heard of the arrival of his third granddaughter at midday. He was not permitted to visit her at the exclusive nursing home in Brunswick Square, his wife could not bear to discuss any aspect of Bridget's unexpected fecundity, and Tollie was at home supervising Olga and Natasha. So Edward took his news down to Bristol Road to share with Sibbie.

'Edward! It's not your day. Is something wrong with Bridie? '

'Nothing. Another girl. I had to come and tell you.' He slammed the door of his car. 'I won't stay long darling. I had to tell someone. Can't I even have a cup of tea?'

'Oh Edward, of course. Come in. Is everything all right? Mother and baby?'

'Fine. She produces 'em like rabbits.' He was proud of that, Alice had been horrified by the whole business. 'Three in just under four years. Not bad, eh?'

Sibbie laughed as she fetched cups and saucers. She liked Edward Williams very much. She remembered how distasteful the seduction of his father had been; this was surely her just reward.

She said, 'Florence Rising had three in three years. Then there was only eight months between April and Teddy.'

'Impossible, darling.'

'Teddy was three months premature. She nearly died.'

'She was always delicate. Bridie is as strong as a horse.'

'It's Tollie who is the surprising one.' Sibbie poured tea, thoroughly enjoying herself.

Edward felt the same; he laughed. 'I reckon it's his way of getting out of the tea dances and the tennis parties and Bridie's silly flirts. Not that they meant anything.' He turned his mouth down. 'Poor baby, she did enjoy a little fling. Not much of that for her these days.'

'She loves it,' Sibbie said sagely. 'She's got a lot of me in her. She likes people to know that she's wanted. And a string of babies is one way of letting them know.'

They were both laughing uproariously at this remark when Will arrived. He had recognized the car as he came over the swing bridge and his alarm had had time to build into anger. He swung open the door with a deafening crash and made his entry like one of Monty's avenging stage heroes.

Sibbie did her best at first, though her heart wasn't in it.

'I think you know Councillor Williams?' She shot warning glances at Will, demanding his co-operation. 'He is just leaving—'

'How long has he been here, that's what I want to know!' Will said truculently. 'Like father like son, eh? I suppose you think you can buy your way into Miss Luker's good books just like he did before you! Is that it? Is that why you come sneaking around here behind my back making a damned nuisance of yourself!'

Edward, aware of the position, mumbled something and picked up his hat.

'Oh no you don't, my fine buck!' Will got between him and the door and adopted a crouching stance. 'You don't leave here just like that. Scot free. Oh no.'

Sibbie abandoned her good intentions. Ever since last January when May had caught them together, her feelings for Will had changed. She was bored with him at last.

'For goodness' sake Will, stop being so ridiculous! Edward and I have been having a cup of tea. Can't you see that!'

'Oh. So it's Edward, is it?' Will crouched lower than ever but now it looked as though he was cowering. 'Edward. Edward and Sibbie. And what else I wonder!'

'You should know, Will,' Sibbie said laconically.

He looked as though she had struck him physically. 'Sibbie!' he protested, his face twisted.

'Look here old man, I think I'll go, and let you discuss this with Sibbie.' Edward tried to touch one of the raised arms reassuringly. It came up automatically and hit him. Will gazed down at the result of his involuntary movement with surprise and horror.

Sibbie's self-control snapped.

'What the *hell* d'you think you're playing at, Will Rising?' She knelt by Edward and dabbed at his bloody nose. 'How dare you come in here – you're the usurper after all! This is my house and I have the deeds to prove it. And this gentleman is *my* caller – I suppose I have a right to have callers?'

'No!' shouted Will. 'Not the sort of caller he is!' He leaned against the back of a chair. His face was mottled. 'You know very well you belong to me, Sibbie! Ever since I rescued you from David Daker you have belonged to me!'

She was furious. 'I belong to no-one, Will,' she said, her voice shaking with sincerity. 'Only myself. You did not rescue me from David. I chose to come with you. I picked you. Don't you understand that after all these years? I have picked other men too when I have felt like it!'

Will sagged, his short legs buckling. His eyes became bulbous.

'And you picked . . . *him*?'

She held Edward close. 'He is different,' she said proudly. 'He is quite different from the rest of you. He has asked me to marry him.'

Will tried to laugh, but bile rose into his mouth. 'How can he marry you? He's got a wife already.'

Edward stood up. 'I'm getting a divorce. I love Sibbie. It's true we'll be married one day.'

Will looked from one to the other. The blood beat in his head. He had thought he would lose Florence and she had been saved for him. Now he knew that it had been an exchange: Florence for Sibbie. He was going to lose Sibbie.

She said calmly, 'It's true, Will. I love Edward. We are going to be married.'

The bile filled Will's mouth and made it impossible for him to reply. Something was pressing behind his eyes, trying to force them out of his head; his collar choked him. He tore at it with one hand, hearing his own breathing as a loud snore in the quiet room. Then he collapsed.

Aunt Sylv opened the door because Florence was arranging the first of the gypsies' daffodils in the dining-room. They called every April, their baskets bursting with the yellow trumpets, their greasy hair gleaming in the pale sunshine as they whined, 'First o' the Newent daffs, lady. Buy some for luck.' Sylv would have turned them away with short shrift, but Florence always liked to fill the house with daffodils.

So it was that when Edward Williams brought Will's body home, the house was filled with the scent of his favourite flower. He had likened April to a daffodil, he had gathered them around his home at Kempley, he was laid in the dining-room among them.

Edward Williams tried to explain and condole at the same time.

Florence, her Rhys-Davies heritage strong in her thin face, stopped him.

'Sibbie, did you say? Little Sibbie Luker?' She seemed to forget that Sibbie was the town's scarlet woman. She looked into Edward's embarrassed face and nodded. 'Hettie always made him happy too. Sibbie's mother. Perhaps it's a gift they have.'

'Mrs Rising, let me fetch your daughter – please—'

'Not yet. Let his mother be with him. And Lottie – fetch Lottie for me, would you? They will lay him out together. Then the girls can see him. And then he and I will be alone together.'

There seemed to be no sign of shock; it was almost as if she was thankful for what had happened. Gran exhibited the emotions Edward had expected, screams and wails and angry accusations against the absent Sibbie. Florence polished the dining-room table and laid blankets on it; then she banked the daffodils along window-ledge and mantelpiece.

Lottie arrived post haste, her eyes snapping; but then, as she looked at the stolid face of her old drinking partner, the wickedness went out of her. She put her knotty forefinger on Will's beard. 'Poor Will Rising. Poor daft Will Rising,' she said.

Florence paused at the door. 'He was rich, Lottie. Rich in love, rich in kindness, rich in joy. Nothing will be the same without him.'

She went to sit in her husband's workroom until the sheer busy-ness of the event should subside. April and March came to her there, tight with anxiety, and she calmed them. There was tea to be made with tea from the caddy emblazoned with the old King's likeness . . . or was it Will's likeness? They had always been so similar. There was bread and butter to be cut, the butter patted and stamped with Mr Goodrich's acorn stamp. There was a telegram to be sent to poor darling May. And there were the undertakers to call.

David and Mrs Daker arrived, then Alf Luker with messages from Hetty and Glad and Fred and Henry; then Kitty Hall. Beds were made up for the visitors the next day: Aunty Vi would come of course to pay her respects to her brother, and May and Victor should arrive by evening. Florence gave instructions in a low voice that did not tremble. When the girls said they would stay with her that night, she shook her head at first, then gave a small smile.

334

'Let it be April then. His daffodil girl.'

So April stayed.

She tried to persuade her mother to come to bed and Florence nodded. 'Perhaps later. You go on darling and make me a warm place. I must be with your father on my own for a little while. Don't worry about me. Not when I'm with him.'

About midnight April crept down the stairs and stood outside the dining-room door. She heard Florence's quiet voice talking . . . talking. After a while April went on down the passage to the kitchen where Aunt Sylv kept vigil, the kettle simmering hopefully on a bead of gas.

'She bin talking to him like that ever since she went in there at eleven,' Aunt Sylv said heavily. 'Talking and talking. As if she'd got to catch up on all the things she never said before.'

'Oh Aunty Sylv, what will happen to her?'

Sylvia came and put her muscular arm across April's shoulders as she sat at the table.

''Tis better she be left than him. Much better. He couldn't 'a done nothing without her.'

'Why? It seems he had someone else anyway!' April couldn't keep the bitterness out of her voice. Sibbie Luker of all people, the reason why David had been ostracized so long ago.

Aunt Sylv massaged her niece's top vertebrae. 'That was 'ow he were, April love. He wanted the moon, but his feet stayed in the cow shit.'

April wept.

'Ah, don't cry, littl'un. He was happy – only in the war when he lost his boys was he ever unhappy. He hardly knew what it was to be miserable. But he couldna done without his Florence. He'd have sunk right into the cow shit . . . hated himself. 'Twouldn't 'ave done, April.'

And in the dining-room Florence whispered, 'Wonderful memories, Will. Don't think I will ever forget them, my darling. We'll share them again very soon . . . so soon. D'you remember when I came to Kempley to get away from the smallpox in Gloucester? You called me a princess, Will. And you made me laugh. My life had been so drab until then, darling. You brought me light and colour and joy. How did you do it, Will, without any money . . . none of the things others consider important? It was in you like a light, wasn't it, dearest? You gave it to Teddy and I thought my heart would break when he went, then I knew I still had it in you. April's got it too, hasn't she? Thank you for sharing it with me, Will. Thank you.'

And in the little house on the canal bank, Sibbie wept into Edward Williams' shoulder.

'I never meant that to happen, Edward. He was always so good – to me and we laughed together . . . I never meant to . . .'

Fred Luker sat with his sister Sibbie in the darkest corner of Saint John's. In front of them in the coloured light coming through the sooty windows, people rustled and whispered discreetly. Will Rising had been a well-known figure in Gloucester, and his funeral turn-out was very respectable indeed. The *Citizen* reporter lingered at the door and people spelled their names carefully for him.

Fred glanced at Sibbie in the gloom. She looked like a drowned rat without make-up and in unbecoming black. He hadn't realized she thought so much of the old boy, and if she really was hoping to marry Edward Williams it was just as well he was out of the way, surely. But Sibbie was mourning her childhood which had gone for ever with Will Rising.

Fred wondered whether Will's death would affect him more personally. Would March give up her big house which meant so much to her and return to live with her mother? Or would that honour fall on May? It wouldn't make much difference either way, he could not keep a personal eye on his son wherever she was. Unless he married her.

And if Will's sudden absence did precipitate a marriage between Sibbie and Edward Williams, what then? Certainly his contracts would disappear. Anything supported by Edward would suffer with his disgrace, that was certain. Could he stand alone yet? He had the gravel pits on a bank overdraft, granted because of Edward Williams' contracts and Marcus Porterman's backing. He needed capital. He remembered Leonie's old and oft repeated joke about Marcus being willing to pay him to keep away from her. How serious was that? And how much could he be pushed to? Without Leonie, he would obviously be without Porterman himself. And Porterman gave the firm a shred of respectability as well as reliability. So he would have to replace Porterman.

He left that thread of a thought hanging in the gloom and thought about his private life. He had a private life . . . a little too private. He had a son and a daughter and no wife and no home. And the Risings had no male head any more. With her father gone and Leonie quite definitely out of the picture, could he batter down March's stubborn pride at last? That thread connected with the previous one and became the perfect solution. March had respectability and money; as far as business went it was the perfect union. She was the mother of his son. And he wanted her . . . he loved her . . . He gnawed his under-lip and glanced at Sibbie again, feeling suddenly that the long, long period of waiting was coming to an end.

Sibbie snuffled up at him, then caught his arm as there was a rustling entrance at the door. The *Citizen* reporter slid into a pew.

'I am the Resurrection and the Life, saith the Lord. Whosoever believeth in me shall not perish . . .'

The white blob of the cleric and the shining rosewood of the coffin appeared, then the mourners. Florence, Sylvia one side of her, Violet the other. Gran would be at home cutting sandwiches with Fred's own mother. March came next, the eldest surviving child, supported by her tall son – by their tall son. Then came Monty, taking all May's considerable weight. Then April, walking erect and slightly away from David so as not to put pressure on his gammy leg. Her chin was tilted as Will's had so often been, she looked very tall and thin in a straight black coat and skirt with her black cloche hiding every strand of hair. But on her lapel and at her waist and in her hand, were daffodils. The violent splash of colour in the grim old church was shocking. People turned their heads to look, and as they did, so she smiled. It occurred to Fred suddenly that if he married March, April would be his sister-in-law. She couldn't very well avoid him then.

The whole family sidled into pews and the pall-bearers placed the coffin. Will's favourite hymn was sung: 'Now the day is ended.' Clear and true, May's soprano led the singing. Beneath it was April's steady voice, and underneath that again could be heard March's. He was proud of them. Dammit, he was proud of all of them. He wanted to belong to their clan.

Beside him Sibbie began to sob. Fred lowered his head and felt tears rush to his eyes.

The hearse was drawn by horses as Will would have wished. Their black plumes nodded ahead of the more mundane cars, and people stood still on the pavement with bowed heads. To the Cross they went, and then down the length of Eastgate and over the level crossing to the Barton. So they came to the cemetery, edged with tall poplars like soldiers. Will was laid to rest quite near his youngest son, Teddy, but this time it did not rain as it had done at Teddy's funeral, and the spring sunshine sparkled everywhere as if Will was laughing. When the earth hit the coffin and the cry went up 'Dust to dust', Sibbie lifted her tear-stained face and met May's eyes across the chasm of the grave. Tentatively, tremblingly, May smiled. She could come back home now; the obstacle to her return to Gloucester had gone.

So March was baulked of the trip with her mother. Not only that, but Florence had chosen April to stay with her that first awful night. March clenched her hands and thought of her father with Sibbie Luker. It was just one more thing to keep the Lukers away from the Risings. Her mother might forgive; March never could.

She watched the earth cast on her father's coffin and the future stretched ahead of her, lonely and sterile. May would come home permanently probably, and live in Chichester Street; and Monty would get a job somewhere and he and Victor and May would be spoiled and pampered by Florence and Gran and Aunty Sylv. Like the prodigal daughter. No-one would realize that she, March, had lost her father twice over and her lover . . . countless times. She shivered and looked sideways at her son who was so like her dead, beloved brother. She still had him, she still had darling Albie. He had set his face in a model of David Daker's, eyes narrowed, jaw line grim; but at such close quarters she could see his mouth was shaking. She leaned towards him and took his hand; he was the one good thing to come out of her life. She could not regret him. She thought back to the terror and loneliness of her pregnancy and what it had meant: the marriage to Edwin, the ensuing degradation when Fred had come home and told Edwin the sordid truth. No . . . she could not regret any of it when she looked at Albert.

He turned his head and met her eyes, and the next minute his head was on her shoulder and he was shaking with silent sobs for the grandfather who had so ably taken the place of a father for him. March held him to her, and at last wept her own difficult tears.

Chapter Thirteen

The interview with Captain Marcus Porterman was cold and businesslike on Fred's side, stammering and outraged on his.

'I've told her I'd pay you a sum to keep away certainly! But – but – dammit all man, a chap says things in the heat of the moment—'

'How much are you willing to pay me, old man?' Fred remembered the condescension of this man at their first meeting; he spared him nothing. 'It'll have to be pretty good because although I can guarantee my absence, I shall have a helluva job to fend her off.'

'You insulting swine! Lee might have enjoyed slumming it for a while but I can assure you once she knows you've said these things she'll have finished with you for good and all! I shan't need to pay you a penny!'

'All right. Try it, Marcus old chap. If you think I have to make any running with your wife, you must be more of a fool than I thought.'

The wrangling went on for the best part of the morning after Will Rising's funeral. At the end of it Fred was richer by ten thousand guineas.

'I want a signed paper,' he said abruptly when he took the cheque. 'Stating that on this day I swore to have nothing more to do with Leonie Porterman—'

'*You* want a signed paper! My God, Luker, you've

got some gall. If you think I'm signing anything—'

'I shall sign it,' Fred said calmly. 'I want your signature as a witness. It's to your advantage after all. It will hold good in a court of law.'

He produced a document already prepared in his own handwriting and Marcus Porterman read it through, breathing heavily.

'Dammit. This says that neither of you must see each other. I thought you were going to take the responsibility for . . . fending her off, as you so elegantly put it.'

'This is it. This is a receipt for the ten thousand and an insurance policy for you. Don't you see?'

Porterman shook his head with a bewildered kind of cunning. 'Wouldn't look too good for you if this became public, certainly.' He scribbled his name under Fred's. Fred took it, folded it with the cheque and put them both into an inside pocket.

'Nor Leonie of course.' He smiled. 'And as you are Leonie's legal guardian, Marcus old man, you are responsible now for keeping her off my back. I suggest a world cruise.'

Porterman stared and began to splutter. 'I could have done that anyway without paying you ten thousand.'

Fred shrugged. 'Maybe. I wouldn't count on it. The shock of knowing that we've made this bargain behind her back might get Leonie on board a boat. But do it quickly, Marcus, for God's sake. Because once she's had time to think it all out, she won't like it one bit. She'll want to stay around to ruin the two of us, and she's brighter than you think.'

There was more spluttering, some vague threats, but eventually Captain Porterman left. Fred followed him soon after and kept an appointment with his bank manager. He explained the cheque briefly.

'Captain Porterman has to leave the firm rather quickly. His wife's health. This is a kind of compensation for loss of his support . . .'

Fred recalled March's expression as she stood at the graveside only yesterday. He knew her thoughts as if they were his own and he cursed Sibbie frequently, though without anger. There would always be something to come between him and March; they had started off on the wrong foot when they were just children. Leonie . . . Sibbie . . Albert-Frederick . . . it amounted to stubborn pride. He wondered how long to wait before he made his frontal attack on her. Because that was what it would have to be; the only way now to win March.

If Florence realized that Will's death had finally revealed his long betrayal to the world of Gloucester, she did not show it. She made his workroom into a small front parlour; the smoked glass panel with his name engraved into it came out of the window and was made into an elegant firescreen. It was replaced by clear glass which she refused to shroud with lace curtains or an aspidistra. That summer she sat in the open window most afternoons with her sewing or knitting, and the neighbours would come over and pass the time of day and ask how she was getting on.

'I miss my husband,' she always said frankly. 'But he's not far away.' And when they left her they said quietly, 'Won't be long before she joins him . . . she was older than him, wasn't she?'

May and Victor did not go back to Harrogate after the funeral, and Monty joined them when he had collected their things. Florence insisted they should have the dining-room for their own, and she moved out of the big front bedroom at last and took Will's smaller room. It seemed the ideal arrangement. Monty left the house at ten to nine each morning and returned at six each evening. May had got what she wanted. She wasn't quite her old self of course; she had lost her father after all, but she was still a devoted daughter to her mother. She saw that Florence ate her mandatory raw liver; she concocted a shopping list with her; she made sure that the three grandchildren visited regularly. There was no way she could ever resume her friendship with Sibbie now, but she could pretend she didn't care about that. She and April and March and Florence presented a united front to the world. Sibbie was never mentioned; she might never have existed. The few titters died away and the integrity of the Rising family was stronger than it had ever been; stronger than when Will himself had led it.

Fred entered the house in Bedford Close very quietly. March was giving one of her rare tennis parties and the garden milled with white frocks and flannels. It was breathlessly hot and had been for a week; a thunderstorm was overdue to clear the air. The front door stood open and he could see right through the large sitting-room to the open french doors. April was there, pushing her hair up at the back to cool her neck, her

344

legs bare and bronzed after this scorching summer. March, head bound about with a ribbon like a Greek goddess, was moving around, pushing some kind of trolley; he could hear the clink of ice; her latest acquisition was a refrigerator. May, frankly fat without a corset, lay in the hammock laughing at Victor and Albie on court. Tollie was there, and Monty, and there were other children he didn't recognize.

He edged along the hall until he came to the staircase. He planned to wait in March's room until this beanfeast was over and she came to bed. Surprise tactics, a showdown. He took the stairs very carefully and slowly, two at a time, loosening his tie as he went. It was hotter still up here. He made for the front of the house and was then baulked. It was obviously March's room, overlooking Bedford Close itself, but it was in use as a cloakroom, the bed piled high with scarves and bags of all descriptions. It was also doubling as a nursery. In a cradle near the window lay Bridget Hall's latest, Beatrice, after Beatrice Webb.

Fred cursed and went to another door. Thank God it was empty and was evidently Albie's room. There was that bloody steam engine he'd mended once, and bits of what looked like a motor cycle on the bed. March would certainly create about that unless Albie got rid of it before she saw it.

From below came April's voice, suddenly raised. He went to the door and listened.

'Bridie, are you sure you're all right?'

Then Bridget Hall: 'Of course I'm not all right April! I'm going to be sick, how can I be all right if I'm going to be sick?'

There were two sets of footfalls on the stair carpet and the bathroom door crashed open. There were awful glugging sounds. April's voice said soothingly, 'There, there darling . . . poor old Bridie . . . it's too soon, much too soon.' Bridget's voice gasped, 'Tell that to Tollie, not me!'

Fred turned back into the room in disgust. Surely she wasn't pregnant again? They were like a pair of rabbits, she and her Tollie.

He waited, sitting on Albie's bed, hands dangling between his knees. An hour passed leadenly. He got up and went into the bathroom himself, then wandered into a room at the back of the house from where he could see the tennis court. They were beginning to pack up. He watched them through the muslin curtains, sharply critical. May could take some tips from Sibbie on how to keep her figure; Monty was just a suit of clothes, and Tollie Hall was . . . what was Tollie Hall? A meek good small boy, always careful of his mother; but what now?

He realized they would be fetching their clothes from March's room and retired again to Albie's bed, wondering what the hell he would say if the boy came in. People seemed to be marching interminably up and down the landing. Then April's voice sang out, 'I'll just collect Davie,' and Albie's door opened and she came in.

'It's all right – all right—' He stood up and held out his hand. 'Don't say anything. Please April.'

Her colour drained away, confirming for him that she was frightened of him. He felt the old resentment against the Risings return; what would she say –

or even do – if he succeeded in marrying her sister?

She said through stiff lips, 'Where is Davie? Albie and Davie, where are they?'

He looked at her incredulously. 'You don't think I've harmed either of them, do you? Hell's teeth April, what goes on in that mind of yours?'

'I . . . nothing. Where *are* they? They were coming up here—'

'For Christ's sake April! I don't know where they are. I've been here for . . . I've been here for some time. Haven't seen them.'

'Then why are you here?'

'I want to see March. Surprise her.'

'Oh.' Her shoulders dropped in relief. She pushed her hair back off her forehead; it was dark with sweat. 'I'll tell her.'

'I said I want to surprise her, April. Look, shut the door a second, will you? Someone's going to come barging in and the whole idea is to catch her off-guard.'

She turned and pushed the door to automatically, then faced him again, still suspicious. 'Why?'

He took a breath. 'I'm going to ask her to marry me.'

She was surprised out of her defensive attitude at last. 'She won't do it, Fred. Four years ago perhaps, after Edwin's death . . .'

'I asked her then. There was something in the way. I've cleared that up now.'

A faint flush showed in her neck. 'She won't do it, Fred. You don't understand March.'

'I understand only too well. Sibbie.' He shook his

head. 'Listen April. March and I have had an . . . understanding . . . for years now. There's always something that holds us back. Now March is on her own and she's not happy – yes, I know that too. I've got to convince her that she should forget Sibbie's existence and marry me. I can do it.'

A smile appeared in April's wary eyes. 'I think you might, Fred. I think . . . it would be wonderful if you could. Wonderful for March.'

He said deliberately, 'What about you, April? How would you feel? It would be much more difficult to treat me like a leper if I were your brother-in-law.'

The flush deepened. 'Fred . . . I know. I'm sorry. That time we talked, when I was still pregnant, at Hucclecote church – d'you remember?'

'Of course I remember. The big brush-off.'

Her eyes darkened. 'There was no other way, Fred. I couldn't . . . divide my loyalties. And over the years I knew you were trying to see Davie. When she was with Mother or Dad, you always seemed to bump into them. Then last winter, at her birthday party . . . and today . . .'

'I shall see more of her if I am married to your sister.'

'But then you will *be* my brother, don't you see? And if you are married to March you won't ever be tempted to . . . ' She trailed off, meeting the real pain in his face.

He said slowly, 'You haven't trusted me then, April?'

'Fred . . . please try to understand. If it had been just my life – but it was David's. And Davie's. And there was talk about your – your business methods. Fred, I'm sorry.'

He drew in a breath and let it go. Then he spoke in measured tones. 'April. Whether March agrees to marry me or not, Davina belongs to you and David. Understand that, once and for all. I shall always love her . . . be interested in her . . . help her if I'm asked. I can't help that. But she does not belong to me.'

There was a long silence. April's flush died away and her darkened eyes cleared to sky-blue. At last she said, 'You make me feel pretty humble, Fred. I won't apologize any more. But . . . oh Fred, I wish you luck. I really do wish you luck.' She came close and her lips touched his cheek. And then she left.

Eventually so did everyone else. He moved at last, opened the door and went down the landing to March's room. All the clothes had gone. He looked through the window: March and Albie were waving at the gate. He wrinkled his nose at the stink of face powder and stripped off his jacket and shirt before collapsing on the bed.

David said, 'Well, my beautiful women. Did you have a nice afternoon? Who won?'

'Mummy won. And Albie's new siding goes unnerneaf the floor and comes up by the window and there's a buffer stop right *there*!' Davina's voice crescendoed with amazement and delight at such ingenuity; David laughed, picked her up and kissed her.

'In other words you watched ten minutes of tennis, then you and Albie played trains for the rest of the afternoon. You're as bad as he is for mechanical contraptions. I don't know where you get it from!'

April looked at him quickly, then remembered her special news and relaxed. 'I know where she gets her antisocial streak from, David Daker!' She encircled them both with her arms. 'Although you're not any more, are you? Oh darlings, what a marvellous pair you are! David and Davina. My family.'

Davina gurgled and ruffled her mother's hair and David tried to look at her properly and could not.

'What's happened? Something nice, I can tell.'

'Tell you later.' April kicked off her shoes and going towards the kitchen sang out over her shoulder, 'Put Davie in the bath would you darling? Then I'll have one and we'll have supper and go to bed.'

'It's six o'clock!' David sat his daughter astride his shoulders and followed April. 'Aren't you well?'

'Never better. I want you to come to bed too.'

He stood in the kitchen doorway, absently unbuckling Davie's sandals which were right beneath his nose. 'Tollie's coming round. There was a library auctioned – Harkworth Hall I think – and he found a first edition of Mary Wolstenholme.'

'How interesting,' April said without any interest at all. She rolled lettuce in a cloth and began to snip the tails from a bunch of radishes. 'I suppose we can spare him half an hour.'

'Generous of you,' David murmured, making it sound like a request for further information. April said nothing, and as Davie was now patting his head and calling 'Gee-up!' he went on into the bathroom.

In the event April postponed her bath and urged

Tollie to stay to supper. She felt a luxuriant freedom from the pressure of time; they had plenty, she and David. She went about getting the meal, clearing it, watching the two men enthusing about some book with the same half comprehending enjoyment she had felt before Davie's birth, when the big living-room of the flat had always been full of people. She knew that somehow this afternoon she had been released from a bondage but she did not – dared not – investigate this knowledge too deeply in case it proved false. Rightly or wrongly she had been bound to Fred; now she was not. It was absurd because if Fred's suit with March was successful she would be doubly bound to him, through Davie's blood and through March's marriage contract. Yet it wasn't so. By revealing his lifelong feeling for March it was as if he had turned his back on April and Davie, indeed his solemn words had confirmed that.

April washed up at the shallow yellow sink, promising herself as usual that she would clean the mottled brass tap tomorrow, then she grinned exuberantly and fetched the Brasso from the cleaning cupboard. From the living-room Tollie's serious voice was interrupted by one of David's explosive laughs that held none of the old cynicism. April sawed away with the Brasso rag and let her grin widen. David was getting younger, not older; he was just about her own age now.

That night she danced for him as she had done long before Davie's birth. With the age-old allure of Salome, she let her tennis skirt drop to the floor and twirled around the bed as she divested herself of her blouse and brassière. David could hardly believe it.

'What has happened? Something has happened.'

He watched her from the bed, half-amused, half-anxious at such a sudden reversion.

She paused, pointed one long elegant leg and looked down its length. 'I often used to dance for you. Don't you remember?'

'Of course I remember. But you're a mother now. And I'm a father.'

He wanted to lean forward and pull her to him and cover her with kisses, but it wasn't possible that her reserve had vanished through a single day. He forced himself to lie there and smile at her.

She smiled brilliantly back at him. 'Yes, that's true.' She held on to the bed rail with one hand, raised the other high above her head and pretended to lift on to ballet points. 'I polished the tap tonight,' she said breathlessly. 'I haven't done it for years. It looks like solid gold.'

'Is that your news?'

She gurgled. 'No. My news is that Fred is going to ask March to marry him.' She left the foot of the bed and leaned over him. 'He's been in love with her since they were children and he thinks that at last it will be all right for them. What do you think, David?'

Her breasts hung pendulously before him. He cupped them with protective hands and said quietly, 'Darling. Everything has always been all right for us.'

'Of course. I didn't mean—'

'And you don't have to dance for me. You never have to prove anything for me, Primrose. I love you, just as you are.'

'Oh David . . . perhaps it's because of that – because it's always been all right for us, that I wanted to dance. To celebrate.'

'Do you mean that? Do you mean you are no longer worried or frightened for me?' He held her off, looking into her eager face. 'Can our love-making be a celebration each time? Whatever happens?'

He used the word in its religious sense and it stilled her too. She stared back at him, savouring the sound of it.

'Celebration . . . celebration. Oh David. That's what it is, isn't it?'

He saw that she was recognizing her own fear over the past few years and he pulled her to him quickly and kissed her face.

'It has nothing to do with dancing, Primrose,' he warned.

'Oh I'm glad . . . glad . . . because it can still happen when I'm an old, old lady and can no longer dance a step.'

He laughed against her mouth and felt her laughter bubble inside him. And for a long time into that hot summer night, they celebrated their marriage.

March went to turn down Albie's bed at nine o'clock that night and the first thing that met her eyes were the engine bits on his clean quilt. She was hot and tired, and though the tennis party had been a success the anti-climax of her aloneness was there as always after a social occasion.

She met Albie ambling along the landing in one of his dreams.

'*What is* all that stuff on your bed?' she demanded.

He blenched. He had forgotten the motor cycle parts in the joy of showing off his train set to April's small daughter.

'A boy gave them to me,' he prevaricated.

'A boy? What boy? Someone from Marley of course. Someone your precious Arnold Baxter encourages—'

Albie interrupted, hoping to divert her wrath. 'Mother, Arnold says I could easily be a first-rate mechanic. He lets me help him fix his car and—'

It nearly drove March mad. 'Do I pay those fees so that you can be the odd job man at that place?' She pointed a trembling finger. 'And I'm warning you, Albert, if Aunty May sends Victor back there next term, you'll leave. I mean it. I'm not having you two boys giggling and tittering over your silly jokes like you were before. At least *that* little partnership seems to have died a death, and I intend to keep it that way!'

'Mother please—'

'Don't argue. Get a box and clear that stuff off your bed and then get into it.'

Albie tried to win her round. 'Into the box?' he enquired.

'How dare you come the smart-alick with me Albert! Just do what you are told.' She followed him into the garage for the box, then back to the stairs. 'Just because you haven't got a father doesn't mean you can walk over me as if I'm a door mat! Just you remember that. And tomorrow you will put on your best suit and you'll take me to church and—' The

354

bathroom door closed on her words. Not too noisily, but not softly either.

She gave up thoughts of a bath herself and decided to drag the tennis court. It was eleven o'clock by then but she knew she wouldn't sleep. She scraped some potatoes for tomorrow's dinner, then strung some kidney beans and cut her finger. It was almost the last straw. She stood in the kitchen, sucking the blood, wishing she could weep and feeling the pressure boil up inside her. And at last she went to bed.

Fred lay very still where he was. The big house had been wired for electric light the year before, but March did not switch on the light. She went to the open sash and stared out at the summer night. He could hear her breathing. After a while she began to undress where she was, letting her tennis dress fall to the floor and stepping out of it unheedingly.

Fred had of course heard everything and had been sorely tempted to intervene on behalf of Albert. But that would have meant a three-cornered row, and he wanted this settled between March and himself alone. Nevertheless his determination to change things increased as he lay motionless listening to her harangue. As a child Fred had had plenty of physical chastisement, but he had never been nagged. Hettie's favourite maxim was 'easy come, easy go' and this attitude had extended to every part of her family life. He had fallen asleep most nights to the sound of bouncing bed springs from his parents' room next door, and before he had realized exactly what they were doing, he had still smiled, knowing they were happy.

355

He wanted to marry March for all kinds of reasons, all selfish. Now he saw that apart from them he was actually needed here.

March's slip joined her tennis dress. She had already discarded pumps and stockings. She stood now in some sort of cotton chemise thing and knickers that looked like a tiny skirt. Leonie never bothered with underclothes, so Fred was not as familiar as he might have been with modern lingerie. March was still adequately covered; but it seemed that was as far as she was going. She stretched with a brittleness that was very far from relaxation, then forced a yawn. Then she turned.

Her eyes were accustomed to the darkness by now and she saw Fred immediately, though she did not recognize him. Her gasp held the seeds of a scream and he spoke to her conversationally.

'It's only me. Hope you don't mind, March. I called and you were busy and I thought I'd wait—'

She let fly. 'You blithering *idiot*! My heart nearly stopped!' She grabbed at a satin dressing-gown thing over a screen and held it against her. 'What did you think you were doing – and how dare you – on my bed – as if it were your own house or something – how long have you – get out before I call Albie!'

Fred swung his legs off the bed and replaced his braces. He went towards the door.

'Well at least tell me what you came for!' March expostulated contrarily. 'You can't just walk out without an explanation of any kind!'

Calmly Fred turned the key in the lock, removed it and put it in the pocket of his trousers.

'I don't intend to. In fact I don't intend to walk out of here until the morning.'

'You . . . what?'

'I think you heard me, Marcie. ' He snapped on the light and grinned as she dropped the covering gown and turned frantically to pull the curtains across the windows. He remembered Leonie's exhibitionism. From one extreme to the other. He pulled forward a basket chair and sat down in it. She surveyed him, incredulous, aghast, but at least blessedly silent.

He said, 'Sit down, Marcie. Pull up that other chair and sit down and let's talk like old friends. That's what we are, my dear. Old friends.'

She said, 'Don't be a fool, Fred. We've never been friends—'

'Lovers then. Lie on the bed and let's be old lovers.'

'Fred, if you've come here to insult—'

'Oh shut up Marcie. For God's sake shut up and sit down. I'm the father of that boy in there.' He jerked his head. 'Have you forgotten?'

'How could I?' She spoke from a deep well of bitterness. But she sat down all the same, though a long way from him.

He smiled at her. 'I told Edwin Tomms once that I'd raped you. But I never had to, did I Marcie? I never had to force you.'

'You told Edwin that? Why?'

'It made our . . . arrangement . . . more acceptable to him.' He stared at her. She was beginning to look old, but she would age well, like her mother. Dammit all he would be so proud of her, standing by his side when he . . . when he became mayor of Gloucester!

Yes, with March by his side he could do anything. He leaned forward and said softly, 'He didn't like the thought of you being in love with me, Marcie. So I told him I raped you.'

She looked startled. 'That's why he . . . perhaps that was why he left the will as it was.' She thought about it and shook her head. 'No. He would have changed it before then anyway. But . . . I'm glad you told him that.' She looked away. 'I didn't mean to hurt him.'

He said quickly, 'I didn't mean to hurt you, Marcie. I swear that. Can't you forgive me like Edwin Tomms evidently forgave you?'

She shook her head dismissively, 'The two cases are completely different, Fred. You can't get round me like that. I had Albie to think of.'

'The first time, yes. But when you went back to Bath five years ago, March . . . it was yourself you were considering then.'

She was furious again. 'You've got a short memory, Fred Luker! Have you forgotten already what drove me back to Bath just then? Wasn't it something connected with you?'

'You mean Leonie. All right, there was Leonie then. I needed her husband and the only way I could keep him was through her. It was a business arrangement, March—' she made an explosive sound of outraged disbelief and he shrugged, partly acknowledging that ' – anyway it's over now. Surely your sources of information have apprised you of that?'

'Don't lie any more, Fred. Please.'

'I'm not lying, Marcie. The day after your father's funeral I saw Marcus Porterman and told him to keep her off my neck. I believe they're going on a cruise this autumn.'

She stared at him. 'Then . . . you've lost Captain Porterman from the firm?'

'Of course.'

Her throat moved on a swallow. 'You – you took your time about it.'

'Yes. I'm sorry, Marcie. I had to establish myself.'

'And you've done that? You can still run the firm? Alone?'

'Yes.'

'It's just coincidental that you're here – just a few weeks later – asking me to marry you?'

He stood up, suddenly enraged with her. 'Good God, woman! Whatever I say – whatever I do – it's wrong with you! What do you want, March – just tell me that? Go on, tell me what you want me to do?'

She didn't move. She didn't even look at him any more. Her eyes stayed where they had been, wide and gazing into the past.

She said, 'It's all too late, Fred. Can't you see that? It's like trying to stir up a dead fire. I suppose I must have loved you to let you . . . yes, I must have loved you then. But I can't even remember. I'm sorry Fred, but I think I'd like you to go away and never try to see me again. You . . . all your family . . . you're an embarrassment to us.'

'Well you can forget that. I'm never going to leave Gloucester. It's my town more than it's yours. My business is here—'

'Then move to the outskirts. Buy a house at Churchdown, or – or Painswick, or somewhere. Take

Hettie and your father and – *all* of you! Just go! You've done enough damage—'

He took her arms and lifted her to her feet.

'Your father could have done much worse than Sibbie! He'd have had to have *someone*, March! Don't you see that? He was married to a nun and no man can take that!'

March's wide stare came back to the present and to Fred. Her face was paper-white.

'My mother is a saint! You know that as well as I do.'

'She is. Exactly. A saint.'

'Let me go, Fred. I can't bear this! You and I are poles apart now and it's hopeless to pretend otherwise. Just let me go.'

He held her closer still and spoke grimly into her ear.

'Listen Marcie. I said I'd never had to rape you. But I will now if there's no other way. I'm going to marry you, March Rising. One way or the other I'm going to marry you. There's always going to be something between us . . . first there was your brother, then Edwin Tomms. Then Leonie Porterman. Now you say my sister Sibbie is coming between us. I won't *let* anything else separate us, March. The only obstacle I can see at the moment, is you. So—'

He felt the panic tighten all her muscles and the next instant she had twisted free and was grabbing at the curtains to pull them back and shout for help. He caught her to him, swung her round and clamped his hand across her mouth. The curtain fitment came down with a clatter and pulled with them as he dragged her to the bed. He fell on top of her and held her down with the weight of his body.

A voice said, 'Mother? Are you all right? What was that noise?'

Fred pressed his hand so tight across March's mouth, he wondered whether her teeth could take the strain. He put his lips to her ear again.

'It's up to you. I can tell him the truth if you like. And I mean the whole truth. Or you can send him away. The choice is yours.' Breath whistled in her nostrils and her body heaved against his. He did not remove his hand but shifted his body slightly. He whispered, 'D'you remember when I took you away from Edwin at the end of the war? D'you remember we spent the night at the George at Almondsbury on the way home? Albie cried and cried that night, but we took no notice.'

The door handle rattled. 'Mother – have you fallen down? Please say something! What has happened?'

Fred raised himself and looked into her eyes. She closed them in surrender. He lifted his hand from her mouth.

She said tremulously, 'It's all right, Albie. I turned over in bed and knocked the table lamp flying. I'll leave it till the morning now. So tired. Good night darling.'

'Oh...' The boy sounded surprised at her tone. 'Oh, good night Mother.' There was a pause, then he said, 'I love you, Mamma.' A moment later his door closed.

Fred said, 'We both love you, Marcie.'

She was weeping. 'Oh Freddie ... Freddie. I can't. You don't understand. I just *can't*.'

'Darling Marcie. You can't do anything else. Neither of us can. Not now. There's only one way we can go on. And that's together.'

She let him kiss her tear-streaked face and her throat. She made no attempt to stop him when he pulled off the brassière.

'So many wicked things we've done, Freddie. Is this one more?'

'You've never done anything wicked, Marcie. Whatever has happened is my fault. And now . . . this . . . I will look after you.'

She remembered that once before he had taken her guilt and made it his. Was it possible he could do it again, and for always?

She held his head in her hands and let memory sweep her away on its tide. The fire was not dead after all. She could feel its warmth thawing the cold sterility of her being. And it was different this time; perhaps not so fierce. A forgiving warmth. Forgiving Fred. And herself.

Everyone was delighted at the news that Fred Luker and March Tomms were going to be married. At one time the match would have been so unsuitable as to be doomed from the start; now, because Florence was so obviously pleased, it was seen as part of a healing process. What Sibbie Luker and Will Rising might have destroyed for ever, was being mended by Fred Luker and March Rising. April, not needing to hug the secret any longer, pondered its advantages a little more objectively with her husband.

'It's so *good* that he's successful,' she said as she sat

one evening pleating a new fan of crêpe paper to fill the blank white radiants of the gas fire. 'I mean, if he'd still been struggling along with the taxi . . . or even just the coal business . . . she'd have been certain he was after Uncle Edwin's money. She doesn't trust anyone. Least of all Fred.'

'Doesn't sound a very good basis for a marriage, Primrose.' David shoved his spectacles to the end of his nose in order to survey his wife properly. He was marking essays on the Pragmatic Economics of Soviet Russia and Tollie had insisted on contributing what amounted to a thesis on the subject. It would take David all week just to read it. He said, 'Surely trust is essential in marriage.'

The paper fan trembled slightly, then April shook it out to a full arc and said decidedly, 'There are certain things in marriage that are better . . . left unspoken. Perhaps.'

'Secrets, you mean.'

'They need not be secrets. They can be common knowledge.' She knelt by the fender and arranged the fan.

'Fred's business methods are suspect, I suppose. But we mustn't make any judgements there, Primrose. He was a prisoner in Silesia, remember. That sort of hell breeds its own morals.'

She glanced at him quickly and sat back in her chair. 'You're right darling, of course. But I think Fred would have done whatever he has done, war or no war.'

David looked at her face and cast off his spectacles, shoved the pile of essays on the floor and got up to take her in his arms.

'You're thinking of other things. Not business methods.'

'Yes,' she said in a low voice.

'Like the name Leonie Porterman? And the old, established firm of Three in a Bed?'

'Yes,' she murmured.

He was silent, looking at her down bent head. Then he lifted her up and tilted her chin so that she had to look at him.

He said, 'Darling April. Has it ever occurred to you that morals were made to suit man. Man was not made to suit morals.'

She stared at him, searching for a hidden meaning. 'What do you mean, David?'

'I mean that Fred might have done things that would make half the citizens of Gloucester throw up their hands and faint.'

'What about the other half?'

'They might say he's a good bloke.'

'Oh David . . .' Her voice shook. 'I hope you're right.'

He grinned at her. 'Perhaps I was over-estimating. I'm not entirely certain about half. Certainly Jack and Austen think he's a good chap. Hettie and Alf . . . Gladys and Henry . . . there's six to start with!'

She laughed along with him a little anxiously. He kissed her. 'March will be a match for Fred, my darling. Don't worry.'

'I'm not worried, David, I'm absolutely delighted. I've always thought, in spite of the gossip, that Fred is . . . all right. I'm glad you think so too.' She looked across the room to where Davina sat on the floor playing with some pieces of meccano that Albert had given her. She murmured, 'Morals were made to suit man. How wise you are sometimes, David.'

He nodded owlishly, 'Sometimes.' Then he laughed like a boy – as he often did lately – and kissed her. 'Not *too* often though, eh Primrose? That wouldn't do at all.'

March told Albert the news at breakfast a week after she and Fred had come together at last. He was anxious and apprehensive.

'Uncle *Fred*? I thought you hated him?'

March, surprised at her son's perspicacity, smiled wryly and in a new, relaxed way that Albert also noticed.

'I thought I did too. I often have in the past, Albie. But we were very good friends once. Before you were born. I think we might have got married then, but Uncle Fred was taken prisoner by the Germans and everyone thought he was dead. And I married Uncle Edwin.'

'You mean Papa?'

'Yes. Yes of course. Then I wasn't very well after you were born, and Uncle Fred came to Bath in his car and took us home to Grandma and Grampa and we were friends again.'

'But after that . . . I mean, when Uncle Fred mended my engine and brought me the meccano and things like that, you would hardly look at him, Mother! You never thanked him once.'

'No. Well, darling, there are things you don't understand—'

He said stoutly, 'I know Uncle Fred isn't a *good* man, if that's what you mean.'

March said quickly, 'He started you off at Marley. He paid your fees for that first term. Before we had money of our own.'

'I thought he might have done. ' Albert saw her surprise and looked away embarrassed. 'Well, he got me out of something rather nasty at school. Saw Miss Pettinger . . . well, it doesn't matter now.'

'I know.' March poured him more tea before he had finished and the cup overflowed. 'Oh dear . . . Then you like some things about him?'

It was his turn to be surprised. 'I like him. I've always liked him. But I thought you disapproved of him so much that you couldn't possibly *marry* him.'

'I don't exactly approve . . . but business is different, Albie. Sometimes – to get a business deal *through* – one has to tell a lie perhaps. A small one. A white lie.'

He looked at her silently and for the first time she saw that his mouth was exactly like Florence's.

She said, 'Albie darling, he has promised me that things will be different. I'm not sure how much you know . . . you and Victor talk about things . . . but Uncle Fred has promised that he will be . . . good.' They exchanged glances. The word 'good' did not fit Fred at all.

'He will reform, you mean,' Albert suggested.

'Yes. Quite. And you see darling, you need a – a man behind you. When you leave school and start out . . . in life . . . Fred will be very useful. Helpful. I mean, he can do things that you and I simply could not. And

366

then, when you are grown-up, I shall need someone –
I shall be lonely—'

Albert said suddenly, 'It won't make any difference
to us will it, Mother? You and me?'

She scrambled up from the table in a rare display of
emotion and took his head on the front of her apron.
'None at all, Albie. We've always been together. No-
one could come between us now.'

With his face hidden he said, 'Will you have more
children? Like Aunt Bridie and Uncle Tollie?'

She said immediately, 'No. No, we shall have no
more children. In any case, we're too old now.'

He waited a while, wondering if he felt a slight
tremor in the hands on his head. Then he said politely,
'Well . . . I hope you'll be happy, Mother.'

May's reaction was also ambivalent. 'Fred used to
follow our March around like a spaniel,' she confided
to Monty. 'It was pathetic. He could hardly string two
words together and she used to make him sit up and
beg almost. I don't think she'll have things all her own
way now.'

Monty, fairly happy at Williams' as Tollie Hall's
assistant, but already anticipating the boredom of the
continuous routine, was optimistic. 'It'll be something
different anyway. And there'll be pots of money there.
March is so damned mean with her windfall. Fred
might let us have enough cash to buy a decent house.'

'We've got a house now darling,' May said edgily.
'Now that poor Pa has gone, this is our home.'

Monty did not reply and May followed up querulously. 'Don't you dare try to borrow money off Fred

Luker, Monty. Just because he'll be our brother-in-law doesn't make any difference. If you put yourself in Fred's power, he'll use you.'

Monty laughed uneasily. 'How could he do that, May?'

'I don't know. But he'd find a way.' She went to the window of the big front bedroom and looked out. Beneath her, Hettie Luker was talking to Florence through the window of the old workroom. May thought she must go down and break it up, it was too much for her mother.

She sighed. 'That's why it's such a good thing for March. Fred will look after her. She won't have to worry about a thing. He'll see to it all.'

Florence, who had looked on Fred as another son ever since he drove Teddy, April and herself back from the infirmary after the children's tonsil operations, felt the same way.

'I know you worried about March, Will,' she said silently as she climbed into her husband's narrow bed that night. 'I think you'd be very pleased about this. It means all the girls are provided for. And soon . . . very soon, dear Will, they will be happy. I know it. I feel it.'

Chapter Fourteen

They were married at Gloucester Registry Office at the end of September. April and David were the only witnesses, but there was a big breakfast at the Cadena afterwards where Davina presented a horseshoe and Bridget's girls a silver rolling pin. Albie was to stay with April while March and Fred went to Paris; at last March was to sample foreign travel. Albie was more than happy to share a roof with April and Davie. To everyone's delight he took his small cousin on his knee for the meal and fed her scraps from his own plate. April snapped them with her Brownie Box camera and promised copies of the print to half a dozen eager requesters.

March surprised herself by actually enjoying the occasion. The Luker family were there in force and should have reminded her of the downward step she was taking, but somehow they no longer irritated her. Gladys had spent years in the office now and had stiffened into a typical, but acceptable, professional spinster. Henry, loose and loud-mouthed, was certainly no worse than Jack or Austen. And Sibbie of course had not been invited. March told herself she would soon forget Sibbie's existence, let alone any connection the girl had had with Will. Hettie and Alf would always be the old neighbours from number seventeen across the road: slightly comical figures acceptable to Florence, therefore bearable, but never mother and father-in-law.

March could hardly believe her own creeping conviction that everything was going to be all right. By marrying Fred she was going to be able to forget the degradation of Edwin; her whole life was going to be legalized at last. And it was more than that. She looked at Fred as he shook hands with Tollie Hall. She hardly knew whether she actually loved him; she had loved her brother Albert and she did not feel the same towards Fred. But there *was* something there: the old link that had been born with his dumb worship when they were children; the passion that had sprung from her terrible grief at Albert's death; and now this new feeling that was so nearly friendship . . . it added up to a lot. And Fred knew about her, he knew . . . what she had done. He was father of her sins as well as her son. March had always wanted to be 'good'. Her brother's love had made her 'good'; so far Fred's love had made her 'bad', but now that they were married it would be different. A husband, after all, was responsible for his wife. She met his eyes unexpectedly and knew he was thinking of that night. They were to spend it in London before catching the boat train. She felt colour rise into her cheeks.

Gran and Aunt Sylv sat next to Hettie and talked of past events as they always did.

'I well remember last time I was here,' Gran said lugubriously. ''Twere at our April's do. Will looked lovely 'e did. One of 'is own tailor-mades 'e wore and a rose as big as a cabbage in his lapel.'

'April looked lovelier,' Aunt Sylv said with unnoticed humour. 'And she still do.' She looked sharply at her youngest niece. ''Fact she looks lovelier than usual I reckon.'

Aunty Vi chipped in. 'I sat nex' March and your Fred.' She nodded at Hettie. 'There was summat goin' on between 'em even then. Bit o' footsie under the table if I recall right.'

Gran shook her head definitely. 'Not our March. She en't like that.' She twisted her head with unexpected speed and surveyed Sylv. 'What you grinnin' at, our Sylv? '

Sylv went on grinning. 'Nothing, our mother. Nothin' at all.'

Gran continued gloomily, ''Twere our May and 'er Monty what was up to Gawd-knows-what that day. May was the side of a 'ouse with Victor and there 'e was a-pattin' of 'er stomach as if they was in their own private quarters 'stead of—'

'They was all right Mother,' interrupted Sylv with finality.

Hettie got her oar in. 'I remember your wedding Sylv. It was in January—'

'Nineteen nought seven,' inserted Sylv.

'It was snowing and after the registry office you came up 'ere, didn't you?'

'Ah. Nothing fancy. Cup o' tea and a cake.' Sylv beamed with remembered pride. 'Yes. Mrs Dick Turpin I was. He made it legal for me. Just like our March and Fred.'

No-one thought anything of this except Gran, who administered another darting look from her lizard eyes.

May said, 'I feel like a lump of suet pudding in this chiffon. It's the same sort of outfit as March's but she gets away with it.'

'She's as thin as a rail,' Monty pointed out tactlessly.

'I'm not *fat*. My muscles were never the same after Victor. You've forgotten what I went through then.'

'No I haven't.' Monty recollected Manchester through rose-coloured spectacles. 'Golly May, d'you remember going to Scarborough that first time with the Mincing? We were theatricals then, people of importance. Top drawer.'

'All I remember is that wretchedly useless Mrs Turner and all her dreadful children and you fainting after Victor.'

It was the first time she had mentioned his faint. He said nothing. But he looked at her as she sat there eating her way through everything in sight and suddenly felt it was her fault he had landed up in this dead hole with all his in-laws. He didn't like Gloucester and he didn't like clerking and Tollie Hall was a solemn sort of a chap. Now, if Will was still alive with his male heartiness and his rabbit shoot and his – his – understanding – it might have been different. Poor old Will. How on earth had he stuck it without a future. That's what Gloucester lacked: a future.

April took some more photographs, put her camera away and went over to Florence.

'Mother, are you all right? Would you like David to take you back home now and lie down?'

'Of course I'm all right, April.' Florence did indeed look better than she had looked since Will's death. 'I'm happier sitting here on my own though darling, so don't bring anyone over. The talking tires me. I like to look . . . quietly.'

'Dearest Mother. You've got us all under one roof for once.'

'Yes. And it happened just as I hoped it would.'

'What? March and Fred getting married?'

'That too. But your father's happiness. It's his legacy to us, dearest. Do you see? He's left it for all of us. I can see it covering March now. Like a shawl.'

April looked across at her sister indulgently, then widened her eyes.

'I do believe you're right. She's different. She looks so – so – young!'

Florence said quietly, 'She looks as she used to look when Albert was alive.' She smiled up at April quickly in case she was suspected of sentiment, then said, 'And you . . . you're bubbling, April! You look like you used to look when you were a little girl and had a secret.'

April nodded. 'Yes. I'm positively fizzing with happiness like Mr Goodrich's ginger beer. As soon as I get Albie and Davie off to sleep tonight I'll come round and tell you why.'

Fred moved up behind them. 'Let me give you some champagne, Mrs Rising. And April too.'

Florence said, 'Oh Fred, no thank you. And couldn't you call me Mother? It would give me such pleasure.'

The way she said that made Fred blush with a kind of schoolboy pride. He said, 'Then . . . thank you, Mother.'

April gave him an open dazzling smile and stood up. 'Fred, Mother wants to be left to look at everyone. Will you come and help me find some anchovies? I've got a craze on anchovies at the moment.'

She linked her arm in his, all very sisterly, and led him out on to the verandah. The Saturday shoppers in the main streets of the Cross could not be seen; the cathedral rose out of a browsing huddle of roofs.

April stood still, looking at it, then she turned to Fred and her eyes were intensely blue.

'Fred, I want to say something.'

He did not meet her gaze. More than anything he wanted to belong to the family of Risings, Florence's request just now had confirmed that for him. If April was about to warn him that she must ostracize him again because of her peculiar conscience, he could not look at her and tell her it did not matter.

She put a hand on his arm. 'I've thought a lot about . . . what you said in Albie's room last month. I mean – I was so pleased about you marrying March that I didn't consider then the other things you had said.' She looked anxious as he still stared above her head towards the cathedral. 'I realize how much my – my attitude – must have offended you, Fred. I realize that you can't just – well, brush the last five years off as if they hadn't happened.'

He said woodenly, 'What you really mean is that *you* can't brush them off – isn't that it, April? Aren't you going to tell me you can't imagine me as a brother-

374

in-law and I had better keep away from you and David and Davina?'

Her hand gripped harder. 'Oh Fred – no! As far as I'm concerned . . . I told you that day how pleased I was. I meant it, Fred. If you can forgive – and forget – then . . . then it will be perfect. Perfect.'

At last he tore his eyes away from the view and looked at her. Her face was so alive, so open, he had to believe that somehow she had squared the whole thing about Davie . . . maybe she had even told Daker?

She said breathlessly, 'Fred, it's only right you should know. Next to David, you've a right to know. I'm pregnant, Fred. David and I . . . we're going to have a baby.'

Her fingers were digging into his arm and her eager face was asking him for something. Approval? Approval from a man she had feared and mistrusted?

She said, 'You've been so good, Fred. So loyal. A lot of people might think . . . your feelings are finer than anyone knows.' She smiled at him. 'But I know, Fred. That's why I wanted to tell you before Mother or anyone else. I've wronged you for a long time, Fred. I can't do anything about it. Ever. But . . . I told David that you must be the first to know about the baby.'

He said, 'That was all you told him, April?'

'Yes. If only he could know, Fred, he would understand. He would understand more than anyone else. He admires you very much. But . . . he can't know.'

He removed her hand from his arm and sandwiched it between his. He returned her smile with great warmth.

'Well then. If I am the first to know about this baby,

I can be the first to congratulate you. You and David are very lucky. A second child. A brother or sister for Davie. A new cousin for Albie and Victor. David must be very proud.'

He had said the right thing. This was what she had wanted. The smile widened to near-tears and he could see the likeness between her and her daughter.

She swallowed and acknowledged his implication. 'He is, very proud. Almost as proud as he was the first time.'

He carried her hand to his lips, a courtly, uncharacteristic gesture for Fred Luker. Well, he was changing. He watched April's cheeks colour faintly with surprised pleasure and determined not to fight the change. He might actually become as honest and upright as April imagined. One day.

They went back into the restaurant and he looked around him for his wife. His eyes met hers and he realized that she too was looking for him. He lifted a hand and walked towards her. This was his family and he was going to make the most of them, as he had made the most of everything that came his way.

It was David who found some anchovies for April and forced her to sit and eat them.

'You've been dashing around all day,' he grumbled proudly. 'You weren't like this with Davie. I hope it doesn't mean we're about to have twins.'

The idea of twins put April into a fresh spiral of joy.

'David. Wouldn't that be just about perfect? If they were girls we could call them Florence and Felicity. And if they were boys—'

'Primrose . . . please don't get so excited. You forget

I'm an old man now and I can't stand too much of it.'

She stared at him to check whether he was serious. Then, once again, they were caught in each other's aura more tightly than in a physical embrace. It happened a lot lately; it was as if a bubble of special atmosphere enclosed them from the rest of the world.

David took a quick breath that was almost a sob. 'Oh my God . . . I do love you.'

And April, gazing into the dark eyes that no longer held secrets, saw mirrored there her own special images: her father and Sibbie, Sibbie and David, David and April, April and Fred. She no longer felt pain. Morals were made for men.

'Yes,' she said. 'I know. Thank God, David, we both know.'

March had started to glance at the new gold watch Fred had given her, when two unexpected guests arrived. The door opened on Edward Williams who ushered ahead of him Sibbie Luker.

For a moment there was an appalled silence. Alf Luker bristled visibly and Hettie looked to right and left with widening eyes. Sibbie had not received an invitation, but then, neither had many of the guests here today. Hettie had been as thankful as March that Sibbie had decided to stay away. But to turn up late like this, certain of catching everyone's attention, and to bring with her her latest what-d'you-call-it . . . Hettie wished herself invisible.

Bridget broke the silence with a sort of whimper. 'Daddy!' closely followed by shouts of recognition from Olga and Natasha. Then Edward himself held up his hand and made his announcement.

'We thought we would call in and wish Fred and March all the best for the future. And to tell you that as soon as my divorce comes through, Sibbie and I will also be married.' He drew Sibbie's hand through his arm and patted it. 'This is unorthodox, we know that, but we're tired of the whispers and the gossip. Those are our plans and this is a good time and place for them to be made public.'

Hettie said audibly, 'Oh my gawd.'

Fred shrugged, 'Sounds all right to me.'

Florence, at the back of the room, stood up and walked towards the door. She looked very old and her straight back was at last bent. She reached Sibbie and without hesitation put her arms around the slender neck.

'I'm so pleased, Sibbie. It will mean – eventually – that you can be friends with May again.'

Such frankness might have been insulting from anyone else. From Florence it was like a benediction. Sibbie, tight as a spring, hanging on to Edward, enjoying the fact that she was stealing the limelight yet frightened in spite of herself, put her arms around the tiny waist and felt unaccustomed tears behind her eyes.

'Thank you . . . thank you, Mrs Rising.' She thought how pleased Will would be. How very pleased. His two worlds coming together at last.

Chatter broke out on all sides. Gran and Aunt Sylv were rigid with disapproval, Hettie fluttered like a nervous hen, Alf cleared his throat and shuffled his feet, Aunty Vi repeated, 'What's to do then, what's to do?' Bridget said, 'I'm going to give birth now, right now, d'you hear me Tollie? I cannot accept that woman – I simply cannot–' and Tollie said, 'Then I think we'd better take this opportunity to feed Beatrice, my dear.' April, feeling she might have conjured Sibbie up out of her own thoughts, said fearfully to David, 'Skeleton at the feast?' And David replied, 'Obviously not for your mother, darling. She probably needed to see Sibbie. She needed to settle that side of your father in her mind.' April still looked at him. 'And for you, David?' He returned her look steadily. 'How can you ask, Primrose? When we've got Davie, Florence and Felicity?'

March said tightly to her new husband, 'Time we went, Fred. The train leaves in an hour.' Fred held her hand. 'March, I want you to do something for me. Go and thank Sibbie for coming, then shake Edward Williams' hand and offer our good wishes.'

'I will do no such thing, Fred.'

He tightened his hold. 'Yes you will. You've just promised to obey me, for one thing. And for another, you want to get rid of Sibbie and that's the way to do it. And for yet another, everyone will think you're just like your mother if you do it. Sweet and forgiving.'

She hesitated, hating having to knuckle under to him, yet seeing exactly what he meant. She shrugged. 'If you think it's best, Fred–' and went forward. It was Fred's decision, not hers.

'. . . good of you to drop in . . .' Edward Williams' handshake was warm. She remembered working for him and finding him kind and just.

He said, as Fred had predicted, 'Thank you, March. We didn't want to steal your thunder. We'll go now.'

Better still, Florence then took her arm and smiled all her love and warmth at her. 'Take me back to my seat darling, will you?' and then very quietly, 'I'm proud of you, March, proud of you.'

March covered the thin, veined hand with her own and stood very straight. Everyone said how like her mother she was. She would make that true in every way.

Sibbie said, 'Goodbye May. Perhaps later – like your mother said – when the talk dies down, we could—?'

May stood up gladly. 'Oh Sibbie, I'm so pleased about you and – oh Sibbie.' The two women, who were no longer girls, looked at each other and smiled. May felt a small spurt of joy somewhere inside her, just as she'd felt on Christmas morning years ago when she first spied the lumpy stocking at the end of her bed.

She drew Monty forward. 'Darling, I know you met Sibbie once – unofficially—' She laughed gaily. 'But let me introduce you properly. Sibbie. Monty. I'd like you to be friends.'

And Monty took the hand that was so frighteningly familiar into his and looked into the bold blue eyes that glinted at him secretly. And he too saw the lumpy stocking of Christmas morning.

'I'm delighted to meet you, Sibbie,' he said and smiled back at her.

March retired into a small room behind the

restaurant to powder her nose and slip into the fox cape Fred had bought her. May and April went with her.

May said, 'March, you look marvellous.' There wasn't a trace of envy in her voice. 'It's so very nice that at last you'll be settled.'

It was a strange way to describe the sort of life that March might be embarking on. She had been settled before, settled into the kind of rut she had known so often, in which she hardly seemed to be alive. Now she was certain of one thing, she would be alive. Fred would see to that.

She smiled, 'Dear May.' Why did she feel no irritation at May's silly, typical remark. 'Dear May. Thank you.'

April said, 'Oh my God. I think I'm going to cry.'

May hugged her. 'Why, little sis? We're going to be together from now on. Doesn't that make you happy? What did that newspaper article call us years ago? Daffodils . . . we're going to blossom together.' And she thought of Sibbie who was so like a Rising – another daffodil.

April smiled. 'I want to cry because I'm so happy. That's all.' She couldn't tell them yet. Florence must be the first to know after David. 'I'm so very happy, girls. I can't explain.'

March said, 'I didn't think I'd get over Father betraying all of us. But after Mother . . . just now . . .'

'Quite.' May nodded eagerly.

April said, 'Let's go back inside and be with her. Come on.'

They went back to Florence and grouped

themselves around her in an unconsciously protective pose. And their husbands, looking at them, were, for a moment, over-awed by their combined beauty and strength.

THE END